THE KEEPER

A SILENT PHOENIX MC NOVEL

SHANNON MYERS

CONTENTS

Cover design by Clarise Tan / CT Cover Creations

Cover images © Serge Lee / shutterstock

Edits by Amy Briggs

First Printing: 2025

Paperback ISBN- 979-8-9925975-1-6

❀ Created with Vellum

ALSO BY SHANNON MYERS

<u>Fictioned Series</u>

(Hayden & Jake's Story)

Protagonized

To Elizabeth Marie and Eliza Lainn for seeing the light at the end of the tunnel and promising me it wasn't a train.

AUTHOR'S NOTE

Please be aware that this is a dark romance, which includes many triggers such as graphic violence, sexually explicit scenes, and other mature content that is not appropriate for readers under the age of eighteen.

For a detailed list, click the QR code below.

If you don't enjoy dark romance, I do NOT recommend reading any further.

Reader discretion is advised.

TERMINOLOGY

1%er (One-Percenter)- *If 99% of motorcycle riders are law-abiding members of society, the rest is the 1%. Advertised through a patch or tattoo, usually on a diamond shaped back field.*

13 - *Patch worn by a biker, usually a 1%er. May stand for the letter "M" (13th letter of alphabet), and indicate the wearer smokes pot, or uses "crank" (methamphetamine). Can also mean "The Mother Club", or original chapter of a motorcycle club.*

1916- *The nineteenth letter of the alphabet (S) and the sixteenth (P). Stands for Silent Phoenix.*

3-Piece Patch- *Configuration of back patches, consisting of: a top rocker (club's name), a center patch (club's emblem), and a bottom rocker (geographical territory).*

69 - *Patch indicating someone who has performed cunnilingus with witnesses present.*

Air Condition- *Riddle with bullets*

ATF- *Bureau of Alcohol, Tobacco, Firearms and Explosives.*

Broad- *A female whose sole purpose is being used as a sexual object; similar to a one-night stand.*

Cage- *Non-biker's car/truck.*

Church- *Club meeting.*

Club Whore- *Also known as a Mama. Sexual equivalent of a public well. Anyone can dip into her, at any time, as often as he wants. These are woman who belong to the club at large. They belong to every member and are expected to consent to the sexual desires of anyone at anytime. They perform menial tasks around the clubhouse, however do not attend club meetings.*

Colors- *Patches, logo, or uniform associated with a motorcycle club.*

Fly Colors - *To ride on a motorcycle wearing club's kutte.*

Gathering: *A scheduled social event or meeting. This is not Church.*

Grocery-getter- *A biker's car/truck.*

Hang Around- *a person that hangs around a motorcycle club and may be interested in joining.*

Jacket- *Arrest record*

Kill-Light- *A flashlight used as a weapon.*

Kutte- *A jacket which has had the sleeves cut off. All club patches are sewn onto kuttes, which are worn as the outer-most layer of clothing. Most, if not all, outlaw clubs have kuttes as their basic uniform.*

Mother- *Founding/original chapter of the club.*

Nomad- *1) "Nomad" on a bottom rocker patch means that motorcycle club member travels between geographical chapters. Kind of like working in a secretarial pool, a Nomad goes where he's needed. 2)"Nomad" on a top rocker patch or car plaque means "Nomad" is the name of that club.*

Ol' Lady- *Wife or long-time girlfriend of club member. She is considered property of the member and is off-limits to other club members.*

Property Of- *displayed on a shirt, patch or tattoo to show who the woman "belongs to." Example: Monica wore a "Property of Torch" vest in Renegade. That meant that she associated herself with Torch and would do anything he needed/wanted.*

———

STRUCTURE WITHIN CLUB

National President- *Many times the founder of the club. He will usually be located at or near the national headquarters. He will be surrounded by bodyguards and organizational enforcers.*

Territorial or Regional Representatives- *In some cases called the National Vice President in charge of a specific region or state.*

National Secretary / Treasurer- *He is responsible for the club's money and collecting dues from local chapters. He also records any by-law changes and records any minutes.*

National Enforcer- *This person answers directly to the National President. He acts as a body guard and gives out punishment for club violations. He has also been known to locate former members and retrieve colors or remove the club's tattoo from them.*

Chapter President- *This person has either claimed the position or has been voted in. He has final authority over all chapter business and members.*

Chapter Vice President- *This person is second in command. He presides over club affairs in the absence of the president. Normally, he is hand picked by the Chapter President.*

Chapter Secretary / Treasurer- *This is usually the member with the best writing skills and probably the most education. He will maintain the chapter roster and maintain a crude accounting system. He is also responsible for collecting dues, keeping minutes and paying for any bills the chapter accumulates.*

Chapter Sergeant (SGT) at Arms- *This person is in charge of maintaining order at club meetings. Because of the violent nature of outlaw gangs this person is normally the strongest member physically and is loyal to the Chapter President. He may administer beatings to fellow members for violations of club rules. He is the club enforcer.*

Road Captain- *This person fulfills the role of a logistician and security chief for club sponsored runs or outings. The Road Captain maps out routes to be* taken during runs, arranges the refueling, food and maintenance stops. He will carry the club's money and use it for bail if necessary.

Members- *The rank and file, fully accepted and dues paying members of the gang. They are the individuals who carry out the President's orders and have sworn to live by the club's by-laws.*

Prospect- *These are the club's hopefuls who spend from one month to one year in a probationary status. They must prove during that time if they are worthy of becoming members. Some clubs have the prospect commit a felony with fellow members observing in an effort to weed out the weak and stop infiltration by law enforcement. Must be nominated by a regular member and receive a unanimous vote for acceptance. They are known to carry weapons for other club members and stand guard at club functions. The prospect wears no colors and has no voting rights.*

Associates or Honorary Members- *An individual who has proven his value or usefulness to the gang. These individuals may be professional people who have in some manner helped the club. Some of the more noted are attorneys, bail bondsmen, and auto wrecking yard owners. These people are allowed to party with the gang, either in town or on their runs; however, they do not have a voting status or wear colors.*

KEEPER

/ˈkiːpɚ/

noun

1. A person whose job is to guard or take care of something or someone.
2. Someone who is worth keeping.
3. One having genuine or lasting merit.

See also: guardian, sentry

ONE

PIPER

Ivy & Piper's Guide to Life Rule Number Thirty-Seven:
You can never have too many books.

Motorcycles, Mobsters, & Mayhem Event 2023

"Good girls get on their knees and ask nicely."

A flush crept across my cheeks as if I hadn't heard the same command at least half a dozen times while waiting in line. Then again, a gorgeous six-foot-something biker hadn't been watching.

It wasn't the first time I'd caught him staring, either. No, I'd felt the heat of his gaze while waiting to get into the ballroom and again when I stopped at a water station to grab a drink. Every time I turned around, he was there.

Had we not been at an event specifically geared toward readers of mafia and motorcycle club romance, I might have thought he was lowkey stalking me. Instead, I assumed he was trying to drum up business for the author who'd paid for him to come or a newbie hoping to kickstart his cover model career by catching the eye of one of the many authors and photographers in attendance.

Although neither theory explained the hours of furtive glances or why he'd stopped in the middle of the busy aisle to watch me deep-throat a shot of liquor.

I knelt on the denim and gold-patterned hotel carpet and pulled my long, dark hair over one shoulder before folding my hands against my lap, playing up the part of demure submissive more for his benefit than anything else.

"Please," I murmured, unable to resist peering up beneath my lashes to see if he was still there.

"Uh, uh, uh," the author chided, placing her fingers under my chin and guiding my face back to hers. "Eyes on me."

I tipped my head back and obediently parted my lips, not catching the hint of cinnamon until it was too late.

Fucking Fireball.

The spicy notes of cinnamon intermingled with distinct undercurrents of regret and memories of my twenty-first birthday, which had subsequently led to the worst hangover of my life.

With tearing eyes, I forced myself to swallow while solemnly vowing never to read another of Avelyn Paige's books for the rest of my life. The books I'd already made the mistake of purchasing would become kindling for my fireplace in the winter.

"Took it like such a good girl," she cooed as she swiped her thumb across my tingling lower lip, effectively reactivating my praise kink and making me rethink my somewhat hasty decision to ban her books from my shelves.

After retrieving my personalized copies from her assistant, plus a few extras I threw in last-second to atone for the ugly thoughts I had when the Fireball was scorching its way down my throat, I picked my way through the gathering crowd to where my best friend, Ivy, stood guarding our book carts.

She smacked my shoulder as soon as I was within reach, exclaiming, "Keanu on a cupcake! That was hot!"

"Really? The spicy aftertaste and burning in my esophagus beg to differ," I croaked, watching as Avelyn ushered the next schmuck to their knees.

"Oh no, it was definitely hot as hell," Ivy insisted with a firm shake of her head before lowering her voice. "And I'm not the only one who thought so."

"What do you mean?" I asked, feigning a neck stretch to casually scan the nearby faces for a certain pair of hooded brown eyes.

"Like you don't know! Dude, I thought the poor guy was going to chew through his bottom lip watching you take that shot. I'm honestly surprised he didn't step in and claim you as his Ol' Lady on the spot."

"Someone's read too many books," I said, playfully nudging her with my elbow. The thought of the gorgeous giant going full caveman and staking his claim, though, sent a shiver of pleasure down my spine —further proof my love of dark romance had warped my mind.

She pointed to my nearly overflowing cart with a snort. "Speak for yourself, missy. And it's obvious to anyone with eyeballs Biker Boy has been lusting after you all day."

"Please! He's probably just some cover model cosplaying as a biker." I consulted my table map, checking off the authors we'd already seen. "Where to next?"

"I don't care. I've picked up all my preorders and met everyone I wanted to, so it's your call," Ivy replied, lifting her shoulder in a half-shrug.

I couldn't recall a single instance in the twenty-plus years we'd known each other in which Ivy had dropped a discussion without a fight. She was like a dog with a bone when it came to uncomfortable conversations, especially when they centered around dating and sex. It was part of what made her a great psychiatrist—well, fourth-year psych resident.

"What?" she asked. "Why are you looking at me like that? Do I have something on my face?"

"No. It's nothing. You're good."

She pursed her lips and studied me through narrowed eyes before shaking her head. "Okay, so can we go now? Or were there more authors you wanted to see?"

"I think Avelyn Paige was the last one on my list—"

"Awesome. Let's beat the crowd and head back to the room," she interjected before promptly steering her cart toward the exit.

"Excuse me—sorry." I cut through the throngs of people loitering near the doors, my short legs struggling to keep up with her gazelle-like stride.

"Jesus, Ivy, slow down! It's not like we've got to rush to catch the elevator! Our room is on the first floor. What are you—oh." My voice broke off in a breathy sigh as I found myself staring up into a familiar pair of brown eyes.

His proximity sent my heart racing but slowed my reaction time, which became glaringly obvious a half-second later when I dragged my loaded book cart across my foot. I clamped my lips together to contain the slew of obscenities bubbling up my throat, trying to play it off like my toes weren't actively being crushed under the weight.

Without a word, he reached for the cart, lifting it up and off my foot before stepping back. Our gazes caught, and all I could think was brown wasn't an adequate enough description for the color of his eyes. Under the ballroom lights, they were so dark they appeared almost black. But up close and with the late afternoon sun streaming in through the glass doors, I was able to make out amber and gold hues I'd missed before.

"I vote for a power nap, early dinner here at the hotel, and drinks by the pool—oh, hey!" Ivy exclaimed as if running into him was a funny coincidence and not her entire plan when she took off for the doors. "How funny. We were just talking about you."

His brow creased, and I shot Ivy a warning glare, which she, of course, ignored. "Yeah, Piper and I were wondering if you and your friends were—"

"Going to the dinner," I blurted, although it came out much louder than I intended. "We were wondering if you were going to the dinner. That's all."

"We are. What about you? Are you going to the dinner, Piper?"

The smoky and deep tone of his voice sent a subtle jolt of pleasure spiking through my veins. I sucked in a breath, my mind filled with visions of my fingernails scoring his muscular shoulders and the heat of his breath against the shell of my ear as he panted my name in his low voice.

"Unfortunately, no. They were already sold out by the time we tried to get tickets," I said, sounding like I needed a few puffs from my rescue inhaler.

"That's too bad."

"But we'll be down by the pool around eight if you want to join us," Ivy offered before going in for the kill. "You should come and bring your friends."

He ran a hand over his bearded jaw before nodding to himself. "Bet we could make that work. I'm pretty sure GQ's free once the dinner's over, and we don't have any plans as far as I know."

I couldn't resist asking, "GQ's a cover model, I take it?"

"He is this weekend."

Score one for Piper.

"And what about you?" I dropped my gaze to read the name stitched onto the breast of his kutte, only to wish I hadn't. "Are you a model, Ghost?" I asked, though I had a sneaking suspicion I already knew the answer.

Ghost.

As in, what he did to women after sleeping with them, or was he a big fan of the Patrick Swayze movie?

Given my recent luck with dating, it was likely the former, which was a damn shame because the man was hot as hell.

He had a broad, muscular body built for heavy lifting and towered over my five-foot-four frame by a solid eight or nine inches. His thick, dark brown hair was cut close to his scalp on the sides, with longer strands on top standing up in messy spikes. Combined with his well-groomed beard, strong jawline, and fuck me eyes, he was just my type. Well, minus the whole love 'em and leave 'em vibe his road name gave off.

"Just a regular biker. Sorry to disappoint," he replied, running his tongue over his teeth.

I willed the hairs on my arms to stand down before lifting my shoulder in a half-shrug. "Never said I was disappointed."

His phone buzzed, and he checked it with a frown before returning his gaze to mine. "I've gotta head out. Eight o'clock?"

"Eight o'clock," I echoed with a grin. Like a heroine in a dark romance, I saw the red flags and ran straight for them like a kid headed for the circus.

TWO

PIPER

Ivy & Piper's Guide to Life Rule Number Twenty-Eight:
No woman left behind.

I stabbed my straw against the ice cubes in my cup with more force than was necessary, noisily slurping up the last remaining droplets of my third watermelon margarita—or was it my fourth?

I'd lost count somewhere between Ghost's friends showing up sans Ghost and the ménage-in-the-making currently playing out next to me in the heated infinity pool.

Not that I was judging. I was a girl's girl through and through, and if anyone deserved to let their hair down for the weekend, it was Ivy. Her entire life revolved around residency. Before tonight, the only Ds in her life were of the psychopathology variety—deviance, distress, dysfunction, and danger.

She tugged the Stetson off Duke's head with a drunken grin and placed it over her icy blonde curls before swimming back over to GQ. "If you want it back, you'll have to come in and get it."

"There are certain rules when it comes to a man's cowboy hat, darlin'," he drawled in his gravelly voice.

"One, the hat always comes off for the three Ps—prayer, patriotism, and when payin' your respects. No exceptions. I'd also recommend taking it off at church, restaurants, and inside your mama's house unless you wanna get cuffed upside the head. I like to take it off when I meet a lady for the first time, like tonight. Two, if you can't hang your hat, set it upside down on the crown—keeps a man's luck from runnin' out and maintains the shape. Three, never mess with another man's hat. That's a fightin' offense."

Duke—whose road name I could only assume was a John Wayne reference—had a whole Marlboro Man thing going on with his cleft chin, clean-shaven face, and jawline that could cut glass. The streaks of silver woven into his close-cropped brown hair weren't hurting, either.

He looked like someone you'd find rustling cattle on the Four Sixes Ranch. He probably opened the car door on dates, helped old ladies cross the street in his spare time, and kept his hand on the small of a woman's back when entering a room, letting every man in the room know she was his.

GQ, on the other hand, looked like the lost member of some trendy alt-rock band. Medium-length strands of dark brown hair fell in strategically messy waves over one eye. He had a nose ring, a diamond stud in his left ear, and a week's worth of stubble dotting his jawline. He was the guy whose photo would have lined my bathroom mirror as a teen—the brooding bad boy I would have been just young and naïve enough to imagine had a soft spot only for me.

They were a juxtaposition—complete opposites save for one exception.

Neither had said a word to me beyond introducing themselves.

The men chatted up Ivy, a few attendees who stopped by on their way to the bar, and even the hotel staff. Meanwhile, I downed one margarita after another while wishing I was literally anywhere else. Like back in the hotel room, binge-eating my way through the emergency chocolate bar stash in my purse and moping over my shitty luck with men.

But Rule Number Eight in Ivy and Piper's Guide to Life Manual—*Never leave another woman in a vulnerable situation*—meant I wouldn't be going anywhere for the foreseeable future.

"Are you challenging me to a duel, Duke?" Ivy asked, tipping the brim of the hat down low over her eyes.

He chuckled and shook his head. "Not quite. If a woman takes a man's hat, it generally implies she'd like to take a few other things off him, too, if you catch my meanin'."

"Wear the hat, ride the cowboy," GQ said bluntly before taking a swig from his beer.

Sober Ivy could handle both bikers and any emotional baggage they happened to have with her eyes closed. Unfortunately, Sober Ivy had been M.I.A. for the past thirty minutes, and there wasn't a snowball's chance in hell I was leaving her alone with two complete strangers, especially not when cowboy hat-related sex acts were being discussed.

"Well, in that case, I'd say it's—"

"Time for another round!" I exclaimed before she could finish that sentence. "My treat."

They agreed and tossed out their drink orders before resuming their conversation, rendering me invisible once again.

Was it too much to ask for some pity small talk?

Or, at the very least, eye contact?

Curious to test a theory, I tapped Duke on the shoulder. "Remind me again, you had the Landshark, right?"

"Yes, ma'am," he replied without turning around. I didn't get so much as a head tip in my direction.

"Great. Be right back," I said quietly, feeling the tears forming in my eyes as I swam over to the stairs.

"I'll come with," Ivy insisted, waiting until we were out of earshot before asking, "Are you okay?"

"Yeah, I'm good," I said, flashing her a fake smile. It was the most relaxed I'd seen her in over a year, and I didn't want to be the one to bring it to an end.

Besides, it wasn't her fault Ghost had, well, ghosted me.

"Really?" she asked, lifting the hat enough to serve me a healthy dose of side-eye. "That's funny because you're doing that squinty blinking thing you do when you're trying not to cry."

"It's just—is there something on my face?"

She scanned me before shaking her head. "You look great. Why?"

"Are you sure? There are no bats in the cave or Alice Cooper mascara thing going on?" I flared my nostrils and lifted my chin for inspection.

"Noooo," she replied, drawing out the vowel with a giggle.

I threw my hands up. "I don't get it! My hair and makeup are good. My swimsuit is covering all the appropriate bits. Even if it wasn't, I can't imagine a biker—or any man for that matter— being too prudish to enjoy a little nip slip."

Her gaze dipped to my cleavage before returning to my face. "I think I'm missing something. Is this about Ghost?"

"Maybe... I don't know." I sighed. "Am I going crazy, or does it seem like Duke and GQ are trying to avoid me at all costs? And please don't think I mean that in like a jealous way or anything, but it's just weird to be ignored completely, you know? They said more to the bartenders than they have me, and I can't help but think it's got something to do with why he didn't show up. I've been racking my brain, trying to figure out what I said or did that might have made him not want to come."

"Don't," Ivy warned, squeezing my shoulder. "Him not coming says more about him than it does you. And for all we know, there might be a solid reason."

"Yeah, like he met someone else at the dinner," I grumbled, tracing a line in the pavement with my big toe.

"My money's on a violent case of food poisoning—what?" she asked when I rolled my eyes. "He was following you around like a puppy all day, Piper. Men don't do shit like that and then flip a switch. I think he wanted to come, but the projectile vomiting and violent diarrhea kept him in the room. It would also explain why Duke and GQ were so vague about why he wasn't there."

My lip curled in disgust. "Thanks so much for that visual. And they could have just been following the bro code and covering for him while he was off boning someone else. Whatever. It doesn't matter now."

She snorted. "Sure it doesn't, Pinocchio."

"Speaking of projectile vomiting," I said, steering the conversation back to her. "Are you good, or should I cut you off?"

"All good, Officer. I'm just past the *I've always wanted to be with two men at once* stage of inebriation, but nowhere close to *let's go back to your room and try out the Eiffel Tower position.*"

"You sure about that? Because from where I was sitting, it looked like you were quickly approaching the *I've forgotten all the reasons why hot tub sex is a bad idea* stage."

After glancing back to ensure both men were still in the infinity pool, she admitted, "It's a social experiment I'm working on. Men are typically on their best behavior on a first date, and by the time you start to see the red flags, you're usually too far in, right? Well, I thought, why not see if I can get them to flash those warning signs up front and save some time?"

"By getting drunk?" I hissed in horror.

"By *pretending* to get drunk," she corrected, tapping the side of her nose.

"Take tonight, for example. I've had five margaritas, but only three contained alcohol. You know when I said I needed to run to the ladies' room? Well, I went back to the bar and instructed the bartender to make ours virgins after the third drink. With each round, they see me getting progressively less inhibited and attribute it to the alcohol. Meanwhile, I'm observing every reaction and comment, gauging what type of men they are."

"And here I thought they were just skimping on the tequila," I muttered dryly, used to being dragged unwillingly into Ivy's little experiments. "Don't keep me in suspense. What's the verdict?"

She shrugged. "Don't know yet, but if the hat comments and them ignoring you completely are any indication, they'll likely fail."

"You're the only person I know who's working even when she's not working." I shook my head and turned around, only to collide with a wall of rock-solid muscle.

The impact knocked me off balance, and I flailed my arms like a cartoon character, desperately trying to regain my footing.

Before I could bust my ass on the wet concrete, which would have been the cherry on top of an already shit sundae, a pair of strong arms locked around my waist to steady me, and I followed the well-defined curve of a bicep up to a pair of eyes that were now as dark as an abyss.

I swallowed hard. "You."

THREE

PIPER

"**M**e," Ghost replied, keeping a firm grip on me like I was a spooked animal in danger of bolting.

God, I wished. If only I were the type of girl who could shut off my emotions on a whim and never let anyone see when they'd slipped past my defenses.

Aloof. Unbothered.

Instead, I was the girl who'd spent the past fifty minutes knocking back mostly virgin margaritas and watching the entrance to the pool area like a loser. My mom often told me I didn't wear my heart on my sleeve but on my face for all the world to see.

"Perfect timing! Piper and I were grabbing another round for everybody. But now that you finally decided to show up, I'll head back if that's cool."

Ivy narrowed her big blue eyes on him like a missile locking onto a target before casually adding, "Or maybe GQ could go with her. You should have seen them together. It was so cute."

He looked down at me with a raised brow. "Is that right?"

Damn Ivy and her damn experiments.

I was distracted. With each breath that filled his giant-sized lungs, his warm skin brushed against mine, activating erogenous zones I wasn't even aware I had and bulldozing through anything remotely resembling a coherent response.

"Yeah, I think initially he felt bad she'd been stood up and was trying to be nice," she continued, hellbent on getting a reaction out of Ghost like she hadn't been the one defending him just five minutes ago.

"And was he?" he asked in a low voice that sent goosebumps scattering across my damp skin.

"Um—" I sucked in a breath as his fingers slowly skimmed up my spine. "Was he what?"

"Nice."

Ivy grinned. "Oh, I'd say he was a lot more than that—"

Ghost flicked a dismissive glance over at the pool before shaking his head. "No, he wasn't."

My head flinched back slightly. "But you weren't here," I said slowly. "How would you know?"

A smile pulled at the corner of his mouth. "Because they were under strict instructions not to try anything, which included looking at, touching, or speaking to you."

The color drained from my face when I realized he wasn't joking. I disentangled myself from his firm grip and backed away in shock.

This asshole couldn't be bothered to show up when he said he would, but god forbid his friends keep me company while I waited. Or, I don't know, not treat me like a leper.

I opened my mouth but found I had no words.

Luckily, Ivy had enough for both of us. "Wow. Afraid she might see that unlike you, your friends actually have personalities to go with their looks? Or maybe it's about the control for you. Is that it? You get off on pulling the strings like some sadistic puppet master?"

Ghost blinked rapidly before stepping back like he was trying to make his hulking frame appear less threatening. "What? No, it's not like that at all. If you could give us a minute alone, I could explain—"

"Why, so you can try to bully your way back into her good graces?" she fired back with a cutting laugh. "Not a chance in hell, pal."

A dark flush spread up his throat and into his face. He pinched the bridge of his nose and took a deep breath before trying again. "Five minutes, Piper. That's all I'm asking for."

"Fine," I agreed, nodding to Ivy to let her know I was good. "But I'm getting a drink before the bar closes."

Without waiting to see if he would follow, I waded into the large pool to the deserted swim-up side of the bar, eager to get the entire thing over with. I couldn't imagine him being able to talk himself out of the hole he'd dug in five minutes, but it would be amusing to watch him try before telling him to go fuck himself.

The stools were level with my chest. Determined to use my buoyancy to my advantage, I placed my palms on the seat and hoisted myself up like The Little Mermaid splashing onto a rock. I almost had it, too, until my hand slipped.

Ghost caught me under the armpits and placed me on the stool before sliding onto the one next to it. Unlike me, he didn't require propelling or special maneuvers.

"Listen, I owe you an explanation," he said, turning to face me.

"You don't owe me anything. I'm good." My throat tightened, and I looked away, feigning a sudden interest in the thatched roof over the bar.

I blamed the sudden heat behind my eyelids and tightness in my throat on my recent string of shitty first dates and not the man in front of me.

He reached out and hooked his fingers beneath my chin, gently guiding my face back to his. Whatever he saw caused the muscle in his jaw to twitch. "You're clearly not good."

"It's allergies," I lied, pulling away as the bartender approached.

"We're closing down in five minutes. Another margarita?" she asked.

"No, thank you. I'll have a—" I blinked back the tears in my eyes and quickly scanned the menu before ordering the one drink guaranteed to have alcohol in it. "A Fat Tire, please. Thank you."

I expected her to try to talk me into a mixed drink, but she just shrugged and turned to Ghost. "And for you?"

"The same, thanks. Can you charge them both to room 702?"

"That won't be necessary," I said, slipping into my customer service voice.

Ghost gave an exasperated sigh. "I'd like to buy you a drink, Piper."

"Well, you're almost an hour and three margaritas too late."

"Four," the bartender corrected, sliding the bottles in front of us with a smirk.

"Excuse me, an hour and *four* margaritas too late," I said, taking a defiant swig. "But I'm sure you've got a great reason, so let's hear it."

"For what it's worth, I am sorry I was late," he admitted quietly, spinning his beer bottle in a slow circle against the countertop. "I was headed down with the guys when my nephew called."

It was the last thing I expected him to say, and I hastily swallowed my mouthful of beer before asking, "Your nephew?"

"Yeah. He's thirteen, and tonight's his end-of-year dance at school. There's this girl in his grade who he's had a crush on for months, so I've been working with him for the past several weeks on how to talk to her."

Something like embarrassment spread across his face before he lowered his head. "I must be out of practice because he went up and asked her to dance just like we talked about, and she laughed in his face."

The bartender, who'd spent the last several minutes pretending to wipe down the bar while clearly eavesdropping, gave me a pointed look before inclining her head toward him. The universal code for *Go on. Say something, you idiot.*

"Oh. Is he okay?"

She rolled her eyes and went back to cleaning with an annoyed huff.

"Other than never coming to me for advice again? I guess," he said before taking a long sip of his drink.

"Well, he could always try following her around for an entire day until she notices him," I deadpanned.

He let his head fall back with an exaggerated groan. "Clearly, I should be the one asking for advice instead of giving it because I thought I was flirting."

"Hey. I'm here, aren't I?"

"For the next five minutes, at least."

I reached for his hand and pulled him closer. "Hate to break it to you, but it's been seven and a half minutes since we sat down."

"And seven and a half minutes ago, I would have taken it as a good sign that you were still here."

"You mean before you discovered you were a stalker?" I asked with a teasing grin.

Ghost's eyes flickered with amusement, and the corners of his mouth quirked up into a genuine smile. "Stalker? I prefer 'discreet admirer,' thank you very much." He squeezed my hand lightly, the warmth from his grip spearing through my chest much like the shot of Fireball had.

Unlike the Fireball, I wanted more.

"Of course. My mistake," I said, my pulse quickening with anticipation. My last handful of dates had been nothing short of disasters. I couldn't remember a time in recent memory when getting to know someone felt fun and not like a job interview. "Biker. Discreet admirer. Anything else I should know about you?"

"Yeah. I give shitty advice and likely ruined my nephew's life."

"Give it a few days and he'll come around," I insisted. Hilarious coming from someone who was an only child, but I'd worked around enough teens to know they bounced back from heartbreak faster than I did at twenty-nine. "Teenage crushes are brutal, man."

He exhaled a laugh. "Tell me about it. I remember my first crush. Mandy Lawrence. I spent almost the entire school year trying to work up the courage to talk to her. When that didn't work, I wrote a note, confessing my love and asking her to the end-of-year awards banquet. I gave it to a buddy to give to her, and guess who she went to the banquet with?"

"Your friend!" I exclaimed with a grimace. "No! That's like the first rule of the bro code."

"Yeah, no honor whatsoever. It's funny; we had to read *Lord of the Flies* in middle school, and I think it stuck with me because it felt like we were living it to some degree every day. Always fighting to be on top and not caring who we stepped on to get there." He shook off the memory before tipping his beer bottle at me with a wry grin. "Your turn."

"Rowdy Thorne in the eighth grade. But instead of passing him a note. I—" I released his hand to cover my face. "No, I can't say it. It's too embarrassing, and you'll laugh."

He tugged my hand down, interlacing my fingers with his. "The guy's name was Rowdy Thorne, so I'm definitely going to laugh, but you're going to tell me anyway."

"Fine. Instead of passing him a note, I called him one night and proceeded to play Celine Dion's *Let's Talk About Love* album at max volume to let him know how I felt. Little did I know he was having a sleepover at the time." My teeth sank into the flesh of my lower lip as I relived the mortifying moment all over again.

"I'm guessing he wasn't much of a Celine fan," he said carefully, the corner of his mouth twitching wildly with the grin he was struggling to conceal.

Despite the flush warming my cheeks, I smiled. "No, Ghost. He was not."

"Dane," he corrected.

"Well, I guess it's a step up from Rowdy."

He let out a low chuckle. "Oh, really? Just a step?"

"Like this much," I said, holding my thumb and index finger about an inch apart.

Sensing things were about to get juicy, the bartender inched closer under the guise of wiping down the bar again. It would have been believable had she been holding the rag and not just making circular motions across the bar top with her hand.

"That's it? That's all I get over the guy who wasn't sophisticated enough to appreciate the Queen of Power Ballads?"

"Eh." I lifted my shoulder in a shrug, and his gaze immediately darkened.

I couldn't decide which I liked better: the reserved giant whose flirting techniques needed some work or the brooding biker who looked like he could eat me for breakfast.

"All right. I see how it is." He cracked his neck from side to side like a boxer limbering up for a fight.

"No, wait!" I scrambled off my stool and swam backward toward the stairs on the opposite side of the pool, doing my best to send a spray of water in his direction with each kick.

Dane disappeared beneath the surface, his muscular body gliding through the water as gracefully as a sea otter. I changed direction and barely made it to the side of the pool when a surge of movement sent ripples through the water. I shrieked with laughter when he burst from the depths seconds later, capturing my ankle in his firm grip.

The determined glint in his eyes was unmistakable as he reeled me in, effortlessly dragging me through the water while I feigned frustration and tried to wriggle free.

"Got ya," he said, holding my gaze. We were close enough that the droplets of water cascading off the ends of his dark hair landed on my face in little splatters. Close enough that I could feel the heat radiating off his body.

His fingers trailed down my spine, and the laughter bubbling in my throat morphed into a breathless gasp. I shuddered, and his dark eyes drifted from my face down to where my nipples were straining against my swimsuit top.

"Cold?"

Not trusting myself to speak, I jerked my chin in a nod.

"Want me to warm you up?" he asked, his deep voice thicker than it had been only a moment ago.

The murmured "Please" had barely left my mouth before he was hauling me up in his arms with a low growl, his palms firmly molded around the curve of my ass.

My legs instinctively wrapped around his waist as he carried me to the edge of the pool. The water lapped gently against us, but I barely noticed. I was too focused on the way Dane's hands kneaded my flesh, sending sparks of electricity through my body.

"Is this okay?" he murmured, his lips brushing against my ear.

I nodded, unable to form words as his mouth trailed down my neck. My fingers tangled in his wet hair, holding him close as he nipped and sucked at my sensitive skin.

"Dane," I gasped, arching into him.

He pulled back slightly, his dark eyes searching mine. "Tell me what you want, darlin'."

The intensity of his gaze made me shiver. "I want..." I trailed off, suddenly feeling shy despite our intimate position.

His thumb traced my lower lip, sending another shiver through me. "Tell me."

I took a shaky breath, my desire overriding my hesitation. "I want you to kiss me."

A slow smile spread across his face. "Thought you'd never ask."

He lowered his head, his lips barely brushing against mine. The light touch was electric, igniting every nerve ending in my body. I pressed closer, desperate for more.

Dane obliged, capturing my mouth in a searing kiss that left me breathless. His tongue swept across my lower lip, seeking entrance. I opened for him eagerly, moaning as his fingertips moved along my jaw, angling my head to deepen the kiss.

"Christ, Piper," he growled, as I rocked against the bulge in his shorts, desperate to alleviate the ache spreading throughout my lower body.

I was vaguely aware of the obscene noises I was making as my wet hands pawed frantically at the hard planes of his chest like a cat making biscuits.

"What would you have done if your friends had been talking to me?" I murmured, hissing out a breath when he thrust forward, dragging the length of his erection over my clit.

"Killed them," he said with a growl.

My nipples pebbled at the lack of humor in his tone, as much as the scrape of his beard against my jaw.

"Sorry to interrupt—"

Dane and I jerked apart, breathing heavily. I could feel the heat in my cheeks as I turned to where Ivy stood at the edge of the pool, arms crossed and a knowing smirk on her face.

She wasn't sorry at all.

"Seriously?" I groaned, dropping my forehead to his shoulder in frustration.

"Yes, seriously," she said, mimicking my voice. "C'mon. We've got a long drive home tomorrow."

"Walk you back to your room?" he asked, his intense gaze boring into mine.

Despite the disappointment surging through my veins, I nodded. "I'd like that."

FOUR

PIPER

Ivy & Piper's Guide to Life Rule Number Twenty-Nine:
Wash your face every single night.

I vy paused in the open doorway to our hotel room and cleared her throat, clearly expecting me to follow.

"Go on, I'll be there in a minute," I assured her with a grin, likely giving away my true intentions.

She shook her head before disappearing inside, leaving me alone with Dane in the quiet hallway.

The air buzzed with electricity, and I was hyperaware of everything from the distant *ding* of the elevators to the rise and fall of his chest. Some part of me knew I needed to commit this moment to memory. My heart pounded like a drumline in my chest as common sense warred with impulsivity.

Before I could talk myself out of it, I grabbed the front of the T-shirt Dane had thrown on when we left the pool and tugged his mouth down over mine.

His lips lacked the softness from before and moved against mine with the desperate urgency of a man shipping off to war. I twisted the material of his shirt beneath my fingers, anchoring myself as much as preventing him from pulling away.

Anyone could walk out of their room and see us, but I was too far gone to care. Nothing else existed outside of the hands braced on the wall on either side of my head and the insistent press of his lips to mine.

"God, I wish you didn't suck at giving advice," I confessed, peering up at him through heavy-lidded eyes.

Dane ran his tongue over his bottom lip as if he was still tasting me, his breaths coming in sharp, shallow pants. "Oh yeah? Why?"

"Because..." I hissed as his hand trailed down the side of my throat.

"Because?" He tilted his head to the side as if he didn't know exactly what had caused my sudden lack of focus. "You wanna elaborate on that?"

My stomach rolled like the loose change on the floorboard of my car as I admitted, "Um, I don't—I don't kiss on the first date ever, but I just broke that rule with this guy I just met."

His laugh was low and husky. "Scandalous."

"And now, I want—" I sucked in a breath as his fingers skimmed along the halter strap of my bikini before stopping just above the swell of my breast.

He nodded, encouraging me to continue. "And now you want..."

"I want more than a kiss goodnight, but I'm not sure if I should." Saying it out loud felt like stepping off a ledge without looking down first, which was admittedly a terrific way to end up dead—*and, oh my god, why was he smiling like that?*

"More, as in you serenading me with 'My Heart Will Go On' and recreating your favorite scene from *Titanic*?" Dane's eyebrow arched suggestively.

I couldn't help the laugh that bubbled up in my throat. "First off, you would be so lucky," I said primly. "Second, there was room for both of them on that door, and I'll die on that hill."

He shook his head with a smirk. "Fair enough. So, the private concert's out. What else could there possibly be?"

"I was thinking of something a little more hands-on, if you know what I mean."

Dane's eyes darkened, his pupils expanding until only a sliver of brown remained. "What kind of hands-on are we talking about here?"

I made a show of glancing up and down the hall before crooking my finger. "Come here. I don't want anyone else to hear."

He obediently lowered his head, and I leaned in, my lips brushing the shell of his ear. "I was thinking maybe we could read together."

"Reading together," he repeated, slowly shaking his head as if waiting for the punchline. "That's more intimate than kissing?"

Even confusion looked good on him. It wasn't fair.

"Mm-hmm." I fought against the insistent twitch at the corner of my mouth, trying not to give myself away. "You don't do that with just anyone."

Dane pulled back with a nod, dropping his hands to his sides. "Okay. We could see if there's a bookstore nearby."

"That's not necessary. I have plenty of books in my room."

"Sure. Sounds good," he agreed, masking his disappointment well. *Unless he wanted to sit and read romance together...*

I licked my bottom lip, noting how his jaw tightened as he tracked my tongue's movement.

Oh, this man definitely wanted more than a book in his hand. And as much as I wanted to draw it out, I was suddenly more interested in a different form of teasing.

"It's not *Titanic*, but I was thinking we could read a few of my favorite scenes, preferably while your hands are on my body. Then, if you're up for it, we could recreate them."

"Christ, woman," he growled, his voice rough with want. "You're killing me here."

"So...is that a yes?"

Dane gripped my hips and pulled me up against the unmistakable evidence of his arousal before asking, "What do you think?"

My breath caught. "That feels like a yes."

"It's a hell yes," he murmured before nodding toward the door. "But how are we going to make this work? Your friend's in there."

My mind raced as I considered our options. The hallway was out for obvious reasons. Duke and GQ likely occupied his room, and while I loved reading about it, I wasn't comfortable having sex with an audience of bikers.

"Once Ivy takes her sleeping pill, she could sleep through a train driving through the hotel," I said, the words tumbling out before I could second-guess the entire thing. "Meet me at the patio door in an hour?"

"You're sure?" he asked, searching my face.

I nodded, my heart racing with a mix of nerves and excitement. "I'm sure."

"One hour," he confirmed before crushing his lips to mine.

Slightly dazed, I forced myself to pull away before I could revise my stance on hallway sex.

With a final heated look, Dane turned and strode down the hallway. I lingered where I was for a moment, admiring the way his T-shirt stretched across his wide shoulders before slipping back into the room.

Ivy was already in her pajamas and moisturizing her face when I entered the bathroom. "That was more than a minute," she observed dryly.

I shrugged, aiming for nonchalance. "We got to talking. You know how it is."

"Uh-huh," she said, reaching for her toothbrush with a bemused smirk. "Last I checked, talking doesn't usually lead to a wicked case of beard burn."

It wasn't just my face. My skin tingled everywhere he'd touched me. But I wasn't sharing any of that with her.

"What's going on with you?" I asked, pivoting to Ivy's least favorite topic. *Herself.* "What's all this?"

"What's all what?" she mumbled through a mouthful of toothpaste.

I gestured vaguely at her reflection in the mirror. "This. One minute, you're laughing it up in the pool with two extremely attractive bikers, and the next, you're all pissy and want to go to bed."

She spit out a mouthful of toothpaste and rubbed her brow like she did when she had a headache. "I'm not pissy. Just annoyed."

"Because they failed your little experiment?" I asked, cocking my head to the side. "Come on, astronauts in space saw that one coming. You're a hottie. They're hotties. Everyone's going back to their regular lives tomorrow. Of course, they're going to try to shoot their shot."

Ivy gave a noncommittal response and took her sleeping pill before replacing the medicine bottle lid. I watched as she meticulously repacked her things, seemingly looking everywhere but at me.

My mouth went slack. "Holy shit!" I exclaimed. "They didn't try to take advantage of you, did they? They passed, and that's why you're so grumpy."

"Fine. They were perfect gentlemen. Are you happy now?" she snapped, her lips pressed into a thin white slash—like it pained her to admit she was wrong. "Why aren't you getting ready for bed?"

I shrugged, trying to keep my expression neutral. "Oh, I'm just waiting for you to finish up so I can grab a quick shower."

Ivy's blue eyes narrowed in suspicion. "You're not planning on sneaking out, are you, Amelia Piper Kelly?"

"What? No, of course not," I said, choking on the saliva in my mouth at her use of my full name. "Why would you think that?"

"Because I know you. And I know that look in your eyes." She folded her arms across her chest and leaned back against the counter. "Remember Rule Number Eleven? No hook-ups on vacation. It's not safe, especially this close to Houston."

"You think Dane's going to try to traffic me?"

She studied me for a long moment, her gaze sharp despite the sleeping pill starting to take effect. "I think leaving this room to meet a stranger for sex is incredibly stupid and dangerous. We may have spent several hours with these guys, but we don't really know them."

I held my hands up in surrender. "Relax. I'm not going anywhere. I just want to wash all the chlorine off before bed. You know how sensitive my skin is."

"Okay," she said after a long pause. "I'm heading to bed. Don't stay up too late."

As soon as the bathroom door clicked shut behind her, I let out a relieved breath before turning on the shower. I didn't feel good about lying to Ivy, even if it was by omission. She saw the darkest sides of people on a daily basis and had every right to be wary.

But I needed to do something to shake myself out of my dating rut. Even if it was a one-night stand with a biker, who was the polar opposite of the men I typically dated.

I waited until clouds of steam billowed over the glass shower door before getting in. The spray of hot water cascaded down my body, washing away any lingering doubts about what I was about to do.

As I lathered up with my favorite candy apple body wash, I couldn't help but imagine Dane's hands gliding over my slick skin instead. I took extra time, shaving my legs and underarms until there wasn't a hint of stubble, pleased I'd had the foresight to get a bikini wax before the trip.

After drying off, I wrapped myself in a fluffy white hotel robe and padded over to the vanity to brush my teeth and touch up my makeup. Nothing too crazy—just enough to feel confident. I brushed the tangles from my damp hair before pulling it up into a messy bun, the best I could do without waking Ivy.

Satisfied with my reflection, I crept into the bedroom to grab some clothes, only to stumble to a stop. The closet doors were firmly shut, with all our shoes and luggage stacked precariously in front.

"Goddammit, Ivy," I muttered under my breath while weighing my options.

Navigating the makeshift barricade would require waking her up, which was clearly her intention when she set it up. Of course, she'd seen right through my plan. That was the problem with knowing someone for almost two decades. You knew all their tells.

I studied the obstacle course before me, debating whether to crawl into bed and admit defeat or find a way to reach my clothes. Unfortunately, a quick glance at the clock on the nightstand between our beds confirmed I was out of time.

Bathrobe it was.

Not ideal, but infinitely better than a wet swimsuit.

FIVE
PIPER

Ivy & Piper's Guide to Life Rule Number Sixteen:
Don't sleep with a man until the third date.

With a resigned sigh, I cinched the belt of the robe tighter and tiptoed out of the bedroom, gently closing the door behind me. The lamps outside filtered through the sheer curtains, bathing the living area in soft yellow light.

My heart jumped into my throat as I caught sight of the massive silhouette waiting on the other side of the glass. I slid the door open as quietly as possible, wincing at the soft scrape of metal on metal.

The humidity enveloped me as soon as I stepped out onto the small sliver of concrete that constituted a patio. "Hey."

Dane's eyes widened as they raked over me. "Hey, yourself," he murmured, his eyes lingering on the deep V of the robe. "Thought you might've changed your mind."

"Not at all," I replied, hoping I sounded more confident than I felt. Goosebumps prickled my skin despite the warm evening, and even with the robe wrapped tightly around me, I felt exposed. I cleared my throat. "Do you, um, want to come inside?"

Where was the bold girl from the hallway when I needed her?

A small smile played at the corners of his mouth, and he inclined his head toward the open doorway. "Ladies first."

I was acutely aware of his closeness as I slid the door closed behind us. The soft click of the latch engaging seemed to echo in the quiet room as I turned to face him.

"Have a seat," I whispered, my voice barely above a whisper. "We just need to be quiet."

Dane stripped off his kutte and placed it on the coffee table before settling onto the sofa, his massive frame making it look comically undersized.

"Come here," he said, patting a sliver of cushion near his thigh.

I perched on the edge and smoothed my damp palms over my lap, willing my body to relax. His fingers brushed against my lower back, and I reflexively jerked away with a nervous squeak.

"You're shaking," he said, pulling his hand back like he'd been burned. "Would you feel better if I left?"

"No." I turned to face him, warmth pooling low in my belly as my knee brushed his thigh. "It's not that. I want you here. I want this. I'm just..." I trailed off, searching for the right words.

"Nervous?" he guessed, his voice laced with amusement.

Heat rushed to my cheeks, and I nodded before admitting, "A little. It's been a while."

His expression softened, and he reached over to cup my jaw, guiding my face toward his. "Hey, we don't have to do anything you're not comfortable with, Piper," he said, his thumb stroking along my cheekbone. "Let's take things slow and just talk."

Something about the gentleness of his touch, so at odds with his imposing presence, calmed my racing heart and settled my rolling stomach. I took a deep breath and nodded. "All right. What should we talk about?"

Dane shifted, pulling me closer until I was nestled against his side. The heat radiating from his body seeped through the lightweight cotton of the robe, easing some of the tension from my shoulders. "Tell me about yourself. What do you do when you're not serenading men with power ballads or entertaining stalkers like me?"

"Discreet admirer," I corrected with a soft laugh before adding,

"I'm a baker. Well, technically, I'm a pastry chef working in a bakery, but six of one, half a dozen of the other."

His eyebrows lifted in surprise. "A baker... Not what I expected."

"What, can't picture me in an apron?"

"Oh no, I can picture it just fine, darlin'," he said, a slow smile spreading across his face. "You look damn good in it too."

My breath caught at the compliment, and I struggled to keep my voice steady as I said, "I'll have you know I'm quite talented in the kitchen. In fact, I've been saving up to open my own place someday."

"Don't doubt that for a second," Dane murmured, lowering his gaze to my lips. "How close are you to making it happen?"

"Pretty close, actually," I said, unable to mask my excitement. "I'm hoping to have a lease signed on a building by the end of the year."

He nodded approvingly. "Impressive. Takes a lot of grit to start your own business."

I relaxed into his side, my earlier nervousness fading. "It does, but it's worth it. There's a certain romantic aspect to taking everyday ingredients and creating something amazing. It's like, in some small way, I get to be a part of someone's big moments, you know?"

As I spoke, his hand began tracing lazy patterns on my arm. "What's your favorite thing to bake?"

"Honestly?" I bit my lip with a grin. "Cinnamon rolls. They're super time-intensive, but the results are so worth it."

"God, I can't remember the last time I had homemade cinnamon rolls. My baking skills are limited to toaster pastries."

"No way. Store-bought doesn't hold a candle to these. I could teach you how to make them," I offered, then immediately felt foolish. What was I thinking, offering to bake for a man I would never see again after tonight?

"The biker and the baker," Dane mused with a low chuckle. "Pretty sure I saw an author selling that exact story at the event."

"Not to brag, but I snagged the last copy," I said, getting up to grab it from the book cart. "Thought it might be a good place for us to start." I bent to retrieve it from the stack before sauntering back to the couch, hips slightly swaying.

Dane kept his eyes on me even as he reached down to adjust

himself. That and the hard set of his jaw were all the motivation I needed.

"Here." I handed him the book before loosening the belt of my robe. His breathing shifted as the fabric slid down my shoulders, the fabric parting just enough to reveal the tops of my breasts.

In one fluid motion, I straddled his lap, my knees sinking into the couch cushions on either side of his muscular thighs. His erection flexed under me, and my lips parted on a strangled moan.

"You okay?" I whispered, leaning down to nip at his ear.

Dane latched onto my hips and lifted me off his lap. The feral growl that tore through his chest as he forced me to my knees had me pressing my thighs together in anticipation.

Instead of reaching for his belt, his fingers slid into my hair, carefully unraveling the messy bun until the dark strands fell in loose waves around my shoulders.

"What?" I asked, suddenly self-conscious under his intense scrutiny.

He exhaled a quiet laugh and shook his head. "Just admiring the view, darlin'. You're so goddamned beautiful. Been waiting all day to see you down on your knees for me."

My cheeks flushed at his praise, a mixture of pride and desire swirling in my belly as I reached for his belt buckle.

Because he was absolutely getting a blow job.

Dane caught my wrists, stopping me. "Easy. We've got all night."

"Please?" I pouted, peering up at him through my lashes.

His resolve crumbled at the plea. With a jerky nod, he loosened his grip, giving me silent permission to continue.

I made quick work of his belt and zipper before tugging his jeans and boxers down just enough to free his magnificent erection. My mouth watered at the sight of him, thick and hard and already glistening at the tip.

He toed off his boots and set his wallet on the end table before stripping off his remaining clothes.

"Go on then," he said gruffly, teeth sinking into the corner of his lip as he fisted his cock.

With a wordless nod, I pushed him toward the couch before shrugging the robe off. I crawled to him, noting the flare of his nostrils and subtle tightening in his jaw as his eyes roamed my body. Like his control was a thread precariously close to snapping.

I took my time, running my hands over the spectacular terrain of his muscular thighs before wrapping my fingers around the base of his dark, swollen shaft.

My breath ghosted over his heated flesh, and Dane hissed out a breath before gathering my hair in his fist. I flicked my tongue out and traced the prominent vein along his cock before swirling it over the precum beading at the tip.

"Fuck, Piper," he said with a groan, his fingers tightening against my scalp.

Emboldened by his reaction, I wrapped my lips around the velvet smooth crown, humming in pleasure when his hips jerked involuntarily.

"Just like that," he gritted out as I slowly took him deeper into my mouth, his voice strained. "You're so good at this."

I relaxed my throat and slid my mouth over him as far down as I could go. Tears pricked at the corners of my eyes as I held him there, using my hand to stroke what didn't fit in my mouth. I peered up through my lashes as his head fell back against the couch, reveling in the way his words of praise cut off in a soft moan. When I pulled back to take a breath, a string of saliva connected my lips to his glistening cock.

Watching the sexy giant come undone because of me was something I wanted to commit to my memory so I could relive it long after tonight.

Without warning, Dane hauled me onto his lap and crushed his mouth to mine, devouring my gasp of surprise. I shivered as my breasts collided with the hard planes of his chest, and he made a low sound in the back of his throat before capturing them in his hands.

His calloused fingers closed around the diamond-hard peaks of my nipples, stroking and tugging the tight buds until I was arching into him with incoherent pleas for more. With a growl, he flipped us so I was on my back on the couch, his massive frame looming over me.

He trailed his fingers along my inner thighs before wrenching them wide open, baring every part of me to his hungry gaze. "So wet for me already," he murmured, stroking my slick folds.

Two thick fingers plunged inside my body, and I bucked against his hand with a whimper, driving them deeper. His thumb found my clit, circling it with maddening precision. "You're perfect," he breathed against my skin.

My eyelids went heavy as he lowered his head to my heavy breasts, running his beard over the stiff peaks before sucking one into his mouth.

"Please," I begged, quickly losing myself to the expert rhythm of his mouth and hand. The coil of tension in my core wound tighter and tighter, my inner muscles pulsing wildly around his fingers. As he continued to stroke my clit with his thumb, I snapped, coming apart with a violent shudder.

While I lay trembling and thoroughly debauched on the sofa, Dane grabbed a condom from his wallet and rolled it on with practiced ease before draping my boneless body across his lap.

"You are so beautiful when you come," he said, nuzzling my neck and jaw.

Goosebumps spread over my skin as he coated himself in my release before guiding me into position. His thick length pressed against my entrance, the blunt head spreading me wide open.

I exhaled roughly as he lifted his hips and forced the first several inches into me, stretching me beyond anything I was used to. The burn of the initial penetration had me clinging to his broad shoulders, nails scoring his skin.

"Relax for me, darlin'," he commanded in a low rumble against my ear.

I nodded, willing my body to accept him. Even so, I had to bite down hard on my bottom lip to keep from screaming as he eased me down another torturous inch.

Sweat beaded on his brow, and he hissed through clenched teeth before filling me completely with one long, hard thrust. His hand clamped over my mouth, silencing my cries.

"Breathe," Dane gritted out. "Nice and easy."

I sucked in a ragged breath and dropped my forehead to his. He arched up to kiss me again while kneading the curve of my ass with his fingers.

Once my body adjusted to his size, I gave a shaky nod, and his large hands settled over my hips. Instead of the quick, hard pace I expected, he rocked me forward and back in a slow, teasing rhythm.

A tremor racked my body as the ridge of his shaft rubbed against my G-spot, and I rolled my hips faster, chasing more of the delicious friction.

His hands tightened on my hips, forcing us back to a slow, sensual grind before stopping entirely.

"Dane, please," I choked out.

"You need to be fucked," he stated, thrusting his hips up in demonstration.

My eyes went hazy, and I rocked shamelessly against him. "God, yes. I want to be so sore tomorrow morning that I can't even move without thinking of you."

He grinned and sucked my lower lip between his teeth before growling, "That's my girl. Hold on."

My warning was cut short when he gripped my ass for leverage and slammed into me, forcing a gasping moan past my lips.

My back bowed, and he dropped his head, sucking my pebbled nipple between his teeth. He bottomed out with every deep, punishing stroke, pushing me toward another peak embarrassingly fast.

"Taking my cock so well."

I writhed against him as he drove me higher and higher, my muscles quivering around his thick length. "I'm going to—" I clamped down around him and came so hard I saw stars.

The low din of a Jimmy Buffet song playing on the TV in the background faded to white noise, drowned out by our labored breaths and the wet sounds of his body pumping into mine.

Dane drove into me like a man possessed, his hips snapping up to meet mine with bruising force. I clung to his broad shoulders, muffling my cries against his neck as the pressure built once again.

"That's it, baby," he growled, his voice rough with exertion. "Ride my cock. Take what you need."

His fingers found my oversensitive clit, rubbing tight circles that had me trembling on the edge. I was so close, teetering on the precipice of another mind-blowing orgasm.

"I can't," I sobbed, overwhelmed by the onslaught of sensation.

"You can," he insisted, scraping his teeth along my jaw. "Come for me one more time."

His command sent a jolt of electricity down my spine, and I plastered my breasts against his chest and climaxed with a silent scream. The peaks of my nipples roughly scraped his skin with each crashing wave of ecstasy.

"Good girl," he ground out through clenched teeth, his strokes becoming erratic.

The words sparked something primal inside me. I rolled my hips to match his frantic pace, desperate to feel him lose control.

Dane's teeth slammed together, and his arms tightened around me before he came with a low, guttural groan. We clung to each other as the aftershocks rippled through our bodies.

I slumped against his chest, utterly spent and content. We stayed connected, our ragged breaths slowly evening out.

"You okay?" he asked.

I nodded, too blissed out to form words. A contented hum escaped my lips as he massaged the base of my skull, lulling me into a dreamlike state.

All too soon, he shifted beneath me. I whined in protest and clutched at his shoulders as he lifted me off his lap and laid me back on the couch. The loss of his warmth left me feeling oddly bereft.

"Don't leave," I said, reaching for him.

I could hear the smile in his voice as he replied, "Not leaving. Just taking care of the condom. Then I'm gonna get you cleaned up."

"Maybe I like being dirty," I teased, stretching languidly on the couch.

He chuckled low in his throat and padded back over to the couch. "Open for me."

I let my knees fall open, expecting him to use the towel in his hand. Instead, Dane dropped to his knees between my thighs. My breath caught as he leaned in, his warm exhales fanning over my sensitive flesh.

"What are you doing?" I whispered, propping myself up on my elbows.

He glanced up at me with a wicked grin. "Cleaning you up."

Before I could process his words, his tongue lapped at the mess between my thighs. I jerked in surprise, a strangled moan escaping my lips.

"Shh," he cautioned, pressing a kiss to my inner thigh. "Don't want to wake your friend, do you? Now, lay back and let me clean you up so we can get you dirty again."

A shiver of anticipation raced down my spine. "Again? Already?"

"Yes, again. And again. And again. A day's not good enough. I wanna make sure you're feeling me for weeks."

SIX

GHOST

Ivy & Piper's Guide to Life Rule Number Three:
Always carry enough cash to get home safely in case of an
emergency.

T he hotel sofa had not been made for men my size. My neck was stiff, and my feet hung over the edge of the arm. Still, I was completely content to stay right where I was.

Piper lay sprawled across me, her chest rising and falling in a gentle, steady rhythm. It should have been enough to lull me to sleep, but I was wide awake and overthinking things…as usual.

I listened to her soft exhales and studied the freckles scattered across the bridge of her nose, wondering if others had done the same. Had other men felt a sudden surge of possessiveness the moment they touched her like I had? The thought was both maddening and irrational, yet it burrowed into my mind, fueling an unexpected jealousy that threatened to consume me.

Piper sighed in her sleep, and her breath was warm against my skin. I tucked her body more firmly against mine and laced my fingers through hers, marveling at how small and delicate they felt beneath mine.

Using my free hand, I continued my exploration, trailing my fingers down her spine and over the seam of her ass, memorizing every dip and curve.

She arched against me, and the feel of her full tits pressing into my skin was all it took to rouse my cock to attention.

The friction temporarily overrode my ability to think rationally. I squeezed my eyes shut and tried to convince my dick to send some of the blood back up to my brain, but it was no use. Every exhale, every tiny movement, only stoked my need to claim her.

This woman would be the death of me.

My hand dipped lower, ghosting over the back of her thigh until I reached her knee. I hitched it higher until she was spread wide open for me before sliding my fingers over her slit.

She was already wet, her body responding to my touch even in sleep. And now that I'd started touching her, I couldn't seem to stop.

After waiting for her breaths to even out, I pumped a single finger into her pussy, grinning when she began drawing me in deeper. I pulled out slowly and brought my finger to my lips, sucking off her thick cream like a man starved.

The taste of her on my tongue only intensified the need pulsing through me. I gently eased out from under her and knelt beside the couch.

"Piper."

"Hmmm?" she mumbled, still caught in the hazy realm between sleep and consciousness.

My jaw tightened as I drank in the sight of her. Tousled brown hair. Legs spread wide. Like a holiday feast just waiting to be devoured.

If she were mine, I'd keep her like this all the time.

My dick jerked at the thought, but instead of fisting my shaft, I used my hands to lift Piper's hips.

Her swollen, pink flesh glistened with her arousal. Unable to resist, I leaned in and licked her from clit to center before sliding two fingers into her slick opening. Piper's breath shuddered when I curled them to hit her G-spot, her thighs automatically slamming shut around me.

The low growl in my throat sounded more animal than human as I forced them open again. I curled my arms around her thighs, anchoring her in place before devouring her cunt like it was my last meal. Alternating between broad strokes of my tongue and gentle suction, I redoubled my efforts until she was rocking back to meet me with little gasps and moans.

"Again?"

I lifted my head to meet her hooded gaze, her juices running down my lips and chin. "Again. Can you take me, or do you need a break?" I asked, already guiding her onto her hands and knees.

She blinked slowly, processing my words. I knew I should stop and let her rest. But the taste of her, the feel of her soft skin under my hands, was like a drug I was helplessly addicted to.

Piper reached back and began jacking my aching dick until precum leaked from the slit. "I can take it," she murmured, guiding the head of my cock into her body.

"Fuck," I gritted out, fighting the urge to slam home in one brutal thrust. She was so tight, her pussy gripping my bare—*oh, fuck.*

Watching her take me raw was almost my undoing. Instead of pulling out, I sank deeper, my hands spanning over the flare of her hips.

Childbearing hips, some might say.

I bit down on my lip until I tasted blood, fighting against every instinct to hold her down and flood her womb with my seed. To breed her. To claim her as mine for all eternity.

It was only the last shred of my moral compass that stopped me.

With a Herculean effort, I managed to pull out. "Condom," I groaned, fumbling for one on the side table and slipping it on.

Piper's disappointed whimper turned into a deep moan when I sank back into her wet heat. She dropped her weight onto her forearms and lifted her ass higher.

"That's my good girl," I growled, gripping her hips tighter.

When she slumped forward, I reached around to squeeze her clit between my thumb and forefinger, coaxing her back to full awareness. "Stay awake for me, darlin'. Okay?"

She nodded drowsily, her inner muscles tightening around me. "How do you want me?"

In every way possible for the rest of my life.

Instead of voicing the dangerous sentiment, I fisted a hand in her hair and tugged her head back. "Like this. Love watching your tight little cunt stretch around my cock from this angle," I growled, surging deeper.

Piper clawed at the arm of the sofa and began fucking back against me with renewed vigor.

"Yeah?" I asked, driving into her with a smirk. "You like that? You like hearing what your perfect body does to me?"

Her breath caught on a moan as she clenched around my shaft. "Don't stop."

As if I could.

As if I'd ever want to.

"You gonna drench this cock?" I rasped, snaking my hand down her belly to massage her clit. Her pussy clamped down like a vise, trying to force me out. I powered deeper with a savage growl, and she exploded, coming around my cock in pulsing gushes.

I released my grip on her hair and rolled to spoon Piper from behind, continuing to thrust into her pliant body. "Still with me?" I asked, placing a small kiss against the shell of her ear and another on her jaw.

She nodded weakly, reaching back to tangle her fingers in my hair.

"You did so good," I praised, squeezing her breast while maintaining my steady pace. "So. Fucking. Good."

"I wish—" Her words cut off in a gasp as I hit a particularly sensitive spot inside her.

"What do you wish?" I asked, my curiosity piqued despite the haze of lust clouding my mind.

Piper turned her head, meeting my gaze with those mesmerizing green eyes. "I wish I had you for more than tonight."

Her words sent a jolt through me, equal parts hope and trepidation. "Oh yeah? Why's that, darlin'?"

"Because then we could do this every night," she whispered, her breaths coming in ragged pants. "But it would be real."

"This isn't—this isn't real?" I stammered, struggling to focus as her pussy fluttered around me.

"N-nuh. Real would be you taking me bare. The way nature intended."

Jesus Christ.

I gripped her hips hard enough to bruise and slammed into her tight cunt, my balls slapping against her skin. The fantasy she'd conjured blurred my vision, pushing me dangerously close to the edge.

"Fuck, Piper. I'm—" I sank my teeth into the soft flesh between her shoulder and neck, muffling my guttural groan as I came in hard, wrenching spurts that caused my body to jerk wildly.

My release triggered hers, and Piper cried out, her body shuddering through another orgasm. She clenched rhythmically around me, milking every last drop.

"Stay inside me," she murmured when I started to pull out, fighting a yawn. "Please. You feel so good."

I settled back against her, burying my face in her hair and breathing in the scent of her shampoo.

"And what if I never want to leave?" I asked, suddenly serious.

Piper pulsed around my cock, and I exhaled a soft chuckle. "I think she likes the idea. You want me to stay—"

"It's one night," she protested, but I heard what sounded like wistfulness in her tone.

"But what if it wasn't?" I countered. "What if I stayed, and we figured out how to make this real over breakfast?"

"Now you're gonna buy me breakfast?" she asked through another heavy yawn before settling against me. "I may keep you forever."

"I like the sound of forever," I murmured, my body finally giving up the fight against sleep.

***

My body jerked violently, ripping me out of a nightmare. Blinking away the remnants of sleep, I checked my watch to find it was just after two. When I shifted, my still-hard cock slid out of Piper's body, followed by a flood of wetness.

Carefully, I climbed over her sleeping form and disposed of the condom in the nearby trash can. When I turned back, my breath caught in my throat. She'd rolled onto her back, one arm flung over her head, lips slightly parted.

The air conditioning kicked on with a low rumble, the cool air pebbling her nipples into tight buds. Unable to resist, I circled one pale pink peak with my finger. She stirred briefly before settling again, her legs falling open.

My cock swelled even more, and I gathered some of her wetness, spreading it over my shaft.

I was debating whether to wake her again when I caught a flash of movement at the patio door. Instinctively, I reached for my gun before remembering I'd left it back in my room, thinking it might frighten her.

Shit.

I tugged on my jeans, moving quietly so as not to wake Piper. Whatever this was, I needed to draw the potential threat away from her.

Heart pounding, I crept toward the patio door, muscles coiled tight and ready to spring into action. When I got closer, the shadow took shape, and a wave of relief washed over me because I recognized the hulking silhouette on the other side of the glass. It wasn't an intruder.

It was GQ.

One look at his grave expression, though, and my relief evaporated. Something was wrong.

"What happened?" I demanded, yanking the door open.

"Need to get home. Now."

A knot formed in my gut, and I swallowed hard before asking, "Is it my dad?"

"Wolverine's fine," GQ said, but his tone did little to reassure me. "We grabbed your shit from upstairs. Duke's bringing the truck around now. Get what you need from inside, and let's fucking go."

Panic clawed at my throat. "Is it my mom? My brothers?" When he didn't answer, I grabbed him by the kutte and growled, "Fucking tell me."

He worked his jaw back and forth before admitting, "It's Levi—"

The world tilted on its axis at the mention of my nephew's name. My grip on GQ's kutte loosened, and I staggered back, bile rising in my throat.

"What about Levi?" I managed to choke out, though part of me didn't want to hear the answer.

I'd just talked to him.

He was fine.

Pissed at me, but fine.

Had he taken off to clear his head after our call and gotten himself into trouble?

GQ's face crumpled, and at that moment, I knew. Whatever had happened was far worse than anything I could have imagined.

"Your brother found him," he said, his voice barely above a whisper.

"Teddy found him? What does that—what does that mean?" I stammered, struggling to make sense of what he was saying. "Is he hurt? In trouble?"

"He hanged himself."

SEVEN

PIPER

Ivy & Piper's Guide to Life Rule Number Thirty:
Friends don't let friends keep secrets.

Motorcycles, Mobsters, & Mayhem Event 2025

I wove through the vehicles parked in front of the valet and past a group of readers and authors getting their nicotine fix before the event. Their loud voices and boisterous laughter echoed off the walls of the hotel, assaulting my already frayed nerves.

It had been one year, nine months, and twenty-seven days since I'd woken up alone on a hotel room couch.

No note. No explanation. Nothing.

Since then, I'd often fantasized about what I would say to Dane if I ever saw him again. I envisioned boldly walking up to him and asking, *Why did you say you wanted to make it real and then leave without a word? Who the fuck does that?*

The daydreams varied, but most ended with me slapping the ever-loving shit out of him before waltzing off with my head held high, like a badass.

Now, faced with the reality of possibly seeing him again, my bravado crumbled. I couldn't do it. I wasn't ready to confront him over his actions if it meant seeing the rejection in his eyes when he learned the truth about our night together.

I'd spent most of the night and part of the morning with my head in the toilet, and exhaustion weighed on me like a lead blanket.

As I approached the entrance, I white-knuckled the strap of my purse, my palms growing clammy. The urge to flee back to my car and speed away from the entire asinine plan was overwhelming.

But my mama hadn't raised a coward.

An idiot, maybe. But not a coward.

So, with my heart pounding out a staccato rhythm, I took a deep breath and entered the lobby like a woman walking to her own execution, wincing when I caught sight of my haggard reflection in an ornate mirror.

Awesome. I looked as wrecked as I felt.

Dark smudges stained the pale skin beneath my green eyes, mocking my futile attempts to conceal them with makeup. The long, wispy bangs I spontaneously gave myself a few days ago looked less trendy and more like a cry for help.

Long months of worry and anxiety had taken a physical toll on me as much as an emotional one. Last night was just another in a long line of sleepless nights spent tossing in rumpled sheets and second-guessing my decision to come. The uncertainty was etched into the lines of my face and the hollows of my cheeks, and I couldn't even remember the last time I'd managed to get four hours of solid, uninterrupted sleep. And the long hours I'd been putting in at the bakery lately weren't doing me any favors either.

On cue, my phone vibrated, pulling me away from the mirror and the shell of a woman who was, as Garth would say, much too young to feel this damn old.

Thinking it might be my mother, I hurriedly snatched it out of my purse, only to see it was a text from my boss, Derek. My jaw tightened as I read his message, another thinly-veiled demand masquerading as a request.

> Derek: Got a last-minute order, and Terri called in sick. I need you to come in this afternoon. You know how it is.

Frustration simmered beneath my skin, a slow burn that threatened to ignite into a full-blown inferno. I requested the day off six months in advance and had already put in nearly fifty hours this week.

My thumbs hovered over the screen, itching to unleash a scathing reply to tell Derek exactly where he could shove his last-minute summons. But I resisted, knowing it was a battle I couldn't win.

Not if I wanted to keep my job anyway. I desperately needed to keep my job.

With a growl, I dropped the phone back into my purse and smoothed a hand over my long-sleeved dress.

The entire hotel bustled with activity, the sounds of book carts being wheeled toward the ballrooms echoing off the marble floors.

I scanned the crowded lobby, searching for familiar faces while simultaneously hoping to avoid them. My pulse kicked up a notch at every glimpse of dark hair or broad shoulders, and I was convinced it was him.

"Piper!" Ivy's voice cut through the chaos, and I turned to see her waving frantically near the back of a growing line.

I forced my lips into what I hoped was a convincing smile and made my way to her, my pulse racing. Every step closer to the ballroom felt like it was bringing me closer to my doom.

What if Dane was already inside?

What if he saw me first?

Or worse, what if he didn't come at all?

As I approached, I noticed Ivy didn't look much better than I did. A slight tremor ran through her body, and her wide blue eyes seemed to dart nervously around the room.

"Hey," I said, feeling the tension in her shoulders as I pulled her into a quick hug. "Sorry, I'm late. Traffic was—"

"Don't apologize!" she interjected a little too loudly. "You're here now, and that's all that matters."

We pulled apart, and I peered into her overly bright eyes with a frown. "You okay?"

"Me? I'm fine!" She let out a startled shriek and spun around, startling the poor woman in line behind us.

"Sorry!" the woman exclaimed, jerking her hand back. "I was just trying to let you know the line was moving."

"Thank you," I told her. After inching forward to close the gap, I turned to Ivy with a raised brow. "Are you sure you're okay? You seem…on edge."

"Just excited and maybe a tad bit overcaffeinated," she insisted, squaring her shoulders with a brittle laugh. "This is fun. I can't remember the last time we had a weekend with just us."

Before I could press further, a familiar figure emerged from the ballroom, and my stomach dropped.

GQ moved with the casual grace of a man used to commanding the attention of women everywhere. But now, the sight of him sent a jolt of panic through my veins because where he was, Dane couldn't be far behind.

Panic clawed its way up my throat, bitter and sharp. Without thinking, I grabbed Ivy's hand and squeezed.

"Piper, what—"

"We have to go," I hissed, my voice trembling. "I can't—I can't do this. I can't be here."

She searched my face, her eyes softening with understanding. "Okay, sweetie. Why don't you wait for me by the entrance, and I'll be right there."

I nodded gratefully and made my way back through the crowded lobby, my heart pounding in my ears.

Once I reached the relative safety of the hotel entrance, I pulled out my phone with shaking hands. I needed a distraction, something to ground me before I completely lost it.

> Me: Just checking in. How are y'all doing?

The reply came through almost immediately.

> Mom: We're perfectly fine and having fun like you should be, missy.

I stared at the screen, the words blurring as tears pricked the corners of my eyes. If my mother knew why I was here, she would have told me not to come. She would have said it wasn't worth the risk, the pain.

But I had to know, didn't I?

I had to see Dane one last time, even if it shattered me.

Ivy's soothing voice broke through my spiraling thoughts. "Hey, I found a volunteer to hold our spot. Let's get you some air."

"You know I hate when you use your therapy voice," I grumbled, as she took my hand and led me outside.

"I have no idea what you're talking about."

The cool air was a welcome relief against my flushed skin. I took a deep breath, willing my racing heart to slow.

"I know it's hard being away from her and doing something for yourself," she said, breaking the silence. "Just know it's completely normal—"

"That's what you think this is—separation anxiety?" I huffed out an annoyed breath and shook my head. "I work all the damn time and only see her three, maybe four hours a day. Sorry, Doctor, but any separation anxiety I may have had is long gone."

"Is it something at work then?" she asked, her voice taking on a dangerous edge. "Or Derek? I swear to all that is good and holy, Piper. All I need is five minutes and a hammer, and that fucking creeper wouldn't bother you anymore."

I choked on a laugh and deadpanned, "A hammer? That's not very love and light of you. Have you asked yourself if this is coming from a place of healing?"

"Screw healing," she growled, balling her hand into a fist. "Sometimes, karma takes too long, and it's up to us to teach the dickheads of the world a lesson."

The reaction was overkill, even for someone as fiercely protective of her friends as she was. I studied her face, noting the tightness around her eyes and how her gaze continuously shifted from one end of the hotel to the other as if she were searching for an unseen threat.

"I'm good," I said, knowing better than to press her over it. Getting Ivy to open up was like trying to break into Fort Knox armed with nothing but a spork. "I think it was just all the people crowding around us—I felt like I couldn't breathe."

"Really?" she asked, her tone skeptical. "You sure it doesn't have something to do with running into Ghost again?"

The blood drained from my face. "Dane's—he's here? You're sure?"

She nodded, watching me with a penetrative gaze that always made me feel like she was peering straight into my soul. "Yeah, I saw him carrying boxes in with GQ and Duke before you got here."

My legs buckled, and I latched onto her to remain upright. My instincts screamed at me to run—from the hotel, from the memories, from him.

"The biker—he's the reason you're on the verge of a panic attack?" she questioned, pulling the corner of her lip between her teeth and studying me like I was a puzzle to be solved.

She knew me all too well—could sense the turmoil churning beneath the surface of my carefully crafted facade.

"What am I missing? You hung out at the pool, and then he walked you back to the room. End of story. Why would seeing him again upset you? It's not like he's the deadbeat who knocked you up—" She stopped abruptly, her face draining of color.

"Dane is Avery's father?" she whispered, her voice barely audible.

I managed a small nod, confirming her worst suspicions.

"Jesus Christ," Ivy breathed, running a hand through her hair. "Why didn't you tell me?"

"Because saying it out loud made it real." Tears burned behind my eyes, threatening to spill over. I swallowed past the lump in my throat. "And I wasn't ready for it to be real."

"Does he know?"

I shook my head, shame and guilt twisting in my gut. "I tried to find him after I found out I was pregnant, but without a last name or phone number, it was virtually impossible. Short of dropping by every clubhouse in the state to see if they knew a Ghost or a Dane, I didn't know what else to do."

"You should have come to me with this. I would have helped you find him."

I shrugged, unable to meet her gaze. "At first, I was too scared to face the reality of the situation. Then, as time went on, it just got harder and harder to bring it up. I told myself it was better this way—that Avery and I were doing fine on our own."

"But you're not fine," she pointed out in a gentle tone. "You're exhausted, overworked, and falling apart at the thought of running into Dane. This isn't healthy, Piper."

"I know," I said, my voice cracking again. "But what am I supposed to do now? Walk up to him and say, 'Hey, remember that night we spent together? Surprise! You have a daughter!'"

Ivy placed her hands on my shoulders, forcing me to look at her. "Yeah, that's exactly what you're going to do. He deserves to know, and more importantly, Avery deserves to know her father."

The thought of confronting him, of seeing the shock and potential anger on his face made me want to vomit all over again.

"You don't understand," I choked out, shaking my head frantically. "I can't just drop this bomb on him out of nowhere."

"Then when, Piper? When Avery's graduating from high school? When she's looking for someone to walk her down the aisle?" Ivy's voice softened. "There's never going to be a right time, but the longer you wait, the harder it's going to be."

The full weight of her words sank in. She was right, of course. But knowing what I had to do and doing it were two very different things.

"What if he wants nothing to do with us? Oh my god. What if he tries to take her away?"

"Breathe," Ivy commanded. "You're catastrophizing. You don't know how he'll react until you tell him."

I paced back and forth across a small section of pavement. "That's just it. I don't know *him*. Not really. We spent one night together, and then he vanished. For all I know, he could be married with three kids."

She latched onto my arm, halting my frantic movement. "Then you need to find out so you can stop torturing yourself with the what-ifs. You also need to consider the possibility that he might want to be involved. Are you prepared for that?"

Was I prepared for Dane to want to be a part of Avery's life? To potentially disrupt the careful balance I'd constructed over the past year?

"Piper?"

I froze, my heart pounding so violently I thought it might burst from my chest. Time slowed to a crawl as I turned around, coming face to face with the man who haunted almost all my dreams.

Dane stood less than six feet away, looking even more devastatingly handsome than the last time I saw him. His dark eyes roamed over me, and memories of that night flashed through my mind like an uninvited guest.

"I thought that was you inside," he said, his presence as palpable as ever. The kutte he wore molded to his muscular frame like a second skin, while the black T-shirt underneath strained against his biceps and broad shoulders.

Had he always been this muscular, or was it a recent development? I couldn't remember.

He took a step closer. "It's been a while."

A while.

As if the past year and nine months could be summed up so casually. As if he hadn't knocked me up and disappeared without a trace.

Not that either of us had known I would end up pregnant when he slipped out in the middle of the night, but still. *A while?* That was the best he could come up with?

A vein pulsed in my forehead. My emotions were rapidly cycling between anger, hurt, confusion, and rage.

Heavy on the rage.

An awkward silence stretched between us, thick with unspoken words and lingering questions. I could feel Ivy's eyes darting between us, practically vibrating with the need to intervene.

I opened my mouth, but the words wouldn't come out. This was it —the moment I'd both dreaded and longed for. And I was completely unprepared.

"You look..." He trailed off, his brow furrowing as he studied me more closely. "Are you all right?"

No, I wanted to scream. *I'm not all right. I haven't been all right since the night you left.*

My throat was bone dry as I replied, "I'm fine."

Dane's eyes narrowed, clearly not buying what I was trying to sell. He took another step closer, close enough now I could smell the faint scent of leather and something distinctly him. My traitorous body reacted instantly, a familiar warmth spreading through my veins.

His forehead creased with concern. "You don't look fine. What's wrong?"

A hysterical laugh bubbled up in my chest. What wasn't wrong?

My entire world had been turned upside down the moment I saw those two pink lines on the pregnancy test. And now here he was, standing in front of me like no time had passed at all, asking what was wrong as if he had any right to know.

"Nothing's wrong," I lied again, my voice trembling. "I just... I wasn't expecting to see you here."

His jaw tightened, a flicker of hurt flashing across his face before he schooled his features into a neutral expression. "Yeah, I wasn't sure if I'd be able to make it this year, but GQ convinced me to come at the last minute. It's good to see you."

Good to see me?

"Well, we better go before we lose our place in line. Bye, Dane." I turned and walked back inside, focusing on the click of my heeled boots against the pavement—anything to keep from looking back.

My mind replayed our brief encounter on a loop. The concern in his eyes and the way his voice softened when he asked if I was all right was almost enough to make me believe he cared.

Almost.

EIGHT

PIPER

Ivy & Piper's Guide to Life Rule Number Seven:
Block, delete, and move on.
AKA- Alcohol and exes do not mix.

Ivy's gaze burned into the side of my head as we made our way back to the line, urging me to go back and tell him the truth.

"What the hell was that?" she hissed, gripping my arm and pulling me into a secluded hallway near the bathrooms. "You had the perfect opportunity to tell him, and you walked away!"

"Why do you care? You're the one who told me not to meet him that night."

"Yeah, Piper. I did," she said dryly. "And you did it anyway. The toothpaste is out of the tube, so to speak."

I bristled, anger flaring hot in my chest. "You think I don't know that? You think I haven't agonized over my decision every single damn day?"

"Then why didn't you tell him?" she pressed, her voice rising.."He was right there, Piper. You could have put yourself out of your misery with a handful of words."

"Because I froze, okay?" I snapped, my eyes stinging with tears.

"Because seeing him again after all this time... It was too much. I couldn't think straight, let alone tell him the truth."

"So you ran away like a scared little girl? That's not like you."

"Mm, you're right. I should have just told him because that worked out so well for my mom," I gritted out, angrily swiping at the tears on my cheeks.

Her expression softened, and she sighed. "Not all men are your father, Piper. Come on. He's here, you're here. It's like the universe is practically screaming at you to come clean. He deserves to know."

I sliced my hand through the air with a groan. "Stop. This isn't about him. It's about what's best for Avery—"

"And you think keeping her father in the dark is what's best for her?" Ivy challenged, arching an eyebrow. "I know you. The guilt will eat you alive. You can't avoid it forever."

"Watch me," I grumbled, digging through my bottomless pit of a purse for my phone. I'd managed to locate it when a large hand wrapped around my shoulder, stopping me in my tracks. I didn't need to look up to know who it belonged to—my body's reaction told me everything. Proving it had a sick and twisted sense of humor, the universe had decided to bring the conversation to me.

"We need to talk," he said, his tone leaving no room for argument.

"I'll, uh, see you inside," Ivy murmured, squeezing my hand as she passed. The silent message was clear—*tell him.*

Take me with you, you traitor.

I took a deep breath before reluctantly turning to face him. "If you're trying to clear your conscience or whatever, you can save your breath," I said, sounding small and uncertain instead of strong and confident. "I'm fine. It was a casual thing—"

Dane tightened his grip on my shoulder, preventing me from fleeing. In one swift motion, he pushed me up against the wall, caging me in with his body. His eyes pierced mine, a storm of emotions swirling within their blackened depths.

My heart thundered against my chest, a mix of fear and something else I didn't want to name coursing through me.

"Bullshit," he growled, his face inches from mine. "You want to write it off as a mistake, fine. But don't act like it didn't mean anything because it did."

I let out a bitter laugh, trying to mask the hurt his words stirred up. "Now, who's bullshitting themselves?"

"I get you're pissed, and you have every right to be. But give me a chance to explain."

"Explain?" I scoffed, shaking my head. "Seems to be a pattern with you, doesn't it? Always needing to explain yourself. Just stop with the excuses and call it what it was. A one-night stand."

"You know it was more than that," he argued, shaking my shoulder as if trying to force me to understand. "Jesus, Piper. I meant every word I said that night."

My chest constricted at the raw desperation in his voice. I wanted to believe him, but the memory of waking up alone, sore, and confused was still too fresh.

"Then why'd you leave, huh?" I demanded, hating the way my voice cracked. Tears blurred my vision, and I blinked them back furiously. "Why take off without so much as a note if it meant so much to you?"

The shrill chime of my phone cut through the heavy silence, startling us both. I used the distraction to try to free myself from his iron grip.

"Let me go." When he didn't immediately release me, I planted my hand on his chest and pushed. "Move."

Dane stepped back and dragged his hands through his hair in frustration while I checked my phone to find an automated text from a local boutique about a sale they were having. Hardly the lifeline I'd been hoping for.

I tucked it back into my purse, steeling myself against the anguished look in his eyes and the dark circles I'd missed before.

"I'll tell you everything you want to know," Dane said, his voice low and urgent. "Just not here."

I rolled my eyes, already anticipating his next move. "Let me guess. You're willing to do it over drinks or back in your hotel room," I muttered, looking up at him with narrowed eyes. "No, thanks."

He ran his tongue over his teeth with a cold chuckle before gritting out, "You want to do this right here? Fine. I left because my nephew, Levi..." His lips trembled, and he pressed them together before dropping his chin to his chest with a pained gasp.

My heart plummeted, the band around my chest tightening. "Dane, what happened?"

"He killed himself the night we were together," he said, his voice little more than a whisper, his dark eyes staring into nothing.

Everything I thought I knew about that night turned on its head. All this time, I'd convinced myself he left because I meant nothing to him when the truth was far more devastating.

"I… I'm so sorry," I managed to choke out, instinctively reaching for his hand before catching myself. The burning anger in my chest I'd carried for almost two years had been snuffed out and replaced by a hollow ache.

"Listen, I don't want to keep you from the event," Dane said, clearing his throat. "But I'd like to take you to dinner after."

I hesitated, torn between the urge to comfort him and the secret still burning a hole in my chest. "I'm actually not staying at the hotel. I have somewhere I have to be as soon as this is over."

Disappointment flashed in his eyes, followed by a resigned nod.

My throat tightened. A part of me wanted to offer some small comfort. But another part—the part that had been hurt and angry for so long—held me back.

"Actually," I began hesitantly. "I'm free now if you want to grab a drink at the bar. I think we could both use one."

He glanced back toward the ballroom with a frown. "You sure? What about your books?"

"I didn't have any preorders," I said, conveniently leaving out the part about how most of my discretionary income went to diapers these days.

Dane's dark eyebrows shot up in surprise. "Really? Figured you'd have a whole stack waiting for you."

I shrugged, trying to appear nonchalant. "Not this year."

He studied me for a long moment before nodding. "All right, darlin'. Let's get you that drink then."

His large hand found the small of my back as he guided me toward the elevators. Even in heels, he still towered over me, his broad frame radiating a sense of safety I hadn't realized how much I'd missed until now. Despite the tumultuous churning in my stomach and my needing to remind myself to breathe, the weight of his palm felt oddly comforting against my skin.

The ride up was silent, the air between us thick with unspoken words and unanswered questions. I fidgeted with the gold band on my thumb, twisting it around and around as I tried to gather my racing thoughts. The confession I'd rehearsed a thousand times in my head suddenly felt all wrong.

When the doors slid open, Dane steered me toward the empty chairs in front of the bar. The terrace was mostly deserted save for a few people taking in the Dallas Steel's practice facility and a couple relaxing in the temperature-controlled pool.

A gust of wind caught my hair almost as soon as I sat down, blowing the long strands across my face. His fingertips grazed my cheek as he reached out to tuck them behind my ear, sending a jolt of longing through me.

"Uh, you go first," I said when the bartender approached to take our order. "I'm still deciding."

"Whiskey, neat," Dane requested before looking at me expectantly.

"I'll have..." I chewed on my lip, weighing my options. It had been ages since I'd had a real drink—motherhood had put an end to my social life. But if there was ever a time I needed some liquid courage, it was now.

"I'll have the same. Actually, you know what? Make mine a double —what?" I asked when Dane did a double take.

"Nothing," he said with a chuckle. "Just surprised."

I snatched up my glass and took a large gulp as soon as the bartender slid it over, hissing out a wheezy cough.

"Jesus," Dane muttered with a low whistle. He held up his own glass. "Cheers, I guess."

"Cheers," I rasped, clinking my glass against his before knocking back the remaining liquor with a shudder.

God, it was like drinking acid.

He sipped his whiskey more slowly, watching me with a mixture of amusement and concern. "You all right there?"

"Fine," I croaked, setting my empty glass down with a *thunk* and signaling the bartender for another round.

The burn in my throat settled into a pleasant warmth that spread through my chest, draining the tension from my shoulders and giving me a false sense of courage.

"I wanted to say I'm so sorry about your nephew. I can't even imagine."

He nodded stiffly, staring down into his glass. "It's been a living hell I wouldn't wish on my worst enemy," he admitted, his deep voice thick with emotion. "I keep thinking about all the signs I missed, you know? The things I could've done differently."

"You have to know it isn't your fault." I reached out, placing my hand over his much larger one.

"Isn't it?" he asked with a humorless laugh, his shoulders slumping under an invisible weight. "I'm the one who gave him shitty advice, and when he called me upset because it all went wrong, I wasn't really listening. I could have stayed on the phone with him instead of rushing to get off so I could…"

He trailed off, but I knew what he meant. So he could meet me.

"Don't," Dane said quietly as if reading my thoughts. "I'm not blaming you. I don't regret anything that happened between us that night, Piper. I need you to know that."

I nodded, biting the inside of my cheek as I absorbed his words. The rational part of my brain knew he was right, that Levi's decision wasn't on either of us. But I couldn't help but feel the sting of culpability.

"GQ was the one who came to get me. By the time I realized I had no way to reach you, it was too late."

He took another small sip of whiskey, the muscles in his throat rippling as he swallowed. "I tried to play it cool earlier but fuck it. I came for you today. I know I fucked up by disappearing on you without a word, but if you give me another chance, I promise things will be different this time."

I stared into the amber depths of my second glass as if it held all the answers I so desperately needed, like some boozy magic eight-ball.

"I can't sleep with you," I blurted out, the words tumbling from my whiskey-loosened lips before I could stop them. Now I remembered why I never drank on an empty stomach because tipsy Piper had no filter. "I mean, I won't. Sleep with you, that is."

Dane ran a hand over his jaw and blinked at me, clearly taken aback. "Shit. At least buy me dinner first."

"I'm serious."

"So am I." The corner of his mouth kicked up in a lopsided grin that did dangerous things to my insides.

The heat from the liquor spread into my lower belly, and I squirmed in my seat. "Things are—they're different now."

"Care to elaborate?"

My eyes flicked to my dark phone screen. "It's just—"

"You're with someone," he guessed, nodding toward the device. "You keep checking it every five minutes, so I assume someone's waiting for you back home."

"Yes. Well, not exactly." I shook my head and blew out a breath, frustrated by my inability to spit it out already. "It's complicated."

His grin widened. "And here I thought you were about to tell me you're happily married. But complicated?" He leaned in, dragging his lips along my jaw before stopping at my ear, his voice taking on a low, sexy edge as he murmured, "I can work with complicated, darlin'."

NINE

GHOST

Ivy & Piper's Guide to Life Rule Number Five:
Be your own sugar daddy.

Instead of leaning into my touch, Piper pulled back as if she'd been burned. "It's not that simple."

"You trying to let me down gently?" I asked, rotating my whiskey glass in a slow circle against the bar top like my entire future didn't hinge on what she said next.

She rubbed at her brow and crossed her legs before answering. "No, that's not it."

I made the mistake of lowering my gaze to the soft curves of her thighs, my mouth going dry as I imagined sinking my teeth into her tender flesh.

The muscles in her calves flexed and tightened as if it was taking everything in her to remain seated. "What do you want?"

Fuck, I wanted her.

I wanted to wrap her legs around my waist and bury myself so deep inside her tight cunt the crease between her brows faded, and she had no choice but to accept that she was mine.

But she was as skittish as a spooked horse—one wrong move and someone was getting kicked in the balls. Likely me.

"What do I want?" I repeated, trying to get myself under control before I fucked this up. "You, Piper. I want you."

Her eyes flashed with something—longing, fear? I couldn't tell. She pulled her plump bottom lip between her teeth, sending a jolt of pure need straight to my cock.

So much for talking it down.

"What does that even look like?" she asked warily.

I lowered my head to hers, inhaling her intoxicating scent. Fuck, she may have looked like sin in that dress, but she smelled like innocence.

"You know exactly what it looks like," I murmured, my voice low and rough with want.

It looked like my ring on her finger. My last name. My baby growing in her belly.

Mine.

"It looks like you in my bed every night, screaming my name while I make you come so hard you see stars." I brushed my lips against the curve of her jaw.

A shudder rippled through her, and her thighs clenched together. I'd barely touched her, and she was already so responsive, so desperate for it, just like our first night.

"You can't say things like that. We barely know each other."

"I know enough." I skimmed my knuckles up her bare thigh, feeling the goosebumps pebbling her silky skin. "I know the sounds you make when you're about to fall apart. I know how fucking perfect you feel around my dick."

Piper made a soft, desperate sound and latched onto my kutte before catching herself. "Stop. We had one night together."

"And?" A muscle ticked in my jaw as I struggled to tamp down my frustration. I didn't give a fuck if it had only been one night. I'd known she was it before ever showing up outside her hotel room, and I would burn the world to ash and destroy anyone who got in the way.

"And you can't build a relationship off one night. Everything you think you know about me relates back to sex. It's superficial."

"That's not true. I know you have a soft spot for power ballads, and your first crush was a douchebag named Rowdy. You're a pastry chef who loves to make cinnamon rolls and..."

Fuck, I was drawing a blank.

"Wait. Weren't you opening your own bakery?"

"My own what?" Piper blinked up at me with those gorgeous green eyes, looking confused and a little lost.

"Your own bakery," I repeated slowly, studying her face for any flicker of recognition. "The one you were close to opening the last time we were together."

Her expression shuttered, and she lowered her gaze, the walls coming back up in an instant. "It, uh, it didn't work out."

"What happened?"

"It's a long story. And not one I want to get into right now," she muttered, knocking back the rest of her whiskey.

The utter defeat in her voice made my chest tighten.

Who the fuck had made her look like that?

I wanted to push—to demand she tell me everything so I could hunt down and destroy the person responsible.

But I needed to tread carefully. If she knew how badly I wanted her and the lengths I would go to keep her, she'd bolt.

"Look at me."

"Why?" she asked, picking at a loose thread on her dress.

I cupped her jaw and tilted her face up to mine until she reluctantly met my gaze. "Because I don't want you to shut me out."

"Who says I'm shutting you out?" Piper jutted her chin up defiantly but didn't pull away. It was a start.

"You don't have to say it. It's right there in your eyes. They give you away." I reached out to brush a loose curl behind her ear, letting my knuckles brush over her cheekbone.

A flicker of something passed over her face.

Guilt? Or was it fear?

In either case, it wasn't the reaction I was aiming for.

"Look, I may not know what makes you laugh or how you take your coffee, but I know that night meant something for both of us," I said, struggling to keep the desperation from bleeding into my voice.

"Tell me you haven't thought about it like I have." I searched her eyes for any hint of the desire I knew she still felt for me. "Tell me you don't get wet remembering how I felt inside you."

She hesitated before bobbing her head in a shaky nod. "I do, but things are complicated."

There was that word again.

Complicated.

As if anything worth having ever came easy. I was a man who knew how to work for what I wanted. And god, I wanted her.

"Then let me un-complicate it for you," I said, tracing the curve of her bottom lip with my thumb.

"But...but there's something you should know first," Piper stammered, her hands fluttering to my chest like she wasn't sure whether to push me away or pull me closer.

I could see the war raging within her, the battle between her head and her heart. A better man would have backed off, but I was too far gone to stop now. I dipped my head, my lips ghosting over the racing pulse point in her neck. She let out a soft whimper as my teeth grazed her collarbone. "Whatever it is can wait."

"Dane—"

The sound of her breathy, pleading voice shattered the last of my resolve. I tugged her head back to expose the slender column of her throat, but before I could capture her lips with mine, her phone buzzed against the bar.

Piper jolted away from me and fumbled for her phone with shaking hands. "I'm so sorry," she said, glancing between me and the screen. "I have to take this."

The breeze caught the hem of her dress as she stood, exposing a brief but tantalizing glimpse of the curve of her ass. It was impossible not to picture the material bunched beneath my fist as she lay across the chair, legs spread wide open and ready to be devoured. My dick strained against my zipper, the image seared into my brain permanently.

She walked a few steps away to take her call, leaving me in a state of frustrated arousal. My eyes followed the sway of her hips, and the way her dress clung to her curves. I tried to regain some semblance of control, fighting against the growl building in my throat.

"She what? Mom, slow down. I can't understand what you're saying."

Piper's voice raised the hairs on the back of my neck. My instincts —honed from years in dangerous situations—were on high alert.

Her hand flew to her mouth, and I was moving before I even consciously registered what was happening. I tossed down more than enough cash to cover our drinks before grabbing her purse, my chair screeching against the concrete as I strode over to where she stood.

"Which hospital?" she asked, the color draining from her face as she listened to the reply.

Her knees buckled, and I locked my arm around her waist before leading her toward the elevator.

I didn't know who was on the other end of the call or what they were saying, but watching Piper fall apart in front of me was like being gutted with a dull knife.

"My purse," she mumbled as we stepped into the elevator, looking around the elevator car in confusion.

"It's right here." I pressed the button for the lobby before turning so she could see it hanging off my shoulder.

Her lower lip quivered. "But my phone..."

"It's in your hand, darlin'," I said, giving her a soft squeeze. "You're doing good. Just breathe."

She nodded numbly and blinked at me, unshed tears turning her already gorgeous green eyes into a deep emerald. "I have to go. My daughter fell," she choked out, her voice little more than a whisper.

Daughter?

The news was as subtle as a sledgehammer to the chest.

She had a kid. Which meant she likely had a man too.

Was that what she'd meant by complicated—baby daddy drama?

I swallowed past the knot in my throat, shoving down the irrational surge of possessiveness at the thought of her with someone else. Of her carrying another man's child. A man I couldn't kill without depriving her daughter of a father.

We spilled out into the hotel lobby, and Piper's phone slipped from her hand, clattering to the floor. I scooped it up and pocketed it before steering her outside.

She clapped her palm over her mouth and lurched toward a nearby flower bed before doubling over to puke up the liquor. I held back her hair and rubbed circles over her back as she retched, quietly encouraging her to breathe.

"Shouldn't have had that second whiskey," she croaked when there was nothing left in her body. "I don't know how I'm going to drive—"

"Oh, you're absolutely not driving," I said firmly before guiding her over to a bench so she could sit while I searched her purse for the keys. "I am. Tell me where you're parked."

***

I kept sneaking glances at the car seat in the back as I drove, searching for any clues as to how old her daughter was.

Had Piper met someone after our night together?

Would he be waiting for her at the hospital?

"I need—"

"Hang on, darlin', we're almost there." I reached across the console to take her hand while navigating the early afternoon traffic like I was running from the cops.

My bike would have been faster, but I didn't have a helmet. That, and I wasn't entirely convinced she would have been capable of holding onto me in the state she was in.

She nodded, tears spilling down her bloodless cheeks. As I approached the exit for the children's hospital, her fingernails dug into the flesh above my knuckles in a silent plea for me to drive faster.

"Almost there," I muttered, pressing harder on the gas pedal.

By the time I pulled into a parking space, my skin was scored with crescent-shaped indentions. Piper sprang from the SUV before I'd even killed the engine and sprinted toward the emergency room entrance with a single-minded focus I knew all too well.

"Piper!" I called after her, pausing to grab my kutte from the backseat and slipping it on before forcing my legs into action. Christ, she was surprisingly fast for someone wearing heels.

"My daughter was brought in," she panted as soon as she reached the front desk. "Avery. Avery Kelly."

Was that his last name or hers?

The receptionist offered her a sympathetic smile, her fingers rapidly tapping against her keyboard. "Just one moment, ma'am."

Less than a minute later, a nurse wearing Winnie the Pooh scrubs and a smile that didn't quite reach her tired eyes arrived to take us back.

We moved through a labyrinth of identical hallways, the fluorescent lights casting a harsh glow on the white walls and linoleum floors. The air was filled with the sterile scent of disinfectant and the sounds of babies crying.

Piper held onto me, her small hand gripping mine so tightly I'd need a crowbar to pry her fingers loose.

We arrived at a nondescript door, and the nurse gently pushed it open before ushering us in. I took two steps before stumbling to a stop just inside the doorway, pressing my fist to my mouth as I took in the bloody gash on Avery's temple. I'd seen plenty of head wounds, but never on someone so tiny.

Piper dropped my hand to rush to her daughter's side.

"We're trying to get her blood pressure, but little miss is not having it," a nurse said as Avery flailed and kicked at her with a hoarse, raspy cry.

"Here, let me see if I can get her calmed down. Mama's here," she cooed, gently rocking her daughter in her arms. Avery clung to Piper, sucking violently on her pacifier for a few seconds before launching into another high-pitched, intense wail.

I couldn't explain it. It was as if someone had wrapped their hand around my heart and was squeezing the life out of it. I hadn't felt this fucking helpless since Levi.

A middle-aged woman, who I presumed was Piper's mother, stroked a hand over the little girl's strawberry curls before noticing me hovering in the doorway.

"Who are you?" she asked, her sharp hazel eyes narrowing when they landed on my kutte.

"Dane Riggs," I answered, offering a hand that was pointedly ignored. "I'm a friend of Piper's."

She looked at me as if I were a stray dog that had wandered into their home and taken a shit on the carpet. "I see. Well, as much as I'm sure she appreciates you being here, this is a family matter, so you should probably go."

"Mother!" Piper hissed before peering up at me. "Dane, I need—"

Avery jerked in her arms with a pained cry, her small body shuddering violently as if she were cold. Piper kissed the top of her head and brushed the tears from her reddened cheeks while humming softly.

"What do you need?" I asked, stepping around the five-foot-nothing obstacle in my way to reach them.

"I need you to stay," she pleaded, her eyes welling up with fresh tears as she stroked Avery's cheek until the cries trailed off into pitiful whimpers. "Please."

"Hey, I'm not going anywhere," I said, ignoring her mother's disapproving glare.

"You're letting this...*biker* near my granddaughter?" she retorted, clutching at her throat as if choking on the idea.

Piper's eyes flashed in warning. "Yes, Mom. This biker has been more help in the last thirty minutes than you've been since we got here. Now, will someone please tell me what happened?"

"She fell out of her highchair," she explained, looking like her daughter when she lowered her gaze to the floor.

"How many times have I told you to buckle her in?" Piper whisper-yelled through clenched teeth.

Before she could respond, another nurse entered the room, carrying a small silver instrument tray. "Looks like Mom and Dad made it here in the nick of time."

"Absolutely not!" Piper's mother interjected. "He is not her father."

I imagined her face was screwed up like she'd been sucking on lemons, but I wasn't looking at her. I was staring at Piper, who suddenly refused to meet my gaze.

The sudden tension in the room was suffocating, leaving my fingers twitching with the urge to reach out and touch her—to force her to look me in the eye.

"Okay," the nurse conceded before checking the white plastic bracelet around Avery's ankle. "And Avery's date of birth?"

"February 17, 2024," Piper replied automatically before awareness dawned on her face, and her eyes widened in horror.

I did the math in my head, counting backward from Avery's birthdate to our night together. A wave of cold realization washed over me when I realized the timing was too perfect, too damning to be anything other than what it was.

Avery was mine.

My daughter.

TEN

GHOST

"Holy fuck," I whispered, the room spinning around me. The nurse continued to ask a series of questions about Avery's medical history and allergies, but my heart thundered against my ribcage so loudly it drowned out every other sound.

The heel of my boot connected with a stool, sending it crashing into the wall with a loud clatter that set Avery off again.

"Dane, wait…" Piper's voice broke as I staggered toward the door, her hand reaching for mine.

But I didn't stick around to hear the rest. I couldn't. The walls were suddenly too close, the floor beneath me giving way as the magnitude of the situation sank in.

My vision blurred as I stumbled out of the room and I had to stop and brace myself against the sterile white corridor wall for a few long seconds to catch my breath.

The maze of hallways we'd stormed through earlier now felt like an endless void where time didn't exist. I moved in a daze, the security cameras overhead glaring down at me from every angle.

Daring me to cause a scene.

My hands were shaking—fuck, my whole body was shaking—but I couldn't stop moving. Not yet. My legs carried me forward on autopilot, past the rows of people slumped over in waiting room chairs, past sick and crying children held tight against their parents' chests.

I barely noticed as I strode through the automatic doors and into the fresh air, my chest heaving like I'd run a marathon.

February 17, 2024.

The date had detonated like a bomb, turning my mind into a goddamned war zone.

Blood roared in my ears as memories of our night together came flooding back—the way Piper's body felt wrapped around me bare, falling asleep inside her despite knowing the risks. Yet when she told me she had a daughter, I hadn't even considered the possibility.

But now, there wasn't a goddamned doubt in my mind.

Avery was mine.

She might have had Piper's eyes, but those red curls were identical to my mother's.

I slammed my fist into a concrete pillar with a low growl, not caring who saw or heard me. My knuckles split open on impact, but it wasn't enough to bleed away the rage coursing through my veins.

"Fuck!" I roared, pinching the bridge of my nose to keep the tears at bay.

A couple of people in scrubs walked by, giving me a wide berth and wary looks as they passed.

Yeah, I imagined I looked like hell. But I felt even worse.

Aware it was only a matter of time before someone called security on the unhinged biker, I moved away from the entrance. My boots scraped against the asphalt, each step heavy and clumsy, but I didn't stop until I reached the parking lot.

The ache in my chest became unbearable, and I dropped to my knees beside Piper's SUV. My breath left my body in shallow, rapid bursts, and I locked my hands behind my neck, leaning forward as if I could fold myself into something small enough to contain this pain.

All the pieces were clicking together now—the way Piper had stumbled over her words when we first reconnected, her skittish deflection every time I brought up our night together, the shadow in her eyes when she talked about complications.

It wasn't another man.

It was me.

I was the complication.

Why hadn't she told me?

Had she thought I wouldn't fucking care—that I wouldn't want to know my own kid? Or had she, like her mother, assumed because I was a biker, I wasn't good enough? Some deadbeat who wouldn't stick around once I knew the truth.

White-hot rage coursed through my veins. I threw my head back and stared up at the endless expanse of pale blue sky. The tears I'd been holding back fell rapidly at the thought of my little girl growing up believing her father never wanted her.

Anger clawed its way to the surface again. I was angry at Piper for keeping the truth from me. Angry at myself for not finding her sooner. Angry at the entire fucked up situation.

The urge to punch something again was overwhelming. I clenched my fists, feeling my bruised knuckles protest. But beneath the anger was a bone-deep fear that threatened to consume me.

I sat with my back against the passenger door of Piper's SUV, trying to get my shit together. The parking lot was quiet, save for the sound of sirens in the distance and the occasional car pulling in or out. I couldn't face going back inside yet.

Not in the state I was in.

I pulled out my phone, my thumb hovering over Wolverine's contact. If anyone could talk me down from this ledge, it was my old man. But I couldn't bring myself to make the call, not with two years of silence standing between us.

Seconds later, my brother Teddy's name flashed across the screen. If it had been the first time, I might have been spooked by his timing, but he'd been calling several times a day for months now. We hadn't spoken since Levi's visitation, and as the night had ended with me on my back in the funeral home parking lot and blood streaming down my face, I wasn't eager for a repeat.

Instead of answering, I scrolled through my camera roll until I found an old picture of Levi, taken when he wasn't much older than

Avery. His tiny-toothed grin stared back at me, reminding me I hadn't been there when he needed me most.

The fear returned, coiling around my chest until I could barely breathe. I hadn't been there for Avery's first breath or her first smile. I was a year late to my own daughter's life. An entire years' worth of moments, gone in the blink of an eye.

Time I would never get back.

What if I fucked up everything else too?

Part of me wanted to go back to the hotel and hop on my bike, riding until the roar of the engine drowned out the chaos in my head. Wasn't it what I'd been doing for the past two years—running from everything?

I let my head fall back against the door with a thud, thinking about my own father. Wolverine wasn't only the founder of the most powerful club in the state and the toughest son of a bitch alive, but he was a pretty kick-ass dad too. He'd not only taught us how to fight but how to know what was worth fighting for.

My old man sure as shit wouldn't have been sitting alone in a parking lot feeling sorry for himself when his family needed him.

Fuck.

My family.

The words felt foreign—like they belonged to someone else. Someone better. Someone who deserved them.

I hauled myself to my feet, swiping the moisture from my face with a shaking hand.

Instead of heading back to the emergency room, I wandered over to the gift shop in the main building. I passed colorful balloons floating above elaborate floral arrangements, greeting cards for every occasion, and enough snacks to feed the entire club.

My eyes landed on a stuffed animal display along the back wall, and I grinned, remembering how my old man would show up with a stuffed animal for me and my brothers after being gone on long runs with the club. When we were teens and well past the age of playing with toys, it was keychains or shot glasses from whatever city he'd been in.

A stuffed animal wouldn't give me back the time I'd lost or erase the sleepless nights Piper had to endure on her own.

But maybe it wasn't about that.

Maybe, much like my dad's gifts, it was my way of letting Piper know I hadn't gone a single day without thinking of her. I picked up a small teddy bear wearing a get well soon T-shirt, its soft pink fur a stark contrast to the mess of a man holding it.

Taking a deep breath, I strode toward the register, ignoring a wary glance from an elderly woman in the greeting card section. The cashier's eyes widened as I approached, her gaze darting from my kutte to the blood streaked across my knuckles.

"Just this," I said, setting the bear down with more force than was necessary.

Her movements were jerky and nervous as she rang me up, and I bit back a sigh because it wasn't her fault I looked like the devil incarnate.

"It's for my daughter," I added, handing her a twenty. The words still felt strange on my tongue, foreign yet undeniably right.

"Aww," she said, her expression softening. "I hope she feels better soon."

I nodded, not trusting myself to speak again.

The lump in my throat threatened to choke me as I made my way back to the emergency room. I paused after entering through the automatic doors, taking a deep breath to steady myself.

Chaos swirled around me, but all I could focus on was the weight of the stuffed animal clenched in my fist as I navigated the winding hallways stretched out like a gauntlet before me.

As I approached Avery's room, I heard Piper's soft voice drifting through the partially open door. She was singing a Reba McEntire song like it was a lullaby, her tone gentle and soothing.

"Mama's here," she said when Avery let out a soft whimper.

The words twisted through my gut like a knife. Then and there, I decided no matter what it took, I would prove to Piper I could be the father Avery needed. I would be the man she needed. I'd take things slow and earn her trust until there wasn't a doubt in her mind I was in it for the long haul.

ELEVEN

PIPER

Ivy & Piper's Guide to Life Rule Number Twenty-Two:
Have a backup plan for your backup plan.

The door swung shut behind Dane with an ominous finality, reverberating through my bones and extinguishing the hope I'd been clinging to for the better part of two years.

"A-ma." Avery stirred in my arms with a hiccupped whimper, her lower lip jutting out pitifully. I smoothed her wispy curls and breathed in her sweet baby scent, my chin quaking as I tried to hold back the tears flooding my eyes.

"Not him, Piper," my mother said while shaking her head in horrified shock. "Tell me you weren't that stupid."

I sucked in a ragged breath and turned away, not bothering to deny the truth hanging over the room like a wet blanket.

Dane was Avery's father.

And my mother's words, while harsh, were only a reminder of the painful reality I'd tried so desperately to ignore.

Because I was stupid.

Stupid enough to think he might be different. That, unlike my own father, he might want to be a part of our lives.

But his sudden and hasty exit said it all.

I wanted to scream, to rage against the unfairness of Dane choosing to walk away when I'd only begun to picture the three of us as a family.

I'd spent so long convincing myself we could make it alone because there hadn't been another option. It was the same way I'd felt when I held Avery in my arms for the first time, knowing everything was on my shoulders. Even then, I'd held onto this naïve hope it wouldn't be forever.

But now I'd watched Dane walk out without a backward glance, and the fear crept back in. Only this time, I knew better.

No one would swoop in and save me.

This time, I was completely and utterly alone.

My mother's eyes drilled into me from across the room, her disappointment especially palpable in the tense silence. If I knew her, she was putting the finishing touches on an epic lecture I was in no mood to hear but would be forced to listen to regardless.

The door handle turned with a click, and my heart leaped in my chest. But it wasn't Dane returning.

"Ms. Kelly? Hi, I'm Dr. Diaz," the woman said as she entered, blissfully unaware of the emotional storm brewing in the room.

After sanitizing her hands, she approached the bed, her face a mask of professional concern. "I understand Miss Avery here took a tumble. Let's take a look."

The fluorescent lights glinted off the bright, rainbow-colored frames perched on the bridge of Dr. Diaz's nose as she examined the angry red gash, and I held my breath, silently pleading for good news. Anything to distract me from the gnawing ache in my chest.

"It's okay," I said when Avery flinched and began fussing. "Be really still so the doctor can make it all better."

Unfortunately, one-year-olds were notoriously bad listeners, and instead of settling, my daughter fought back with everything she had. By the time Dr. Diaz finished her poking and prodding, I felt as if I'd just wrestled a honey badger. Sweat ran in rivulets down my spine, and I was certain at least one of the kicks would leave a bruise.

"Good news," Dr. Diaz announced before straightening. "It's shallow enough that it won't require sutures. We'll clean it up and apply Steri-Strips to help keep the wound closed while it heals. It's important to keep the area clean and dry while those are on, okay?"

"So, she's going to be okay?"

She nodded reassuringly. "She should be just fine. Concussions aren't always easy to spot in little ones, though, so keep a close eye on her over the next twenty-four to forty-eight hours. If she's acting sleepier than normal or begins vomiting, bring her back in so we can run some more tests."

I nodded numbly, already imagining another sleepless night ahead. "Thank you."

My mother waited until she left the room before rounding on me. "How could you be so reckless, Amelia? A biker? Really?"

"It's not like I planned it," I said through clenched teeth, trying to focus on Avery's soft breaths and not my rising blood pressure.

"Oh, that's blatantly obvious." She pinched her lips together and shook her head. "Mark my words. A man like that is trouble with a capital T."

"He's her father—"

"And where has he been while you've been raising his daughter?" she asked, her eyes flashing with frustration. "Riding with his club, free from all responsibility? That's not a father, Amelia. That's a stranger who happens to share her DNA."

Her words landed with all the subtlety of a whip, but it wasn't as if I could argue. We'd both watched Dane walk out when he put two and two together. Avery reached up, her tiny fingers grazing my cheek as if sensing my distress.

"Owie, A-ma."

"Mama's here." I stroked the back of her hand with my thumb, softly singing a song that had helped me through my pregnancy and many sleepless nights as a new mom.

The door swung open, and I froze mid-verse, convinced I was seeing things. My heart lodged in my throat when Dane stepped into the room, his broad shoulders filling the doorway.

"Well, look who decided to grace us with his presence again," my mother said, her eyes narrowing to slits.

His jaw tightened, but he didn't take the bait. Instead, he approached the bed, each step slow and measured, like he was trying not to startle us. In his hand was a small stuffed bear, its fluffy pink fur matted from being squeezed too tightly.

"I thought," he began, his voice gruff with emotion. "I thought she might like this."

The simple gesture threatened to unravel me completely. I blinked rapidly, fighting back tears as Avery reached for it with both hands.

"You think a cheap toy makes up for—"

"Mom," I said in a carefully controlled tone. "Why don't you head home?"

She looked ready to argue, but I cut her off with a sharp look. "Please. I need to do this alone."

"Fine." She shot Dane a withering glare. "But don't come crying to me when he breaks your heart." The door slammed behind her, leaving an awkward silence in its wake.

He sank onto the edge of the bed, his gaze never leaving Avery's face. "I'm sorry I walked out like that. It was...a lot to take in, and I needed a minute."

My eyes brimmed with tears. "I'm so sorry, Dane."

"She's mine," he said flatly.

It wasn't a question.

I nodded. "I should have told you back at the hotel—"

He held up a hand, cutting me off. "Not here. Let's get her taken care of first. The rest can wait."

Was he angry?

Did he hate me now?

"Okay," I finally said, unable to read his expression.

We slipped back into an uneasy silence. My mind swirled with the what-ifs and could-have-beens until the nurse returned.

"All right, sweetie, let's get you patched up," she said before turning to me. "Just try to keep her as still as possible, Mama. She's not going to like me messing with it."

She didn't. Avery whimpered and clung to me as soon as the nurse touched her head. I stroked her damp hair with my free hand while the nurse cleaned the wound.

"It'll be over soon."

In response, she arched her back and let out the unholiest shriek while battering my thighs with her heels.

I was seconds from joining her when Dane's hand found my shoulder, giving it a gentle squeeze. I leaned into his solid presence, letting myself pretend we were a normal family.

Even if it wasn't real.

"You're being so brave," he said. I didn't know if he was referring to me or our daughter, but his low voice calmed us both. By the time the nurse finished, Avery was asleep in my arms.

The nurse went over the discharge paperwork, explaining what to give her for pain and when to follow up with her pediatrician. I nodded along, trying to absorb it all while simultaneously worrying about the conversation still looming over us.

"Someone will be in shortly to discuss payment options," she said as she headed for the door.

My stomach tightened. The last thing I needed was another medical bill.

"I'll take care of it," Dane said, releasing his grip on my shoulder.

I craned my neck to look up at him. "You don't have to—"

"Not asking for permission, Piper," he said, silencing me with a look.

After settling the bill, Dane led us out to my SUV. I buckled a sleeping Avery into her car seat while he stripped off his kutte and placed it on the backseat.

I reached for the driver's side door handle before hesitating. "I can take you back to the hotel."

"Why would I want to go back to the hotel?" he asked, adopting a challenging tone.

"Um, I didn't know if you wanted to get your motorcycle or..." I trailed off with a shrug.

He frowned. "Thought we'd go back to your place to talk...unless that's a problem."

"No! I mean, no, as in it's not a problem, not that I don't want you to come to my house. That came out—"

"Piper," he said, opening my door with a heavy sigh. "Just get in."

My knuckles were white against the steering wheel as I drove home, each familiar street leading me closer to a conversation I wasn't sure I was ready to have.

Dane didn't say a word, but I could feel the tension radiating off him in waves.

I pulled into the driveway before turning to him, noting the rigid set of his jaw in the glow of the lights over the garage. We're here," I announced unnecessarily.

He nodded, his eyes fixed on the large two-story house. "Nice place."

"Oh...thanks. It was my grandparents'," I said, glancing back at Avery, pacifier dangling from her bottom lip.

He got out and opened my door before I could reach for the handle.

"She doesn't like men," I blurted when he moved toward the backseat next, realizing how it sounded as soon as the words left my lips. "It's just—she's more comfortable with women...that's all."

"Got it," he clipped, backing away from the SUV with his hands raised.

I carefully lifted Avery from her car seat, tucking her sweaty body against my chest before heading around to the gate on the side of the house. I shifted her weight to one side long enough to punch in the code, breathing a sigh of relief when she didn't stir.

Dane held it open for me to enter, his eyebrows pulling together in confusion. "Any reason you don't use the front door?"

"Because that's my mom's house," I explained before nodding toward the small guesthouse across from the pool. "We live back here."

I fumbled with my keys, hands shaking slightly as I unlocked the front door. Once inside, I disarmed the alarm and dropped my keys on the entry table before carrying Avery to her room. Dane followed close behind, his heavy footsteps echoing off the hardwood floor.

In a routine almost as familiar as breathing. I changed her diaper and put on her favorite unicorn pajamas while he stood in the doorway, taking in every detail.

"Do you mind watching her for a minute? I need to grab her sippy cup from the fridge."

He slowly released a deep breath and nodded before taking my place at the changing table.

When I returned, he was tracing the back of her hand with his index finger. My breath caught at the unmistakable look of love in his eyes, and I hesitated in the doorway, feeling like I was intruding on a deeply intimate moment.

Dane stepped back when I approached, letting me lift Avery and settle her in her crib. I tucked her favorite blanket around her and placed the sippy cup within reach before turning on the white noise machine.

"She's so perfect," he said, putting the stuffed bear in next to her.

I nodded, unable to speak past the lump in my throat. We stood there for a long moment, watching her chest rise and fall with each peaceful breath.

Finally, Dane turned to me. "We should talk."

TWELVE

PIPER

Ivy & Piper's Guide to Life Rule Number Thirty-Three:
Pick your battles wisely.

"If she hadn't fallen, would you have told me?" Dane asked from the opposite end of the couch.

I fidgeted with the sleeves of my dress, guilt and fear churning in my stomach. "I—I don't know," I admitted, unable to meet his eyes. "I wanted to. God, Dane. I wanted to tell you so badly."

He exhaled sharply and dragged a hand through his hair, frustration evident in every line of his body. "Why didn't you?"

"Because I was terrified," I said, wrapping my arms around myself. "That, and I didn't even know your last name until today."

"You could have gone to the club."

I shook my head. "I couldn't remember the name. What was I supposed to do? Put out an APB for every Dane with a motorcycle? Even if I had remembered, showing up alone and pregnant at a clubhouse didn't seem like the safest option."

"No, you're right," he said, pinching the bridge of his nose with a groan. "Sorry, I just hate how I've missed out on so much already."

I lowered my head to hide the tears welling up in my eyes. "I swear

I was working up to telling you before I got the call about her fall, but I didn't know how you'd react."

"You really thought I wouldn't want her? That I'd walk away?" he asked, moving closer.

I took a shaky breath and forced myself to meet his gaze. "I never knew my father. He took off before I was born, and the thought of Avery going through that too…"

"Hey," he said, reaching out to brush a tear from my cheek. "I'm here, aren't I?"

It was the same thing I'd said to him the night we met, and that, coupled with the feel of his hand on my face, broke past my defenses. "You don't hate me?"

Dane chuckled. "Darlin', I don't think there's anything that could make me hate you. Hell, if I could go back, there are a lot of things I'd do differently to prove it to you. But I can't. Best I can do is be here for Avery now. For both of you. That's what I want—to be the father she deserves."

"I need more than that," I said, my voice betraying a tremor. "I need to know you'll still be here even when it gets hard."

Dane's eyes softened, and he shifted closer, his large frame dwarfing mine on the couch. He cupped my jaw in his rough hand, forcing me to look him in the eye. "Not going anywhere. I know I've got a lot to prove, but I swear to you, I'm in this for the long haul. All I'm asking is for the chance to be a part of her life."

As much as I wanted to throw myself into his arms and trust everything would work out, I couldn't shake the lingering uncertainty. Bridging our world with his came with an entirely new set of risks.

"I want that, too," I said, trying to focus on our daughter rather than the heat radiating from his body. "But I'd be lying if I said your lifestyle didn't scare me."

A flash of hurt crossed his face before he masked it. "You're talking about the club."

My gaze dropped to the patch on his kutte. "That one-percent patch tells me you're not exactly on the right side of the law. Avery's safety is everything to me, and I don't know how to shield her from—"

"From what I am?" Dane finished, his hand falling away from my face.

I reached for his hand. "Hey, I didn't mean it like that."

His eyes hardened, and he pulled back. "You think because I wear this patch, I can't be a good father? That I'd put our daughter in danger?"

"No, that's not..." I trailed off, blinking back fresh tears and struggling to find the right words in my exhausted, overly emotional state. "It's just—I've worked so hard to give her a stable, safe life. I can't risk that, Dane. I won't risk that. Not even for you."

He stood abruptly, pacing the small living room. The pain in his eyes made my chest ache. "You think I'd put my daughter at risk? Christ, Piper."

"But how can you guarantee her safety?" I asked, padding over to his side. "What happens if—"

"If what?" he demanded, backing me up against the wall. "If the feds come knocking on your door? If a rival club tries to start shit? If a deal goes south? You think I haven't considered a million and one scenarios just like that since learning she's mine?"

Aware we were both emotionally raw and needed sleep, I placed my palm on his chest, hoping to soothe his wounded ego. "I want us to be able to co-parent peacefully, for Avery's sake," I said carefully.

"Did you just offer to co-parent our daughter with me?" he asked. His low voice was tinged with anger and hurt, but the intensity in his gaze was sending conflicting signals to my brain.

I swallowed hard. "Um...yes?"

He threaded his fingers through my hair with a dark chuckle before tugging my head back. "Is that what you think I'm interested in, baby —some new-age, bullshit term divorced couples use to make themselves feel like they're still a team? Do I look like that kind of guy to you?"

"I—"

His mouth came down over mine, hard and demanding. I gasped, my hands flying up to grip his shoulders. His tongue slipped past the seam of my lips, claiming me with a possessiveness that made my knees weak.

We had so much left unresolved and so many issues to work through. But the feel of his body against mine, the taste of him on my lips, overrode all logic, and I kissed him back.

Dane growled low in his throat, his hands roaming down my sides to grip my hips. He lifted me easily, and I instinctively wrapped my legs around his waist. The hard length of him pressed against the seam of my underwear, wrenching a strangled moan from my throat.

"In case I didn't make myself explicitly clear earlier, I'm not fucking interested in co-parenting or custody arrangements," he rasped against my throat, nipping at the sensitive skin. "Is that what you want, huh? To keep me at arm's length so you can play house with another man, only seeing me when it's my turn to have Avery?"

"No." I rocked against his erection, whimpering when his teeth grazed my collarbone. "That's not what I want."

His breath was hot against my neck. "Then what do you want, Piper? Tell me."

I shuddered against him, trying to collect my thoughts into something resembling a complete sentence. What did I want? As much as I ached to tell him to take me to bed and leave the problems for future Piper, we couldn't fix this with sex. Sex had gotten us into this mess in the first place.

With more than a bit of reluctance, I pulled back to catch my breath. "I want you. I want us to be a family. But I'm scared. I'm scared Avery will get hurt." I swallowed before admitting, "I'm scared I'll get hurt."

Dane's eyes softened as he set me back on my feet, his hands still gripping my waist. "I get it, darlin'. I'm scared, too. This is all new territory for me."

"According to the back of your kutte, you live in Lubbock. How do we even begin to make this work when we live five hours apart?"

He pressed his forehead against mine, his breath mingling with my own. "We'll take it one day at a time. You don't need to have all the answers tonight. You just need to trust me."

"And the club?" I asked, desperate to silence the nagging voice in my head, which sounded a hell of a lot like my mother.

"The club is part of who I am, Piper. Once you're in, you're in. I can't walk away from this life," he said before pausing. His brow creased as though he were carefully weighing his following words. "But family comes first over everything, and I swear to you, I'll do whatever it takes to keep stuff with the club separate from us."

It wasn't a perfect solution, but it was a start. The tension coiled tightly in my chest began to unravel, replaced by a tentative hope.

I let out a slow breath. "Okay. I think I can work with that, but I want to take things slow. For Avery's sake."

"Baby, nothing about us has ever been slow," he drawled with a lazy smirk.

My cheeks warmed, and I twisted my thumb ring to keep my fingers occupied... To stop myself from latching onto his kutte and losing myself in his kiss again. "True. But this time around, we've got a lot more at stake. This is going to be a big adjustment for us all, and I don't want to make it more complicated than it needs to be."

Dane nodded, his expression growing serious. "No, you're right. We'll do this at your pace."

Relief washed over me, quickly followed by exhaustion. I stifled a yawn and glanced at the clock to find it was after midnight. I had gotten into the habit of going to bed when Avery did and couldn't recall the last time I'd been up this late.

"Been a hell of a day. Let's get you to bed," he finally said.

Too exhausted to argue, I let him lead me down the hall to my bedroom, suddenly self-conscious of the dirty clothes strewn across the floor and the disorganized stack of books taking up space on my nightstand. I had planned to clean it all up, but there never seemed to be enough hours in the day. I kicked off my boots and twisted my arm behind my back, struggling to reach the zipper on my dress.

"Turn around," he commanded, sweeping my long hair over my shoulder before sliding it down.

I shivered as his fingers grazed my bare skin. Every nerve ending in my body sparked to life at his touch despite my exhaustion. I turned to face him, clutching the front of my dress to keep it from falling.

"I should, um..." I gestured vaguely toward the bathroom. "Get ready for bed."

"Need help?" he offered.

My tongue darted out to wet my dry lips. "I thought we were taking things slow."

He moved closer, his large frame crowding me against the dresser. "We are. Doesn't mean I can't admire the view, though, darlin'."

Keeping my eyes on him, I slipped my arms out of the sleeves of my dress before letting it pool at my feet. While comfortable with the ways my body had changed since having Avery, I was painfully aware I didn't look like I had the last time he saw me naked. My arms moved back up to hide the stretch marks and baby weight I was still carrying.

Dane's dark gaze raked over me, lingering on the soft swell of my breasts spilling over the top of my bra before dropping down to the curve of my hips. When he noticed my arms crossed protectively over my stomach, a look of something like understanding crossed his face.

He reached out, gently grasping my wrists and pulling my arms away. "You're even more gorgeous now than I remembered," he said, his calloused hands tracing the marks on my skin.

His lips brushed over mine in a tender kiss, and I melted into the warmth of his body. Unlike the encounter in the living room, this kiss was slow and sweet. When we broke apart, I was light-headed and second-guessing my decision to take things slow.

"Why don't you go ahead and get ready for bed?" Dane suggested. "I'll be here."

Slipping into the bathroom, I rushed through my nightly routine and changed into an oversized T-shirt. When I returned, Dane was studying the framed photos lining the bedroom wall. I climbed under the comforter, sinking into the mattress with a relaxed sigh.

"I wish I'd been there the day she was born," he said, pointing to the picture of me holding Avery in the hospital, my face a mix of exhaustion and pure joy.

My chest tightened at the wistfulness in his voice. "I wish you had been too."

He sat down on the edge of the bed, taking my hand in his. "What was it like?" he asked, stroking my knuckles with his thumb.

I let out a shaky laugh. "Honestly? It was intense—sixteen hours of labor. I was exhausted and in so much pain. But the moment they placed her on my chest..." I trailed off, emotion clogging my throat. "It was like the whole world shifted. Nothing else mattered except this tiny, perfect human we'd created."

Dane listened while I recounted the details of Avery's birth—how tiny she was, how she'd gripped my finger with surprising strength, and the overwhelming love I'd felt the moment I held her in my arms.

A yawn caught me by surprise, and I covered my mouth before apologizing.

He released my hand before getting up. "Don't apologize. It's been a long day. You should get some rest."

Panic seized me when he turned to leave. The thought of waking up alone, of this all being some elaborate dream, was too much to bear.

"Don't go," I blurted, hating how needy I sounded.

"Not going anywhere but to the couch," he said, jerking his thumb toward the doorway.

"Stay." I patted the space beside me. "Please."

He hesitated, his lips pressed together in a slight grimace. "Fucking hanging on by a thread here, Piper. You sure you want me in your bed?"

I wasn't sure of anything anymore, but I knew I didn't want to be alone. "Please," I repeated. "Just to sleep."

Dane searched my face for a long moment before shrugging off his kutte and draping it over a nearby chair. My breath caught as he pulled his T-shirt over his head, revealing tattoos that covered almost his entire back. I forced my gaze away when he unbuckled his belt, focusing instead on smoothing imaginary wrinkles from the comforter.

He switched off the lamp and slid in beside me, the mattress dipping beneath his weight. I rolled onto my side to face him. Even in the darkness, I could make out the conflicted emotions playing across his face.

"This okay?" he asked gruffly, his arm hovering uncertainly above my waist.

I nodded and scooted closer, letting out a shaky breath as his arm settled around me. The warmth of his skin against mine sent a shiver down my spine.

"You cold, baby?" he murmured, pulling me tighter against his chest.

"No," I whispered, my fingers tracing the muscular line of his bicep. "Just...overwhelmed, I guess."

Dane's hand came up to cup my cheek, his thumb brushing away my tears. "Sleep, Piper. I'll still be here when you wake up. I promise."

Exhaustion tugged at me, and I drifted off before jerking awake seconds later. "Don't leave me again, Dane. I can't survive it. Not again."

His arm tightened around me, his voice a low rumble against my ear. "Never again, darlin'. I swear it. You're mine—both of you—and I'm never letting you go."

I nodded against him, feeling the steady thrum of his heartbeat beneath my cheek. The rhythmic sound and the warmth of his body slowly lulled me toward sleep. Before I drifted off completely, I felt Dane press a soft kiss on my forehead.

"I love you, baby," he murmured so quietly I wasn't sure if I'd imagined it.

I tried to fight the fog settling over me and failed. Maybe I'd never woken up because men like that only existed in books.

THIRTEEN

PIPER

Ivy & Piper's Guide to Life Rule Number Ten:
No is a complete sentence.

The shrill ring of my phone jolted me awake. I fumbled for it in the darkness, squinting until the name flashing across the bright screen came into focus. My boss.

"Hello?" I mumbled, my voice thick with sleep.

"Piper, where the hell are you?" Derek's voice boomed through the speaker. "You were supposed to open at three. It's five!"

I bolted upright, panic flooding my system. "Shit. I'm so sorry. I completely forgot—"

"This is the second day in a row you've missed your shift," he said, cutting me off. "Being a manager doesn't mean you can blow off work whenever you feel like it."

My throat tightened, and I shook my head even though he couldn't see me. "No, I didn't. I requested off yesterday. Remember?" I asked, rubbing my stinging eyes. I was a grown-ass woman. A grown-ass woman who was dangerously close to tears because she was being reprimanded by her boss.

"As a manager, you're technically always on call," he reminded me, his tone patronizing. "The higher wage and guaranteed hours come with more responsibilities. I can't have you disappearing without notice like this. What kind of an example does it set for the rest of the employees?"

When I realized the other side of the bed was empty, a sense of déjà vu washed over me, and my stomach dropped. The memory of his arms around me and his promise to be here when I woke up had felt so real. But the cold, empty sheets beside me told a different story.

Dane was gone. Again.

"Please, Derek. I'm so sorry," I said, trying and failing to mask the emotion in my voice. "Avery fell, and we were at the hospital until late last night. I should have called, but everything's been such a blur…"

"If you'd called to let me know what was going on, I could have made arrangements," he said, his tone softening slightly. "But I can't run a business effectively if I don't know when my employees will show up."

"You're right," I admitted, kneading my chest with the heel of my hand like it might stop it from aching. "It won't happen again, I promise."

Derek sighed heavily. "Look, I know you're in a difficult situation as a single mom. But if you can't manage your time effectively and be available when I need you, we may need to reevaluate your position."

Tears clung to my lashes before spilling over onto my cheeks. I couldn't afford to lose this job. "Please, Derek. I'll do anything," I said, choking back a sob. "I need this job."

There was a long pause on the other end of the line. "Fine. I'll find someone to cover your shift today, but you better be prepared to work double shifts for the next few weeks to make up for it," he said gruffly.

"Of course, absolutely. Thank you so much." Relief washed over me even as dread settled in my stomach at the thought of seeing my daughter even less than I already did.

The call ended, and I collapsed back onto the bed, my hands shaking as I placed the phone on the nightstand. As if Dane walking out again wasn't bad enough, now my job was on thin ice, too. I pressed my hands over my face to muffle the sound of my sobs, not wanting to wake Avery.

When there was nothing left to cry, I dragged myself out of bed and down the hall, only to freeze as soon as I reached the living room.

Dane lay sprawled across the couch with Avery on his bare chest, his massive frame dwarfing the furniture. One muscular arm was draped over her back, protecting her even in his sleep.

The magnitude of the moment struck me, and I sagged against the wall. My sweet, cautious girl, who had been wary of men since she came into this world, looked right at home in her daddy's arms. Like it was where she was always meant to be.

Fresh tears sprang to my eyes as I thought of the long, sleepless nights I'd spent wishing I didn't have to do it alone. Now he was here, stepping into the role of father as if he'd been doing it all along

I crept closer, my bare feet silent against the cool hardwood. His face was relaxed in sleep, softer somehow, making him look younger and more vulnerable. A lock of dark hair had fallen across his forehead, and I fought the urge to brush it back.

As if sensing my stare, Dane's eyes fluttered open, instantly alert. His arm tightened around Avery before his gaze found mine. The tension in his body eased, replaced by a slow, sleepy smile that made my heart skip a beat.

"Mornin'," he rumbled, voice rough with sleep. Avery stirred at her father's voice, her tiny fist clutching his chest as she burrowed closer.

"Morning," I whispered back once I found my voice. "How long have you two been out here?"

He glanced down at Avery, his expression softening even further. "Since about three. She was fussing, so I brought her in here so you could sleep."

Guilt twisted in my gut. "I'm so sorry. I usually hear her through the monitor. You should have woken me up."

"Piper." The way he said my name, low and firm, did something to my insides. "You needed the rest. Besides, we were just fine."

Dane studied me for a long moment before shifting Avery to one arm and extending his free hand toward me. "Have you been crying?"

"It's nothing," I said, swiping at my cheeks. "Just work stuff."

"C'mere, let me hold you."

Against my better judgment, I took his hand and let him pull me down onto the couch beside him. His skin was warm against mine, and I fought the urge to curl into his side like Avery had.

"What happened?" he asked, keeping his voice low so as not to wake our daughter.

I exhaled a shaky breath, feeling the weight of everything crashing down on me again. "My boss called. I was supposed to open the bakery this morning and completely forgot. He's—well, let's just say I'm not his favorite person right now."

Dane's arm tightened around me. "He giving you a hard time about taking care of our daughter?"

"Not exactly," I said, absently stroking Avery's hair. "But he did threaten to demote me if I can't manage my time better."

His chest vibrated with a low growl. "Manage your time better? The fuck? You were at the hospital with our kid. What's he expect you to do?"

"I should have called to let him know what was happening," I said quickly, though I couldn't deny the warmth spreading through my chest at his protective tone. "I promised to work double shifts for a while to make up for it."

"And when the hell are you supposed to see Avery if he's got you working double shifts?" he asked, his jaw flexing and tightening.

I shrugged. "I'll figure something out. I have to—I don't have another choice."

He remained silent for a long moment, his thumb drawing circles on my hip. "What if you did?"

"What do you mean?" I asked, tipping my head back to peer up at him.

"I mean, I work for a security firm and can take care of both you and Avery. You wouldn't have to work for some asshole who doesn't give a shit about you or our daughter."

My heart raced at his words, equal parts tempted and terrified by the offer. "Dane, I can't just quit my job and depend on you. We barely know each other."

He raised an eyebrow. "I beg to differ. We made a baby together, darlin'. I'd say I know you pretty damn well."

The offer was tempting. So tempting. But the rational part of my brain knew it was too soon.

"Has she had meds recently?" I asked, shifting to a safer topic. The swelling on Avery's head appeared to have gone down significantly overnight.

"I went off the discharge paperwork and gave her some pain meds when she woke up at three after checking to make sure she wasn't running a fever. She settled pretty quick, so I'm hoping that means we're in the clear."

"I'm—"

His brown eyes narrowed. "The next word out of your pretty mouth better not be an apology."

"It isn't. I was going to say I'm not used to having help." Although, I was more than a little curious to know what he would have done if I had apologized.

Something dark and possessive flickered in his eyes. "Guess you'll just have to get used to it because I'm not going anywhere."

There was nothing erotic in what he said, but the words sent a thrill of sensation down my spine. I was keenly aware of how thin the material of my tank top was when my nipples peaked against his chest.

Dane's fingertips skimmed the curve of my breast when he noticed my body's reaction, and I pulled my bottom lip between my teeth to keep from moaning.

"Baby," he murmured, voice husky with desire. "You keep looking at me like that, and I'm gonna have to do something about it."

"Like what?" My breath caught when he slid his hand down to squeeze the back of my thigh.

"Like put little miss back in her crib so I can bend you over the back of the couch and fuck your cunt with my tongue until I'm drowning in your juices." His fingers moved higher until he was cupping my pussy through my panties.

The air between us crackled with electricity. I wanted nothing more than to climb onto his lap, pull my underwear to the side, and lose myself in the feel of him.

"Dane," I whimpered, torn between desire and the awareness of our sleeping daughter nestled between us.

"But we're taking things slow," he reminded me, returning his hand to my shoulder.

"Right." I bobbed my chin in a shaky nod and shifted slightly, trying to ease the throbbing ache when Avery stirred against his chest. She smacked her lips together several times before exhaling.

"Tell me something," he said once her breaths evened back out. "We talked about the day she was born, but what was she like as a newborn?"

A lump formed in my throat as I thought back to those first overwhelming days. "She was perfect," I whispered. "So tiny and fragile. I was terrified I'd break her."

He chuckled, the sound vibrating against my cheek. "I can imagine. What else?"

"She hardly ever cried," I said, smiling at the memory. "Just these little whimpers when she was hungry or needed changing. And she had the most expressive face, even then. You could see every emotion play across it."

"Just like her mama." Dane's finger hooked under my chin, tilting my face up to his. "Every thought that crosses your mind shows up right here. It's how I knew Avery was mine without you saying a word."

Aside from my mother and Ivy, no one had ever read me so easily before. It was both thrilling and terrifying to be seen like that.

"What else?"

I let my fingertips trail over her pudgy arm. "She was so alert, always watching everything with her big green eyes. And she had the most adorable little snore…"

As I spoke, sharing the memories I'd tucked away over the past year, something inside me began to soften. I'd carried the weight of being a single parent for so long, but watching Dane eagerly soak up every detail about our daughter made me realize that I hadn't ever given myself a chance to stop long enough to take it all in.

We lay there talking in hushed voices the room slowly brightened with the dawn. When Avery's eyes popped open, she blinked sleepily up at us, her little face scrunching in confusion as she took in her surroundings. For a heart-stopping moment, I worried she might burst into tears at finding herself in an unfamiliar position.

But then her gaze settled on Dane, and a grin spread across her face. She reached up with one chubby hand, patting his stubbled cheek as if to make sure he was real.

"Mornin', princess," he said, his voice cracking slightly.

She babbled happily in response, her tiny fingers exploring the planes of his face with unabashed curiosity.

The tenderness in his expression made my chest ache. I'd dreamed of this moment so many times, but the reality was infinitely sweeter than anything I could have imagined.

"A-ma," Avery chirped suddenly, twisting in Dane's arms to reach for me.

I gathered her close, smoothing a hand over her wild curls before peppering her face with kisses. "There's my sweet girl. Are you hungry, baby?"

Her tummy let out an impressive growl as if on cue, making us both laugh.

Dane sat up and stretched his arms overhead with a low chuckle. "I'll take that as a yes."

The movement drew my attention to his ab muscles, and my throat bobbed up and down in a slow swallow.

"I should get her breakfast started," I said, forcing my gaze away from his sculpted torso.

"Let me." He held out his arms, and I sat in open-mouthed shock when Avery went to him without hesitation. "Why don't you grab a book and take a long bubble bath, darlin'? We'll rustle up something to eat."

A protest rose to my lips, but the determined set of his jaw told me it was pointless to argue.

I lingered in the doorway, watching as he expertly secured Avery in her highchair. He moved around my kitchen with easy confidence, narrating his every move, much to our daughter's delight.

"You sure you don't need any help?" I called out, unable to completely let go of my routine.

Dane shot me a pointed look over his shoulder. "Piper. Bath. Now."

The firmness in his tone sent a shiver down my spine, and I forced myself to turn away, padding down the hall to take a bath.

With a hiss of pleasure, I sank beneath the lavender-scented bubbles, letting the hot water melt the tension from my muscles. For the first time in over a year, I was allowing myself to unwind, knowing Avery was in good hands.

I tried to focus on the psychological thriller I'd grabbed on my way in, but after reading the opening paragraph four times, I gave up. My thoughts kept drifting back to Dane. I slid a hand down my belly, grazing my fingers over my clit as I recalled the heat in his gaze, the effortless way he took control.

A gasp of relief slipped past my parted lips as I circled the tight bundle of nerves before moving down to my slit. I draped my right leg over the edge of the clawfoot tub and imagined it was his fingers pumping in and out of me.

Water lapped gently against the sides of the tub. The thought of him barging in, seeing me spread out and desperate for his touch, only fueled the motion of my hand. Heat coiled low in my belly, and I pinched the sensitive peak of my breast, teetering on the edge of climax when a sharp knock at the door sent me hurtling back to reality.

"Piper?" Dane's deep voice called from just outside the door. "Breakfast is ready whenever you are, darlin'."

I froze, my fingers still buried inside my body. "O-okay," I called back, wincing at how breathy I sounded. "I'll be out in a minute."

There was a pause, and I could almost feel his suspicion radiating through the door. "You all right in there?"

"Fine!" I squeaked, no longer aroused but mortified at the thought of him catching me. "Just...super relaxed."

The bathroom door creaked open, and I jerked my foot back into the tub, sending water sloshing over the side in my rush to hide what I was doing.

Dane leaned against the counter with a knowing smirk. "You sure about that? You look a little worked up."

I sank lower in the bubbles, praying he couldn't see how hard my nipples were. "Just the hot w-water," I stammered, face flaming.

His dark eyes raked over the water. "Let me help,"

"But Avery—"

"Avery is securely fastened in her highchair and watching cartoons. We've got about two minutes before I need to check on her unless you feel like things are moving too fast between us."

The bastard was making fun of me, but I was too far gone to care.

"Stay," I said, letting my legs fall open.

In two long strides, he was on his knees beside the tub. His hand plunged beneath the water, finding my slick folds with unerring accuracy.

"Fucking soaked," he said before moving up to circle my clit. "How long's it been, baby?"

I arched into his touch with a whimper. "One year, nine months, and three weeks."

The corner of his mouth lifted in a barely there grin. "No one since me."

"No one," I admitted breathlessly. "What about you?"

His dark eyes, so brown they were almost black, held mine. "One year, nine months, and three weeks."

My smile froze in place. "Wait—no one since me?" I asked, trying and failing to mask my surprise.

With me, it was to be expected. *But him?*

"No one else *but* you."

I shivered at the sincerity in his voice. He looked so genuine, so open and unguarded, that it made my heart ache in a way I couldn't describe.

Dane increased the pressure on my clit, drawing me back to the present. "Tell me what you were thinking about."

"You...walking in on me," I said, letting my head fall back against the tub.

"And what did I do in this fantasy?"

"You...oh god," I hissed as he slid two thick fingers inside me. "You —you touched me. Fucked me with your fingers until I came."

"Like this?" He curled them, hitting my G-spot.

I clutched at his forearm, my hips rolling forward to meet each thrust of his hand. "Yes, just like that. Please don't stop."

His free hand came up to cover my mouth. "Shh...gotta be quiet, darlin'. Don't want our little girl hearing what Daddy's doing to Mama."

I nodded frantically against his palm, desperate for release.

"That's my good girl. Let go, I've got you," he growled, pumping his fingers in a steady rhythm.

He lowered his head to my breasts, flicking his tongue over my soapy nipples before sucking one between his teeth. My hips bucked involuntarily, drawing broken moans from my throat. Water sloshed over the sides of the tub, but I was beyond caring.

"Don't stop," I said, my walls clenching around his fingers.

Dane popped off my breast. "Come for me, Piper."

The command in his tone sent me hurtling over the edge. I cried out, my back arching as waves of ecstasy crashed over me. He continued, wringing every drop of pleasure from my body and only slowing his movements when I slumped bonelessly against the tub.

"Gorgeous." He pressed a tender kiss to my sternum before lowering his voice. "But next time, I want it on my tongue."

With that, he strode out of the bathroom, leaving me breathless and trembling in the cooling bathwater.

FOURTEEN

GHOST

Ivy & Piper's Guide to Life Rule Number Thirty-Six:
Know your limits.

"C'mon, princess," I coaxed, bringing the syringe of liquid Tylenol to her pursed lips. "Open up for Daddy. It'll make the owie feel better."

Avery stared at me like I'd sprouted a second head before jerking her chin away.

Seemed my daughter was familiar with the *Just Say No* campaign. Unfortunately for her, this wasn't my first rodeo, and after a series of ridiculous facial expressions and exaggeratedly pretending to drink it myself, the medicine was in her system.

"That's my good girl," I praised, wiping her face with a damp paper towel. "Now, let's take care of that diaper."

She babbled happily as I laid her on the changing table, oblivious to my watering eyes and the toxic sludge in her pants. The smell could have knocked a buzzard off a shit wagon, but I soldiered on while she reached for anything and everything she could get her tiny little hands on.

Who'd have thought diaper changes were a full-contact sport?

"All done," I panted, dropping the soiled diaper into the pail and scooping Avery up. She giggled, patting my cheeks with her chubby hands.

"A-ma!" she bellowed, twisting in my arms to look for Piper.

"Mama's taking a bath, sweetheart," I explained, carrying her to the living room. "How about we watch some cartoons while we wait?"

She immediately grabbed a fistful of my beard, tugging with surprising strength for such tiny fingers.

"Easy there. Daddy needs that to stay attached to his face." I gently pried her fingers loose and pretended to nibble on them. "Nom, nom, nom!"

Avery let out a belly laugh and patted my cheek, babbling something that sounded suspiciously like "Da-da."

"That's right," I said, pressing a kiss to her cheek. "I'm your daddy. Can you say Da-da?"

"A-ma!" she yelled, her green eyes sparkling with mischief. Great. She was a brat…just like her mama.

"We'll work on that one."

She snuggled against my chest as I scrolled to find her show, her little legs bouncing in excitement.

"Boo!" she exclaimed when the opening notes of *Bluey* filled the air, looking to me for a reaction.

"Bluey," I echoed before pointing at the screen. "And who's that? Is that Bingo?"

"Beh-beh!" she babbled, reaching toward the colorful characters dancing across the screen.

I couldn't help but grin, marveling at how such a simple thing could bring her so much joy. Then she wrapped her little hands around my fingers and gazed up at me with a look of complete trust and innocence, and suddenly, I felt like the luckiest son of a bitch alive.

The lump in my throat threatened to choke me. I never imagined loving someone I just met this fiercely, but Avery had stolen my whole damn heart.

I had heard my dad say he was willing to lay down his life if it meant keeping his kids safe, but I never truly understood it until now.

She was everything I never knew I needed. As I watched her giggle and clap at the characters' antics, I knew I would protect her until I took my last breath.

God help any bastard who got in my way.

The bathroom door creaked open, and Piper appeared, hair damp and cheeks flushed.

"Feeling better after your bath, darlin'?" I asked, quirking an eyebrow suggestively.

She blushed deeper. "Much better. Has she eaten?"

I glanced down at our daughter, who was so transfixed by the cartoon dogs prancing across the screen she hadn't even noticed her mother come in.

"Tell Mama you had a container of yogurt and two of the blueberry muffins on the counter," I said, grinning at Avery. She was still completely engrossed in Bluey, her tiny brow furrowed in concentration.

Piper's eyes widened. "My goodness, Avery. You were a hungry girl!"

"Wasn't sure about giving her eggs, so I stuck with what looked kid-friendly," I explained, aware of how much I still had to learn.

"Oh, yeah," Piper said, realization dawning on her face. "She doesn't have any food allergies. I'm sorry. I should have said something."

"No worries. We figured it out." I nodded toward the kitchen. "There are eggs and bacon in the microwave, so eat up."

I couldn't resist adding, "Hope you're a hungry girl, too, because you're gonna need your strength for what I have planned."

"A-ma!" Avery shrieked, finally noticing her mother and pointing excitedly at the TV.

"I see, pumpkin," Piper managed, her eyes wide and voice slightly strained. "We should get your diaper changed—"

"Already done," I cut in. "And she's had her pain meds. Now, sit your pretty A-S-S down and eat your breakfast."

The weight of Piper's gaze burned into me as I turned my attention back to the TV, watching as Bluey and her friends played at the park. "I can feel you staring at me," I said without turning around. "You gonna eat, or do I need to feed it to you myself?"

She inhaled a sharp breath before grumbling, "I can feed myself."

"Prove it," I said, grinning at the sound of silverware clinking against the plate.

When she finished and headed toward the sink to start cleaning up, I shook my head. "Leave your dishes and come sit."

"But I can do it."

I narrowed my eyes, twisting to look at her over the back of the couch. "I know you can, darlin'. You've been doing it the whole damn time. Now, it's my turn to take care of both of you. End of discussion. Come here," I said, patting the space next to me.

She hesitated, conflict clear on her face, before she finally sank down beside me.

"Careful, or she'll rope you into an all-day *Bluey* marathon," Piper said, looking up at me with a bemused smirk.

"Better than singing sharks," I drawled, pulling her closer.

She rested her head against my shoulder, her damp hair tickling my neck. I breathed in the scent of her shampoo, enjoying the feel of her in my arms.

"You're handling the whole fatherhood bombshell pretty well," Piper said after several minutes of silence. "Most men would be freaking out or demanding a paternity test—"

"A paternity test?" I scoffed, bristling at the implication. "Why the hell would I need that?"

"Well, I mean, look at her, Dane. Red hair. Ghost-white skin. She doesn't exactly look like either of us."

I chuckled, shaking my head. "That's all Lucy Riggs right there. My mom's hair has more white in it these days, but it used to be the same color as Avery's."

Avery perked up at the sound of her name, her green eyes wide and curious. I searched her little face, soaking up every detail. "There are parts of you in here," I murmured. "I see you in her eyes and her little button nose."

Piper stroked her cheek, a soft smile playing on her lips. "These dimples are yours."

I nodded, seeing more of us in our daughter with each passing moment. Our eyes met, and my heart damn near burst out of my chest at the vulnerability in her gaze. A single tear tracked down her cheek, and I thumbed it away before cupping her face in my palm.

She leaned into my touch, eyes fluttering shut. "Sorry," she whispered. "It's just surreal, having you here."

"Too late to change your mind now. You're stuck with me." I tilted her chin up toward me. "Hey, I'm serious. We're a team now. A family."

Her breath hitched. "I want to believe that, but..."

"But you're not there yet," I finished. "I get it. Trust doesn't happen overnight, but I'm not going anywhere. And I'm willing to do whatever I can to prove it to you."

She turned to bury her face in my neck, breathing deeply as if to ground herself. Knowing her old man hadn't bothered to stick around, her reluctance made sense. Piper had been let down one too many times to believe someone might want to stick around for the long haul.

It was evident in the guarded look in her eyes and how unused she was to accepting help.

And as much as I'd love to place blame solely on her old man's doorstep, I hadn't exactly given her much reason to trust men either. Regardless of what my intentions had been, I'd hurt her just as much, if not more, than her father. He'd walked out without a word. I'd been the bastard who said he wanted more than one night before bailing on her without a word.

Earning her trust wouldn't come easy, but it'd be worth it.

As we sat there, wrapped up together with our daughter between us, I felt a sense of peace settle over me. This was where I belonged—with my family, my whole world within these walls.

Eventually, Avery's mouth stretched in a wide yawn, her eyelids growing heavy as she snuggled deeper into my chest. I plucked her sippy cup off the table and offered it to her, gently rocking her as she drank.

"You're like scary good at this," Piper whispered, watching us with a mix of awe and something else I couldn't quite place.

I shrugged, trying to play it cool even as pride swelled in my chest. "I've had plenty of experience with my brothers' kids," I admitted, a pang of grief hitting me as I thought of Levi. I pushed the feeling aside, focusing on the warm weight of my daughter in my arms. "You think I should lay her down?"

She checked her watch. "Yeah, she usually takes her morning nap around this time."

"Come here, sweetheart. Let's get you to bed."

Piper followed as I carried Avery to her room.

"Sweet dreams, princess," I murmured, kissing her wild curls before lowering her onto the crib mattress. I tucked her blanket around her and placed her teddy bear beside her, marveling at how tiny she looked.

Piper launched herself at me as soon as the bedroom door was closed, wrapping her arms around my neck and crushing her lips to mine. I groaned, backing her against the wall as heat flared between us.

"Take me to bed," she said against my mouth, her fingers tangling in my hair.

FIFTEEN

GHOST

Ivy & Piper's Guide to Life Rule Number Thirty-One:
Establish clear boundaries upfront.

I didn't need to be asked twice. I carried Piper into the bedroom and tossed her onto the bed before stripping off her yoga pants, growling when I encountered nothing but damp, bare skin.

No panties.

Fuck, she was trying to kill me.

"Jesus, darlin'," I said, running my hands up her thighs.

She spread her legs and arched her back invitingly. I could see how wet she was already, her arousal glistening on her inner thighs.

"Please," she whimpered.

I smirked, enjoying her desperation. "Please what? Use your words. Tell me exactly what you need."

Piper ground shamelessly against my hand. "Touch me. Please."

I slid my middle finger inside her, slowly pumping in and out while using my other hand to push her shirt up.

"Goddamn. These are new," I said, cupping her tits in my hand. Last night, with her bra on, it had been hard to tell. But there was no denying her breasts were fuller now, heavier in my palms. I brushed my thumb over them, her nipples already stiff and begging for attention.

"Having a baby does that," she said with a gasp.

"Fuck, I wish I'd been here while you were knocked up. Because these—" I leaned down to tease her nipples with my tongue before sucking one into my mouth with a groan. "These would've been in my mouth every damn day."

My cock strained painfully against my jeans just thinking about it. I added another finger, stroking along her front wall until her back came off the bed.

"More," she gasped, tangling her fingers in my hair. "Please, I need more. I'm close."

"Close? Well, that just won't do," I drawled as I guided a third finger into her tight pussy and increased the pace before working my jeans down just enough to free my shaft, stroking it as I fingered her.

"Come for me, darlin'," I demanded. "Let me feel that sweet pussy dripping all over my hand."

Piper's eyes rolled back, her walls fluttering around my fingers. I couldn't tear my eyes away from her as she writhed beneath me, lost in pleasure. Her lips parted on a breathy moan, and I surged forward to capture them with my own, greedily swallowing her cries as I drove her closer to the edge.

Her body shuddered beneath me, her inner muscles clamping down on my fingers as wave after wave of pleasure washed over her. I kept stroking, drawing out her orgasm until she was a trembling, whimpering mess.

"That's it, darlin'," I said against her neck, pressing open-mouthed kisses along her throat. "So fucking beautiful when you come for me."

"Dane," she panted, wrapping her hand around my shaft. "I need you inside me."

I struggled to maintain control even as my hips rocked into her touch. "I don't—I don't have a condom."

Piper's green eyes met mine, pupils blown wide with lust. "I need to feel you," she said, guiding the head of my cock to her soaked entrance.

"Wait, baby." I braced myself on my forearms before gritting out, "Are you on birth control?"

She bit her lip and shook her head. "No…"

Jesus fuck. The thought of taking her bare, of potentially getting her pregnant again…

The rational part of my brain knew we should stop, but my body had other ideas. I pushed forward and breached her with the tip of my cock, both of us groaning at the sensation.

"Not like this." I clenched my jaw and forced myself to pull back, everything in me rebelling against it. "Our first time together in two years isn't going to be a rushed fuck while our daughter naps in the next room. You deserve better than that."

Piper trailed her fingers down my chest, a pretty blush staining her cheeks as she admitted, "But I want to make you feel good."

The protest died on my tongue as she pushed me onto my back and straddled my hips. She stripped off her shirt and bra before leaning down to capture my mouth in a searing kiss.

My hands roamed her soft skin, relearning every curve. I traced the pronounced curve of her hips and the stretch marks on her belly with reverence, amazed by how her body had changed to bring our daughter into the world.

When she began rocking back against my cock with little breathy moans, I had to squeeze her hips in warning.

"Don't be a brat," I forced out through clenched teeth.

"I'm not," she said, hissing through her teeth as the tip hit her clit just right.

I groaned as she rocked against me, her slick heat teasing my aching cock.

"You need to come again, don't you?" I asked, already knowing the answer.

She managed a shaky nod. I put my hands under her thighs and adjusted her position so the length of my cock nestled against her pussy lips.

"Ride it," I said. When she reached down to guide me inside, I stopped her. "Like this."

Piper shuddered as I dragged her forward and back, using my cock to create friction against her clit. "Right there," she pleaded, bracing herself on my chest.

"Good girl. Tell me what else you need."

"You inside me," she whispered, her mouth curving up at the corner as she reached between us.

I caught her wrist and flipped her onto her stomach, bringing my palm down against her ass cheek before thrusting two fingers inside her dripping cunt. "Starting to think you like being a brat, baby."

She slammed herself back on my fingers, begging, "More."

I added a third finger, growling at the sight of her stretching around me.

"Harder."

The sounds of her wet pussy filled the room as I fucked her with my hand, her inner walls rhythmically squeezing my fingers before she came with a strangled sob.

"That's my girl. Keep going," I said, changing up the speed to prolong her orgasm until she was squirting against my hand.

And fuck, if that wasn't the sexiest thing I'd ever witnessed.

"Dane," Piper whimpered, her leg muscles quivering. "I can't."

"You're doing so good, baby," I said, adjusting my angle to hit her G-spot better. "You can give me one more, can't you?"

Her hips bucked wildly in response as she grabbed a fistful of the comforter, coating my hand and the comforter in her cum.

I brought my fingers to my lips, groaning as soon as the taste of her hit my tongue. "Goddamn, you taste good."

Piper peered back at me through a curtain of dark hair, her cheeks flushed. "I bet you do, too," she whispered before crawling over to me. "Can I touch you?"

I made a guttural sound in the back of my throat and nodded, tracing the curve of her bottom lip. She gazed up at me with those big green eyes before swiping her tongue across my thumb.

"Suck," I commanded, slowly pressing it into her mouth.

She obeyed instantly, working her tongue around the digit as if it were my cock.

"That's it, baby," I praised, unable to tear my eyes away from her mouth.

Piper reached down to grip my shaft, and my nostrils flared with the force of my breaths. I was already so close to coming, and she'd barely touched me.

"Do you want to watch me suck you?" She circled her fingers

around the base and leaned in, lapping up a bead of precum glistening on the tip.

I fisted my hand in her hair and pressed my cock against her lips with a groan. "Fuck yes. Show me what that pretty little mouth can do."

My head fell back as Piper took me into her hot, wet mouth. The feeling of her lips wrapped around me was even better than I remembered. She hollowed her cheeks, sucking hard as she bobbed her head.

Her tongue moved along the underside of my shaft, tracing the vein there, and my hips jerked involuntarily, forcing more of my length past her lips. What little control I had left snapped, and I thrust in as far as I could. The feel of her throat spasming around me nearly pushed me over the edge.

Piper pulled back to gasp for air, her eyes watering. "I want you to come on my stomach," she panted before diving back down.

I managed a jerky nod, finding it difficult to focus on anything beyond the incredible suction of her mouth. Fat tears streamed down her cheeks as she deep-throated me, but she kept working my cock like a pro.

"Look at me while you suck my cock," I ordered. When she gazed up at me through shimmering eyes, spit dripping down her chin, I thought I might lose it right then. "Good fucking girl."

She hummed in pleasure at the praise, the vibrations shooting straight to my cock. One hand moved down to caress my balls while she bobbed her head, and I clenched my jaw so hard I thought my teeth might crack.

My pulse thundered in my ears as pressure built at the base of my spine.

"I'm close," I grunted, my muscles tensing as I fought to hold back.

Piper pulled off me with an obscene pop, a string of saliva connecting the tip to her swollen lips. She lay back and spread her legs wide. With her hand wrapped around my shaft, she teased her clit with the blunt head, quickly jacking me to orgasm.

The muscles at the base of my cock contracted, and I came with a roar, painting her stomach and the thin strip of hair between her legs with ropes of cum.

Piper continued milking my cock, smearing my release across her skin. I watched through heavy-lidded eyes as she circled her clit with cum-slicked fingers.

It was the hottest fucking thing I'd ever seen.

"What are you doing, darlin'?" I asked, my spent cock twitching with renewed interest.

"Playing," she said innocently, her lips quirking into a grin.

"Such a brat."

"Is it wrong to want the real thing?" Piper pouted, releasing her grip on my cock to tease her nipples.

"Oh baby, this is real," I assured her, squeezing her hip.

She shook her head in disagreement. "Remember? Real would be your cum inside me."

Fuck me.

I groaned, raking a hand over my face as all the blood rushed south. "You can't say shit like that."

"Why not?" She grabbed my hand and pressed it to the curve of her belly. "You're the one that said you wanted to see me pregnant."

Mine. All fucking mine. Possessiveness blazed through me like a wildfire.

I let my head fall back, nostrils flaring with ragged breaths. Every shred of self-control I had left was hanging by a thread.

"Fucking do it," I rasped. "Put my cum inside you where it belongs."

Piper's eyes darkened with lust as she coated her fingers in the mess on her stomach and positioned them at her entrance, teasing herself.

A little closer, baby…

Before she could push them into her body, a loud robotic voice announced, *"Alarm. Front Door,"* followed by a shrill beeping.

"Stay here!" I yelled, yanking on my jeans and snatching my gun from the nightstand.

Piper clutched a pillow to her chest, her eyes wide with fear. "What—"

"It's all right, baby. Stay put." I quickly cleared the house room by room, surprised to find Avery still asleep when I entered the nursery.

With my gun raised and every sense on high alert, I crept down the hall into the living room to find the front door sitting open about an inch.

Heart pounding, I checked the perimeter outside, searching for any sign of an intruder. Nothing seemed out of place, but the hairs on the back of my neck stood up regardless.

Something wasn't right.

The system was disarmed when I returned, and Piper was pacing the living room in her robe. "Did you find anything?" she asked, worry etched on her face.

"Nothing," I said, shaking my head.

"I can't remember if I locked up last night. Maybe it was the wind? The damn thing is glitchy as hell. I swear it goes off for no reason."

I frowned, my instincts screaming it was more than just a glitchy system. "I checked all the locks before I crashed on the couch. Everything was secure."

Piper chewed her lip, clearly unsettled. "Are you sure? Maybe I forgot..."

"I'm sure," I said firmly.

Her eyes darted nervously to the front door. "So someone tried to break in?"

I didn't want to scare her, but I didn't want to downplay the situation. "It's possible it was the wind, but I'll reach out to some of our sub-contractors tomorrow about upgrading your system."

She nodded, wrapping her arms around herself. I pulled her close, running my hands over her back.

"It's okay, baby. I've got you," I murmured. "No one's getting past me."

"My hero," she said, a hint of playfulness returning to her voice. Her hands slid down my chest to the waistband of my jeans. "I think you deserve a reward."

I groaned as she palmed me through the denim. My body was already responding to her touch, but my mind was still racing. "Wait—"

She cut me off with an insistent kiss, backing me toward the bedroom. "Talk later—need you now."

When she untied her robe, letting it fall open to reveal her naked body, my resolve crumbled. My lips collided with hers as I carried her to the bed, my earlier concerns fading to background noise.

"You're going to kill me, woman," I growled against her lips.

She rocked against me with an impatient whine. "Please…"

I notched myself at her entrance, gritting my teeth as I guided the head of my cock into her tight pussy.

Piper rolled her hips, urging me deeper when a piercing wail erupted from the baby monitor.

We froze, staring at each other with wide eyes before I reluctantly withdrew from the warmth of her body.

"No!" She threw her arm over her face with a muffled curse as Avery's cries increased in volume.

I dropped a quick kiss to her sternum before tucking myself back into my jeans with a low chuckle. "I've got her."

SIXTEEN

GHOST

Ivy & Piper's Guide to Life Rule Number Twenty-Five:
Never date or sleep with someone from work.

I drummed my fingers against the steering wheel, waiting for Piper's shift to end, which should have occurred—I glanced at the clock on the dashboard—eighteen minutes ago.

"A-ma!" Avery shrieked from the back seat, her little face screwed up in irritation.

"Hang on, princess," I said, twisting around to face her. "Mama will be out soon."

She bucked against the safety straps on her car seat, her cheeks turning an alarming shade of red. I sighed, knowing exactly what that look meant. I'd learned it well over the last week.

Baby girl needed a distraction and fast.

I unbuckled my seatbelt. "Tell you what? How about we go inside and get you a little snack while we wait for Mama? How's that sound?"

"A-ma!" she agreed, bouncing excitedly as I busted her out of her car seat prison. Getting her to hold still long enough for me to get her jacket zipped up took a little more convincing.

The jingle of the bell over the door to the bakery might as well have been a fucking air raid siren with all the attention it drew. Customers tensed, and conversations halted mid-sentence.

It felt as if the entire shop froze, eyes locked on us like we were some freak show.

Some tried to hide their stares, burying their noses in their phones or suddenly finding the pattern on their paper coffee cups interesting. Others didn't even bother to be subtle, openly gawking at my kutte and the bandages on Avery's forehead with pinched expressions.

It was why I'd avoided bringing her anywhere other than the park. People took one look at me and immediately jumped to all the wrong conclusions.

I shoved down the familiar mix of anger and shame and squared my shoulders, refusing to let the judgmental assholes know they'd gotten under my skin. But deep down, an ache bloomed in my chest. This wasn't solely about me anymore. It was about Avery too.

Would she always be seen as the biker's kid? The one parents whispered about at PTA meetings and warned their precious angels to stay away from?

"Co-ku," Avery said, oblivious to the tension around us. Her chubby fingers released my kutte to reach for the display case.

I forced a smile, trying to focus on her and not the whispers spreading through the bakery. "Let's see," I said as we approached the case. "They've got cupcakes. You want a cupcake?"

She shook her head. "Co-ku."

"All right. Not a cupcake. What about—" I went down the menu, rattling off anything that sounded remotely close to what she was saying. "Cheesecake? Cake Pops? Ooh, how about a cinnamon roll?"

She pushed her pink lips into a pout and mashed her forehead to mine. "Co-ku," she repeated, slower this time since I was clearly a moron in her eyes.

"Cookie?" I guessed, bracing myself for a meltdown.

Avery's mouth lifted in a grin that showcased her little teeth before nodding. "Co-ku!"

"Could we get a chocolate chip cookie and a cinnamon roll?" I asked since they were Piper's favorite thing to make, and I'd yet to try one.

The guy behind the register was probably the only person in the joint who didn't look at me like I was a threat. He rattled off my total, giving me a chin tip when I told him to keep the change.

"Where do we want to sit?" I asked, so focused on finding an open table I damn near collided with a delivery guy as he came through the front door. "Sorry, man. I didn't see you there."

"Nuh, no, owie!" Avery growled with a furrowed brow that looked almost comical on her small face.

"What's your deal, sassy pants?" I asked, tickling her side before moving out of his way toward an empty table near the back.

She arched her back and squawked when I tried to put her in a highchair. Not willing to draw even more unwanted attention, I settled her on my lap and broke off a small piece of cookie for her.

"Co-ku." She snatched the cookie from my hands and crammed it into her mouth like she hadn't been fed all day.

"Little bites, remember?" I said, cutting off a piece of my cinnamon roll in demonstration. "See? No, that's Daddy's."

I managed to catch her grabby hands before she could snatch my dessert, smacking my lips loudly against her cheek until she was shrieking with giggles.

A clean-cut guy in khakis and a polo shirt emerged from the back, making a beeline for our table.

"Hey, folks," he said with a smile that didn't quite reach his eyes. "I was wondering if I could grab a couple of to-go boxes for you."

"Nope. We're good. Thanks, man," I said, keeping my voice level despite the anger bubbling up inside me.

"Nuh-no," she repeated, wagging her finger sternly before reaching for her cookie.

He glanced at Avery, then to my kutte, and his lips curled in barely disguised disdain before he caught himself. "Listen, I'm cool with y'all being here," he said before lowering his voice like we were buddies sharing a secret. "But your presence is making some of the other customers uncomfortable. I'm sure you can appreciate the position it puts me in as the owner."

I clenched my jaw, fighting the urge to tell him exactly what position he'd be in by the time I was done with him. But Avery was watching, her green eyes wide and curious. I couldn't lose my shit in front of her.

"Look," I said, leaning in. "Piper wasn't even scheduled to work today, but here we are. I'm sure you can appreciate the position it puts me in when my girl was supposed to be off a half-hour ago, and my kid missed her naptime because she wasn't."

The guy's eyes widened at the mention of Piper, and his composure slipped. "You—you're Piper's boyfriend?"

"Dane," I said, breaking off another piece of cookie for Avery before extending my hand. I didn't give a fuck about niceties, but he was Piper's boss. I wouldn't disrespect her or set a bad example for our daughter, even if the guy's face was begging for a fist. "And you are?"

"Derek." He reluctantly placed his hand in mine, his gaze lingering on my kutte. "Kinda ironic, isn't it?"

I tightened my grip before releasing him. "What, me and Piper?"

He yanked his hand back, hiding a wince. "N-no. Ghost," he blurted out, nodding to my kutte. "I mean, look at you. You're kinda hard to miss. It's the exact opposite of a ghost."

"Yeah, that's not why they call me Ghost," I said, pausing to wipe a smear of chocolate off Avery's mouth before turning back to him with a bemused smirk. "But good guess."

The story behind my road name wasn't all that intimidating or interesting. I was the youngest of Wolverine's four boys and incredibly shy, so it was no surprise to anyone when my old man saddled me with the name Ghost.

But Derek didn't know that, and I enjoyed watching the color drain from his face.

"Oh, yeah. Of course," he quickly agreed.

Avery watched our exchange with raised brows before ripping off a chunk of my cinnamon roll and stuffing it in her mouth.

"You know, I always wanted a motorcycle when I was younger," Derek said.

"That so?" I drawled, sliding the cinnamon roll out of reach. The last thing she needed was a sugar crash on top of the missed naptime.

He nodded. "Yeah, but they're so dangerous. It's not just the bike either—you've got to worry about everyone else on the road. One wrong move, and it's game over."

"No shit? I had no idea," I said dryly.

Derek shrugged, unfazed by my sarcasm. "Don't shoot the messenger, *Ghost*. I'm just saying it's not something I'd do. Can't imagine any family man taking a risk like that."

The implication in his words was clear, and it took every ounce of self-control not to knock his teeth down his throat.

I ran my tongue over my teeth with a low chuckle before pushing back my chair to stand, using every inch of my height to tower over him. "I'll keep that in mind."

Derek took a step back, clearly unnerved by my proximity. Good. Because of him, I hadn't gotten to try a bite of my cinnamon roll before Avery decimated it with her grubby little hands.

"Speaking of risks," I said, keeping my voice low and even, "Think it goes without saying that threatening Piper with fewer hours or a demotion to get her to come in and cover shifts on her days off won't end well for you. Am I clear?"

His eyes widened, and he held up his palms. "Sure thing, man. She's never mentioned you before, so I was under the impression she was doing it all on her own and needed the extra shifts to provide for this little one."

He reached for Avery, and she jerked away with a whimper, burying her chocolate-covered face against my kutte. "Nuh-no!"

"She doesn't like men," I growled, pulling her closer. "And for future reference, Piper's personal life is none of your goddamn business."

"Hey, no problem, man," Derek said, a condescending smirk tugging at the corner of his mouth. The guy was slicker than a boiled onion. "My employees are like family. But if she's got someone looking out for her now, that's great."

His placating tone only served to piss me off even more.

Keeping my upper body turned to the side to shield Avery, I stepped closer, invading his personal space. "Stay the fuck away from my family."

The door to the back swung open, and Piper emerged, her cheeks flushed and wisps of dark hair escaping from her ponytail. Her eyes went wide when they landed on us. "Dane? What's going on?"

"Hey, darlin'," I said, trying to keep my tone light. "Your shift was supposed to end a while ago, so we were having a snack while we waited for you."

"Didn't you get my text?" she asked, her gaze darting between the two of us in suspicion. "I said I was staying a little later to finish up an order for tomorrow."

"A-ma!" Avery squealed, nearly toppling out of my arms to reach for her mama.

Piper's face softened as she scooped up our daughter, using her thumb to wipe the chocolate streaks off her face. "Hi, baby. Looks like you missed your mouth."

"Fuck!" Avery bellowed with a giggle.

Shit.

Piper's green eyes locked on mine like a missile, the muscle in her jaw ticking. "Where'd you hear that word?"

"Is that a word?" I asked. "Didn't sound like a word to me."

"We'll talk about this later," she muttered, shifting Avery to her hip. The tension in the air was thick enough to choke on when she turned to Derek with a forced smile. "Sorry about that. I'm just finishing up and should be out of your hair in a few minutes."

His earlier nervousness was gone, replaced by another smarmy grin. "No rush. Family comes first, right?"

I clenched my fists at my sides, biting back the urge to wipe the smile off his face. Piper must have sensed my rising anger because she quickly handed Avery back to me.

"Why don't you two wait in the car?" she suggested through clenched teeth.

Derek cleared his throat. "Nice meeting you, Dane. I'm sure we'll be seeing more of each other."

I sensed a hint of challenge in his tone but simply nodded, not keen on digging my grave any deeper than I already had. The bell jingled again as we left, and I could feel the weight of everyone's stares on my back.

Once we were settled in the SUV, I glanced in the rearview mirror to see Piper having what looked like a heated discussion with Derek.

Her cheeks were flushed, and she was gesturing animatedly with her hands.

"A-ma?" Avery's small voice pulled my attention back to her. She was watching me with wide, worried eyes.

I faked a smile, reaching back to smooth her hair. "Mama will be out in a minute."

True to my word, Piper stormed out of the bakery moments later, her face a thundercloud as she yanked open the passenger door and slid inside.

"What the hell was that?" she hissed, keeping her voice low so Avery wouldn't hear.

"Look, I'm sorry if I overstepped—"

"Overstepped? You threatened my boss, Dane. Do you have any idea how that makes me look?"

"Didn't threaten him, per se," I argued, gripping the steering wheel tighter. "I just made it clear he can't keep jerking you around with your schedule. That's all."

Piper huffed out a laugh. "Oh, is that all? Look, I've been handling things just fine on my own for years. I don't need you swooping in to save me like I'm some damsel in distress."

The words stung more than I cared to admit. "Not trying to save you, darlin'," I gritted out. "I'm trying to help."

"Well, don't," she said, turning to stare out the window. "I can take care of myself."

The rest of the drive home was tense and silent, save for Avery's occasional babbling from the backseat. By the time we pulled into the driveway, my jaw ached from clenching it so hard.

Piper was out of the car before I'd even cut the engine, slamming the door behind her. I sighed, rubbing a hand over my face before grabbing my kutte and Avery from the backseat.

"Looks like Daddy's in the doghouse, princess," I murmured, lifting her onto my hip.

She gave a little yip and grinned up at me, oblivious to the mess I'd made.

SEVENTEEN

GHOST

Ivy & Piper's Guide to Life Rule Number Thirty-Five:
If it feels like a bad idea, it probably is.

Inside, I found Piper aggressively wiping down the kitchen counters, her movements jerky and tense. "This whole damn place is a mess!"

We'd only been living together one week, and the growing pains were becoming more evident by the day.

I set Avery down and rubbed the back of my neck. "Yeah, sorry about that. I didn't get a chance to clean up before we left to come get you."

"And look! Your laptop and work shit are spread out all over my kitchen table like it's your own personal office again!"

"Like I said, I didn't get a chance to clean up before it was time to leave," I repeated, this time through clenched teeth. I started gathering my things, stacking them neatly.

Piper paused her frantic cleaning and leaned against the counter, brandishing the dishrag like a weapon. "It's not just that. It's everything. Your shit's all over the table. Your boots are in the middle of the bedroom floor. Your clothes are piled up in the chair in my bedroom. I like things a certain way, and it's like you don't even care!"

If she were willing to give up an inch of closet space, none of this would be an issue, but I bit back the retort, knowing it would only add fuel to an already raging dumpster fire.

Instead, I held my hands up in surrender. "I'll keep my stuff contained. I'm still adjusting to sharing space, too. Give me some time."

"Avery needs a bath," she said without looking up. "Can you handle that while I clean up in here?"

"Already planning on it," I replied, grabbing Avery before hesitating in the doorway. "Again, I'm sorry—"

"Never mind, I'll take care of the bath too." She tossed the dishrag into the sink with an annoyed huff before trying to pull her from my arms.

"Jesus, Piper!" I snapped, catching her wrists in my hand. "I said I'd fucking do it. Just forget all of this for a second and talk to me."

She avoided my gaze. "Not now. Can you give Avery her bath, or is that too much to ask?"

I nodded tightly and stalked down the hall. No point in pushing her when she was already in a shitty mood.

As I helped Avery out of her chocolate-stained clothes and into the tub, my mind replayed the scene at the bakery. I knew I'd fucked up, but I couldn't for the life of me understand why Piper continued to work for someone who clearly didn't respect her or her time.

Why hadn't she quit and opened her own place?

Avery tossed a handful of bubbles over the side of the tub, her eyes widening in mock surprise. "Uh-oh…"

I shook my head, unable to resist the smile tugging at my lips before wiping it up with the towel. "Think you and I have made enough messes for one day, squirt."

Once she was clean, I dressed her in her unicorn pajamas and brushed out her curls, my mind frequently drifting back to how to fix things with Piper. Avery rubbed her eyes with a yawn, the missed naptime finally catching up with her.

"No, nigh-nigh," she grumbled, laying her head on my shoulder.

She was as bad as my old man when he fell asleep on the couch and claimed he was only resting his eyes.

Piper's bedroom door was closed, and I lifted my hand to knock before deciding to give her some space to cool down.

"All right, kiddo," I said. "Let's get some dinner in you before you pass out."

Avery perked up long enough to decimate several reheated dinosaur-shaped chicken nuggets before dozing off with mixed vegetables smashed beneath her cheek.

While she slept, I cleaned up the kitchen and started the dishwasher. After one last sweep to ensure everything was pristine, I cleaned Sleeping Beauty's hands and face. She grumbled an unintelligible protest but was out cold again by the time I laid her in the crib.

After easing the nursery door shut, I paused in the hallway. Deciding to face the music sooner rather than later, I knocked softly on the bedroom door. "Darlin', you hungry?"

No answer.

Fuck. I'd really stepped in it.

Bracing myself for round two, I opened the door. Piper lay curled on her side with her back to me. Her arms were wrapped around her stomach, making her appear even smaller than she was. I thought she was sleeping until she sucked in a ragged breath.

The raw sound of her pain ripped through me like a blade, and I would have given anything to take it away, to make things right between us. I didn't think before climbing onto the bed to pull her into my arms.

"I'm sorry," I murmured into her hair. "Talk to me...please."

"What do you want me to say, Dane?" she asked through tears. "You moved in and took over everything. You decided my security system wasn't good enough and changed it without consulting me first."

"Without consulting you? I said I'd reach out to some subcontractors and see about upgrading your system—"

"Seeing about upgrading my system and having a brand new one installed while I'm at work are two totally different things!" she hissed. "And then today, you went all alpha male and caused a scene in front of my coworkers because you didn't like that my boss called me in on my day off."

"You're right," I admitted softly. "I overstepped, and I'm sorry. I'm still finding my footing here as a dad and with you. This is all new to me. I want to help make things easier for you, but I'm not always going to get it right."

Piper rolled over to face me, her green eyes rimmed with red. "I'm not a girl who needs her big bad biker boyfriend to fight her battles. Do you know how hard I've worked to build a reputation there? To be taken seriously?"

"That asshole doesn't take you seriously," I said, brushing a strand of hair from her damp cheek. "He takes advantage of you, and I put a stop to it."

She shook her head, fresh tears spilling down her cheeks. "And what happens when he decides it's not worth the hassle and fires me? Did you stop to think about that? Because I need this job."

"Bullshit," I growled, my chest tightening at the defeat in her voice. "You could open your own place. You were so close. I don't understand why you haven't told Derek to go fuck himself and pulled the trigger on your own dreams."

Piper pulled away from me to sit up. "Why the fuck do you think? All the money I saved went to Avery. Diapers, formula, doctor visits— it all adds up fast. Starting a business takes more than just capital. You've got to put in long hours if you want a snowball's chance in hell at succeeding. Kinda hard to do with a newborn." Her chest heaved, but she held the sob back, pressing her fist against her mouth.

Me. I was the reason her dream never came true. And had Avery not woken up from her nap when she did a week ago, I would have given in and fucked Piper without protection, never stopping to consider how another baby would impact her life. The only reason we hadn't tried again since was because she was on the rag and had been dealing with severe cramps.

I sat up, the weight of my failure crushing me. "Jesus, Piper. I'm sorry. I had no idea."

"We both made choices that night, Dane. Nothing we can do about it now." Her shoulders sagged, the fight draining out of her body. "I'm going to grab a shower, and then we can figure out dinner."

"Want some company?" I asked, needing to hold her in my arms and bury my face in her hair while I came up with a solution.

She swiped the tears from her lashes before getting up. "I'm still on my period," she said. "And I really just need a few minutes to myself right now."

I nodded, swallowing the lump in my throat. "Take your time. I'll go start dinner."

The click of the lock echoed in the quiet room, an audible reminder I hadn't given her many reasons to trust me. Scrubbing a hand over my face, I let out a heavy sigh and headed for the kitchen. There had to be a way to earn her trust and help her achieve her dream without overstepping.

While pulling ingredients from the fridge, I noticed a slip of paper sticking out of the top of Piper's purse. After listening to ensure the shower was still running, I slid it out of her bag. My eyes scanned the neat, masculine handwriting, a chill creeping down my spine with each word.

Hope these help make your time of the month more bearable. I swung by your favorite French chocolatier—dark chocolate ganache with sea salt, just like you like. I also included some extra-strength ibuprofen because I know how bad your cramps can get. Let me know if you need anything else...even if it's just a massage to ease the tightness in your muscles. And remember, no matter what happens, I'm always here for you.

I crumpled the note in my fist, my vision going red at the edges. The sound of the shower faded to a dull roar in my ears, drowned out by the pounding of my pulse.

That fucking piece of shit.

I smoothed out the paper, forcing myself to re-read it to ensure I hadn't misunderstood. But no, the words were crystal clear. The writer knew intimate details about Piper—her favorite chocolates, when she was on her period, and how bad her cramps got. Not the kind of information one would typically share with a boss.

How long had it been going on? What else didn't I know? Had she and Derek—

No. She said she hadn't been with anyone since me, and Piper wasn't the type to start a sexual relationship with someone she worked with.

But then, why was he leaving her gifts? Offering massages? Acting like he had some claim on her?

The shower shut off, and I carefully refolded the note with shaking hands before slipping it back into her purse exactly as I'd found it. My movements were mechanical as I prepared dinner while trying to come to terms with what I'd read and what it meant for our relationship.

I wanted to confront her, to demand answers. But I knew that would only push her farther away. I'd already overstepped once today, and there wasn't a chance in hell she'd ever learn to trust me if I admitted to going through her things.

But how the fuck was I supposed to ignore it?

"Something smells good," Piper said, padding into the kitchen. Her hair was damp, and she'd changed into yoga pants and one of my T-shirts.

I plastered on a smile, hoping she couldn't see the turmoil churning inside me. "Just throwing together a stir fry. Nothing fancy. How was your shower?"

She shrugged, reaching past me to grab a glass from the cabinet. "Fine. The hot water helped with the cramping some."

I tensed at the mention of her cramps, the note burning in the back of my mind. "That's good," I managed, focusing intently on the vegetables sizzling in the pan. "You need anything for the pain?"

"I'm okay," she said, filling her glass with water. "I took some ibuprofen earlier."

My jaw clenched. Had she taken the pills he'd left for her? The thought made my stomach turn.

"You sure?" I asked, unable to keep the edge from my voice. "I could run to the Dallas clubhouse and get you something stronger."

Piper gave me a puzzled look. "I'm fine, really. What's going on with you?"

"Nothing," I said, pushing away from the stove to stand behind her at the sink. I lifted the hem of her shirt and gently kneaded her lower back.

"Just making sure you're comfortable." I forced myself to focus on the task at hand, working out the knots in Piper's lower back as she leaned against the counter. Her soft sighs of relief helped ease some of the tension coiled in my chest, but the knowledge of the note still burned hot in the back of my mind.

"That feels amazing," she murmured, her eyes fluttering closed. "Thank you."

I kissed her damp hair. "I'm sorry about earlier. You're right. I shouldn't have made a scene like that. It won't happen again."

She turned in my arms, her green eyes searching mine. "We're both still figuring this out, and while I appreciate you wanting to protect me, maybe we can talk about some boundaries—like what's okay and what's not when it comes to me and Avery?"

I nodded, swallowing hard. "Yeah, that's probably a good idea. And I mean it. I'll do better, I promise."

"Thank you." She stretched up on her toes to press her lips to mine.

I returned the kiss, trying to push my swirling thoughts aside. But even as I held her close and breathed in her scent, the note taunted me from where her purse sat on the counter. Who else was trying to take care of her? Who else knew intimate details about her that should have been reserved only for me?

"Hey, are you sure you're okay?"

I lifted my head, my eyes locking on the scrap of paper. Seeing an opening, I casually asked, "What's that?"

Piper followed my gaze to her purse, her eyebrows drawing together in confusion. "What's what?"

I nodded toward the note. "That—the piece of paper sticking out of your purse."

A brief flash of panic crossed her face before she shrugged. "Probably a grocery list or something. I'm always leaving myself notes and forgetting about them."

"I'll take it," I said, managing to keep my voice steady. "I was planning on running to the store tomorrow anyway, so I don't mind grabbing whatever you need while you're at work tomorrow."

She reached her purse before I could, and I went still, searching her face for a reaction as she skimmed it.

"Never mind, it's about some new product we've got coming in next week," she said before tucking it back inside her bag. "Nothing exciting."

She was lying to my face.

I forced myself to remain calm, even as rage bubbled up inside me. "Sounds exciting to me. What kind of new product?"

Piper turned back to the stove to monitor the stir fry. "Just some new baking supplies. Specialty flours and stuff. Derek is really particular about ingredients and wants to try out a new supplier."

Each lie that fell from her lips was like a knife twisting in my gut. I wanted to ask if she was fucking her boss, demanding she tell me the truth, but I was also fond of my balls and wanted to keep them attached to my body.

I ground my teeth together, fighting to keep my expression neutral as I said, "That's cool. I didn't realize Derek was so...hands-on."

She continued stirring the vegetables, avoiding my gaze. "Oh, yeah. He likes to be involved in all aspects of the business. You know how it is when you're passionate about something."

Another lie.

"Yeah, I get that," I said, my voice strained. "Speaking of, maybe I should carve out some time tomorrow to swing by and smooth things over with Derek."

Piper spun around. "That's really not necessary, Dane," she insisted, her voice rising in pitch. "I talked it over with him, and everything's good."

"I don't mind. Might be good to—"

She stretched up onto her toes and pressed her lips to mine. I froze for a moment, caught off guard by the sudden kiss. But as Piper's lips moved against mine, I found myself responding instinctively, my hands coming up to cradle her face. The kiss deepened, and I could taste the desperation on her tongue, feel it in the way her fingers clutched at my shirt.

She was trying to distract me.

"What was that for?" I asked when we broke apart to catch our breaths.

Piper plucked an invisible piece of lint off my T-shirt. "Nothing. I just... I'm sorry about earlier. I overreacted."

"Hey, you don't need to apologize," I said, hooking my fingers beneath her chin and guiding her face back up to mine. "I'm the one who fucked up."

Her green eyes searched mine, almost as if we were playing a mental game of chicken. "Let's just forget it and enjoy the rest of our evening. Since Avery went down early, maybe we could watch a movie—what? Why are you looking at me like that?"

I brushed a damp strand of hair from her forehead and shook my head. "Nothing. Just thinking about how lucky I am to have you and Avery in my life."

Piper's eyes softened at my words, but I could still see the tension in her shoulders. "I'm lucky to have you, too," she said, brushing her lips over mine in a brief kiss.

I wanted so badly to believe her, to ignore the gnawing doubt eating away at me. But the lies she'd told played on a loop in my mind.

I forced a smile, trying to hide the turmoil churning in my gut. "You know you can tell me anything, right? No matter what it is."

The irony wasn't lost on me. Here we both were, harboring secrets and telling lies. What a fucking pair we made.

I'd promised to stay out of her work life, and I would. I'd play along with her lies and half-truths. Let her think she had me fooled.

For now, at least.

After dinner, Piper curled into my side on the couch, her head resting on my chest. I wrapped my arm around her shoulders, breathing in the familiar scent of her shampoo. For a moment, I could almost pretend everything was normal between us.

But as the movie played, my mind kept drifting back to the damn note. Who else knew such intimate details about Piper? Who else was trying to take care of her in ways that should have been reserved for me?

EIGHTEEN

PIPER

Ivy & Piper's Guide to Life Rule Number Seventeen:
Always share your location.

The bakery was silent except for the steady thump of my fists against the stainless steel worktable. With every resounding smack, puffs of flour rose, swirling through the air like tiny snowflakes. They clung to my sweaty face and coated every surface in a powdery white layer.

Early morning shifts like this one were usually my favorite. I liked the stillness and having the entire bakery to myself, at least for a few hours.

There was a sort of alchemy to turning flour, sugar, and yeast into elaborate pastries and sweetbreads. One I'd mastered over the years. Maybe that was why I'd always been drawn to baking—it was the one aspect of my life that offered consistency and guaranteed results.

But this time, the rhythmic push and pull against the dough wasn't enough to silence my mind. It had been almost a week since I'd discovered the note in my locker. It wasn't the first time an anonymous person had left me gifts, but it was the first time they'd left a message.

Someone wanted me to know they were watching me, cataloging my habits down to my menstrual cycle. The invasion of privacy made my skin crawl, and no matter how hard I tried to shake off the paranoia, it stuck to me like the flour dusting my arms.

Thinking about it made my stomach churn. I'd lied to Dane when he asked about it, afraid he'd overreact. Initially, I planned to tell him everything, but after his run-in with my boss, I was afraid he'd force me to quit my job or, worse, go after Derek even though his handwriting and the writing on the note were completely different.

Lying had seemed like the lesser of two evils at the time, but now, the distance between us had grown into a living, breathing thing.

From the outside, everything looked perfect. I came home to a clean house. He cooked dinner every night and had taken over bath and bedtime duty with Avery, but the heat between us had gone ice cold. I often found him watching me with guarded eyes, almost like he was waiting for me to crack, to confess.

At night, he'd taken to sleeping on the couch, if he slept at all. More often than not, he'd disappear after dinner on his motorcycle, citing club business in a way that wasn't open for discussion.

The weight of my lie pressed down on me, making it hard to breathe. I wanted to come clean and bridge the gap between us, but every time I opened my mouth, the words died on my tongue.

I was already losing him. What would he do when he found out I lied? That I'd kept something so important from him?

He'd leave. This time for good.

My palms dampened with sweat, making the dough beneath my fingers sticky. I kneaded harder, trying to channel my fear and frustration into something productive. When it began to tear beneath my knuckles, I forced myself to set the overworked dough aside to rest before moving on to the next one.

A noise from the back hallway yanked me from my spiraling thoughts. My hands froze mid-knead, flour-covered fingers splayed against the half-formed dough. The clock on the wall read 4:17 AM— far too early for anyone else to be arriving.

I knew the sounds of this old building—the creak of settling wood, the low hum of the walk-in, the whir of the commercial mixer—but this? This sent a chill up my spine and prickled the skin along my arms. Suddenly, the bakery felt too large...too empty.

My heart slammed against my ribs as I strained to listen. The silence stretched on, broken only by the hum of the refrigerators. Maybe it was just my imagination, fueled by lack of sleep and mounting anxiety. But then I heard it again. A soft scraping sound echoed in the pre-dawn quiet like someone trying to move quietly and failing.

Fear clawed its way up my throat, threatening to burst out in a scream. I forced it back down and glanced frantically around the kitchen, searching for anything I could use as a weapon. The gleam of a chef's knife caught my eye, but it may as well have been miles away on the opposite side of the room.

My revolver. My revolver was in my purse on the back counter. Before I could move toward it, two figures stormed through the kitchen doors, their faces obscured by black ski masks. My body tensed, ready to flee, but there was nowhere to go. They had me cornered.

"Don't even think about it," the shorter of the two snarled, following my gaze to my phone.

I froze, my muscles rigid with fear. The taller one stepped forward, his eyes narrowing as he studied my face.

"Shit, man," he said with a dark chuckle. "It's Ghost's Ol' Lady. Well, well, well. This just got a whole lot more interesting."

My mind reeled. How did these men know Dane? The questions swirled in my head, but terror clogged my throat and choked off any words I might have spoken.

"Let's go." The shorter one gestured toward the doors with his gun. "Now."

They herded me toward Derek's office, keeping their weapons pressed against the back of my neck. My legs felt like jelly, threatening to give out with each step.

One shoved me roughly from behind, sending me stumbling into the office. My hip collided with the sharp corner of Derek's desk, and I fell to my knees with a muffled cry.

"Open the safe," the shorter one demanded, jabbing the barrel of his gun against my temple.

"I-I don't know the combination," I stammered through chattering teeth.

He laughed, the harsh sound sending shivers down my spine. "Don't lie to us, sweetheart. We know you're the manager. Open it. Now."

I bobbed my chin in a frantic nod and knelt in front of the safe, my heart pounding so violently I thought it might burst from my chest.

"Tick-tock," the taller one taunted. I could almost hear the smirk in his tone, the perverse pleasure he took from my fear.

My hands trembled violently as I entered the combination, and the keypad blurred before my eyes. Instead of clicking open, the safe gave a series of beeps, indicating I'd entered the wrong code.

I tried again, my dough-covered fingers slipping on the dial. "I'm sorry. I can try—"

The taller man yanked my head back so forcefully that he tore off my skull cap and a chunk of hair, wrenching a sharp cry of pain from my throat. He pressed the cold barrel of his gun against my trembling lips, tracing them with sickening deliberation.

"One more chance, sweetheart," he growled, his breath hot against my ear. "Or I'll give you something else to do with that pretty mouth of yours."

Despite the bile rising in my throat and the tears streaming down my face, I managed to steady my shaking hands enough to enter the correct code. The soft click of it opening seemed deafening in the tense silence.

They shoved me aside and began greedily scooping stacks of bills into a duffel bag while I stumbled back, my legs threatening to give out. Once they had the money, they would leave.

But the taller man wasn't done. Instead of leaving with his prize, he shoved me against the wall, using his body to pin me in place.

"Maybe we should send Ghost and his Silent Phoenix boys a message before we go," he said, his eyes raking over me.

"I did what you asked me to do," I said, panic surging through me. "J-just take what you want and go."

The shorter man shifted uneasily. "Come on, man. We're just supposed to scare her. Let's grab the cash and go before someone catches us."

"You go," the taller one snapped, tearing my chef coat open with a vicious yank and scattering the buttons across the floor. "I'm not done with her yet."

His retreating footsteps echoed through the bakery, followed by the slam of the back door. Then silence descended, broken only by my ragged sobs.

I was alone with a monster.

Dane's world had come crashing into mine, and I was suddenly the currency in a game I never wanted to play.

"No, please don't do this," I begged, thrashing against him as he forced my sports bra up over my breasts.

Images of Avery flashed before my eyes. What if I didn't make it home to her?

"Please. I have a baby." My broken pleas fell on deaf ears, his eyes utterly void of empathy.

"I have a baby," he parroted in a high-pitched voice, tracing the column of my throat with the gun before dragging it down to my breasts. He pressed the barrel against my nipple, pushing the tight bud down like a button, and let it spring free before moving to the other side.

"Please let me go," I said through chest-heaving sobs.

He changed tactics and began scraping the barrel over my nipples, flicking them up and down like someone would a light switch. "Be a good girl, and I'll let you go after."

Black spots danced at the edges of my vision, my breaths coming in short, shallow bursts because I knew as well as he did I wasn't leaving this room alive.

I'd go to my death with pastry dough wedged beneath my fingernails and his hot, rancid breath filling my nostrils.

He jammed the gun into my breast just beneath my heart before fumbling with his pants. The metallic clink of the buckle coming undone echoed in my ears like a death knell.

"Ghost is gonna feel this one."

Something snapped inside me. Fueled by fear and desperation, a primal rage surged through my body. I wouldn't let this happen.

I clawed at his eyes, my nails raking across the exposed skin. He roared in pain and fury before backhanding me so hard my head snapped to the side. The force of the blow left me reeling, my vision exploding in a burst of white-hot pain. My legs buckled beneath me, and I crumpled to the floor.

He was on top of me in an instant, pinning my arms beneath his knees. I thrashed wildly, but he outweighed me by at least a hundred pounds.

"Shouldn't have done that, bitch." He licked a wet stripe up my throat. "Even Ghost won't be able to put you back together when I'm done with you."

Beads of sweat trickled down my temple to mingle with my tears. I squeezed my eyes shut, willing this to be nothing more than a horrible nightmare. But the acrid stench of his sweat and the feel of his hands on me was all too real.

"No!" I screamed, my voice raw and desperate. "Please, don't—"

A deafening bang drowned out my screams, followed by a warm spray across my face. For a split second, I thought I'd been shot. But then my attacker's body collapsed on top of me.

I shoved him off with a strangled cry, my ears still ringing from the gunshot. Blood and gray matter pooled beneath his masked head, his empty eyes fixed on nothing.

Derek stood in the doorway, his face ashen and the gun trembling in his outstretched hands.

"I didn't mean to kill him," he mumbled, his eyes wide with shock. "You were screaming. I just wanted him to stop. I didn't mean to kill him."

The full weight of what had just occurred crashed over me, and I scrambled backward, my hands slipping in the sticky red puddle spreading out from his body. My back hit the wall, and I curled in on myself, violent sobs racking my body. The coppery scent of blood filled my nostrils, mixing sickeningly with the lingering smell of yeast and sugar.

Time seemed to stretch and warp, each second an eternity. The ringing in my ears faded, replaced by the pounding of my own heartbeat and Derek's ragged breathing.

"We have to call the police," I managed through chattering teeth.

He continued staring blankly at the floor as if he hadn't heard me. I tugged my bra down and fumbled with the torn edges of my coat, struggling to hold it closed as I unsteadily made my way over to where he stood, holding his gun on the man's body. His index finger hovered over the trigger in a way I didn't trust.

With shaking hands, I carefully pried it from his fingers and laid it on the desk before turning back to him. "Give me your phone."

He fumbled for his phone and unlocked it before passing it over. "You were screaming. I didn't mean to kill him."

"I know. You did the right thing," I said, my voice barely above a whisper. My fingers left bloody smears on the screen as I dialed 911.

The police arrived in a flurry of flashing lights and barked orders. I huddled in the corner, arms wrapped tightly around myself as they swarmed the bakery. Their voices blurred together, an endless barrage of questions I couldn't begin to process.

"Ma'am, are you injured? Can you tell us what happened?"

I opened my mouth, but no sound came out. My throat felt raw as if I'd been screaming for hours instead of minutes. Maybe I had been.

A female officer knelt beside me, her face swimming in and out of focus. "Can you tell me your name?"

"P-Piper," I managed to choke out. "My full name is Amelia Piper Kelly, but I go by Piper."

"Okay, Piper. We're going to get you checked out by the paramedics, all right?"

I nodded numbly, allowing her to help me to my feet. My legs wobbled, threatening to give out with each step.

As we passed the body on the floor, now covered by a white sheet, bile rose in my throat. I barely made it to the trash can before retching violently. The acidic burn of the vomit mingled with the metallic tang of blood in my mouth.

The officer kept her hands on my shoulders as I emptied the meager contents of my stomach before guiding me out of the bakery and into a waiting ambulance. The brisk morning air hit my face, and I shivered violently before clutching the edges of my jacket a little tighter.

The paramedics peppered me with questions, shining lights in my eyes and probing at the bruise blooming on my cheek. I hugged my knees to my chest, rocking slightly as I tried to make sense of what had happened. The world felt hazy and distant, as if I was watching everything unfold from behind thick glass.

All I could focus on was the sticky feeling of my attacker's blood drying on my skin and the knowledge that those men had known Dane.

They knew about me, about my connection to him.

And they had used that knowledge to target me.

NINETEEN

PIPER

Ivy & Piper's Guide to Life Rule Number Fifteen:
Know where the exits are in any situation.

"Amelia!" My mother's voice cut through the fog. I looked up to see her pushing past the officers, her face pale with fear. "Oh my God, baby."

She pulled me into her arms, and I broke down completely, sobbing into her shoulder like a child.

"I'm here, sweetheart. I'm here," she said, stroking my hair. "You're safe now."

Once my attacker's blood was cleaned from my skin, the police resumed their endless questioning, their voices growing more insistent.

What happened?

Did I know the men?

How did they get in?

Why did they target the bakery?

I squeezed my eyes shut, trying to block out their demands for answers I couldn't give.

"That's enough," my mother finally snapped, her arms tightening around me protectively. "Can't you see she's been through hell? She needs rest, not an interrogation."

The lead detective backed off, holding up his hands in a placating gesture. "We understand, ma'am. But we need to get her statement while the details are still fresh."

I took a shuddering breath, forcing myself to meet the detective's eyes. "I-I'll try to answer your questions."

My mother squeezed my hand reassuringly. I swallowed hard, fighting back another wave of nausea as I recounted the robbery and assault. But I hesitated when it came to their comments about Dane and Silent Phoenix.

"They...they seemed to know who I was," I said carefully, omitting any mention of Dane or the club. "But I'd never seen them before."

The detective's eyes narrowed slightly, sensing there was more I wasn't saying. But before he could press further, my mother intervened.

"No more," she stated firmly. "My daughter needs medical attention."

He gave a reluctant nod. "Of course. Here's my card if you need to reach me. Once we get an ID on the man inside, we'll likely need you to come to the station for a formal statement. We'll be in touch as soon as we have an update."

After what felt like an eternity later, he walked away, and I exhaled a breath of relief. The sick feeling in my gut was growing worse by the second, but I couldn't bring myself to tell them about Dane and the club.

Not yet.

Not until I understood what was going on.

My mother helped me to my feet, wrapping her arm around my waist as we made our way to her car. The familiar scent of her perfume mixed with the sharp tang of the antiseptic they'd used to clean my skin, heightening my sense of disorientation.

The drive passed in a blur. I stared out the window, watching as the sun crept over the horizon and the city came to life. It seemed unfair that the world was operating as if it were business as usual when my own felt like it had just been hit by a meteor.

"We need to get you cleaned up," she murmured as we pulled into the driveway behind Dane's motorcycle, her voice tight with barely contained emotion. "Then we'll figure out what to do next."

I shook my head slowly. "I can't let Avery see me like this."

Her knuckles whitened against the steering wheel. "I know, sweetheart," she said gently. "That's why we're going to my house first."

The home had been built in the 1930s. My grandfather grew up in it, followed by my mother and, eventually, me. It was the place of some of my happiest childhood memories, but even the familiar comfort of home couldn't chase away the ice that had taken up residence deep in my bones.

She helped me upstairs to my old bedroom while she ran a bath. I sat on the edge of the bed, staring blankly at the sheer voile curtains hanging above the windows. The crimson was the same color as the blood on my jacket...

"Amelia, honey?" My mom's voice drifted through the fog in my mind, and I blinked, slowly coming back to reality. "Tub's ready."

It felt like I'd only been sitting for seconds, but given her worried expression, it must have been longer. I let her usher me into the bathroom, feeling numb—disconnected from my own body.

"I'll find you something clean to wear," she said, her movements gentle but purposeful as she removed my torn jacket before directing me to raise my arms overhead. She peeled off my blood-stained sports bra before sucking in a sharp breath.

I caught a glimpse of myself in the mirror and flinched. A stranger stared back at me, her cheek swollen and eyes haunted. Dark bruises bloomed across my breasts and belly, and I looked away quickly, unable to face the broken woman I'd become.

She reached for the drawstring on my pants before pausing. "Do we need to go to the hospital...for a kit?"

"A kit?" I echoed with a frown.

"Baby, did they rape you?"

"No," I whispered, shaking my head. "He tried, but Derek stopped him before..." My voice trailed off, unable to finish the sentence.

Relief flashed across my mother's face, immediately replaced by concern. She helped me out of my pants and into the steaming tub. The warm water stung against my bruised skin, but I welcomed the pain. It was proof I was still alive.

To my surprise, instead of leaving, Mom knelt beside the tub. She dipped a washcloth into the water and began gently cleaning the dried blood and flour from my face and neck.

"You don't have to do this," I mumbled, embarrassed by my helplessness.

She gave me a watery smile. "Let me take care of you, baby. Just this once."

The tenderness of her touch broke something inside me, and I started to cry again, silent tears streaming down my cheeks. For a moment, I was a little girl again, safe in my mother's arms. But the illusion shattered as pain flared across my bruised ribs.

"You're safe now," she murmured, a tear sliding down her cheek and into the water. "Let it out. I've got you."

I felt raw, exposed in a way that went beyond my naked body. All my carefully constructed walls had crumbled, leaving me as vulnerable as a newborn.

An anguished sob tore from my throat, followed by another and another until I was weeping uncontrollably. My mother held me as I cried, murmuring soft words of comfort and love as she washed away the last traces of blood.

When she was finished, she helped me into an old T-shirt and sweatpants of hers that were soft with age before leading me downstairs to the kitchen.

"Here, this'll help take the edge off," she said, pressing a mug of what smelled strongly of bourbon into my hands. "Drink. You're shaking."

Was I?

I hadn't even noticed the tremors running through my body until she pointed them out. I took a swig, immediately shuddering at the taste. The bourbon burned a fiery path down my throat before settling in my stomach with a pleasant warmth. I took another sip, letting the alcohol numb my frayed nerves and settle the tremors in my hands.

My mother settled across from me at the kitchen table, her own mug cradled between her hands. The silence stretched between us, heavy with unspoken questions.

"Mom, I…" I took a deep breath, trying to steady my voice, but the air caught in my throat. "I didn't tell the police everything."

"What do you mean?"

I took a deep breath, steeling myself. "The men who robbed the bakery knew about Dane and his club. They said they wanted to send a message to Silent Phoenix."

Her face paled, and for a moment, I thought she might be sick. "Jesus, Amelia," she breathed, running a trembling hand through her hair. "What the fuck has he gotten you into?"

"I don't know," I said, my voice cracking. "I thought I knew him, Mom. But now… I'm not sure I know anything."

She took a long pull from her mug before nodding to herself. "Okay. We'll figure this out."

"How are you so calm right now?" I asked, searching her face in confusion. "I thought you'd be freaking out."

She sighed heavily, tracing the rim of her mug with a fingernail. "Believe it or not, I've seen much worse. Your father—he's a biker."

I stared at my mother in disbelief, her words echoing in my head. My father…a biker? The mug in my hands trembled, and I set it down before I could spill. "What? But you said he was a musician who left us."

Her hands shook as she took another swig of bourbon. "I lied. Your father…his name is Red. He's with the Outlaws up in Oklahoma."

"Why are you telling me this now?" I whispered, my throat tight.

She met my eyes, her gaze haunted. "Because you need to understand how dangerous this world can be. Red didn't leave us, sweetheart. I left him."

"What happened?"

"He put me in the hospital," she said, taking a deep, shuddering breath. "It wasn't the first time, but it was the worst. I ended up in the ER with three broken ribs, a fractured cheekbone, and…" Her voice broke. "It's where I found out I was pregnant with you."

I reached across the table and squeezed her hand, feeling the slight tremor beneath my fingers.

"One of the nurses who treated me had seen it all before. Told me if he beat me, he'd likely beat our baby too." My mother's eyes met mine, filled with a fierce protectiveness that took my breath away. "I didn't have a dime to my name, but she helped me contact your grandparents. They drove through the night to get me. My mama had to help me bathe just like I did with you..."

"Oh my god, Mom," I whispered, my voice cracking. "I had no idea."

She exhaled a bitter laugh. "That was the point, sweetheart. I never wanted you to know that kind of fear."

"So when you saw Dane that first time..." I trailed off as the pieces of my childhood suddenly snapped into sharp focus. My mother's overprotectiveness...her wariness of men...her insistence that I learn how to use a gun and never be dependent on a man.

It all finally made sense.

The father I'd imagined all these years—a nameless, faceless man who'd walked away—had been replaced by something far more sinister. A violent biker who'd beaten my mother so severely she'd fled for both our lives.

"It was like seeing a ghost," she said, her expression pained. "The kutte, the bike...it all came rushing back. I was so scared for you and Avery."

"You think he could be like Red?" I whispered.

Mom glanced down at the table, considering the question before shaking her head. "No. From what I've seen, Dane is nothing like your father. The way he is with you and Avery... Red never had an ounce of that tenderness in him."

"Then why have you been so against us being together?"

"Because even if Dane himself isn't dangerous, the world he's tied to is," she explained, her eyes pleading with me to understand. "What happened to you this morning is proof of that."

I stared into my mug, watching the amber liquid ripple beneath my trembling hands. The weight of my mother's revelation pressed down on me, threatening to crush what little composure I had left.

"Do you really think Dane could be involved in something like that though?"

"I don't know," she said. "But I do know good men can do terrible things when they're caught up in that life. I've seen firsthand how quickly things can spiral out of control."

"What do I do now?" I asked, feeling lost and overwhelmed.

My mother squeezed my hand. "Talk to Dane. Find out if his club has enemies who would hurt you to get to him and then let him and the club clean this mess up."

"What does that mean?"

"Men like Dane live and die by code, and they aren't known for playing nice when someone comes for the people they love. I may not like his world, but I admire their brand of justice."

Her eyes clouded with a pain so deep it made my chest ache before she continued. "I've spent almost thirty-one years looking over my shoulder, wondering if today would be the day your father tracked us down. I don't want you to live like that, and I sure as hell don't want you to have to relive the shit you went through today in a goddamned courtroom." She squeezed my hand. "But ultimately, it's up to you to decide whether being in Dane's world is worth the risk."

What if everything between us had been a lie?

I tried to reconcile the gentle giant I was falling for with the dangerous world he was tied to. The Dane who made Avery belly laugh and massaged my back when I was cramping seemed worlds away from men like my attacker.

But hadn't I seen a sliver of that darkness when he threatened Derek? Wasn't that why I'd kept the note from him? Because some part of me knew that beneath his gentle exterior was a man who had taken lives.

He sure as hell hadn't earned that kutte for his kindness.

A wistful look crossed my mother's face as she took another sip of bourbon. "I wish someone had taken care of Red back then," she murmured.

"Someone did," a gruff voice said from behind us.

We both jumped, whirling around to face the intruder. A tall, imposing man with long salt-and-pepper hair stood in the doorway. But it was the kutte he wore, emblazoned with a president patch, that stole the air from my lungs.

"Ethan?" my mother gasped, her face draining of color.

"Hey, Nik," he said, his weathered face creasing with a rueful smile. "Sorry, I didn't knock. Old habits die hard."

I glanced between them, noting how her hands shook as she gripped her mug. "I take it you two know each other?"

"We went to high school together," he replied, his eyes never leaving her face.

She shot him a look that could have melted steel. "It was a hell of a lot more than that, Ethan Diaz."

He ran his tongue across his teeth and chuckled, the tension between them palpable. I shifted uncomfortably in my seat, feeling like an intruder in my childhood home.

"What are you doing here?" my mother finally asked, her voice barely above a whisper.

Ethan's expression sobered. "Got a call from one of our guys at the Dallas PD. He tipped us off about the bakery robbery."

"But why would they do that?" I asked, confusion momentarily overriding my fear.

His piercing gaze shifted to me. "Because I told them to alert me immediately to anything involving Nicole or Amelia Kelly."

"I don't understand," my mom said, her brows pinching together.

Ethan's jaw clenched, a muscle ticking beneath the skin. "Made your old man a promise. He came to me after they got you back home. He was worried Red would come after you."

My mother's sharp intake of breath echoed in the quiet kitchen. "Did Dad know about your connection to Silent Phoenix? Is that why he went to you?"

Ethan shook his head. "No, Nik. He came to me because he knew I'd die before letting anything happen to you." His eyes softened as they met hers. "Sure enough, Red showed up less than a month later, and I took care of it."

It didn't take a rocket scientist to figure out his meaning.

Ethan had killed my father.

"All this time?" she asked, running her knuckles over her sternum. "But why didn't you come to me—why didn't you tell me?"

His head jerked back, and he let out a rough bark of laughter. "Because of this, Nik," he said, tugging at his kutte. "That fucker damn near killed you. The last thing you needed was another biker showing up to remind you."

Mom's eyes widened, a mix of shock and something like frustration flashing across her face. Ethan stood rigidly as if bracing himself for her reaction.

I cleared my throat. "The men who robbed the bakery mentioned Silent Phoenix. Said they wanted to send a message."

He ran his knuckles over his beard, eyes narrowed on my bruised face. "Doesn't make a goddamned bit of sense. It's an unspoken rule that family members are off-limits. Can't see how anyone could have made a connection between us. I've been careful to keep my distance."

"The message wasn't for you," I said quietly, picking at my broken thumbnail. "They called me Ghost's Ol' Lady. He's with the Lubbock chapter—"

Ethan chuckled again. "I know who Dane is, sweetheart. His old man, Wolverine, founded Silent Phoenix."

I had a baby with him and didn't know that. The realization of how little I actually knew about the man I was living with left me feeling off balance.

"Still doesn't make sense, though," he muttered. "What does he say? Any guesses as to who's behind it?"

I grimaced. "I haven't, uh, haven't told him yet."

His eyebrows shot up, and he let out a low whistle. "You waiting until he sees it on the morning news, or what?"

"You can't blame her for being reluctant to talk to him, Ethan. This isn't her world—"

"Not yours either, is it, Nik?" he snapped, his eyes flashing with hurt. "Now you know why I've stayed away."

My mother pushed her chair back and stood, her eyes never leaving Ethan's face. She walked toward him like she was in a trance, and for a moment, I wondered if she might slap him. Instead, she tucked herself against his chest with a choked sob, her small frame fitting perfectly in his arms.

Ethan stroked her hair, murmuring something too low for me to hear. There was clearly a long history between them, one that ran deeper than old classmates.

After a moment, he gently pulled back, his hands resting on my mother's shoulders as he addressed me. "I'll reach out to Bear, the mother chapter's Pres, but Ghost needs to know someone's targeting his family."

I nodded, suddenly exhausted. The adrenaline that had been keeping me going was fading fast, leaving me hollow and drained.

As we headed out into the backyard toward my house, I heard Ethan mutter to my mother, "That boy's gonna go scorched earth when he finds out, especially since they used his name to get to her."

An icy chill traveled down my spine. I'd seen glimpses of Dane's darker side, but I had a feeling I was about to witness it in full force.

Scorched earth.

What exactly did that mean when it came to the world of outlaw bikers? I wasn't sure I wanted to know.

The morning sun cast long shadows across the dewy grass, and a cool breeze raised goosebumps on my arms. Or maybe that was just the dread coursing through my veins.

Because if Dane's lifestyle had the potential to put us in danger, then I needed to be ready to take Avery and run.

No matter how much it hurt.

TWENTY

GHOST

Ivy & Piper's Guide to Life Rule Number Two:
Trust your gut. That bitch knows what's up.

The morning sun filtered through the open blinds, illuminating the mountain of clean laundry piled high on Piper's bed. Avery emerged from the closet with a scarf draped over her head like a wedding veil and one of Piper's sky-high heels on her foot.

"Da-da-da!" she exclaimed, her wobbly but determined steps echoing off the hardwood.

It was a twisted ankle waiting to happen, but I was more concerned with the scarf.

"I see. Come here, princess," I said, kneeling to tie it around her shoulders like a cape. "Your head's still healing. Let's try to get through the day without a visit to the ER. Can you do that for Daddy?"

She patted my arm before toddling back toward her bedroom, clearly unbothered that her foot kept slipping in and out of the shoe.

I chuckled and went into the closet for more hangers.

As I hung up the last of Piper's shirts, the chirp of the front door sensor sliced through the quiet morning. My blood ran cold because I had Piper's SUV, and Nikki would have knocked first.

I bolted down the hall, sidearm already in hand and my heart thrashing in my ears. Rounding the corner into the living room, I skidded to a stop to avoid colliding with Nails, the Dallas chapter president. An uncontrollable shudder swept through my entire body when I registered the figure leaning against his side.

"What the fuck happened?" I asked, shaking my head as I took in the bruises on Piper's face and neck. "Who did this to her?"

Nails subtly positioned his body in front of hers before nodding to my sidearm. "You wanna put that away first?"

Fuck.

I holstered my weapon and forced myself to take a deep breath before reaching for Piper. She stumbled into my arms, her eyes glassy and unfocused with shock. I caught her gently, cradling her trembling body against my chest.

"Jesus Christ," I breathed, gently tipping her face up toward mine. "Baby, can you tell me what happened?"

Her bottom lip quivered as she opened her mouth to speak, managing little more than a choked sob.

"Two men hit the bakery this morning," Nails explained in a low voice. "Said they wanted to send a message to Ghost and Silent Phoenix through his Ol' Lady."

My jaw clenched so hard I thought my molars might crack. "And where are they now?"

"One's dead, and my crew's hunting the other."

"A-ma owie?" Avery's small voice cut through the tension. She stood in the hallway, still wearing Piper's shoe and staring wide-eyed at her battered mother's face.

"Hey, princess. Mama's okay," I lied, forcing my mouth into what I hoped was a reassuring smile. "Why don't you go with GiGi for a little bit?"

Nikki stepped forward, her eyes shimmering with unshed tears. "Come on, sweetheart. You can help me feed Mr. Fish."

Avery hesitated, her little brow furrowed as she looked between me and Piper. I nodded encouragingly, and she finally made her way over to Nikki.

"She can stay with me as long as you need. Until things…settle," Nikki said, distracting our daughter with a list of things they were going to do as she carried her out.

"Nuh-no, owie?" Avery asked, peering back at us over her grandmother's shoulder.

Nails squeezed my shoulder. "I'll be at Nik's, making calls to your chapter as well as the Tulsa crew. Might reach out to Carnage too, see if he and Jimmy can't help us track down this other guy."

I nodded, waiting until the front door clicked shut behind them before leading Piper to the couch and easing her down onto the cushions. Her entire body shook violently, teeth chattering together noisily. She looked so small, so fragile—nothing like the woman I'd dropped off at work hours ago.

"Don't leave," she whispered when I turned away.

"Just grabbing a blanket to warm you up," I said, draping the soft throw over her shoulders. It was a piss-poor attempt at protection after what she'd endured, but it was all I could offer at the moment.

I carefully examined the swelling on her cheek, my hands trembling with the need to shed blood. Piper flinched at my touch, and a soft cry spilled past her lips, the sound gutting me.

"Sorry," I said, carefully brushing away the tears leaking from her eyes with the pads of my thumbs. It was a foreign feeling, this mix of impotence and protective fury.

Things between us had been shit for the past week, ever since I found the note in her purse. It seemed like such a small thing now, in light of what had happened. None of that mattered anymore. All I wanted was to put her back together and make the bastards responsible pay.

My mind raced with vivid scenarios of vengeance, each one more gruesome and satisfying than the last. Images of bloodied faces and broken bodies played out like a horror movie in my head. I could almost hear their agonized screams and pleas for mercy.

Mercy that I would deny again and again.

I'd never gotten off on torture like some of the other men in the club did. But the thought of hunting down the person responsible for hurting Piper and slowly carving his body into little chunks left my heart pounding with a dark excitement.

"Baby, look at me." I crouched in front of her, my hands hovering uncertainly over her thighs. "Need you to tell me what happened."

Piper's breath hitched, her gaze distant as she relived the nightmare. "It was just after four, and I was prepping the pastry dough."

She described the robbery in halting fragments—two masked men storming the kitchen, a gun pressed to her temple as they forced her to open the safe.

"I did what they wanted. I thought they'd leave once they had the cash, but the taller man—he said he wanted to send you a message. The other guy said they were just supposed to scare me."

Ice flooded my veins. It sounded as if the entire thing had been orchestrated solely to get to her, but why? Why go after her at all if it was me they wanted?

"He—he tore my coat and put the gun on my..." Piper's voice trailed off, and she curled in on herself, fresh tears spilling over onto her cheeks.

The air left my lungs in a growl that was more animal than human. My hands clenched into fists, knuckles blanching at the thought of anyone putting their hands on her.

"I thought he was going to kill me, so I tried to fight back," she continued, her hand unconsciously moving to her bruised cheek. "But he hit me. Said you wouldn't be able to put me back together once he was done with me."

My vision tunneled, rage building like a tsunami in my chest. I wanted to tear the room apart—to hunt down everyone involved and rip their throats out with my bare hands. My nostrils flared, the need to send someone to the Reaper threatening to consume me.

But she needed me calm. I pushed the fury back down, letting it simmer until the time when I'd have them on their knees.

"Did he...?" I choked on the word, unable to bring myself to say it.

"Derek showed up and shot the guy before he—before he—" Piper gulped in a breath of air before releasing a strangled sob.

Doing my best to avoid aggravating the injuries I could see, I pulled her onto my lap on the floor, holding her while she fell apart. She hadn't been raped, but it was little consolation. Cold sweat ran down my back as I tried to piece it together, racking my brain for anything that might point to the people responsible.

Our enemies wouldn't take a piss in our territory without getting permission first, and an attack on an Ol' Lady was tantamount to a declaration of war. If a rival club were looking to send a message and start another war, they'd go after a ranking officer.

But Piper wasn't my Ol' Lady, at least not in an official sense. And that wasn't the only thing that didn't add up for me. Aside from GQ, Duke, a handful of the Dallas chapter guys, and our president, Bear, no one knew Piper existed.

"Baby, these men, were they wearing colors?" I prodded gently.

She tilted her head to the side, lips pursed in confusion. "Colors?"

"Kuttes, darlin'. Leather vests with patches," I clarified, my fingers absentmindedly stroking her hair.

"No, they were wearing all black," she replied, hiccupping through a ragged breath. "Their faces were covered with those ski mask things. I could only see their eyes."

I nodded, filing the information away. No colors meant it likely wasn't a rival MC, but the person had used my road name and made the connection to Piper.

Son of a bitch.

A vein in my forehead pulsed, but I tried to keep my tone calm as I asked, "Why was Derek there so early?"

Her eyebrows drew together as she tried to remember. "One of the afternoon girls quit. He said he was coming in early to rework the schedule."

"Awfully convenient," I muttered.

Piper studied my face with a frown. "What's that supposed to mean?"

I sighed, knowing she wouldn't like what I had to say. "The whole thing reeks of bullshit. Two guys happen to know you're connected to the club, and Derek just happens to show up at the perfect moment?"

"What are you saying? That Derek's behind this—that he's trying to, what? Set you up?" Her voice rose an octave, disbelief clear in her tone.

"All I'm saying is it's a hell of a coincidence," I replied, holding her gaze. "And in my experience, there's no such thing as coincidences."

"He literally saved my life—"

"Or he showed up at just the right moment to play hero," I countered, my own temper flaring. "Wake up, sweetheart. If it walks like a duck and quacks like a duck…"

She scrambled off my lap, wincing as she straightened. "Do you realize how completely unhinged that sounds? Seriously, are you cracked out of your head right now?" Why would he want his own bakery robbed?"

I rubbed the back of my neck. "I don't know, Piper. Maybe he's got a gambling problem. Maybe he owes the wrong people money. Or maybe he's so fucking delusional that he thinks making me look like the bad guy will convince you to give him a chance. There are a hundred reasons why a prick like that might be willing to put your safety at risk."

"Or maybe it has nothing to do with Derek!" she shot back, jutting her chin up at me like the defiant brat she was. "How do you know it's not some enemy of your precious club?"

The rage I'd been holding back erupted, and I was on my feet before I realized I'd moved. "Because that's not how it fucking works!"

Piper shrank away from me, and I forced myself to sit, trying to dial it back before continuing. "Family is off-limits. Always has been. There's only been one group stupid enough to try it, and it led to an all-out war. After we wiped out the Sons of Death eight years ago, they reinstated the syndicate. No one in the country is willing to risk another war when the first one nearly destroyed us all."

She swiped at the tears on her cheeks while slowly pacing the length of the couch. "Forgive me for not having a lot of faith in your 'biker moral code' at the moment, but I had a fucking gun held to my head, Dane. Because of you."

I ran my tongue over my teeth with an exhaled chuckle. "You don't need to have faith in it, darlin'. You just need to know it's gonna be dealt with accordingly."

"What does that even mean?" she grumbled, raking her hands through her damp hair. "I feel like you're speaking in riddles."

"It means your little buddy Derek better pray he's not involved, or he's about to have a really bad fucking day."

My phone buzzed in my pocket, and I pulled it out to find a text from Nails.

> Nails: ID on the dead guy. Timothy Ellis. 23. No known gang affiliations. Petty criminal record. Whoever these guys are, they're not operating under another club's orders. Looks like someone closer to home. Who else knows about you and Piper?

The list of people with that knowledge was even shorter, and I didn't like the direction my thoughts were going.

> Me: Look into Derek Williams. Convenient that he decided to show up early today of all days. Could be an inside job.

I glanced up to find Piper clawing at her arms, leaving angry red slashes across her skin. I set the phone aside, pushing my suspicions to the back of my mind for the moment.

"Come on, darlin'. Let's get you cleaned up," I murmured, gently taking her hand and guiding her toward the bathroom. She swayed unsteadily, and I locked an arm around her waist, supporting most of her weight until we reached the doorway.

"Please don't leave me alone," she pleaded when I turned to go, her face flushing with shame.

The fear in her eyes left me feeling sick, and I nodded before helping her out of her clothes, my eyes darting over the bruises mottling her breasts and belly.

I'd start with their skin, peeling it off layer by layer.

"I bathed at my mom's, but I still feel so dirty," Piper admitted, trying to cover herself with her arms.

Without a word, I carried her into the shower, not even bothering to strip off my boxer briefs. My hands moved gently over her skin and scalp, the hot water washing the suds down the drain.

"You're safe. I've got you," I said, wishing it was as easy to wash away the memories.

She sucked in a sharp breath and turned, striking my chest with her palm in a stinging slap. "You promised me you'd keep your club shit away from us!" she roared before collapsing against me with an anguished sob.

"I know," I said, cradling her head against my shoulder. "I'm so sorry." I held her tight as she cried, her tears mixing with the shower spray. Her accusation cut deep, but I couldn't deny the truth of it. I had promised to keep her and Avery safe, and I'd failed spectacularly.

She blinked up at me, water and tears mingling on her lashes. "I can still feel him," she choked out. "His breath on my neck. The gun against my skin…"

Helplessness clawed at my insides. "Tell me what you need, baby. Anything. I'll do it."

Her fingers curled against my chest as she met my gaze. "I need you," she breathed. "I just… I need to feel safe. Even if it's only for a few minutes."

My throat tightened as she guided my hand to her bruised cheek. I pressed my lips to the tender flesh, releasing the sob that had been lodged in my throat since she walked through the door.

"Where else does it hurt?"

With a stuttered exhale, she guided my hands down to her breasts. "Here."

I trailed kisses over the marks on her pink skin, my lips barely grazing the bruised flesh. When I pulled back to search her eyes, they were heavy-lidded, a mixture of pain and need swirling in their depths.

"Where else?" I asked, my voice rough.

"Here," she whispered, guiding my hands down to her thighs.

I sank to my knees, skimming my fingers over the angry red crescents before pressing my mouth to each mark. "I'm sorry, baby," I breathed against her skin. "I'm so fucking sorry."

She shuddered at the warmth of my exhales against her sensitive skin. I wanted to erase every trace of his touch with my tongue, to reclaim every inch of her body as mine. But I forced myself to pull back, not wanting to push too far.

Then her hands were in my hair, urging me up. Our mouths collided roughly, her tongue slipping between my lips. Her hands moved frantically over my muscles before anchoring against my chest, her fingernails scoring my skin.

I gripped her hips to steady her as she pressed against me. Her mouth was desperate and demanding against mine, seeking comfort and oblivion. I wanted to give her both, to erase the horror of the morning from her mind, even if only for a little while. But I let her set the pace, afraid of pushing too far.

When we finally broke apart, both of us panting, Piper rested her chin against my chest. "I'm sorry."

"Don't apologize, darlin'. Not to me."

She took a shaky breath, her voice cracking as she admitted, "I lied to you."

"About what?" I asked, bracing myself for her confession.

Piper's teeth sank into her lower lip, tears spilling onto her lower lashes. "The note that was in my purse. It wasn't about baking supplies."

I wanted to stop her, to tell her I didn't want to know. But a larger part needed to hear the truth, no matter how much it hurt.

"Someone left it in my locker with some chocolates and painkillers when I was on my period," she said, her flushed cheeks turning a darker shade of red.

"I know," I said, swallowing past the lump in my throat. "I saw it when you were in the shower."

"Why didn't you say anything then?"

I shut off the water and grabbed a couple of towels before answering. "I thought about calling you out on it and forcing you to tell me the truth, but that's not really a great way to build trust," I said dryly. "Also, I wasn't sure I wanted to know if you were involved with someone else. I'm still not."

Piper's eyebrows shot up. "You—you thought I was cheating on you? Oh my god, no wonder you've been sleeping on the couch," she said, groaning into her hands before huffing out a breath. "I lied about the note because I thought you'd make me quit my job or, worse, show up and cause a scene."

"Is it from Derek?"

She shook her head. "I don't think so. I mean, it's not his handwriting. Honestly, it's not the first time stuff has been left in my locker, but it was the first time there was a note attached. And I don't know who left it or if it's connected to what happened today, but I wanted you to know."

I took the towel from Piper's hands and wrapped it around her body. "How long has this been going on?"

"A year, maybe?" she guessed with a shrug. "It's typically little things like candy or gift cards for my favorite coffee shop. I assumed everyone was getting them until a few months ago when I mentioned it to one of my coworkers."

"And you never thought to mention it?" I couldn't keep the edge out of my voice.

"Because I didn't think it was a big deal, Dane," she said softly. "And things have been so strained between us lately. I was afraid you'd overreact."

I bit back a growl of frustration. "Overreact? Someone's been stalking you, and two men just held you at gunpoint. I'd say any reaction I have is pretty fucking justified."

Piper winced at my tone, and I immediately regretted snapping at her. I took a deep breath, forcing myself to calm down.

"I'm sorry," I said, pulling her against my chest.

She melted into my embrace with a shuddering sigh. "I hate how things have been lately and just want us to be okay again."

"Hey, we will be. I promise." I lifted her in my arms, trying to ignore the penetrating ache in my chest as I carried her to the bedroom. Her skin was still damp from the shower, and she began shivering when I lowered her onto the bed.

"I don't want to be scared," she said, catching my hand as I slipped one of my T-shirts over her head. The dark bruises on her skin stood out in stark contrast to the pale blue fabric, each one a reminder of how I'd failed to protect her.

"You're scared?"

She mashed her lips together before nodding. "Not of you, exactly. But of what being with you means."

I knelt in front of Piper, taking her hands in mine. "Listen to me, baby. What happened today—that's not normal. Not for me, not for the club. I know it's scary as hell, but I swear to you, I'm going to find out who's behind this and make it right."

My old man often said that if you put enough people down, the others quickly learned their place. That bastard had signed his own death warrant the second he entered the bakery, and I was willing to flood the streets with blood to send a message to anyone stupid enough to think they could lay a finger on my family and get away with it.

TWENTY-ONE

GHOST

Ivy & Piper's Guide to Life Rule Number Thirty-Two:
Always question the rules.

"You going to be able to keep your shit under control, or do you need to wait out here in the truck?" Carnage asked as we pulled into the bakery parking lot.

I shook my head at the irony of getting a lecture on control from the man who'd waltzed into the Crows' territory five years ago and abducted a woman against club orders.

"That's real fucking rich coming from the guy who lost his goddamned mind when his Ol' Lady gave me a lap dance," I drawled with a hard smile, dropping the visor to block out the sun glinting off the windshield of his truck. "She wasn't even your Ol' Lady then…just the stripper you drugged and chained up in your basement like a fucking serial killer."

He clicked his tongue against his teeth before shifting his neck from side to side. "Really? You want to go there right now? Because I'm more than happy to provide a repeat performance if you don't watch your fucking mouth when it comes to my wife."

A sane person wouldn't try picking a fight with their boss and the club's Sergeant at Arms—a guy who was six-foot-six and built like a fucking tank—but I was craving a release. It had been two weeks since the robbery, and we didn't have a single goddamned lead.

"Let's just get this shit done," I muttered, reaching for the door handle only to find it locked. "Seriously?"

He crossed his arms over his broad chest and leaned back. "What's your old man always saying, huh? Better to have the enemy thinking you're weak while you come up with a strategy than to run in and get your fucking head blown off."

I mashed my thumb against my knuckles, cracking them one by one. "And making this douchebag a client is your strategy? The guy who leaves notes and chocolates for Piper when she's on the rag?"

"Unless you have video evidence, then yeah, that's the fucking strategy," Carnage bit out. "Why would you automatically assume Derek knows when her period is? Are they fucking?"

My jaw flexed at the thought, rage bubbling to the surface. "No. She said their relationship is strictly professional."

He tilted his head down, his gray-blue eyes boring into me. "Then fucking drop it. Derek's our best bet to finding out who's behind this, so we do this by the book. No accusations, no threats. Got it?"

I nodded tersely, swallowing the urge to tell him to go fuck himself. As much as I hated to admit it, he was right. Going in guns blazing wouldn't get us access to the security footage.

Carnage unlocked the doors, stopping me when I reached into the backseat for my kutte. "Leave it. We're not here on club business."

The bell chimed as we entered, but unlike my last visit, nobody gave me a passing glance. Then again, I wasn't dressed like a biker. The scent of fresh-baked bread and cinnamon normally would have made my mouth water, but today, it just turned my stomach.

Staff bustled in and out of the double doors leading to the kitchen, refilling the glass display cases and taking orders, oblivious to the tension crackling through the air. Everything looked normal, but my skin crawled. The threat was here somewhere. I could feel it.

Derek materialized from the back, all fake smiles and nervous energy. "Let's talk in my office."

The sleek, modern furniture and chrome accents clashed with the retro vibe of the rest of the bakery. He settled behind his desk, gesturing for us to take the two leather chairs opposite him.

"Thank you for agreeing to meet with me so quickly," he said, his fingers tapping out an erratic rhythm against the polished wood of his desk. "I've heard nothing but great things about Phoenix Security, and that's why I'd like to hire you to investigate the robbery. The police have been completely useless, and I need someone who can get me answers."

I made a conscious effort to unclench my jaw and forced a smile as I noted, "Funny, you seem pretty jumpy for a guy who claims to want answers."

Before he could respond, Carnage's boot connected with my shin under the desk. I bit back a curse and forced myself to lean back in the chair.

"What my associate means is that we understand how stressful this situation must be for you," Carnage said smoothly, his eyes flashing with an unspoken warning for me to shut the fuck up. "Why don't you walk us through everything you know."

While Derek recounted the events surrounding the robbery, my eyes wandered to the framed photos on the shelf behind his desk. Most were of the bakery and people I assumed were his family, but one caught my attention. It was Piper, laughing as she frosted a cake. The sight of her carefree smile made my chest ache.

"That's a good picture of Piper," I said, nodding to the frame.

He glanced over his shoulder. "Yeah, I took that when we were updating our website photos a few years back. Not bad for a phone camera, right? I may have missed my calling as a photographer."

I ground my molars together, resisting the urge to tell him he was liable to throw his shoulder out, yanking his own dick the way he was. Instead, I settled for, "What if our investigation leads back to you? What then?"

His eyes narrowed, a flicker of irritation crossing his face before he laughed. "I take it you're not familiar with Ross Williams."

"The oil guy?" I asked, thrown by the sudden change in topic.

Derek's laugh immediately set my teeth on edge. "Yeah, the 'oil guy.' Number 302 on the Forbes 400 list of richest people in America and my old man." He leaned back, resting his arms on the chair rests. "What possible motivation would I have to rob my own bakery?"

The question hung in the air, effectively shutting me up. I glanced at Carnage, who gave an almost imperceptible shake of his head.

"Look," Derek continued, his tone softening. "I get it. You're protective of Piper, and you want answers. So do I. My employees should feel safe coming to work."

Carnage nodded, his expression unreadable. "We'll draw up a contract and get started as soon as it's signed. You have my word. We'll find whoever's responsible."

His shoulders relaxed slightly. He reached into his desk, pausing to check his phone before retrieving the thick folder lying beneath it and sliding it across to us. "Here's everything I thought you might need— past and present employee records, regular customer information, and details on the neighboring businesses. I've also arranged for you to have full access to our security feeds. Maybe you'll be able to spot something I haven't."

As we stood to leave, Derek pulled me aside. "One more thing, Dane. About Piper..." He lowered his voice. "She's out of vacation time. I've got her on the schedule starting tomorrow, but I don't want her feeling pressured to come in before she's ready. I'm willing to put her on paid leave until then, but I wanted to get your thoughts on it."

I eyed him warily, taken aback by the unexpected generosity. Was this the same guy who'd been pressuring Piper to pick up shifts just a few weeks ago?

"That's...actually really decent of you," I said, struggling to keep the surprise out of my voice. "I appreciate it, and I know she will too."

Derek nodded, his expression softening. "I get it, man. If I were in your shoes, I wouldn't want her leaving the house until we knew who was behind this shit."

I found myself agreeing before I could stop myself. Fuck. Had I been reading this guy all wrong? His actions didn't match up with the picture I'd built in my head of Piper's asshole boss.

"There's, uh...another reason it might be good for her to stay away for the time being," Derek continued, hesitating before reaching into his desk drawer. He pulled out a manila envelope and held it out to me with a grim expression. "One of my employees found this in the back this morning."

My stomach dropped as I opened it to find a crudely photoshopped image of Piper's face on a bound and naked body being gang-banged by a group of bikers.

No words accompanied the image.

None were needed.

The message was crystal fucking clear.

Stay with the biker, end up as a club whore.

———

My laptop screen flickered with surveillance footage, casting an eerie glow in Piper's darkened kitchen. Despite the high resolution, my eyes burned from the strain of scrutinizing every goddamned pixel.

I pressed the pads of my fingers against my eye sockets and leaned back in my chair, feeling a tension headache coming on. Its vise-like grip tightened around my temples, souring my mood even further. I'd spent the entire day combing through security footage, refusing to stop until we had a lead.

Carnage pulled his glasses off, pinching the bridge of his nose with a heavy sigh. "Without a clear shot of the back hallway, there's no way to see who left this."

My jaw ticked, rage gnawing at me like a relentless itch I couldn't scratch. I wanted to tear the metroplex apart brick by fucking brick until I found the piece of shit responsible.

I scrubbed a hand over my face in a bid to stay awake when something caught my eye—a delivery guy I hadn't noticed before entering through a side door.

"Hey," I said, tapping the screen. "We get IDs on the people who make deliveries?"

"A few. Jimmy's still working on it," Carnage muttered, slipping his glasses back on before leaning in to study the figure. "Looks like the SKS Food Distribution logo, so he is—" He turned to his tablet. "Isaac Scott. No criminal record. He's been working for SKS for two years."

"He's at the bakery multiple times a week and would have had full access to the lockers in the back. Any of them would, for that matter."

It was a lead, albeit a thin one.

Carnage stood, bones cracking as he stretched. "I'll get with Jimmy when I get back to the hotel. See if we can't turn up something. For now, let's call it a night. You need sleep."

"Yeah, sounds good," I lied.

Sleep could fuck right off.

I waited until he left before pulling up the footage from the morning of the robbery. Derek had sprung for the high-quality security cameras, and seeing my worst nightmare play out in 4k resolution was like a shot of adrenaline to the heart.

"Please don't do this. I have a baby."

I swore my molars were going to crack under the pressure as I watched Timothy taunt Piper with the gun, toying with her body while she tearfully pleaded for mercy. My fists clenched so tight I could feel my nails digging into my palms.

It was the most helpless feeling in the world. And no matter how many hours I spent trying to track down the person responsible, it wouldn't change what had happened to her. I'd thought living without her for two years was hell.

But I was wrong.

It was seeing the terror on her face and knowing I hadn't been there to stop it.

Exhaustion weighed on me like a physical thing, my eyes drifting shut despite my best efforts. My chin dipped toward my chest, and I jolted awake before forcing myself to my feet.

My fingers itched for a cigarette or a neck to snap. Preferably the latter, but I settled for the former and stalked out onto the front porch.

The craving clawed at my insides like an animal fighting its way out of a cage, and I fished the pack from my pocket with trembling hands. It had been a bitch to quit smoking the first time around, but the need to quiet the chaos in my head since the robbery outweighed the hell of withdrawals.

I lit up and took several long, desperate drags, the nicotine hitting my brain with all the subtlety of a sledgehammer. The neighborhood was quiet, almost eerily so, and it made me wonder what other threats lurked in the shadows, waiting to strike.

After taking a final drag, I crushed my cigarette beneath my boot and immediately lit another before leaning my head back against the side of the house. I'd deal with quitting again later, assuming we made it out of this clusterfuck alive.

Tension coiled between my shoulder blades like a snake poised to strike, my body bracing for the sound of blood-curdling screams or cries for help. I should have been used to Piper's nightmares by now. They'd become a nightly occurrence since the robbery, which was why our daughter had been sleeping over at GiGi's, and I'd given up on it altogether.

She was slipping away a little more each day, and there wasn't a goddamn thing I could do to bring her back. After finishing the second cigarette, I trudged back inside and rewound the robbery footage to the beginning.

As much as I wanted to turn it off, I forced myself to watch the entire thing—to relive the assault alongside her, over and over again, reminding myself what was at stake if I failed again.

TWENTY-TWO

PIPER

Ivy & Piper's Guide to Life Rule Number Nine:
Don't shrink yourself down for anyone.

I bolted upright in bed with a choked gasp, my face damp with tears. The room felt too small, the walls closing in, trapping me with the remnants of another nightmare that had felt all too real.

The dreams were different every time. Sometimes, I fought back and managed to escape, only to find myself trapped inside the bakery like a rat in a maze. In others, I stood paralyzed while each man took what he wanted from me.

My mind was caught in an endless loop of the robbery, leaving me barely able to focus on the most basic tasks. Everyday stressors, like Avery shrieking at something on TV, sent me into a fight or flight response.

This was what they'd turned me into. Someone who jumped at shadows and didn't feel safe even in her own home.

But tonight's? Tonight's nightmare took the fucking cake.

Instead of a stranger, it was Dane holding the gun. His dark eyes were cold and clinical as he groped my body, his touch both familiar yet terrifyingly foreign. When I begged him to stop, he told me to be a good girl. And the worst part? My traitorous body responded to him, leaving me feeling sick and confused.

I reached across the bed for him, needing his warmth to thaw the ice in my veins and reassure me it was all in my head, but found only empty sheets.

Alone.

Of course, I was alone.

Dane had taken to spending his evenings in the makeshift command center he'd set up in the kitchen, poring over surveillance footage from businesses in the area while I wrestled with tangled sheets and nightmares.

With a shuddered breath, I reached over to flip on the lamp, wincing at the sudden brightness. A book Ivy brought over about the effect of trauma on the body lay untouched on the nightstand along with a prescription bottle of anxiety meds. I didn't want any of it.

I just wanted things to go back to normal.

Knowing there wasn't a chance in hell of falling back asleep, I reached for my phone to find it was close to two, almost time for my alarm to go off anyway.

My two-week-long reprieve from the bakery was over, and my first day back loomed ahead of me like a mountain I wasn't sure I could climb.

But I couldn't endure another second of being cooped up in this house, a prisoner of my own fear.

I swung my legs over the side of the bed, my bare feet hitting the cold hardwood floor. The chill sent a shiver up my spine, but I welcomed the sensation. Anything to ground me in reality and shake off the nervous energy churning in my gut.

With trembling hands, I pulled on my black chef pants, sports bra, and tank top. Part of me was terrified to return to the scene of the crime, while another was eager to escape the suffocating atmosphere of my own home. I longed for my familiar routine, to feel like myself, even if it was only for a few hours.

My hopes of slipping out unnoticed were dashed as soon as I entered the hallway and heard low voices coming from the kitchen. I crept closer, straining to hear over the blood rushing in my ears.

Dane paced the kitchen like a lion in a cage, his muscular form taut with tension. His dark hair stood on end from running his hands through it, and dark circles shadowed his eyes.

But it was his eyes that stopped me cold. They were dark, almost black, filled with the same nothingness as the version of him I saw in my nightmare.

"Please don't do this," a voice cried out from his laptop.

My voice.

"Shhh... Be a good girl, and I'll let you go after."

I clamped my hand over my mouth, resisting the urge to puke. Or cry. My cheeks flooded with heat, knowing there was video evidence of me at my most vulnerable. I didn't want anyone seeing me like that, least of all him.

A floorboard creaked beneath my foot, giving me away. Dane's head snapped up, his eyes locking onto mine with an intensity that made me shiver. In an instant, he slammed the laptop shut, cutting off the haunting echo of my terror-filled voice.

"Christ, Piper," he said, his jaw tightening as he took in my work clothes. "I forgot to tell you Derek's putting you on paid leave until this is resolved."

While thrilled they weren't at each other's throats and seemed to have come to some truce, I didn't appreciate anyone making decisions on my behalf. I snagged my purse and keys off the counter, biting the inside of my cheek to keep from starting a fight.

"Did you not fucking hear me?"

I gritted my teeth. "I heard you just fine, but I'm going anyway. I need to get out of this house."

In two long strides, he was in front of me. "You're not going anywhere but back to bed."

"No." I planted my feet, refusing to give up what little independence I had left. "I'm going to work, Dane."

"Wasn't a request. Get your ass back in bed. Now."

Anger flared in my chest, hot and bright, my voice deadly as I hissed, "I'm not a child you can order around."

"Yeah? Well, you're fucking acting like one right now."

"And you're acting like a dick!" I planted my hands on his chest, trying to shove him back, but it was like trying to move a building. A stupid, pig-headed building. "I'm done with you thinking you call all the shots around here. Now move."

The tension radiating off him was palpable. Like a rubber band stretched to its breaking point. "Not doing this with you right now," he stated flatly, the muscle beneath his eye twitching wildly.

Having had enough of being pushed around by men to last a lifetime, I ducked under his arm and made a beeline for the front door. "Cool. Have fun being an asshole. I'm going to work."

I made it three steps before his hand clamped around my wrist, yanking me back. "Like hell you are," Dane growled, the muscles in his neck straining as he fought me for control. "I swear to Christ, Piper, I'll handcuff you to the fucking bed if you don't stop being such a brat."

Fury and hurt ignited inside me like a lit match on gasoline. "A brat?" I exclaimed, struggling against him. "I'm not the one playing vigilante!"

"Those motherfuckers held a gun to your head—they laid hands on you! What the fuck did you expect me to do?" he snapped, releasing me to drag his hands through his hair in frustration.

"Let the cops handle it!"

Dane laughed—a low, menacing chuckle that raised the hairs on my arms. "I look like the kind of guy who's gonna sit back and wait for the cops to handle it, sweetheart? Someone touched my Ol' Lady—"

"I'm not your Ol' Lady," I interjected, jabbing a finger into his chest. "I'm not some piece of property for you to defend. I'm a person. A person who's trying to heal from a traumatic experience. You can't pull your biker bullshit and call dibs on me like I'm the last slice of cake!"

His eyes flashed dangerously. Before I could blink, he had me up against the wall, his muscular body caging me in, radiating heat and barely contained fury.

"I don't need your permission to do shit, sweetheart," he growled, his breath hot against my ear. "It's cute you think you get a say in the matter, but you're mine. And I protect what's mine."

A shiver ran through me, equal parts fear and arousal. It didn't matter whether I was awake or asleep, my body responded to him, even when I didn't want it to. "By breaking the law?" I challenged, meeting his gaze defiantly. "How is that protecting me?"

"In my world, we don't wait around for the law. We are the law," he said, his voice deadly calm.

I shook my head and squeezed the pads of my fingers into my palms, overwhelmed by the sheer stupidity of his statement. Was that what my mother had meant by club justice?

"Let me get this straight. You're going to interfere with an active police investigation?"

"No. Told you already. I'm going to find the fuckers involved and make them pay," he said.

Needing to put some distance between us before I did something foolish—like strangle him with my bare hands—I brushed past him.

"Where the hell are you going?" Dane caught me by the elbow, his grip like iron.

"Away from you," I muttered, trying to wrench free.

He chuckled. "I see. You're good with the softer sides of me, but the minute the not-so-nice parts come out, you're ready to run."

"Fuck yes, I am! Because I know how this story ends!" I had a little girl to worry about, and my number one priority was keeping her safe.

The cold look in his eyes returned. "What the fuck does that mean?"

"My father was a biker. He used to beat my mom. The last time, she ended up in the hospital, where she discovered she was pregnant with me. A nurse helped her contact my grandparents, and they drove up to Oklahoma to get us out." My voice cracked, and I swallowed hard before adding, "If we'd stayed, we'd both be dead."

Dane's grip on my arm loosened, his expression shifting from anger to shock. "You think I could do that—that I could hurt either one of you?"

I glared up at him in stony silence, still tugging against his hold.

"Fucking talk to me, Piper."

"What's the point?" I looked down, angrily blinking back tears. "You're going to do what you want even if it puts me and Avery in danger. Fuck what I need, right?"

"What you need is to feel safe," he said, cupping my chin and forcing my eyes up to his. "Not spend the next few weeks, months, or years looking over your shoulder and jumping at every little noise."

"But the police—"

"Are going to follow their law. That means the man who hurt you has the right to a fair trial, the right to a lawyer, and the right to confront you in a courtroom. Let's say the jury manages to find him guilty. Then he's looking at five to twenty-five years behind bars with the possibility of parole in five," he said, stroking my jaw with his thumb.

"What happens when he's back on the streets, Piper? You going to trust that legal system to keep him from coming after you or Avery?" His eyes burned into mine, dark and intense.

"So you're—" I licked my dry lips, my pulse thrumming against his fingertips. "You're good with killing…for me?"

Dane kept his eyes on mine, his grip on my chin tightening. "Darlin', I'd burn the whole fucking world to the ground for you."

The intensity in his voice sent a tremor down my spine. "That's what scares me," I whispered, my voice cracking. "I don't want what happened to turn you into something you're not."

The muscle in his jaw flexed. "I'm a monster, sweetheart. Have been since long before you came along."

I shook my head, tears spilling onto my cheeks. "No. No, you're not. The Dane I know is kind and gentle. He takes our daughter to the park almost every afternoon and buys me flowers just because. That's the man I—" I caught myself before I could say it. I couldn't think of a worse time to admit I loved him, especially when I still wasn't convinced I hadn't been dreaming the night I heard him say it. "That's the man I know."

Something flickered in his eyes—a hint of the warmth I was used to seeing. But it was quickly swallowed by cold darkness.

"That man can't protect you," he growled. "He can't make sure those fuckers never lay a hand on you again."

"And this version of you can?" I challenged, finding a shred of backbone. "By what, torturing them? Killing them? How is that going to help me feel safe?"

His nostrils flared on a sharp inhale, and for a moment, I thought he might lash out. Instead, he scraped a hand over his face as if trying to wash away any trace of emotion before taking a step back.

"You think I don't see how you flinch whenever someone touches you? How you can barely sleep through the night without waking up screaming?" he asked, his voice strained. "It's killing me to see how this is tearing you apart. And knowing that bastard's still out there..."

Dane's shoulders sagged, and he leaned against the wall, suddenly looking exhausted. "You want to know why I can't let this go—why I have to handle it myself?"

I nodded, hardly daring to breathe.

"Because I can't lose you too," he said, his voice barely above a whisper.

The raw grief reflected in his eyes gutted me. I reached out, wanting to comfort him, but the anger still pulsing off him in waves held me back.

"What happened with Levi wasn't your fault," I said, lowering my arm back to my side.

He huffed out a bitter laugh and shook his head. "People keep saying that, but I could have done a hundred things differently, and he'd still be here. My brother wouldn't have gotten divorced and fucked off to Colorado." He absently ran his knuckles along his jawline.

"Way I see it, I can sit back and watch you suffer, or I can do what needs to be done. You may not like it, but this is who I am, Piper. The parts of me you've seen before? That was just the surface. This—this is the real me."

"The real you," I repeated. "And what exactly does that entail? Because I need to know what I'm getting into here, Dane. No more secrets."

He closed the distance between us. "It means I'll tear the entire fucking metroplex apart and break every single law to find the man responsible for hurting you," he said, his hand coming up to rest against the base of my throat. "And when I find him, I'm gonna make him suffer in ways that'll have him begging for death long before I'm done."

"How?" I asked, leaning into his touch as an involuntary shiver worked through my body.

Dane cocked his head to the side, clearly caught off guard by my response. "Well, I've always been partial to slow slicing. Slip the tip of the blade just beneath the surface of their skin, carving off bits of flesh a little at a time.

"From there, you move onto the limbs. I'll probably start with his hands, removing every finger that touched you, joint by joint. Since there's no way to know which fingers touched you and which ones didn't, I'll have to take them all," he said, watching me closely. "When it comes time for the final cut, I'll go for the head, making sure mine is the last face he sees while he chokes to death on his own blood."

The cold certainty in his voice should have terrified me, but instead, a perverse sense of excitement coursed through my veins. The idea that this man—this dangerous, powerful man—would go to such lengths to protect me and our daughter called to something dark inside me. A wave of heat spread up my throat, and I clutched at his kutte, wanting to erase the remaining distance between us.

Dane's eyes darkened as he took in my flushed cheeks and heaving chest.

"That turn you on, baby?" he murmured, applying just enough pressure to the sides of my throat to make my pulse race. "Knowing what I'm willing to do for you?"

I swallowed hard, unable to deny the heat pooling low in my belly. "It shouldn't," I whispered, even as I pressed closer to him.

"But it does," he growled. His muscular thigh slipped between my legs, and I ground against him, seeking the friction from the denim. "Tell me, Piper. Tell me how it makes you feel."

My breath hitched as his free hand skimmed down my side, coming to rest on the curve of my hip. "Powerful," I admitted, my voice barely audible. "Safe."

A predatory smile curved his lips. "It's in our nature. The need to protect...to possess," he said, his open mouth trailing over my jaw and down the column of my throat. "To punish anyone stupid enough to touch what's ours. And make no mistake, baby. You're mine."

Dane's teeth grazed my pulse point, sending goosebumps spreading across my skin. His words should have angered me, should have made me want to push him away and remind him I wasn't something he could claim for himself.

Instead, I tipped my head back and bared my throat to his mouth before whispering, "Prove it."

TWENTY-THREE

GHOST

Ivy & Piper's Guide to Life Rule Number Twenty-One: Always
pee after sex.

P iper yelped in surprise when I hauled her up over my shoulder and stalked toward the bedroom before tossing her onto the bed. I could feel her eyes on me as I pulled my sidearm from my holster and placed it on the dresser, her gaze burning into my back. When I turned around, she was spread out on the bed like a fucking feast, and I had to clench my fists to keep from pouncing.

I knew I needed to walk away and get my head on straight before I did something we'd both regret. But the storm raging inside me demanded release.

"What are you going to do?" she asked as I loomed over her, her tongue darting out to wet her lips.

I growled low in my throat, pressing my fists to the mattress on either side of her body. "What I should've done the moment I found out what that fucker did to you."

My fingers tangled in her hair, freeing the strands from the tight bun before yanking her head back to expose the delicate column of her throat. I dragged my teeth along her pulse point, feeling it race beneath my lips. Piper whimpered, her body arching into mine instinctively.

"Tell me to stop," I rasped against her skin, tracing the bow of her plump pink lip with the pad of my thumb, my body shaking with restraint. "Tell me this isn't what you want."

Instead of pushing me away, the heels of her feet dug into my lower back, urging me closer. "Make me forget," she pleaded. "Make it all go away."

The last threads of my control snapped, and I crushed my mouth to hers in a raw, bruising kiss. My tongue invaded her mouth, claiming every inch as she moaned against my lips.

Her fingers clawed at my shoulders, nails biting through the fabric of my shirt. I ground my hips against hers, letting her feel how hard I was, how much I wanted her.

"Is this what you need, baby?" I growled, nipping at her earlobe. "You want me to prove you're mine? Want me to fuck the pain away?"

Piper nodded frantically, her eyes wild with desperation. "Please, Dane. I need to feel something else. Anything else."

I tugged at the drawstring of her pants and ripped them down her legs, leaving her in just the tank top and a pair of panties.

The bruises had faded to a greenish-yellow hue but seeing them was enough to put logic back in the driver's seat instead of my dick.

If I took her now, in the fucked-up headspace I was in, I was liable to kill her. At the very least, I'd add to the growing list of emotional scars.

"Wait," I said, rolling off her with a frustrated groan. "I can't."

"You can't what?" she demanded, her voice cracking. "Can't fuck me? Can't stand to touch me now that I'm damaged goods?"

The rejection in her tone killed me. But I couldn't let this go any further, not when we were both so fucked up.

"That's not it," I growled, running a hand over my face. "You have no idea how badly I fucking want you, but this isn't right."

Piper let out a bitter laugh. "Right? Nothing about this situation is right, Dane. I was assaulted in my own bakery. I'm trapped in this house like a prisoner. And now the one person I thought I could count on thinks I'm some fragile little doll who can't make her own decisions."

My cock wanted nothing more than to give her exactly what she was asking for—to lose myself in her body and make her forget everything else. But the monster inside me was too close to the surface. If I let it out now, I wasn't sure I could control it.

"You don't understand," I said through clenched teeth. "If I touch you right now, I won't be able to stop. And the things I want to do to you..."

Her eyes flashed defiantly. "Maybe I don't want you to stop. Maybe I need you to lose control."

"I don't want you to regret this later."

She planted her palms against my chest and shoved me back against the bed. My heart thumped painfully against my ribcage at the feel of her pussy grinding over the front of my jeans.

"You want to know what I regret?" she asked, moaning as she slipped her hand beneath the waistband of her panties. "I regret letting you decide what's best for me."

Goosebumps pebbled her soft skin and puckered her nipples into tight little points against the thin material of the tank top. "Piper..."

"What, Dane?" she challenged, her eyes locked on mine as she touched herself. "Oh, I forgot. You're my jailer. You going to stop me? Maybe handcuff me to the bed like you threatened to earlier?"

The scent of her arousal filled the air, making the rational parts of my brain short-circuit. I gripped her hips tighter, torn between pulling her closer and pushing her away.

I clenched my jaw so hard I thought my teeth might crack. "You don't want this. Not like this. Not with how fucked up things are right now. You're not thinking clearly."

She wrenched away from me, her voice rising. "You don't get to tell me what I'm thinking or feeling. You weren't there when it happened."

"Thanks for the reminder, sweetheart," I growled, finding myself slipping into a dark place. "Like it's not all I've fucking thought about since it happened."

The monster I kept caged was rattling the bars, demanding to be let loose. It craved blood, vengeance...but would happily settle for her body beneath mine.

"Good," she said, her fingers defiantly working between her legs. "If I have to suffer, so do you."

My hand shot out, wrapping around her throat like a collar. Not squeezing enough to hurt her but enough to get her attention. I tugged her mouth down over mine, fucking it with my tongue in a way that wasn't like me. Not soft. Not gentle.

Maybe that was what she needed.

"Is this what you want?" I whispered against her lips. "You wanna be held down and fucked senseless until you can't remember your own name, let alone what he did to you?"

Her eyes went hazy with lust, her fingers moving a little faster beneath the lace. "If it means feeling whole, even temporarily, then fuck yes. That's what I want."

Fuck if I didn't want it too. But I was in no condition to give her what she needed. I was somewhere north of buzzed and more in the mood for murder than making love. If I gave in now, I'd be no better than Timothy.

"Baby, we can't. Not like this." I tugged her hand out of her panties with my free hand, resisting the urge to suck the juices off her glistening fingertips.

She yanked her hand out of my grip. "What happened to the guy from a few weeks ago? The one who couldn't keep his hands off me?"

"He's trying real fuckin' hard not to take advantage of you right now."

"Then give me the biker," she stated calmly, rocking against my painfully hard cock.

"Piper," I warned, my nostrils flaring with each ragged breath I took. "I'm not in a good place right now."

"That makes two of us."

I shook my head, my throat bobbing up and down in a hard swallow.

She took a deep breath before nodding to herself. "I'm not asking for soft or gentle. I'm asking for my biker to fuck me so hard it resets my brain back to its original factory settings. Give me the bad guy."

My fingers flexed against her throat. "You don't want that side of me, baby. Not tonight."

"I survived being assaulted," Piper said, her eyes flashing with determination. "I think I can handle you."

Something snapped inside me at her words. The monster broke free of its cage, roaring to the surface. I flipped her onto her back, pinning her to the mattress and letting her feel every rigid inch of my cock through our clothes.

Instead of fear, I saw need in her eyes. She arched up, pressing her breasts against my chest. "Fuck me, Dane. Make me forget everything but you."

With a feral growl, I tore her tank top straight down the middle and shoved her sports bra up over her tits before pinning her wrists above her head with one hand, using my body to keep her spread beneath me.

The position was eerily similar to how Timothy had her during the robbery, but the monster in me was focused on her heaving tits. I dragged my free hand down her body to roughly palm one, brushing my thumb over the stiff peak before pinching it. Hard.

I greedily swallowed her cry before taking her lower lip between my teeth and sucking hard enough to draw blood.

"Yes, please...more..."

I released her wrists. "If you need me to stop, yank or squeeze my shoulder. Got it?"

Piper quirked an eyebrow. "What, no safe word?"

I hooked my fingers in the waistband of her panties, tearing the delicate lace clean off her body in one sharp tug.

"Gonna be hard to use a safe word when your mouth is full, darlin'," I growled, shoving the ruined panties between her parted lips. "Bite down. You're going to need it."

Her pupils dilated, nearly eclipsing the green of her irises. The monster in me was absolutely feral at the sight of her spread out and gagged beneath me.

As I settled between her thighs, I caught sight of a thin white string and grinned wickedly.

"Well, well. What do we have here?" I twisted it around my finger and tugged, sliding the tampon free in one smooth motion.

Piper spit out the makeshift gag, her cheeks flushing. "Shit, I forgot—"

"You cramping or in pain?" I asked, searching her face for any sign of discomfort.

She shook her head. "No, but—"

"Good," I growled, shoving her panties back between her lips. "Because I'm not going to let a little blood stop me from taking what's mine."

The thought of taking her on her period and having her mark me only turned me on more. I stripped down to my briefs, my cock straining against the fabric as I spread her thighs wide.

My mouth watered at the sight of her glistening pussy. She was already so wet for me that I didn't need to coat my fingers before sliding two into her slick channel, curving them to hit her G-spot.

"That's it, baby," I growled as her inner muscles clenched around me. "Fuck my fingers. Show me how bad you want it."

Piper's hips bucked frantically as I increased my pace, driving her closer to the edge. I waited until her thigh muscles tightened and her breaths grew ragged before withdrawing my hand. She whimpered in protest, her eyes flashing with frustrated desire.

I made sure she was watching as I brought my blood-stained fingers to my mouth, sucking them clean with a low groan. The metallic tang mixed with her juices sent another surge of possessiveness through me.

"You're mine," I said, dragging my teeth over her peaked nipples. "Nod for me, baby."

She shook her head, playful defiance sparking in her lust-glazed eyes.

"Be a good girl and submit to me," I demanded, wrapping one hand around her throat, putting pressure on the sides. Enough to make her lashes flutter.

Piper spit out the gag. "Make me," she panted before pulling my mouth down over hers, nipping and sucking my lip until she drew blood.

The pain only spurred me on, and I growled against her lips, the taste of blood mingling between us. "You want a safe word? Red. That's your safe word. Use it the second you feel uncomfortable, and I'll stop immediately."

Her eyelids went heavy, and she nodded.

"I'm fucking serious, Piper. Don't hesitate or try to tough it out," I warned, dragging my thumb over the blood on her lip. "You want me to stop, say red, and it ends right there. Are we clear?"

"Say red if it's too much or I need you to stop," she repeated, her tongue tracing the same path my thumb had. "Now, are you going to fuck me or not?"

"Always a brat." I ground my cock against her slick folds. The thin barrier of my boxer briefs was torture, but I wanted to make her beg for it.

I trailed biting kisses down her neck, leaving marks on her pale skin in my wake. My hand slid up to cup her breast, thumbing her nipple roughly as I sucked a bruise onto her collarbone.

Mine.

"Who do you belong to?"

"No one," she hissed, jutting her chin up in defiance.

I grinned and sank my teeth into the soft flesh where her neck met her shoulder, drawing a cry from her lips. "Wrong fucking answer."

My head dipped to her breasts, and I exhaled a warm breath over the hardened points before flicking them with my tongue. "Whose tits are these?"

"Mine," she said, her breath catching as I rubbed my beard against them.

"You're really bad at this game," I said, capturing a nipple between my teeth. I sucked greedily at the puckered flesh before switching sides until she was a writhing mess beneath me.

I released her nipple with a wet *pop* and slid my hand between her thighs. "Try again, darlin'. Who owns this pussy?"

She ground her clit against my palm before groaning, "Fuck...you do, Dane. You own me. Only you."

"That's my girl," I praised, curving two fingers inside her.

I worked her mercilessly, bringing her to the edge over and over, only to deny her release. The tension built until every muscle in her body was shaking.

"Please," she begged, her fingers twisting in the sheets. "I need you inside me."

I pulled back and hooked my thumbs in the waistband of my briefs and dragged them down until my cock sprang free, achingly hard and leaking precum.

Piper's eyes widened, her tongue darting out to wet her lips.

"This what you want, darlin'?" I growled, fisting my length. "To be fucked hard and filled up?"

She nodded, spreading her thighs wider in invitation.

I positioned myself at her entrance, teasing her slick folds with the head of my cock before pulling back. "Nah. I'm not done playing with you yet."

"You bastard."

"You knew what you were getting into, sweetheart," I said with a low chuckle.

With a smile I didn't trust, she reached into the top drawer of her nightstand to grab her vibrator. "Never mind. I'm good," she said, switching it on with a raised eyebrow as if daring me to stop her.

I snatched it from her hand and tossed it out of reach. "Nice try, brat. But the only way you're coming is on my cock."

Piper pouted, her eyes flashing with annoyance. "Then stop teasing and fuck me already."

"Patience." I grabbed a condom from the dresser, tearing open the foil with my teeth. I rolled it on and positioned myself at her entrance when my phone suddenly blared to life.

"You've gotta be fucking kidding me," I gritted out, pressing my forehead against her. "Every fucking time I get you naked…"

She wrapped her legs around my waist, drawing me closer. "Ignore it."

I rolled my hips forward, sinking into her tight, wet cunt with a groan. Her inner muscles clenched around me, pulling me deeper, and I had to grit my teeth to keep from coming on the spot.

The ringing stopped, only to immediately start up again. With a muttered curse, I reluctantly pulled out and fumbled for my jeans on the floor.

"I have to take this," I said apologetically, sliding my thumb over the screen to answer. She guided my cock back into her body as I brought the phone to my ear, and my eyes slammed shut at the sensation.

"Yeah?" I managed to grunt out.

"Bad time?" Carnage's dry voice came through the line. I could practically hear his smirk.

I worked to keep my voice steady as I slowly rocked into Piper's tight pussy. "You calling because you found something or just to shoot the shit?"

"Bit of both," Carnage drawled. "Think I might've found the vehicle used in the robbery. Tracked it to a rental car place out by Love Field."

"Right there," she moaned.

I thrust deeper and clamped my palm over her mouth to muffle the sound.

He cleared his throat. "Look, as much as I'd love to be home fucking my Ol' Lady, I'm stuck in Dallas, helping your sorry ass. So if we could wrap this the fuck up tonight, that'd be great."

"Uh…" I stilled my movements, trying to coax the blood back up to my brain so I could think. Piper squirmed impatiently beneath me, and I gave her a warning look. "I can meet you in twenty—"

"The fuck you can," he replied. "Not after the drinking you did. I'll be there in twenty. Should be plenty of time for you to finish up your...activities."

"Make it thirty," I said through my teeth, struggling to focus as her pussy clenched around me. I ended the call and tossed the phone aside, turning my full attention back to the woman beneath me.

I slowly withdrew from her body before dropping my mouth to her throat. "Might have a lead on the vehicle used in the robbery, baby. Carnage and I are going to check it out, but Nails will stick around to keep an eye on things."

A flicker of fear passed over her face before she masked it. "Good. That's...good, right?"

"Depends," I said, taking her peaked breasts in my hands and tracing circles around her tight nipples until her eyes went hazy. "You gonna let me take care of this, or do you still want the cops to handle it?"

"I want…" Piper hesitated, her teeth worrying her lower lip. She wasn't built for the kind of violence I was capable of inflicting. But then her gaze hardened, and she surprised the hell out of me. "I want them to suffer."

"Good fucking girl," I said, fusing my mouth to hers before directing her onto her hands and knees. My hand splayed across her upper back, pinning her in place. "Tell me if it's too much or if you need me to stop."

She peered over her shoulder with a cocked eyebrow. "I was expecting something a lot rougher. You know, for a biker, you're awfully soft—"

Such a fucking brat.

Her words cut off in a sharp gasp as I slammed into her, burying myself to the hilt in one powerful thrust.

"You were saying?" I asked, bringing my palm down on her ass cheek, the sharp smack echoing through the room.

All my pent-up rage and frustration poured out as I pounded into her willing body, fucking her with an intensity that bordered on feral. I gripped her hips hard enough to bruise, pulling her back to meet each brutal snap of my hips.

"This what you wanted, baby? Or do you need more?"

"God, yes," she whimpered, pushing back to meet my thrusts. "Harder."

"You're gonna feel me for days, brat," I promised darkly, driving into her with enough force to make the headboard slam against the wall. "Every time you move, you'll remember who you belong to."

My hand came down on her ass again, leaving a perfect red handprint on her skin. When I felt her inner walls start to flutter, I reached around to rub tight circles on her clit.

"Come for me, baby," I demanded through gritted teeth, my balls tightening. "Soak my cock with that pretty little pussy."

Piper babbled a string of gibberish in response, her body convulsing around me in rhythmic spasms. The vise-like grip of her pussy triggered my own release, and I came with a low, guttural groan.

We collapsed onto the bed in a tangle of sweaty limbs, both of us panting heavily. After padding to the bathroom to dispose of the condom and her tampon, I wet a washcloth with warm water and returned to clean her up.

"You okay?" I asked, gently wiping between her thighs.

She nodded, a drowsy smile playing on her lips. "Much better. Was there—" Her voice dropped to a whisper. "Was there a lot of blood?"

"Nah, just a little," I said, tossing the washcloth in the hamper and pulling her against my chest. "Nothing to worry about."

I pressed a kiss to her forehead before checking my watch. As much as I wanted to stay curled up with her, Carnage was due to arrive in the next couple of minutes.

With a groan, I extricated myself from her arms and threw my clothes back on. I grabbed my sidearm off the dresser and checked the magazine when Piper sat up straighter.

"Does having it on you all the time make you feel safer?" she asked.

I paused, considering her question. "I guess I never really thought about it. I like knowing it's within reach if I need it." I studied her face. "Why? Are you interested in learning how to use one?"

She let out a short laugh before shaking her head. "I have a .38 Special I keep in my purse."

"Since when?"

"Since I was old enough to get my concealed carry permit," she said with an easy shrug. "My mom's always carried, so it seemed natural. I thought it was just because we lived in a big city, but now I wonder if it had more to do with her being afraid my dad might come after us someday."

"No shit?" I raised an eyebrow, impressed. "What the hell do you need me for then?"

"Sex mostly," she bluntly replied, her lips quirking into a wry smile. "And free babysitting."

I slid my sidearm back into the holster with a chuckle. "Pretty sure that's called parenting, brat, but I'm glad I still have some use around here."

Piper nodded, her expression turning pensive. "I keep thinking if I'd had my gun on me that night at the bakery, maybe…"

"Hey," I said firmly, sitting on the edge of the mattress and pulling her onto my lap. "Don't go down that road. Two armed men caught you off guard. Having a gun might've made things a hell of a lot worse."

She nodded, but I could see the wheels turning in her head. "Maybe, but I never want to feel that helpless again."

I cupped her cheek, forcing her to meet my eyes. "I get it, believe me. How about this? We'll look at some concealed carry options when

I get back, okay? Find something that you feel comfortable wearing every day."

"Thank you," she said, kissing me.

With the lead on the vehicle, I was confident we'd find and eliminate the remaining threat, but I also wanted her to feel she had a way to protect herself if she needed it.

If it helped ease her fears, I was willing to do whatever it took.

The familiar rumble of Carnage's truck sent a rush of anticipation through me. We were one step closer to finding the fucker responsible for hurting Piper.

And once we did, God help him.

Because I sure as fuck wouldn't.

TWENTY-FOUR
GHOST

I stood outside the rental car company, watching planes take off in the distance. One after another, they disappeared into the darkness until they became indistinguishable from the faint stars in the night sky.

The ground beneath my boots vibrated with the low-frequency rumble of engines, creating a subtle thrumming sensation I felt in my bones. Then again, it might have been the aftermath of the rough sex still reverberating through my body. I shifted uncomfortably, wincing at the twinge in my ass.

Fuck, I definitely pulled something.

I took a slow lap around the building, trying to walk off the ache. Christ, I felt old, and I was only thirty-eight. Still, the memory of her thick ass rippling beneath my hands as she begged for more made every second of discomfort worth it. Despite the protest from my muscles, my cock revived at the image in my head, leaving me eager to get back home. I raked a hand over my face, desperately in need of a cold shower.

A gravelly voice cut through the noise from the planes. "You look like hammered shit."

"Still better than looking old as shit," I drawled as the club's former president and one of my old man's closest friends stepped out of the shadows like the motherfucking ghost of biker's past.

Grey snorted and tapped a cigarette from his pack before passing it and his gold lighter to me. "Last I checked, I ain't the one limpin' around the parking lot. The fuck did you do?"

I lit up and took a long drag before admitting, "Might have pulled a muscle."

"Pulled a muscle? Shit, son," he said with a chuckle, smoke lazily drifting out from between his lips. The ember on his cigarette glowed bright in the darkness, illuminating the lines etched deep in his weathered face. "Maybe you need to hit the gym more so you can keep up with your Ol' Lady."

I flipped him off, but there was no real heat behind it.

We stood in silence for a few moments, the only sound the distant roar of jet engines and the soft crackle of burning tobacco. I could feel his eyes on me, studying me like I was some kind of puzzle he couldn't quite figure out and knew what was coming next.

"So," he finally said, flicking ash onto the pavement. "You talk to your brother lately?"

"Don't ask questions you don't want the answers to," I ground out with a stream of smoke before letting my head fall back against the building.

Grey grunted before taking another drag. "There's a sayin' about assumptions and the assholes who make 'em, kid."

"There's also one about minding your own damn business."

He turned to face me, his blue eyes hard in the dim light. "Quit bein' so goddamn hard-headed and sit down with Crow. Between you, me, and the fencepost, Wolverine ain't no spring chicken, and this shit between y'all ain't doin' him any good."

I exhaled slowly, watching the smoke curl into the night air. "Old man, you don't know what the fuck you're talking about."

Grey wasn't the first to confront me over the shit with my family. It seemed everyone had an opinion on me keeping my distance and felt the need to try to bring me back into the fold.

"I know everything, kid. And as your godfather—"

"You're not my godfather," I interjected before taking another drag off the cigarette, reveling in the familiar, almost comfortable burn in my lungs.

He let out a rough bark of laughter that held no humor and waved his hand dismissively. "Semantics. Point is, you've been runnin' from this shit for too long."

His voice softened a fraction. "I've watched you self-destruct for two goddamn years, and I'm sick of it. As a good friend of mine once told me when I was standing where you are, 'At some point, you gotta man the fuck up.'"

Man the fuck up?

What did he think I'd been doing for the past two years?

A vein pulsed in my neck. "And say what? Sorry I drove your kid to suicide and destroyed your marriage."

"Jesus fuck. You must be more powerful than the fuckin' Wizard of Oz if you're singlehandedly responsible for all that," Grey said dryly. "You don't know shit about fuck when it comes to your own family, son. If you did, you'd know it didn't have a damn thing to do with you. Surprised you didn't bail on your girl after the robbery because you 'failed.'"

I saw red. In an instant, I was in Grey's face, snarling, "Watch your fucking mouth."

Using the sides of my kutte as handles, he shoved me up against the side of the building with a surprising amount of strength for a man pushing sixty. "The fuck you gonna do about it, huh?" He exhaled a stream of smoke into my face because, unlike me, he'd managed to hold onto his cigarette during our scuffle.

"Now you listen to me, you stubborn little shit," he hissed. "You think you're the only one who's ever fucked up? Who's ever lost someone? Pull your head out of your ass."

I struggled against his grip, but he didn't budge.

"I've been in your shoes," he said, shaking me. "I know about the nightmares and the drinkin' you have to do to try to forget. I know how it feels to wake up every morning hatin' yourself. But take it from an old man with a mile-long list of regrets, pushin' everyone away ain't gonna bring that boy back or make your Ol' Lady safe. You wanna throw yourself a goddamn pity party? Fine. But at least get all the goddamned facts first. 'Cause what went down with Levi ain't on you."

"Yeah? Tell that to Crow," I said, remembering the things Teddy had said to me when we were at the funeral home.

And I'd deserved every bit of it.

"The fuck you expect him to do, huh? That was his baby. Whatever he said or didn't say, ain't a chance in hell it had anything to do with you. You just happened to be the closest target. You think you know grief? Boy, that is a whole other ballgame."

Grey mashed the cigarette between his quivering lips and worked his jaw back and forth several times before continuing, "Parents ain't supposed to—" His nostrils flared. "They ain't supposed to bury their kids. It's a hell I wouldn't wish on my worst enemy."

The fight drained out of me at the anguish reflected in his eyes, leaving me slumped against the wall. It was the attack on his Ol' Lady that had led to the war with the Sons and caused her to lose their baby.

He took a deep breath before continuing. "I've known you since you came into this world. I've watched you grow into a man I'm proud to call family. But this chip on your shoulder is going to eat you alive if you don't deal with it."

The door to the rental office swung open, cutting off whatever bullshit was about to spew from my mouth. Carnage and Bear stepped out, their eyes narrowing when they saw us.

"We interrupting something?" Carnage asked dryly.

Grey released me and stepped back, smoothing down his kutte. "Just havin' a heart-to-heart with our boy here."

Bear snorted. "Funny, from where I'm standin', it looked more like you were about to rip his heart out."

"If I wanted details on what it looked like, I'd have asked for 'em, Pres," he replied with a shit-eating grin.

Already feeling the familiar itch for another cigarette and needing some good news, I approached Carnage. "Tell me this guy didn't use a fake ID to rent the van."

He held up his phone to reveal a screenshot of a driver's license. "Dumbass rented the van using his real name. Isaac Scott. Twenty-one years old, no priors."

Finally, a fucking lead.

"The fucking delivery guy?" I asked when the name clicked. "No shit?"

Carnage nodded grimly. "One and the same. Explains why he didn't flag when we ran background checks on the drivers. Squeaky clean record."

"Until now," Bear added.

"Why the fuck would a kid with no priors knock off a bakery?" Grey asked, voicing the question on everyone's mind, mine included. "Why not choose a more obvious location if he was looking for cash? Like a convenience store or a laundromat."

Carnage ran his knuckles over the bristles of his beard before shaking his head. "Maybe it's not his first run, and he's just damn good at covering his tracks?"

"That, or someone else is pullin' the strings," Grey finished, pinching his lower lip between his thumb and forefinger, a tell I'd seen at least a thousand times.

"Only one way to find out," Bear said, cracking his knuckles with a grin. "Got an address in South Dallas…about twenty minutes from here."

"What the fuck are we waiting for?" I growled, already stripping off my kutte and heading for Carnage's truck. "Let's go pay the little shit a visit. He wanted to start a war. We'll bring it to his motherfucking doorstep."

———

Twenty minutes later, we arrived in a neighborhood that had seen better days. It was the kind of place where no one saw shit, and even if they did, they weren't calling it in.

Carnage killed the engine, and we sat in the darkness, surveying the dilapidated house. Paint hung off the siding in long strips, exposing rotted wood underneath. The yard was overgrown, littered with rusted car parts and broken bottles.

"Nice curb appeal," Bear muttered dryly from the back seat.

My fingers twitched against my thigh, itching to wrap around someone's throat. "You sure this is the right place?" I side-eyed the decrepit structure. The windows were dark, with no signs of life inside.

Carnage double-checked the address on his phone. "This is it."

"Don't think I need to remind anyone here how this is gonna go down. In and out through the back door without a trace," Bear said, giving us the green light.

After slipping on our gloves, we moved stealthily through the shadows, with Carnage leading us in a tight military formation. His Army Ranger background was evident in every calculated step.

He knelt to pick the lock before silently easing the door open. The house was deathly silent, but we kept our weapons raised as we entered. Despite our best efforts to mask our presence, the floorboards creaked beneath our weight.

The stale air reeked of mold and neglect, but as we crept farther into the house, another smell hit me—one that was all too familiar.

"Got a body somewhere in here," Grey said unnecessarily.

The sickly, sweet stench of death clung to the inside of my nostrils and the back of my throat. My stomach roiled, and I fought the urge to gag as we moved through the darkened house, systematically clearing each room.

We followed the putrid odor to the hallway. With his flashlight and sidearm raised, Carnage nodded. Bear pushed it open, and the full force of decay assaulted us like a physical blow.

My eyes watered, and I swallowed hard against the bile rising in my throat. A body lay on the bed, partially covered.

I approached cautiously, keeping my M17 trained on the ratty comforter as I slowly eased it down with a gloved hand. If the rotting odor hadn't given it away, the bloated, mottled gray-green skin and vacant eyes staring at nothing would have. Bloody foam leaked from his nose and mouth onto the sheets below.

"Jesus. Fucker's ripe," Bear muttered, covering his nose and mouth with his bandana. "How long's he been here?"

Carnage leaned down to examine the corpse, seemingly the only one of us not affected by the stench. "Based on decomp, I'd say anywhere from three to five days," he guessed before peering at Isaac's hands and arms.

"There are no obvious signs of a struggle or defensive wounds.

Given the drug paraphernalia on the nightstand and the track marks on his arms, I'm leaning toward overdose for cause of death, but there's no way to know for sure without an autopsy."

"So, it's him?" I asked, my voice muffled behind the crook of my arm.

He nodded grimly. "Matches the photo from his license."

"Shit," I growled, resisting the urge to drive my fist through the already crumbling drywall. Our one lead, dead before we could get any solid answers as to whether there was anyone else involved. "There's got to be something here that'll tell us if these guys were working alone or not."

We spread out, meticulously combing through the rest of the house. I took the kitchen, rifling through drawers and cabinets, but nothing jumped out at me. Just overdue bills, dirty dishes, and takeout menus.

I moved on to the living room, methodically searching every nook and cranny for anything that might give us a clue. My frustration mounted with each passing second. This kid had to have left something behind.

"Get Ghost out of the fucking house," Carnage directed Bear and Grey in a low voice that sent the hairs on the back of my neck up. There was only one reason he'd use that tone.

He'd found something.

"Let's grab a cigarette," Grey said, holding his hands out like I was some skittish animal he was trying to calm.

I pushed past him, trying to get to the room at the end of the hall, when Bear stepped into my path and latched onto my upper body, trying to haul me back.

"Dane, don't," he warned, shaking his head. The last time he'd called me by my real name, I was still a kid.

Their faces were ashen, and I knew—I fucking knew that whatever I was about to see was going to wreck me. But my feet continued moving as if on autopilot. The moment I stepped inside, my world tilted on its axis, horror washing over me in icy waves.

Hundreds, maybe thousands of photos of Piper littered every square inch of wall space. Some had clearly been taken from a distance—at work, the grocery store, while she was at the park with Avery.

But it was the ones taken inside our home that made my blood run cold.

There were shots of her in the shower and sleeping in our bed, her face peaceful and unaware. In some, she was visibly pregnant, her swollen belly on full display. One section of the wall appeared to be devoted solely to images of Piper nursing Avery.

"Jesus fucking Christ," I choked out, feeling as if I was going to puke. I reached out to touch one of the photos with shaking hands, half-convinced this was some fucked up nightmare.

"Don't touch anything," Carnage warned, pulling on a fresh pair of gloves before moving to the desk in the corner where a laptop sat. With a few keystrokes, he'd hacked into the system, revealing an entire folder of videos.

"Wait," I said, but he'd already clicked on one.

The screen flickered to life, showing Piper naked and masturbating in our bed, her belly swollen with Avery. The camera angle suggested the person filming was somewhere in our bedroom, yet she seemed oblivious to their presence.

"Shut it the fuck off," I snarled, my hands clenched at my sides.

Carnage quickly closed the video and opened another file. I steeled myself, expecting more footage of Piper, but what I saw made my blood run cold.

The camera was in Avery's bedroom, focused on my baby girl huddled in the corner of her crib. Her little face was red and tear-stained, her lower lip quivering.

"Nuh-no, owie," she whimpered, her little voice quietly pleading with the person holding the camera.

Ice flooded my veins as I recalled Avery using that phrase at the bakery. What if it hadn't been random babbling but her trying to tell her daddy the delivery guy was the monster who had been hurting her?

Jesus.

The person filming chuckled cruelly before holding a pillow over her face, and I dropped to my fucking knees with a pained howl that didn't sound human. Carnage shut it off, but not before I saw her tiny arms and legs flailing as she struggled to take a breath, her muffled cries barely audible.

"Fuckin' Christ," Grey said, his voice catching.

She'd been so fucking quiet, almost like that fucking monster had trained her not to cry out for Piper.

"I'll fucking kill him!" I roared, tears streaming down my face as I lunged for the laptop. Carnage caught me around the chest, restraining me as I thrashed against his grip. "Let me go! My baby—he fucking touched my little girl! I'm going to tear that motherfucker apart!"

"Hey, hey. He's already dead," he said, his voice rough with emotion. "It's over."

I shoved him off me, my chest heaving as I fought to catch my breath. The walls seemed to close in around me, the evidence of my failure to protect Piper mocking me from every angle. My failure to protect my daughter.

"Jesus, how the fuck did he get these? How the fuck did he get that close to them?" I drove my fist into the doorframe, splintering the wood. But the physical pain was nothing compared to the anguish ripping me apart from the inside. "I'll bring him back from the dead just to kill him all over again."

"There are detailed floor plans for both Piper's house and her mother's place on here, as well as notes on entry points and how to bypass the security system remotely," Carnage said before slamming the laptop shut.

"Son of a bitch." My hands shook as I raked them through my hair, tugging at the roots. "He was trying to find a way back in after we upgraded the system. To disable it—"

I couldn't finish the thought. The image of that monster's hands on my girls sent my stomach lurching. I barely made it to the trash can in the corner before emptying the liquor from my stomach.

Carnage tucked the laptop under his arm and stood, jaw ticking as he surveyed the walls. "I want to get back and do a full sweep on both houses. There are obviously hidden cameras, and we need to make sure Isaac was the only one with access to them. But first, we need to pack all this up."

While they stripped the pictures off the wall, I knelt by the trash can, paralyzed by a toxic cocktail of rage and guilt. If I'd left my number at the hotel that night for Piper, none of this would have happened. My daughter wouldn't have come face to face with a monster.

"Hey," Grey's gruff voice cut into my self-flagellation. "Reached out to Nails and had him check on your girls. He laid eyes on 'em, and they're both safe."

I wiped my mouth with the back of my hand and rocked back on my heels, still trembling with rage and nausea. "Safe? Did any of that look fucking safe to you?"

Isaac hadn't been some kid with a crush. He was a sick fuck who had gone to great lengths to get close to Piper, methodically stalking her for years.

He knelt beside me. "They're safe now because they've got you. We'll figure out the rest, but right now, we gotta move before someone notices we're here."

I nodded numbly and got to my feet, forcing myself to focus on the task at hand. We took every shred of evidence that could potentially link back to Piper or Avery.

We did one final sweep of the house to ensure we hadn't missed anything. As we headed for the door, I paused, my gaze drawn back to the bedroom where Isaac's body lay. Something didn't sit right. The entire thing felt too neat, too convenient.

"You coming?" Carnage called from the doorway.

I shook my head, unable to shake the nagging feeling. "Give me a minute."

Ignoring the stench, I entered and began methodically searching every inch. Under the mattress, behind picture frames, inside drawers. My fingers probed along the baseboards, looking for any loose sections.

Nothing.

There was no smoking gun. No closure. No sense of relief. Instead of suffering the way he'd made my girls suffer, Isaac had taken the easy way out and OD'd, robbing me of the opportunity to send him to the Reaper myself.

Maybe that was why it didn't feel like it was over.

TWENTY-FIVE

PIPER

Ivy & Piper's Guide to Life Rule Number Thirty-Four:
Don't wait for perfect.

I entered the living room to find Dane slumped in the armchair with Avery curled up against his bare chest. His arms were wrapped tightly around her little body as if protecting her from nightmares.

Since finding the man responsible for robbing the bakery dead of an apparent overdose two weeks ago, this had become their nightly routine.

Almost as soon as Dane's eyes drifted shut, he jolted himself awake again with a panicked gasp. He refused to let himself sleep, and aside from telling me they found pictures of me in Isaac's house, he refused to discuss anything about that night.

With a sigh, I padded over to where he sat, brushing a strand of hair from his brow before reaching for Avery. "I'll take her. You should try to get some sleep."

Dane's arms reflexively tightened around our daughter in a silent plea not to separate them. My throat constricted at his unspoken desperation.

"Hey," I whispered, blinking against the sting of tears. "She needs to sleep in her own bed. And so do you."

He reluctantly let me take her before settling back against the chair. "I'm fine."

There was nothing fine about his clenched jaw and the dark circles rimming his eyes, but I wouldn't waste my breath arguing. My vision blurred, and I turned away before the tears spilled over onto my cheeks.

I carried Avery to her room, gently laying her in her crib and tucking the teddy bear Dane got her in beside her. She stirred briefly, little fingers clutching the stuffed animal before she stilled.

As I quietly closed the door behind me, Dane's low voice drifted down the hall from the living room. It sounded like he was on the phone, but he was speaking too softly for me to make out what he was saying.

My stomach clenched when he stepped out onto the front porch, and I wrapped my arms around myself, fighting back a fresh wave of tears.

A small, traitorous part of me wondered if he was talking to another woman. He hadn't touched me since the night they found the rental car. I'd spent the last week racking my brain and replaying every moment, trying to pinpoint what had gone wrong.

Was it the role-playing?

The fact that I was on my period?

I didn't know, but I couldn't keep living like this. I needed answers.

Taking a deep breath, I slipped out onto the porch. Dane was leaning against the railing, his broad shoulders hunched forward. A cigarette dangled from his fingers, wisps of smoke curling into the night air. His head hung low, and for a moment, I thought he'd fallen asleep standing up until I heard the sharp intake of breath.

He was crying.

Without a word, I wrapped my arms around him from behind, pressing my cheek against his back. I could feel the tension in his muscles, the slight tremors running through his body as he fought to maintain control. My hands splayed across his abdomen, rubbing small, soothing circles.

Dane's body went rigid for a moment before he turned, pulling me tight against his chest. His massive frame vibrated with silent sobs as he buried his face in my hair. I held him tightly, my own tears falling freely now.

We stood for what felt like hours, the weight of unspoken words hanging heavy between us. Finally, I forced myself to voice the fear that had been gnawing at me for days.

"I feel like you're pulling away," I whispered, my voice barely audible. "Have you...have you changed your mind? About us? About me?"

He stiffened, then gently disentangled himself from my arms, and I knew I'd guessed right.

"Sit down, darlin'," he said, leading me over to a chair. "There's something I need to tell you."

My heart plummeted to the porch, and I dropped onto the chair, my legs suddenly weak. Dane crouched in front of me, his red-rimmed eyes filled with a mixture of guilt and anguish, leaving me with a sick feeling in the pit of my stomach.

"Levi's death...it put me in a bad place. I did something that—" He broke off, nostrils flaring as he tried to rein in his emotions. "In light of recent events, I'm afraid it might change how you feel about me. It's already changed how I feel about myself."

A sickening dread flooded my veins, and I pressed a hand to my sternum, feeling like I might hyperventilate. My mind raced with possibilities, each worse than the last. I knew he was capable of killing to protect me. Had he done something even more extreme? Or was it simpler but no less devastating? Another woman. A child I didn't know about.

"Just tell me," I said, bracing myself for the implosion.

"There are 3,123 Pipers living in this country," Dane said abruptly.

I blinked, caught completely off guard. Of all the things I'd imagined him saying, a random fact didn't make the top ten.

"Okay," I said slowly. "That's...interesting, I guess?"

"I'm not done," he continued, his eyes never leaving mine. "There are 3,123 Pipers living in the United States. I know because I've spent the last two years tracking down every single one. Had I been searching for an *Amelia* Piper, I might have found you sooner."

My mouth fell open in shock. "You...what?"

"At the time, it seemed romantic," Dane said, his voice thick with self-loathing. "But after seeing the extent of Isaac's obsession with you... Christ, Piper, I can't help but feel I'm no better."

His hands shook as he reached for me, his grip desperate. "I'm disgusted with myself. I've been making all the decisions since I came into your life, and it's not right. You deserve to know the truth, to decide for yourself if..." He trailed off, throat working. "I'll understand if you want me to leave."

My mind reeled, trying to process the enormity of what he'd done. Two years of his life, dedicated to finding me. I thought back to when we met, how he'd looked at me even then like it was more than a one-night stand.

Because it was.

Men like Dane Riggs were typically only found in the pages of a romance novel, and I would have been an absolute fool to let him go.

A small smile tugged at my lips as I echoed the words I'd said to him that first night. "Hey, I'm here, aren't I?"

Something like hope ignited in his brown eyes, and he swallowed hard, his Adam's apple bobbing up and down. "What are—what are you saying, darlin'?"

I slid from the chair and into his lap, wrapping my arms around his neck. "I'm saying I want you. All of you. The guy who searched the country for me. The daddy. The biker—" I hesitated for a moment before softly adding, "The husband."

Dane made a low noise in his throat, his eyebrow lifting in surprise. "The husband? Are you proposing?"

A flush crept up my cheeks. "Well, you said I was your Ol' Lady, so I figured..." I trailed off, suddenly unsure.

Had I misread everything?

His large hand cupped my chin, tilting my face up to meet his intense gaze. He searched my eyes for a long moment before his lips curved into a slow smile that made my heart skip.

"Come here," he murmured, scooping me up as he stood.

Dane carried me bridal style into the bedroom and gently set me on the edge of the mattress before stepping into the closet. When he emerged, he had one hand behind his back and an uncharacteristically nervous expression on his face.

"I thought when I did this, I'd have some grand speech prepared. Wouldn't be sleep-deprived and emotionally wrung out." He lowered himself to one knee before me, suddenly looking almost bashful. "But hell, baby. When have we ever done things the conventional way?"

I pressed a hand to my mouth when he pulled a small velvet box from behind his back, opening it to reveal a stunning emerald-cut sapphire ring flanked by diamonds.

"Bought this a few weeks after we met," Dane admitted. "Carried it with me for two years, hoping I'd find you again so I could tell you I never wanted one night. I want them all." His voice grew husky with emotion. "Marry me, Amelia Piper Kelly. Be my wife and my Ol' Lady."

Tears spilled down my cheeks, and I nodded frantically, choking out, "Yes. God, yes."

For the first time in weeks, Dane's face broke into a genuine smile, dimples and everything. He slid the ring onto my finger before capturing my mouth with his.

I melted into him, wrapping my arms around his neck as he deepened the kiss, his tongue sweeping into my mouth. A moan slipped past my lips as his hands skimmed down my sides, and I broke away, panting, "Make me yours, Dane."

My back hit the mattress with a bounce, and I pushed myself up onto my elbows, watching with hungry eyes as he stripped off his kutte and shirt.

The dim light from the bedside lamp cast shadows across the muscled planes of his torso, highlighting every ridge and valley. He turned to toss the clothes onto the dresser, and I drank in the full expanse of ink covering his broad back.

I'd seen glimpses of the intricate tattoos before, but never like this —never with the knowledge that this beautiful, dangerous man was all mine.

"See something you like, baby?" he asked with a cocky smirk, his hands moving to his belt buckle.

"Yep. Everything," I replied honestly, too far gone to lie or play coy.

He chuckled darkly as he worked his jeans and boxer briefs down over his muscular thighs. My mouth went dry as his hard length sprang free, eagerly jutting up against his abdomen.

Dane crawled onto the bed with predatory grace, caging my body beneath his larger frame. His skin was hot against mine, and I could feel the barely restrained power in his muscles as he hovered above me.

Slowly, he peeled off my T-shirt before moving to my panties until I was bare beneath him. One hand circled my wrists, pinning them above my head before he claimed my mouth in a searing kiss.

"Tell me to stop, and I will. No questions asked," he said when he broke away, his voice rough with need.

I shook my head frantically. "Don't you dare stop."

A low groan rumbled in his chest as he lowered his head to my breast, rolling one nipple between his thumb and forefinger while taking the other in his mouth. "Mine."

I gasped at the sensation of his teeth grazing the sensitive bud before he soothed it with his tongue. "Yes, yours. All yours."

"Christ, you're gorgeous," he murmured against my skin, switching his attention to my other breast.

When he finally released my nipple with a wet *pop*, I forced my heavy eyelids open to find him staring down at me with an expression of awe. The corners of his eyes crinkled as he studied my face, and I inhaled sharply, suddenly fighting back tears.

I'd seen the same look in his eyes in the hotel room the night we met and again when he saw Avery for the first time. It was one I'd seen so many times since then that its meaning never fully registered.

Until now.

"You love me," I breathed, shaking my head in open-mouthed disbelief. I thought of the words he'd whispered the night he learned about Avery, the words I thought I'd dreamed.

Dane's eyebrows pulled together, creating two vertical lines of confusion between them. "Was that not clear with the whole wanting to marry you and make you my Ol' Lady?"

"No, you love me," I repeated before trying again. "You loved me even the first night—"

"Loved you then," he interjected, dropping his head to kiss the space between my breasts. "Love you now." His mouth moved lower, reverently tracing the stretch marks on my belly before he moved between my thighs. "I'll love you until I take my last breath, darlin'."

I pushed myself up and wrapped my hand around his thick length. His breath hitched as I slowly pumped his shaft, using my thumb to spread the bead of moisture at the tip.

"Mine," I whispered, guiding him to my entrance.

Dane's eyes locked on mine. "Yours."

Slowly, I guided him inside me, both of us releasing a groan as he stretched my body around his. He held still for a long moment, letting me adjust to his size.

"Fuck, you feel so damn good," he said, lowering his forehead to rest against mine.

I nodded and wrapped my legs around his waist, silently urging him to move. When that didn't work, I rolled my hips experimentally, drawing a sharp hiss from between his clenched teeth.

Bracing himself on his forearms, he began to thrust in a slow, deep rhythm. My walls clenched around him, each drag of his cock sending shockwaves through my body.

"Look at me," he said, waiting until my eyes fluttered open before moving again. "You're mine. No one else gets to touch you like this. No one else gets to make you fall apart. You hear me?"

"Only you," I gasped, keeping my eyes locked on his.

He groaned and buried his face in my neck, his movements growing urgent. "Say it again," he growled, nipping at my earlobe.

"I'm yours," I said, clinging to his shoulders to anchor myself. "Only yours. Always."

Dane's hips snapped forward with more force. "That's right, baby. Mine." He slowed his thrusts, gazing down at me with a soft smile. "My woman. My Ol' Lady. My wife."

The words sent a shiver through me, and I reflexively tightened around him, drawing a low groan from his throat.

He shifted our position, rolling onto his back and pulling me on top of him without breaking our connection. I braced my hands on his broad chest, relishing the new angle as I began to ride him.

His hands gripped my hips, controlling my movements as I rose and fell on his thick length. "That's it, baby," he said. "Use me. Take what you need."

I leaned back, changing the angle and gasping at the increased friction against my clit. "So good," I babbled, rocking my hips faster.

Dane watched me through hooded eyes before sliding one hand between our bodies, coating his fingers in my wetness.

My breath caught when he reached around to cup my ass, kneading the flesh as he guided me into a faster rhythm.

"Gonna claim you here next," he said, circling my puckered entrance with one slick finger. "You'd like that, wouldn't you, having me stretch this tight little hole?"

I gasped at the unfamiliar sensation, my hips faltering in their rhythm. "I've never…"

"Shh, I know, baby." He pressed his lips to my collarbone. "We'll take it slow. I'll make it so good for you."

The promise in his voice sent a thrill through me. I'd never let anyone touch me there before, but the thought of Dane claiming every part of me was intoxicating.

"Yes," I breathed. "I want that. Want you to have all of me."

His finger continued to tease my rim as I rode him, each brush sending jolts of pleasure through my body. I gasped when he pushed his finger past the tight ring of muscle, tensing up at the unfamiliar sensation.

"Relax for me," he murmured.

I forced myself to take a deep breath, focusing on the taboo sensation of having him in two places at once. Gradually, the tension eased, and his finger slipped deeper.

"Oh, fuck—" The burn of the intrusion mixed with the pleasure coursing through me, and I came with a breathless cry, my body clenching rhythmically around him.

"That's it," he growled, working a second finger into my ass as I trembled through my orgasm. "Keep being good for me."

I whimpered at the fullness, continuing to rock desperately against him. "I can't…it's too much."

His free hand gripped my chin, guiding my eyes down to his. "Breathe for me, baby. You're doing so good. Just a little more."

He curled his fingers inside me, gently stretching me until the initial discomfort faded into pleasure so intense it bordered on pain. I ground down against his hand with a soft whine, spiraling toward another climax embarrassingly fast.

Dane sat up suddenly, wrapping an arm around my waist to hold me close as he thrust up into me, growling, "There we go. Come on my cock like a good girl,"

The change in position had him hitting even deeper, and my eyes rolled back in my head. I was reduced to breathless moans and whimpers. When he sucked my nipple into his mouth, I came apart with a scream. It was almost too much, but I never wanted it to end.

"Fuck, Piper," he panted, burying his face in my neck as his movements became erratic. "Where do you want it, baby?"

"Inside me," I gasped, squeezing his shoulders. "Want you to fill me up."

Dane pulled back to search my face. "You know what you're asking for?"

My teeth sank into my bottom lip, and I nodded. "Real."

His fingers dug into the soft flesh of my hips as he thrust upward with a guttural groan, flooding my body with his seed. I clung to him, shuddering through the aftershocks of my own release as he pulsed inside me.

We stayed like that for several long moments, our bodies still joined as we caught our breath. He peppered soft kisses along my neck and shoulder, his beard tickling my sensitive skin.

"You okay?" he murmured, gently easing his fingers from my body.

I gave him a thumbs up, feeling boneless and utterly sated. "Super duper."

He chuckled and carefully lifted me off his cock before laying me on the bed. "Don't move. I'll be right back."

Moments later, he returned with a warm washcloth and carefully wiped away the evidence of our lovemaking before tossing it in the hamper and climbing back into bed. He draped himself over my body like a blanket, nuzzling his cheek against my breasts.

"I love you," I whispered, cupping his jaw in my hand.

"Love you too, darlin'." Dane turned his head to kiss my palm, his fingers tracing lazy patterns on my hip. "More than you know."

I stroked his damp beard, savoring the feel of the coarse bristles beneath my fingers. The room was quiet except for the occasional rustle of sheets. "I have a question about being your Ol' Lady…"

Dane tilted his head back to meet my gaze, his brow furrowing slightly. "Having second thoughts already?"

"No, not at all," I assured him quickly. "I just... I have some questions."

He relaxed slightly, shifting to prop himself up on one elbow. "Shoot."

I bit my lip, trying to find the right words. "Will I have to give up my career and just blindly obey whatever you say while being stuck at home all day? Because that's not who I am."

His expression softened. "Baby, the last thing I want is for you to be something you're not. This is a partnership. I want you by my side, not behind me. So work if you want to work and call me on my shit when I'm being a dick. I can take it."

"Honestly, I don't think I want to go back to the bakery," I quietly admitted. "After everything that's happened... I'm not even sure I'm cut out to live in the city anymore."

Dane's arm tightened around me protectively. "You're one of the strongest women I know, darlin', and there's not a doubt in my mind you could live anywhere and make it work."

I nodded even as my heart sank. Because when it came down to it, I didn't feel very strong.

"But I wouldn't be the man you chose to spend the rest of your life with if I let you step foot back in that building." He paused, his forehead wrinkling as if he was debating his next words. "Truth is, I was hoping you and Avery might want to move to Lubbock."

Relief flooded through me at his words. "Really?"

"You've already given up a hell of a lot because of me, so I don't want you to feel pressured. If you're open to the idea, I reached out to Carnage," he continued. "He's into commercial real estate and bought a shopping center for his Ol' Lady's dance studio."

I nodded, not quite following.

"There's an empty space next to it," he said, his eyes lit with excitement. "Prime location, lots of foot traffic with people coming and going to classes. Could be the perfect spot for a bakery. Your bakery."

My heart raced at the possibility of owning my own place before reality quickly set in. Between medical bills from Avery's birth and just trying to keep my head above water as a single mom, I hadn't exactly been able to save up.

"Dane, that sounds amazing, but I don't have the capital for something like that," I admitted, my voice small. "And starting a business from scratch—"

"Hey," he interrupted, gently gripping my chin and forcing me to meet his gaze. "You carried our daughter for nine months and raised her alone for her first year. Now, it's my turn to take care of you both. This is part of being my Ol' Lady."

Tears pricked at my eyes as the full weight of his offer sank in, and I blinked rapidly to keep them at bay. "I don't know what to say."

"Say yes," Dane murmured, his lips brushing over my jaw. "Let me help make this happen for you."

I opened my mouth to argue further, but Dane silenced me with another kiss. "Stop overthinking it, Piper. You want this. Just say yes."

My own bakery. A fresh start in a new place. A future with the man I loved. A giddy laugh bubbled up from my chest, and I nodded.

"Okay, yes," I said, unable to keep the smile off my face. "Let's do it."

"That's my girl." He rolled so I was beneath him once more, trailing kisses down my throat. His beard scraped deliciously against my sensitive skin as he made his way down my body, and I shivered.

"Now, spread your legs for me, baby, so that I can celebrate our engagement with a proper meal," he growled before burying his face between my thighs.

TWENTY-SIX

PIPER

Ivy & Piper's Guide to Life Rule Number One:
Never let a man break up the band.

I folded one of Avery's sweaters and added it to the cardboard box on the floor of her bedroom, trying to ignore the tension knotting my shoulders. The movers would be arriving first thing in the morning, and I hadn't even made a dent in my bedroom or the kitchen.

When Dane proposed and asked us to move to Lubbock, a month had seemed like more than enough time to get everything squared away. It didn't help that Avery's new favorite pastime was going behind me and unpacking the boxes faster than I could pack them. Thankfully, Dane had taken her with him to run some last-minute errands this morning while Ivy and my mom helped me finish.

"You know, there's more than enough room in the moving truck," I said, glancing at Ivy as she loaded Avery's books into a box. "We could probably squeeze in your stuff, too. You're always saying you don't want to live in the city forever. Now's your chance to make it happen."

She shook her head, her long, icy blonde hair falling across her face. "We've been over this," she said, donning her therapist's voice. "As much as I would love to stowaway in your suitcase, I can't uproot my whole life and leave my patients high and dry."

"Don't think of it as uprooting. It would be more like... transplanting to better soil. Your own practice soil, perhaps." I forced a smile, but it felt brittle on my lips.

We'd lived within a half-hour of each other since junior high. Even if we didn't see each other often due to our work and life schedules, we were at least within easy driving distance.

Ivy's bright blue eyes met mine, filled with a mix of affection and exasperation. "You're completely ridiculous, you know that?"

"I'm persuasive," I countered, tossing a stuffed giraffe at her. She caught it deftly, a small smile tugging at her lips.

"You're going to be fine without me," she added, holding my gaze. "You've always been stronger than you think."

There was that word again.

Strong.

I swallowed hard, looking down at the half-packed box next to me. The weight of the last two years pressed down on my chest. "I'm scared," I admitted, my voice barely above a whisper. "Scared that the nightmares won't ever go away. Scared that I'm jumping into a marriage and a brand-new life without a safety net."

Ivy set down the book she was holding and moved to sit beside me on the floor. "How are the therapy sessions going?"

"They're..." I trailed off, deciding how to best describe them before releasing a shaky breath. "Intense. Dr. Carlson says I'm making progress, but some days, it doesn't feel like it. The nightmares are still there, vivid as ever. I wake up in a cold sweat, my heart racing, convinced it's happening all over again."

"Trauma affects everyone differently. Just because you're struggling doesn't mean your relationship is doomed to fail. The two aren't mutually exclusive." She reached over and squeezed my hand. "Be kind to yourself, and don't be afraid to lean on the people who love you when you need to. Like Dane."

Deep down, I knew she was right. But the thought of voicing my fears out loud and adding to his already full plate when he was grappling with his own demons felt wrong.

As if reading my mind, she asked, "Has he been sleeping any better?"

"No," I replied, my nose stinging with the threat of tears. "When he does, he tosses and turns, mumbling things I can't quite make out. More often than not, though I wake up to find him on the couch with Avery curled up against his chest. She's become his little security blanket."

I twisted my engagement ring around my finger, a nervous habit I'd developed over the past month. "He told me they found pictures of me inside Isaac's house. But I feel like there's more to it that he's not telling me. Like maybe he gave me a watered-down version because he didn't want to upset me further. Why else would he be acting the way he is?"

Ivy's lips pressed together, her eyes darting away from mine for a split second. That subtle tell was all the confirmation I needed. She knew more than she was letting on.

"What is it?" I demanded, my voice sharp. "If there's something else, I deserve to know."

She hesitated, seeming to weigh her next words carefully. "You're right. It was more than just some photos. He had hidden cameras all over your house. There were videos and images of you in private moments, completely unaware you were being watched."

Nausea rolled through me in sickening waves. How had he gained access to my house? He would have needed to know both the gate code and the passcode to disarm the house alarm. To override everything remotely, he would have needed my phone, which was even less feasible than him knowing the codes.

"That's...that's insane," I whispered, my voice trembling. "He couldn't have..."

Ivy bit her lip. "Supposedly, he had detailed floor plans for both your house and your mom's. I think he also had notes on how to bypass the security system."

I stared at her, a chill running down my spine despite the warm afternoon. "And how exactly do you know all this?"

She looked down at the hardwood floor before meeting my gaze again, clearly uncomfortable. "I overheard some of the guys from the club talking. I'm so sorry, Piper. I can't even imagine."

I felt disgusted, violated on a level I couldn't even comprehend. The thought of Isaac—or anyone, for that matter—having intimate access to my life without my knowledge or consent made my skin crawl.

And now those videos and images were out there, being discussed openly by the bikers at the club. Were they being passed around, the subject of crude jokes and lewd comments?

Bile burned the back of my throat. "Oh god, how many people have seen them?"

"As far as I know, only Dane and Carnage know the full extent of what was in Isaac's house," Ivy rushed to assure me.

"And they told you instead of me?" I asked, my voice rising with each word.

She grimaced before shaking her head. "GQ and Duke told me. But they haven't actually seen anything themselves."

I held up my hand, momentarily distracted from the horror swirling inside me. "Back up. GQ and Duke? What in the what?"

A faint blush colored Ivy's fair cheeks. "We've kept in touch since Motorcycles, Mobsters, and Mayhem. But it's nothing. I mean, they live in Lubbock, and I'm here…"

"All the more reason to come with us then," I said, mustering a wan smile before gesturing around the room. "I really think we could fit you into one of these boxes if we really tried."

She laughed softly, bumping her shoulder against mine. "Speaking of, do you think your mom's back yet from picking up more packing tape? It's been over an hour."

I pulled my phone from the back pocket of my jeans to check her location, expecting to see her still at the office supply store. But the blinking dot on the map showed she was indeed back at home.

"It says she's here, but where's our tape?"

Ivy quirked an eyebrow suggestively. "Maybe she was going to bring it but got…distracted by a certain silver fox who can't seem to stay away?"

I wrinkled my nose, even as a tiny part of me was glad for the momentary levity. "Please don't make me think about my mom's sex life. I'm still trying to come to terms with the fact that her high school boyfriend is the president of a biker club."

"Well, he seems to be finding any and every excuse to drop by lately, so it's not crazy to think he's looking to rekindle an old flame."

I shrugged. "She's been very tight-lipped about the whole thing, says she's too old for a relationship at this point."

"Too old?" Ivy scoffed. "Please. She's only fifty! That's like the new thirty these days. Think about it. You're past all the bullshit body insecurities women deal with in their twenties and thirties. You know exactly what you want in the bedroom, and you're not afraid to ask for it. Perfect age to get a little friends-with-benefits action going—"

I groaned. "Ew, I don't want to walk in on that! Could you maybe sneak over there and grab the tape? I'll love you forever."

"You already owe me forever for helping you clean up that awful diaper blowout when Avery was a newborn," Ivy retorted with a grin. "But fine. I'll brave the potential awkwardness for you. But when I get back, we are definitely brainstorming bachelorette party ideas."

Dane and I still hadn't decided whether we were going to do the big white dress affair or go down to the courthouse. We already skipped a few steps by having the baby before the love and marriage bit.

Still, I forced a smile, not wanting to dampen her enthusiasm. "Deal."

Minutes later, the front door chirped, signaling Ivy's return. "Please tell me they weren't doing it on the kitchen table," I called out jokingly as I turned.

But the playful smile quickly slid from my face. Derek stood in the doorway, one gloved hand fisted in Ivy's hair, the other pressing the gleaming blade of a knife to her throat.

"Derek? What...what are you doing?" I asked, trying to keep my voice steady despite the icy fear flooding my veins

His expression was unsettlingly calm, almost bored, as if this were a normal day at the bakery and not a hostage situation.

My heart seized in my chest, adrenaline flooding my system. I held up my hands in what I hoped was a non-threatening gesture, my mind racing. Dane wasn't due back until the afternoon, and with my phone in the kitchen, there was no way to alert him to the very real danger we were in.

"Where's my mom?" I asked, fighting to keep my voice steady. "Is she okay?"

His lips curled into a smile that sent a chill down my spine. There was no warmth, no hint of the easygoing guy I'd worked with for years. Just a cold, calculating emptiness.

"She's a bit...tied up at the moment." He chuckled at his own morbid joke.

Ivy's eyes met mine, and I could see her training as a psychiatrist kicking in as she tried to reason with him. "Derek, you don't want to do this. Whatever's going on, we can talk about it. Just put the knife down, and let's figure this out—"

He pressed the tip of the blade into her throat until a bead of crimson welled up in a thin line. "Shut up," he stated, with no inflection in his tone. "You sit there and play like you're some expert on the human mind, but I know what you really are."

Ivy winced as he dug the knife tip deeper into her flesh. "And what is that exactly?" she asked, her voice trembling slightly despite her attempt at calm.

Derek leaned in closer, his lips brushing the shell of her ear. "I've been watching you just as closely as I've watched Piper, but don't waste your time trying to psychoanalyze me, Doc. I needed to know what kind of influence you had over what belongs to me."

He turned his empty eyes to me, sending a fresh wave of terror coursing through my body. "Do you know what kind of person your best friend really is, Piper? She's a slut. While you were at the hospital with Avery after her fall, Ivy was back at her place, fucking two bikers in her hot tub. The model and the cowboy." His lips twisted in a cruel smirk. "You just couldn't decide, could you?"

She paled but said nothing, a muscle ticking in her jaw. My stomach churned with revulsion, and I wanted to throw up, knowing he'd given himself front-row access to our personal lives.

Instead, I focused on the knife at her throat, trying to figure out a way to get us both out of this alive. The lower half of my body was hidden behind a couple of stacked boxes. I pressed my hand to my chest in feigned shock before slowly sliding it down toward my abdomen, where my .38 Special was strapped in a hidden holster around my abdomen.

I wasn't confident I could draw and fire before he hurt Ivy. I had to keep him distracted long enough for me to retrieve it. "Derek, if you had feelings for me, why'd you wait until now to say something?"

His cold gray eyes bore into me. "I gave you every opportunity, Piper. Every chance to make the right decision. But you still chose a fucking biker over me."

"If you wanted a relationship, you could have just asked me out like a normal person. We could have—"

"Could have what?" he interjected. "Played house? Pretended like anything about our relationship would be normal?"

He laughed, a chilling sound devoid of humor. "You would have strung me along for a few dates until someone better came along. No, I had to take matters into my own hands. I even killed for you. And did I get so much as a thank you?"

Killed for me?

"You shot Timothy because he was hurting me. That's what you said," I whispered, my mind refusing to accept that the entire thing had been staged. That he'd put me in the situation so he could play hero...just like Dane said.

"Killing him at the bakery wasn't part of the original plan," he said with a casual shrug. "But he touched what belongs to me, forcing me to go off-script."

"Why?" I demanded, my voice shaking with barely contained rage and fear. "Why would you do this?"

His lips curled into a macabre imitation of a smile. "For you. I've spent years putting in the work. Leaving you your favorite chocolates on the days you were on your period. Complimenting you on how beautiful you looked, even when you were exhausted and had flour all over your face. But you never appreciated any of it."

I thought of the note left in my locker. "But how...how did you know when I was on my period?"

"I cloned your phone," he said as if it were the most obvious thing in the world. "It was a necessary evil. You were so private, and I needed to know your every thought, every picture you took, and every message you sent. Right now, I know you're in your fertile window."

His eyes flicked down to my stomach before meeting my gaze

again. "I was the second person to know you were pregnant with Avery. Not that I was happy about that piece of news."

"You...you've been watching me for years?" I finally managed, my voice sounding distant and hollow to my own ears.

"Of course I have," he replied, sounding almost affronted I would question him. "I thought you were making progress, but then you went to that book convention and fucked some idiot biker you just met."

He'd followed me to Houston.

I slipped my hand beneath my shirt, curling my fingers around the grip before inching it out of the holster. My eyes met Ivy's, silently communicating I would get us out of this, no matter what it took.

But Ivy, having dealt with her share of unstable psych patients, gave an almost imperceptible shake of her head, warning me not to make any sudden moves.

Swallowing hard, I forced myself to meet Derek's cold, empty gaze. "If you were the one watching me, then why frame Isaac?"

A slow, sinister grin spread across his face. "I needed you to call off your guard dogs. Get them to stop sniffing around while I put the rest of my plan in motion."

"Dane won't let you get away with this," I warned, keeping the gun hidden beneath my shirt. "He'll throw everything into hunting you down. The entire club will—"

"Oh, I'm counting on it," Derek interrupted, sounding amused. "Unlike your big dumb animal, though, I'm not an idiot. I never make a move unless it's airtight. And my insurance policies are firmly in place."

He adjusted his grip on the knife, and Ivy let out a pained gasp.

"Ghost took every piece of evidence out of Isaac's house. With all of it in his possession, it looks like he's got quite the obsession with you. His fingerprints are all over that note left in your locker, and I have video proof he was inside Isaac's house."

My blood ran cold as the pieces clicked into place with sickening clarity. Derek had orchestrated all of this, framing Dane for everything to get him out of the way.

"Once you found out what he was doing to Avery, you confronted him and he snapped—"

"Avery?" I cut him off, raw panic seizing my chest. "What did you do to my daughter?"

Surprise flickered across his face. "Your fiancé really has been keeping secrets, hasn't he? I have to say, he did not react well to the video. Now that I think about it, none of them did. Strange to see tough bikers break down like scared little boys."

"What did you do?" I repeated, my voice shaking with barely contained fury even as tears blurred my vision. My mind raced with scenarios, each one more sickening than the last.

"Nothing much," Derek said with a careless shrug. "Before you invited a biker to live with you and went all Fort Knox with your security system, I used to sneak into her room for a little playtime."

"What did you do to my baby?" I demanded again, freeing the gun from beneath my shirt.

His lips curled into a cruel smile. "I held a pillow over her face just to watch her struggle for air. It's funny how that fight to live is ingrained in us from such a young age. She fought so hard, tiny fists flailing, little legs kicking. All for nothing, of course. She never stood a chance against someone like me."

White-hot rage coursed through my veins, momentarily eclipsing the icy terror. In one fluid motion, I raised the gun and aimed it at his head, my hands surprisingly steady.

"You don't have it in you," he taunted, positioning Ivy in front of him like a shield. The blade pressed harder against her throat until a thin rivulet of blood trickled down her pale skin.

My finger tightened on the trigger as I thought of Avery in this very room, fighting to breathe while I slept unaware down the hall.

I met Ivy's terrified gaze. Mindful of the knife against her throat, she gave me a subtle nod, encouraging me to take the shot. But I couldn't. Not without hitting her.

"Sweet, innocent Piper. Always needing to be protected and coddled. You've never had to get your hands dirty. Not like me." Derek pushed Ivy's head forward and ran the blade across her throat.

Time seemed to slow to a crawl. Her blue eyes went wide with confused shock, and she brought her hands up over the wound before dropping to her knees with a gurgled cry.

I could hear myself screaming as I pulled the trigger, the gunshot reverberating off the bedroom walls. He jerked back as the bullet tore through his shoulder.

I'd aimed for his heart but missed by mere inches.

He lunged at me as I fired again, the bullet lodging in the doorframe where he'd been standing. We crashed to the floor in a tangle of limbs, both of us wrestling for control of the gun.

"Finally decided to grow a fucking backbone!" he snarled against my ear, trying to pin my arms beneath his legs. "Sadly, it won't do you any good now."

His face hovered inches from mine, his eyes wild and crazed, spittle flying from his curled lips. "Dane had to kill you and Ivy to keep you from going to the police. It's a fucking shame, but no one's really surprised that a biker would commit such an act of violence. And then to go after your mother...tragic. Don't worry. I'll step up to adopt Avery, ensuring she's as safe as I want her to be."

"You're not getting anywhere near my daughter," I gritted out, fighting to maintain control of the gun with every ounce of strength I possessed.

"Sweetheart, with the connections my family has, I could have custody of the brat today if I wanted it."

I couldn't get the gun up, but that didn't stop me from firing two rounds into his thigh and another into his stomach. He roared in pain and anger before knocking the gun from my hands and sending it skittering across the hardwood. Not that it mattered. It was empty.

Knowing what would happen to Avery if I failed kicked my maternal instincts into overdrive. I fought him like a feral animal— biting, kicking, clawing at any part of him I could reach. Ivy had grabbed one of Avery's blankets and was holding it to her throat while dragging herself over to where her phone lay on the dresser.

Determined to keep Derek distracted long enough for her to call for help, I arched up and sank my teeth into the area between his neck and shoulder.

His hand closed around my throat, squeezing mercilessly, and cutting off my air supply. Black spots danced before my eyes, but I bit down harder until the sharp, coppery tang of blood flooded my mouth.

"You crazy bitch!" Derek hissed, punching my side with his free hand. "What happens when you get tired, huh? You can't fucking do this all day."

I could feel his blood seeping through my clothes. Four of my five bullets had struck his body. I just had to hold on long enough for him to die from blood loss.

My lungs burned for oxygen, and my vision dimmed at the edges, but before I could succumb to the encroaching darkness, Derek was suddenly and forcefully yanked off my body. I sucked in a ragged breath before rolling onto my side, coughing and spitting blood.

"She's got me, you piece of shit motherfucker!"

I blinked hard, my vision clearing enough to see Dane had Derek pinned against the wall by his throat. His feet kicked wildly from where they dangled above the floor as he clawed at Dane's hands, his face turning a mottled purple as he fought for air. But Dane's grip was relentless, fueled by a blind, all-consuming rage I'd never witnessed before.

There was an audible crunch, and then Derek's body went limp, his head lolling at an unnatural angle as he crumpled to the floor in a lifeless heap.

Head still spinning from lack of oxygen, I pushed myself across the blood-slicked hardwood, trying to find Ivy. The acrid stench of gunpowder and blood mingled in the air, making my stomach churn.

Dane reached me in an instant, his face a mask of rage smoothed into concern as he caught sight of my battered form. He grabbed my shoulders, keeping me grounded and viscerally present despite the chaos.

"Don't move, darlin'," he instructed urgently, the timbre of his voice revealing his own barely constrained panic.

"I need to get to Ivy," I managed through clenched teeth, my voice hoarse from screaming and the stranglehold Derek had had on me. Sharp, blinding pain lanced through my torso when I attempted to push myself up, knocking the air from my lungs and forcing me back down.

"Piper, need you to look at me," he insisted, his hands gentle yet unyielding as they held me down. "Carnage is getting Ivy to a hospital—"

"My mom," I said with a strained groan. "You have to check on my mom."

Dane's brow furrowed as he inspected my side. "Nails has your mom. She's okay, but he's taking her to a hospital just to be sure, okay? Fuck," he muttered, his fingers probing gently under my shirt where warm wetness clung to my skin. "I can't tell how deep these are."

He brushed over the spot Derek had struck me with his fist, causing my vision to go black for a second.

"Stop," I whimpered, batting his hand away. "It's his blood. Not mine. The bastard just hit me. We need to check on Ivy and my mom."

Had I said that already? I couldn't remember.

His expression shifted, the grim lines deepening. "Baby, you've been stabbed."

"No," I argued, hissing out a breath when he lifted me in his arms. "Don't leave Ivy here with him. I need—" Whatever I intended to say next faded into a choked gasp as a wave of dizziness washed over me, and my vision tunneled into darkness.

TWENTY-SEVEN

PIPER

Ivy & Piper's Guide to Life Rule Number Eighteen:
Never make major life decisions when ovulating.

I jerked awake with a sharp, shuddering breath, my body twisting before a bolt of blinding pain ripped through my ribs, stealing the breath from my lungs.

"Easy, baby. Try not to move too much." Dane grasped my shoulders before easing me back against the bed. He adjusted the pillow behind my head, and I clenched my teeth, biting back a slew of curse words.

"Where…" I blinked against the harsh fluorescent lights, the sharp, antiseptic smell synonymous with hospitals invading my nostrils. I struggled to orient myself, my heart rate spiking on the monitor beside the bed. "Any updates on Ivy?" I croaked, my voice rough and gravelly.

Dane smoothed his hand over my blood-crusted hair, his touch grounding me. "She's still in surgery, but as soon as I hear anything else, I'll let you know. I promise."

It was the same answer he'd given me the last few times I'd surfaced from the murky depths of oblivion.

I nodded, letting my eyes drift shut again. My mind felt like it was shrouded in a thick fog, thoughts slipping away before I could grasp them, blurring together until I couldn't distinguish my dreams from reality. I had the short-term memory of a goldfish. The IV drip of pain meds wasn't helping matters.

"And my mom?" I forced my eyes open again, needing reassurance she was okay, too. Dane's expression softened with a mix of exhaustion and understanding.

"She's got a concussion, but last I heard, they're going to discharge her later today."

Some of the tension bled out of my shoulders at his words. I shifted restlessly and immediately regretted it when pain lanced through my side. "Seriously, what's taking so long? I want to get out of here."

My ultrasound and X-rays had come back clear, showing no internal bleeding or broken ribs. It seemed Derek's hand had been slick with blood when he'd tried to stab me, causing his grip to slide down the handle.

I was covered in bruises, and a couple of slashes across my ribs required a handful of stitches to close, but it could have been so much worse.

"We can't leave until they give us the results of your rabies test."

"Rabies test?" My brows knitted together in confusion before I realized he was joking.

Knowing there was a chance I might have ingested some of Derek's blood and wanting to err on the side of caution, the on-call doctor, Dr. Wallace, decided to run a full panel.

None of which involved rabies.

"You're such a dick," I said, my chuckle morphing into a hiss as the vibrations reverberated into the wound at my side. The pain was blinding. I took several deep breaths, squeezing my eyes shut until it let up.

When I opened my eyes again, I found Dane studying me with a look of concern. He'd taken up residence in the uncomfortable-looking chair beside my bed, his large frame dwarfing the small space.

Mindful of my IV line, I reached over and took his hand in mine, running my thumb over his bruised and bloodied knuckles. His skin was warm against mine, the calluses rough yet familiar. Grounding.

"What happened?" I asked quietly, taking advantage of the fact that we were alone, with no nurses hovering nearby. "How did you know to come back when you did?"

It was the question I'd been asking myself for hours, the one thing I couldn't wrap my head around.

His expression darkened, and he hesitated before admitting, "It was Avery."

"Avery," I echoed with a slight headshake. "I don't understand."

He scrubbed a hand over his face, looking as if he'd aged a decade in the span of a few hours. "I stopped by the bakery on the way to get her a mid-morning snack. She was getting hangry...like her mama does."

A ghost of a smile touched his lips before fading. "She was covered in frosting by the time she finished her cinnamon roll, so I took her to the bathroom to get her cleaned up. And she just... she started crying and clinging to me, burying her face against my neck."

His nostrils flared, and I squeezed his hand tighter in silent support as he struggled to get the words out.

"I turned around, expecting to see someone behind us, but the hallway was empty. And then I realized...she was pointing to a picture on the wall. A picture of Derek."

Icy dread slithered down my spine, my stomach turning at the thought of what Avery had endured, what she'd been too young to verbalize.

Dane's voice was strained as he continued. "She just kept saying, 'owie,' and my gut told me to get home to you. I didn't even think. I knew Carnage was in town, so I reached out and told him to meet me at the house. No questions asked."

My stomach roiled, knowing the bloodbath we'd left behind. "Avery didn't—she didn't see anything, did she?"

He shook his head. "Absolutely not. Carnage's Ol' Lady, Harper, took her back to their hotel room."

"Nothing screams romantic, kid-free weekend quite like babysitting a one-year-old," I said, trying to inject some levity into the heavy moment.

His lips curved into a rueful half-smirk. "Probably not, but when I checked in a little while ago, Avery was happily trying on Harper's high heels and enjoying some room service chicken nuggets, so I think she's got plenty to keep her entertained."

Leave it to our daughter to find the silver lining in the midst of tragedy.

Dane glanced down at our joined hands, his throat working in a hard swallow. "I lied to you, Piper."

I froze, steeling myself for the bomb he was about to drop. "What do you mean?"

"Lied is probably too strong a word," he amended, pressing his fingers into his eyes. "But I omitted certain details about what we found in Isaac's house."

Nausea swelled like a tidal wave, the acrid taste of bile scorching my tongue. "I know about the photos and videos. Not the specifics, but enough to know I never want to see them."

My chin quivered, but I forced myself to continue, needing to get everything out in the open. "I also know about what he did to Avery. The sleepless nights and your need to rock her to sleep make a lot more sense now. What doesn't make sense is why you kept it from me. She's my baby too. I have a right to know if someone's hurt her."

Dane's jaw clenched, his eyes filled with anguish as he met my gaze. "I was trying to protect you. After everything you'd been through, I didn't want to add to your trauma. I thought I could shoulder it alone and keep you both safe without burdening you with the knowledge."

He tilted his head back, blinking quickly to keep from crying. "Seeing that video…watching what he did to our baby? Christ, Piper. I don't know if I'll ever be able to unsee it. I didn't want you to have to carry that too."

Tears welled in my eyes as I imagined what he must have witnessed. The thought of anyone hurting Avery made me feel physically ill.

I cupped his jaw in my hand, feeling the tension thrumming through his body. "You said it yourself. This is a partnership. If we're going to make this work, we need to face these things together, no matter how awful they are."

He nodded, turning to press a kiss to my palm. "You're right, darlin'. No more secrets between us."

"No more secrets," I agreed, huffing out a pained breath as I shifted to get more comfortable. "Though I have to admit, knowing what that monster did makes me wish you'd made him suffer more before killing him."

A dark gleam flashed in Dane's eyes. "Believe me, baby, if I'd known the full extent of what he'd done, then I would have put a bullet in his head the first time I laid eyes on him. But, in the interest of transparency and no more secrets, you should know I didn't kill him. You did."

I jerked my head back, the movement pulling at my bruised and aching ribs. "What do you mean I killed him? I heard the...the snap when you did the thing."

My words were coming out all wrong, but the idea that it had been me, not Dane, who ended Derek's miserable existence was crazy.

He leaned in until his lips brushed against my ear, his voice little more than a low growl. "You must have jaws of steel, darlin' because you bit down hard enough to sever an artery or vein. Fucker was barely conscious when I pulled him off you and dead before I could finish. I snapped his neck anyway so I could at least feel like I contributed."

"Am I going to have to go in for questioning?" I asked with a sinking feeling in the pit of my stomach.

He cocked his head to the side. "You really think I'd allow that to happen, baby? The club's taking care of everything. That's all you need to know."

I knew better than to press for details. There were some aspects of club business I was better off not knowing about. Still, I couldn't help but wonder how they planned to explain away the bloodbath in Avery's bedroom to the authorities.

As if reading my thoughts, Dane added, "Carnage called in some favors. As far as the police are concerned, Derek broke in and attacked you. You acted in self-defense. Case closed."

I nodded, grateful for the simplicity of the cover story. It wasn't far from the truth, after all.

"And the house?" I asked, dreading the answer.

"Nails has a clean-up crew there now. I also hired a company to finish packing up the house before the movers come tomorrow...which is what I wanted to do in the first place, but someone stubbornly insisted she could handle it."

I shrugged, wincing as the movement pulled at my stitches. "In my defense, I didn't know I was going to end up in a knife fight with my former boss."

"That's not fucking funny, Piper," Dane grumbled, trying to resist the smile tugging at the corner of his mouth.

"I mean, it's better than the alternative, which involved panic attacks and uncontrollable sobbing," I pointed out just as Dr. Wallace entered the room.

"Are you getting any relief?"

"Honestly, I still feel like I got hit by a truck," I replied.

She nodded sympathetically as she logged into the computer on the wall. "I'm not surprised, given what you've been through. We collected a baseline serum, and the nurse will go over long-term follow-up care. To be on the safe side, we'll start you on a post-exposure prophylaxis, which is safe to take while pregnant."

"Pregnant?" I spluttered, my heart rate spiking on the monitor.

"Based on your hCG levels, I'd estimate you're about six to seven weeks along."

I blinked in shock, my mind reeling. "But... I took a test two weeks ago when I missed my period. Several of them, in fact. They were all negative."

"Could be your hCG levels weren't high enough to register," she explained. "I'd recommend making an appointment with your OB as soon as possible to confirm and start prenatal care. I'll step out and give you two a moment, but the nurse will be in shortly to go over follow-up care and get you discharged."

Pregnant?

"Hey, hey," Dane said when my eyes welled up with tears. "Piper, talk to me. What are you feeling?"

"I'm feeling pregnant, Dane. That's how I'm feeling. How did this happen?"

He eased onto the narrow hospital bed facing me. "Well, I'm pretty sure I know how it happened," he said with a soft chuckle, using his thumbs to wipe away the tears streaming down my cheeks.

I let out a watery laugh before my ribs protested. "You know what I mean, smartass. We were careful... Well, except for the night we got engaged. But we were careful all the other times..." I trailed off, dissolving into another round of tears.

Dane cradled my belly in his palms, his eyes misting with tears as he gazed at me in awe. "We made another baby, Mama," he whispered, pressing his lips to my still-flat stomach.

"And I'm happy," I choked out between sobs. "I am. But I'm also terrified. Avery's only one, and we're still trying to find our footing..."

"Darlin', listen to me," he said, his voice thick with emotion. "I know you're scared. Hell, I'm scared too. But you are the strongest person I know. We've been through hell and back, and we're still standing. This baby? This is a gift. A new beginning for our family."

"But I wanted to get moved and settled before... this." I waved vaguely in the general direction of my stomach, still sniffling.

He lowered his head against mine. "I know it feels like the timing's all wrong, and it's not what we planned. But we'll figure it out together, okay? You're not alone this time."

I gave him a shaky nod before brushing my lips against his. "I love you."

Dane's mouth curved into a tender smile against mine. "I love you, too, baby."

His hand drifted to my stomach again, his touch reverent as he caressed the spot where our baby was growing. "I'm gonna be here for every part of it this time. Every check-up, every milestone—"

"Every craving, every mood swing, waking up every hour to pee," I finished helpfully before covering his hand with mine. "You do realize you're basically signing up for nine months of hell, right? I was a nightmare when I was pregnant with Avery."

He chuckled, the rumble vibrating through his chest. "Baby, I can handle anything you throw at me."

I arched an eyebrow. "Even if I wake you up at three a.m. demanding ice cream and french fries?"

"I'll have the food delivery app already pulled up on my phone."

"What if I cry because my shoes don't fit?"

He grinned. "Then I'll buy you new ones in every size."

"Uh-huh," I said, unconvinced. "What about when I'm the size of a house and feeling about as sexy as a beached whale?"

Dane's eyes darkened with desire as he leaned in close, his breath fanning hot against my ear. "I'll strip you down and spread you out on our bed, worshiping every fucking inch of your body until there's not a goddamn doubt in your head that you're the sexiest woman on the planet."

I bit back a moan, suddenly very aware of how thin the hospital gown was. "Jesus, Dane. You tell me this when I'm stuck in a hospital bed?"

His lips curved into a wicked grin. "Just giving you something to look forward to, darlin'."

I shook my head, trying to ignore the way my body responded to his words. "You say that now, but wait until I'm waddling around looking like I swallowed a beach ball, and my sciatic nerve is being compressed—"

Dane captured my lips with his, silencing my objections. I tilted my head to deepen the kiss while stroking his beard with my fingertips.

"You'll be gorgeous," he murmured, leaning down to press his lips to my stomach. "Carrying my baby... there's nothing sexier."

I rolled my eyes but couldn't help smiling as I said, "You're ridiculous, you know that? You and your super sperm."

"What can I say, baby? I'm good at marking what's mine," Dane replied with a cocky grin, his brown eyes twinkling with mischief. "We'll probably have to get a bigger house for all the babies I'm gonna give you."

"Nice try, Romeo," I said, shaking my head. "But I'm getting on birth control as soon as this one is born. Two kids under the age of two is more than enough for now."

My smile faded when I glanced up to find Duke standing in the doorway, looking as if he'd aged a hundred years in the span of a few hours. His red-rimmed eyes and vacant expression made my stomach drop.

"Did she?" I couldn't bring myself to finish the sentence. I tried to move, but my body protested vehemently, pain flaring through every nerve. I stopped, taking in shallow breaths as I tried to mitigate both the physical and emotional agony.

Duke quickly shook his head before dropping onto the empty chair beside the bed, the skin around his eyes bunching. "She made it through surgery. The cut severed her jugular but missed her carotid by, like, a millimeter or something."

He mashed his lips together and stared down at his lap, trying to compose himself before continuing. "The surgeon said that had Carnage not known to pinch off the vein and put pressure on her collarbone, she wouldn't have made it."

"Have you seen her yet?" I asked as Dane reached over to squeeze Duke's shoulder.

"No," he replied, pinching the bridge of his nose. "She was still in recovery. They did say she lost a lot of blood, so we won't know if she has any neurological damage until she's conscious."

She was alive but not out of the woods yet. Relief battled with renewed fear at the thought of Derek stealing any part of Ivy's brilliant mind. It was unfathomable to imagine a world where my friend woke up with no memory of the people who loved her.

Tears pricked my eyes and blurred my vision. "Does GQ know?"

He ran a hand through his disheveled hair before exhaling a soft, humorless laugh. "Oh, yeah. He's outside chain-smoking and wearing a path in the parking lot concrete. I think he'll relax once we can see her." A muscle in his jaw ticked, and his eyes went distant. "That is *if* we get to see her. As you can imagine, her parents aren't exactly thrilled about us wanting to check on their daughter."

I grimaced, imagining how well that was going over. Brian and Cheryl were notoriously conservative and had never approved of her more free-spirited lifestyle. Finding out she was involved with not one but two tattooed bikers was likely sending them into conniptions.

"I'll talk to them," I said, trying to get up only to sag back against the pillows with a groan. "Just give me a minute. I can smooth things over and put in a good word for you guys."

Dane's eyes narrowed. "The hell you will. You're gonna sit your happy ass right here and wait to be discharged."

I rolled my eyes at his overprotective tone but didn't argue. Truth be told, I wasn't sure I could make it more than a few steps without collapsing.

I rolled my eyes at his overprotectiveness but didn't argue. My body felt like one giant bruise, and the thought of getting up made me want to curl into a ball and sleep for a week.

"Fine," I conceded with a sigh. "But I'm texting her mom as soon as I get my phone back. Cheryl may not approve of Ivy's life choices, but she knows how close we are. She'll listen to me."

Duke nodded, his eyes filled with gratitude. "Thanks, darlin'. I appreciate that. I'm gonna check on GQ and get back up there."

He stood and headed for the door, pausing to look back at us. "I'll let you know if there are any updates."

As soon as Duke was out of earshot, Dane turned to me with a quizzical expression. "All right, you wanna tell me what the hell's going on with those three?"

I bit my lip, debating how much to share. "Honestly? I'm not entirely sure. Ivy was pretty vague on the details. All I know is they hooked up at some point after the Motorcycles, Mobsters, and Mayhem event."

Dane ran his tongue over his teeth with a low chuckle. "Hooked up? Baby, a hookup doesn't look like that. You don't camp out in a hospital for a hookup. You don't fall apart over a hookup."

When he put it that way, I had to admit, it felt like there were some real feelings involved.

"Do you spend two years searching the country for a hookup?" I teased, earning another grin from him.

"You do not," he said, his hand coming to rest on my thigh. "How are you doing? I know the stuff with Ivy is heavy."

I mashed my lips together with a small nod, tears immediately welling in my eyes again. "I feel guilty for being happy about this baby when everything else is such a mess."

Dane's expression softened as he cupped my face in his hands. "Hey, listen to me. You have nothing to feel guilty about. This baby is a blessing, and being happy about it doesn't take away from how much you care about Ivy or anyone else."

"You're right. It's just...everything feels so out of control right now. We're supposed to be moving tomorrow, and instead, I'm in a hospital bed while my best friend is fighting for her life down the hall."

He gathered me carefully into his arms, mindful of my injuries. "And we'll get through it, just like we've gotten through everything else," he promised, brushing the tears from my lashes. "One minute at a time. Isn't that what Ivy's always telling you?"

"Yeah," I whispered, letting myself relax against his chest. "I just wish she was here to celebrate with us. We've shared every major milestone in our lives. It feels wrong not having her here for this one."

"I know it's hard right now," Dane murmured, pressing a kiss to my forehead. "But she's gonna pull through this, and before you know it, she'll be planning some over-the-top baby shower that'll make you want to throttle her."

"Knowing her, she'll insist on a biker-themed shower, and I'll have to make cookies that say 'Future Prospect' or something equally ridiculous," I said with a smile.

Dane chuckled. "I wouldn't put it past her."

We slipped into a comfortable silence, his hand resting protectively over my stomach. The steady beep of the heart monitor and the occasional squeak of shoes in the hallway were the only sounds.

"Marry me," I whispered, craning my neck to look up at him.

He gave me a confused look, his dark brows scrunching together. "Darlin', we're already engaged. Did they give you the good drugs? Should I call the nurse?" He glanced at my IV drip with mock suspicion.

I exhaled a laugh, wincing at the resulting twinge of pain. "No, I mean, marry me now. I don't want to wait."

"What brought this on?"

I took a slow, deep breath, trying to put my thoughts into words.

"Let's just say my brush with death put things in perspective for me," I said. "I don't want to wait or plan some big, elaborate ceremony. I want you, me, our babies—oh, and a justice of the peace, obviously. I'm ready to start the next chapter of our lives."

A slow smile spread across Dane's face, his eyes crinkling at the corners. "You sure about this, darlin'? You're not gonna regret skipping out on the whole white dress affair?"

I met his gaze steadily. "I've never been more sure of anything in my life. I don't need a fancy dress or some overpriced venue. I need you. We've already done everything backward anyway—baby, then love, then marriage. Might as well keep the trend going, right?"

Dane's smile widened, his dimples deepening. "Well then, I guess we're getting hitched, Mama."

Happy tears spilled down my cheeks as I leaned up to kiss him, ignoring the protests of my battered body. He cupped my face in his hands and moved his lips against mine like I was the most precious thing in his world.

When we broke apart, he rested his forehead against mine. "I can't wait to make you Mrs. Riggs."

I grinned up at him like some love-struck idiot. "Piper Riggs. It has a nice ring to it."

"Hell, I'd marry you right here in this hospital bed if that's what you wanted."

"Hard pass on that one," I replied, wrinkling my nose. The weird, medicinal stench was not one I wanted to associate with my wedding day. "I want to be wearing something other than a hospital gown when we tie the knot."

Dane's eyes darkened as he leaned in close, his breath hot against my ear. "Doesn't matter what you wear, baby. It's all coming off again as soon as we say I do."

My face heated at his words. "Such a sweet talker."

"Must be doing something right. Knocked you up twice now, didn't I?" he asked with a challenging smirk.

"No, I let you knock me up because of your irresistible charm and rugged good looks. The dirty talk was just a bonus."

Dane laughed, the deep rumble vibrating through his chest. "Oh, I see how it is. You only want me for my body."

I brushed my lips against his and murmured, "That, and I'm really into the whole protective daddy vibe thing you've got going on."

He raised an eyebrow, his smirk widening. "Didn't realize your praise kink was really a daddy kink in disguise, darlin'. You should have said something sooner."

Maybe it was the pregnancy hormones. But the thought of calling him Daddy in a completely different context sent a shiver of desire down my spine. Feeling bratty, I murmured, "Sorry, Daddy. I'll be sure to remind you next time."

Dane's eyes darkened to a molten amber as he leaned in closer, his lips brushing the shell of my ear. "Keep calling me that, baby girl, and you'll be pregnant again before this one's even born."

I licked my suddenly dry lips, my heart rate picking up speed on the monitor. "Is that a promise or a threat...Daddy?"

He chuckled. "Both, darlin'. Definitely both."

Despite my injuries, his words sent a fresh wave of heat flooding through my core. I shifted restlessly against the hospital mattress, trying to ease the ache building between my thighs. "At the rate we're going, we'll have our own little army."

"You say that like it's a bad thing," he murmured, nuzzling into the crook of my neck. "Personally, I'm looking forward to seeing you all round and glowing with my baby in your belly."

"I'd like to see the terms and conditions around middle-of-the-night diaper changes and feedings before I sign anything," I said, fighting back a yawn.

He chuckled, his hand lazily stroking my stomach. "Oh, I plan on being right there with you for every single one, darlin'. No way I'm missing out on a minute of it this time."

"I'm holding you to that." I couldn't help the soft smile that tugged at my lips as I snuggled into his side as much as my aching body would allow. The adrenaline from earlier was wearing off, leaving exhaustion in its wake.

"I think I've had enough excitement to last me several lifetimes," I murmured, my eyelids growing heavier by the second. "I'm ready for some boring married life with kids now. The most drama I want is squabbling over whose turn it is to get the kids to bed."

Dane pressed a tender kiss to my temple. "I could get on board with that. We can argue over preschools and whether to sign Avery up for ballet or soccer. It'll be a blast."

I hummed in agreement, my eyes already fluttering shut. "Love you," I mumbled, the words slightly slurred.

"Love you too, darlin'," he whispered back, smoothing my hair away from my face. "Get some rest. I'll be here when you wake up."

For the first time in what felt like forever, a sense of peace washed over me. We'd made it through the nightmare. Not completely unscathed, but alive. Together.

A family.

The road ahead wouldn't be easy. Ivy still had a long recovery in front of her, physically and emotionally. And god only knew what fresh hell this pregnancy would bring. But for now, in this moment, I let myself believe that the worst was behind us.

That maybe, just maybe, Dane and I had suffered enough to earn our happily ever after.

I'd spent most of my life waiting for the other shoe to drop. Preparing for the worst and hoping for the best. But as sleep pulled me under, a new, unfamiliar feeling took root in my chest.

Hope.

EPILOGUE

GHOST

Ivy & Piper's Guide to Life Rule Number Twenty-Six:
Whatever you're going through, Celine and Taylor have a song
for it.

The rumble of my bike seemed magnified as I pulled into the parking lot. It was just after four in the morning, and every storefront in the shopping center was dark, with the exception of one.

I parked my bike next to my Piper's SUV and killed the engine, the sudden silence broken only by the jingle of my keys as I swung my leg over the seat.

Today was *Swoonworthy Pâtisserie's* grand opening. While I still wasn't entirely sure what the difference was between a bakery and a pâtisserie, I'd seen how hard she'd worked the past six months to bring her vision to life, and I'd be damned if I wasn't going to support my wife and take some of the stress off her plate.

Even if it meant stumbling my way through baking.

I scanned my fingerprint when I reached the door, waiting for the soft beep and click of the lock disengaging before entering. After the shit that went down in Dallas, Carnage and I installed top-of-the-line security systems on every building in the shopping center.

The scent of butter and sugar hit me as soon as I stepped inside. Well, that and Celine Dion's powerhouse vocals blasting through the mounted speakers on the ceiling.

Piper was so focused on the dough beneath her hands that she didn't hear me come in. I leaned against the doorframe, content to watch her in her element for a moment.

Her long brown hair was piled into a messy bun atop her head, wisps escaping to frame her face. She swayed to the music as she kneaded, the swell of her pregnant belly straining against the flour-dusted apron.

Finally sensing she wasn't alone, Piper lifted her head and promptly let out a startled yelp before clutching her chest. "What the fuck, Dane? You know I hate it when you do that."

"Sorry, darlin'," I said with a chuckle, crossing the room to pull her into my arms. "Didn't mean to sneak up on you."

She smacked my chest playfully. "You're such a creeper."

"Hey, you created this monster, sweetheart," I said, lowering my head to trail kisses over her throat before sliding a hand down to cup her belly. "How's Oliver this morning?"

"Pretty chill, actually," Piper said, placing her hand over mine. "Which is a blessing, considering how hectic today is going to be."

I brushed my lips against hers in a quick peck before crossing the room to grab one of the hot pink aprons off the wall. "That's why I'm here, boss lady. Put me to work."

Her eyes lit up. "Really? You want to help?"

I stripped off my kutte and rolled up the sleeves on my black henley before donning the apron. "Why the hell else would I show up here at the ass crack of dawn, darlin'?"

She let her gaze drift over my body before raising an eyebrow suggestively. "I can think of another reason."

"Not when we've got to make..." I scanned the list hanging above the long, stainless steel counter before switching to a heavy French accent. "Pain au Chocolat, éclairs, canelés—oh, cinnamon rolls. I actually know that one."

Piper grimaced as I butchered the pronunciation of every French dessert on her menu before shaking her head. "That was... something. Let's get started on the cinnamon rolls and go from there."

"Funny story," I said as I washed up. "I had a one-night stand with this pastry chef who promised to teach me how to make the best cinnamon rolls of my life...supposedly. I was worried she was gonna try to flake out on me, so I went ahead and knocked her up so we had a reason to run into each other again."

Piper laughed, her eyes twinkling mischievously. "So crazy. I actually had a one-night stand with this biker who promised me breakfast after sex and then bailed on me before I woke up the next morning. Coincidentally, he also knocked me up."

Chuckling, I leaned in close, the kitchen's warmth enveloping us both. "Sounds like it was a really special night. Guy must have known what he was doing if you're still thinking about him all these years later."

"Keep it up, and you'll find yourself on frosting duty for the entire day," she said, rolling her eyes.

"If you need me to frost something, sugar, all you have to do is ask," I teased, catching her around the waist and pulling her back against my chest. "I can give you as much frosting as you want, as many times as you want."

"Really? As many times as I want?" She craned her neck, peering up at me with an arched brow.

"Well, within reason," I conceded. "I'm a man, not a machine."

Piper wriggled out of my grip to cover the dough. "Maybe try proving yourself with these cinnamon rolls first before promoting yourself to Head Frosting Technician."

While she dusted flour across our work surface, I pulled a large tray of dough from the roll-in proofer. After demonstrating how to roll the dough into a large rectangle, she turned to me with the rolling pin and a smirk I knew all too well. "Make yourself useful."

Accepting the challenge, I dusted the rolling pin with flour, my hands forcefully moving over the heavy dough."

"Here," Piper said, stepping in to guide my hands. "Front to back and left to right to start. You wanna start with lighter pressure at first. Think of it like revving up slowly."

Her analogy drew a low chuckle from me. "Baby, if this were a bike, we'd have crashed already."

She leaned over to correct my technique, her curvy body pressing against mine, making it hard to concentrate on baking. There was something incredibly erotic about watching her hands move skillfully, shaping and molding the dough as if it were the most precious thing in the world.

"Start in the center and press a little harder as you roll out diagonally toward the corners. Just make sure you work from the center out every time."

We worked side by side, with her watching me with those bright green eyes that could either cool me down or set me on fire. Today, they did a bit of both.

"That's not too bad," she said after a moment, her shoulders relaxing as she observed my work. "But let's see how you handle the filling."

"Everyone knows the filling is crucial," I played along, spreading the softened butter over the dough as evenly as I could manage. Piper mixed the brown sugar and cinnamon together, handing it over so I could sprinkle it across the buttered surface. The rich, sweet scent filled the air around us, mixing with the light trace of her candy apple body wash.

"Spread it all over. You wanna coat every inch," she instructed, her hand briefly covering mine as she guided it. Her touch sent an inexplicable pulse through me, brief but potent in its ability to draw my full attention to her.

I wasn't sure baking was supposed to leave me with a hard-on, yet everything she said felt as if it was laced with innuendo. Her subtle touches weren't helping either.

"Okay, now we need to roll this into a tight log," she explained, stepping back so I could get my hands on the dough. Her voice dipped an octave lower. "Make it tighter, Dane. We want them nice and tight."

I couldn't help myself. "Are you sure you're just talking about cinnamon rolls here, darlin'?" My words were playful, but the underlying tension was palpable.

She snorted. "What? You don't you like it nice and tight?" Her laugh didn't quite hide the flush spreading across her cheeks.

"Baby, I fucking love it nice and tight."

Rolling the dough into a log shape took more finesse than I'd anticipated, forcing me to pull back on the banter and focus on the task at hand.

Piper had to adjust my grip a few times, her hands guiding mine with a gentle firmness that made my heart pound harder than usual.

After rolling the dough into a perfect log and slicing it into rounds, Piper placed them onto a baking tray with practiced ease. "Now we'll let these beauties proof before they go in the oven," she said, wiping her brows with the back of her flour-dusted hand.

"And what am I supposed to do while waiting for the buns to rise?" I quipped, leaning against the counter close enough that our hips touched.

"You can help me clean up."

Our bodies subtly brushed against each other while we worked. It felt like a dance—choreographed yet instinctual, familiar in its routine but still hot as fucking hell.

I'd just finished wiping down the counter when Piper tugged my apron off and arched onto her tiptoes to whisper, "I have another job for you if you're *up* for it."

I ran my tongue over my teeth with a grin. "What'd you have in mind?"

Without a word, she grabbed my hand and led me toward her office, closing and locking the door behind us before stripping her T-shirt off. "I need to come. Badly."

Her statement was plain, direct, and hit me like a shot of pure adrenaline. I untied the drawstring on her pants, yanking them and her panties down before moving to her bra. Her heavy tits spilled over into my waiting palms.

"Goddamn, baby," I growled, teasing her nipples with my teeth and tongue while guiding her onto the tan leather couch in the corner of her office.

Piper's pregnant body was something straight out of every deep-seated fantasy I had. Her curves were more pronounced, drawing me in like a moth to a fucking flame.

Her breath caught as my lips closed around her swollen nipple, a gentle moan escaping her lips. I reveled in the sound, knowing only I could draw that kind of response from her.

"Please, Dane," Piper murmured, her voice laced with urgency and desire. Her hands tangled in my hair, gently but firmly pulling me toward the place she needed me most.

My lips moved lower, tracing a path down her swollen belly before settling between her legs. My beard scraped against the delicate skin of her inner thighs. I inhaled deeply, the scent of her arousal flooding my senses and making my cock strain against my zipper.

"You smell so fucking good," I murmured against her slick flesh before dragging my tongue through her folds. "Taste even better."

Piper's back arched off the couch as I focused all my attention on her clit, alternating between flicking it with the tip of my tongue and sucking it between my lips.

"Oh god, Dane. Don't stop," she panted, her fingers gripping my hair almost painfully as she ground her hips against my face.

I had no intention of stopping. Not until she was coming all over my tongue and screaming my name. I slid two fingers inside her, groaning at how tight and wet she was.

Her hand fisted in my hair as I worked her over with my mouth and fingers, her breathy pleas and whimpers spurring me on. I loved seeing her like this—wet and needy, surrendering to the pleasure only I could give her.

"Baby, please... I'm so close..." Piper's thighs began to quake and tremble against my shoulders. "I need more."

Sliding a third finger into her slick heat, I groaned at how tight she was around me. "You gonna be a good girl and squirt for me?"

"Oh, fuck!" Her inner walls clamped down on my fingers, and she came hard, gushing over my hand and arm. I kept licking and sucking at her clit, drawing out her orgasm until she was shaking and pulling away from the overstimulation.

"That's my girl," I praised, pressing kisses to her inner thighs. "So fucking beautiful when you come for me."

Her chest heaved as she tried to catch her breath. "Holy shit," she panted. "That was..."

"We're not done yet, darlin'," I growled, sliding my fingers back inside her still-quivering pussy. "I wanna see how many times I can make you come before those cinnamon rolls are ready."

I worked her body relentlessly, bringing her to climax again and again until she was a trembling, whimpering mess beneath me. My cock throbbed painfully behind the zipper of my jeans, beads of precum already leaking from the tip, but I ignored it. This was about Piper.

"Dane," she gasped after her fifth orgasm, a satisfied smile playing on her lips when she looked down at me. "You look good with me all over your face."

I moved up her body to capture her lips in a deep kiss, letting her taste herself on my tongue. While we kissed, Piper's hands worked at my belt and jeans, shoving them down my hips. She broke away with a gasp when she realized I'd gone commando.

"Fuck, baby," she breathed, wrapping her hand around my rock-hard shaft.

I groaned as she took me into her hot mouth, her tongue swirling over the blunt head before she hollowed her cheeks and took me deeper. My jaw clenched as she dragged her tongue along the underside of my shaft, tracing the prominent vein there.

"Goddamn," I grunted, threading my fingers through her hair. I could already feel my climax building at the base of my spine and knew I wouldn't last long with my wife's talented mouth working me over. Reluctantly, I pulled out from between her lips and guided her onto her hands and knees, facing the back of the couch.

Her belly swayed as she pushed her hips back, presenting her glistening pussy to me. I took a moment to admire the view before lining myself up and pushing inside her in one smooth thrust, both of us groaning at the sensation. Her pussy gripped me like a velvet vise, hot and slick from her previous orgasms.

"You feel fucking amazing," I panted, setting a steady rhythm. One hand gripped her hip while the other snaked around to tease her sensitive nipples.

Piper pushed back to meet each of my thrusts, breathy moans escaping her lips. "Harder, baby. Please…"

I picked up the pace, pounding into her with abandon. The sound of skin slapping against skin filled the small office, punctuated by our grunts and gasps of pleasure.

My fingers found her clit, rubbing tight circles as I fucked her. "Come for me again, darlin'. One more time."

Her inner walls fluttered around me as she neared her peak. With a strangled cry, she came undone, her whole body shaking as waves of pleasure washed over her. The pulsing of her pussy pushed me over the edge, and I came with a hoarse shout, spilling inside her.

We collapsed onto the couch, panting heavily. I held Piper close, caressing her belly and feeling the slight movements within. "So, about that Head Frosting position," I teased, catching my breath as I brushed a stray lock of hair off her damp forehead.

She giggled, the sound bright and clear in the quiet of her office. "You think you've earned it after one morning's work?" she quipped, her green eyes still hazy from the orgasms.

"Darlin', after that, I think I've earned a fancy title." I pressed a soft kiss to her lips, the taste of her lingering on my tongue.

Piper hummed thoughtfully, a playful smile curving her lips. "Maybe we should make it an official position. You being here is good for staff morale."

"It sure as shit better be," I replied, tightening my arms around her. "If the benefits package includes exclusive private baking sessions with the owner and quality control taste tests by the Head Frosting Technician himself, count me in."

"You're hired," she said, her voice husky, her body relaxed against mine. We lay entwined on her office couch, a tangle of limbs and satisfied sighs, the stress of the bakery's grand opening forgotten until the timer on Piper's watch went off.

"All right, Head Frosting Tech," she said with a groan. "Break's over. Back to work."

***

Pride swelled in my chest as I watched Piper move through the busy bakery, completely in her element as she chatted with patrons and recommended sweets with her infectious smile.

The day had flown by in a tornado of non-stop activity, with customers lining up at the door before we'd even opened. Not that I was surprised.

Swoonworthy was Piper's vision brought to life, combining her love of romance novels with her passion for baking to create a bakery unlike any other.

Forest green bookshelves lined the walls, displaying some of her favorite romance novels, along with hanging baskets of plants and colorful artwork depicting classic romance novel covers. Low couches and overstuffed armchairs were scattered among the tables and chairs, creating what my wife had referred to for the last six months as a "bohemian café vibe."

She'd poured her heart and soul into this place, and it showed in every carefully curated detail down to cleverly named menu items inspired by her favorite tropes—enemies-to-lovers eclairs, secret baby beignets, cinnamon roll hero.

When the late afternoon crowd thinned, I joined Piper's mom on one of the couches, watching my wife work her magic. Even seven months pregnant, she was a bundle of energy, flitting from table to table.

"This is amazing," Nikki said, shaking her head in amazement. "I mean, I knew she had talent, but this...this is something else."

I nodded in agreement, unable to keep the grin off my face. "She's incredible. I don't know how she's still going strong. I'm dragging ass, and all I've done is stand around looking pretty for most of the day."

She laughed. "Well, you know Piper. Stubborn as hell and twice as determined."

"That must be where this little stink gets it from," I said, reaching over to ruffle Avery's curls. She pushed my hand away with an annoyed grunt, intently focused on the movie playing on her tablet. "Gets her brattiness from her mama too."

The bell above the door chimed, and I glanced up to see a familiar face enter, watching with amusement as Nikki's demeanor instantly shifted. She sat up straighter, her fingers fidgeting with her long, dark hair.

"Nails," I said, standing up to clap him on the shoulder when he approached our table. "You're a hell of a long way from home, brother."

"Yeah. I, uh, had some club business with Bear. Thought I'd stop in on my way out of town," he answered distractedly, his eyes locked on Nikki's. "Hey, Nik. Been a while."

His smooth drawl held a thrum of something deeper, and her lips twitched into a barely there smile, leaving me feeling like I was on the outside of some inside joke between them.

"Ethan," she said, her cheeks flushing pink.

The chemistry between them was nothing short of a badly kept secret. Everyone could see it—everyone except them, of course. An awkward silence fell over our table as the two continued stealing glances at each other.

Nikki tucked her hair behind her ear, exposing a large hickey on the side of her neck. Maybe they weren't so oblivious after all. I bit back a smirk, deciding to have a little fun.

"Looks like you've got a little something on your neck right there, Nikki," I said casually, leaning in to inspect it closer. "Almost looks like you got bitten by something…or someone."

Her eyes widened for a fraction of a second before she composed herself, her hand darting up to cover the mark. "Oh, this? Just a little mishap with my flatiron earlier."

Nails didn't even bother hiding his grin, his gaze intense as he looked at her. "Yeah, I've heard those flatirons can be tricky," he added, the double meaning clear in his voice.

I chuckled before standing with a stretch. "I've gotta get back to work before the boss lady catches me slacking. You two think you can manage Avery and avoid getting bitten by any more flatirons while I'm gone?" I asked.

"Think we can handle it," Nails said with a wink, settling into the seat I'd vacated.

When I returned to the kitchen, Piper was deep in conversation with Ivy near the industrial mixers, her green eyes pinched with concern. Ivy had flown in for the grand opening yet had spent most of the day hiding out in the kitchen or Piper's office, only venturing out front a handful of times.

It was hard to reconcile the guarded, withdrawn woman with the vibrant, outgoing Ivy who'd chased me down at a reader event two years before, wanting to introduce me to her friend.

The bright blue scarf around her neck concealed the scar left from the nearly fatal attack, but she couldn't hide how profoundly she'd changed since.

I hung back, not wanting to interrupt, but I couldn't help overhearing snippets of their conversation.

"I just don't feel ready," Ivy was saying, her voice barely above a whisper.

Piper squeezed her hand. "I know, but you can't hide forever. Maybe just come out for a few minutes? GQ and Duke have been here all day, hoping to see you."

"Don't tell them I'm here, please," Ivy insisted, the color draining from her face. "I'm not in the right place mentally to deal with...all of that."

Piper pressed her lips together before nodding. "Okay. I'm gonna head back out there. Uh, just text me if you change your mind."

I slipped back into the hallway, catching Piper's arm when she emerged. "Hey, you okay?" I asked, nodding toward the kitchen.

She blinked rapidly before shaking her head. "No. I feel so helpless, Dane. She's so closed off. I don't even know how to reach her anymore."

Piper snuck a furtive glance toward the kitchen before gesturing for me to follow her back up to the front, waiting until we were out of earshot before continuing. "And, to make matters a million times worse, Ivy's parents convinced her to quit her job and sell her house. She's moving in with them next week. Oh, and she didn't even talk to anyone about it because, according to her, her parents know what's best for her," she said with an exaggerated groan.

I'd only had the briefest of interactions with Brian and Cheryl while Ivy was in the hospital. They'd seemed more concerned about controlling the narrative around what happened than they had with their daughter's well-being, which was why they'd refused to let Duke or GQ anywhere near her.

"That seems like a recipe for disaster," I said dryly. "What's their plan? Keep her locked up in her old bedroom until she's 'normal' again?"

Piper dug her thumbs into her lower back with a shrug. "Honestly?

I have no idea. They're two of the most uptight, emotionally repressed humans on the planet, and suddenly, they know what's best for someone trying to work through the emotional trauma of her attack? Give me a fucking break. She's gonna end up like Cheryl, strung out on benzos and booze, and there's nothing I can do to stop it."

"What if she didn't move in with them?" I asked, stepping in to work the tension out of her back. "What if she moved in with us for a while? Get her out of that environment and give her some space to heal without all the pressure."

She raised her eyebrows, peering up at me with a questioning gaze. "You'd be okay with that?"

"Why wouldn't I be? She's your best friend, and we have a spare bedroom," I replied, kneading her tight muscles. "Jesus, darlin'. You're gonna need to soak in a hot bath when we get home."

"As nice as that sounds, we've still got an hour before closing," she said, glancing down at a notification on her watch before straightening.

A visible tremor passed through her body, and I frowned, instantly on high alert. "What's wrong?"

Piper bit her lip, avoiding my gaze. "Just...don't be mad, okay?"

"Can't agree to that without knowing what the hell's going on, darlin'," I gritted out, searching her face for answers.

She took a deep breath, her eyes darting toward the front door. "I may have done something..."

Before she could answer, the bell above the door chimed. My whole body tensed as I turned, coming face to face with someone I hadn't seen in over two years.

Teddy.

My oldest brother still carried himself like he owned every inch of ground he walked on, his long, dark hair pulled back in a low knot, beard streaked with gray. His eyes scanned the bakery before landing on me, and for a moment, I was that desperate little kid again, wanting nothing more than to make my big brother proud.

I pinched the bridge of my nose, fighting back the tears that threatened to fall. Two years of silence, of avoiding his calls and texts, and here he was, standing in my wife's bakery on opening day.

Grief, guilt, and anger sucker-punched me, flooding my mind with the memory of the last time we saw each other. The funeral home parking lot. His fist connecting with my jaw. The raw grief and rage in his eyes as he'd blamed me for not doing more to save Levi.

"Remember how much you love me," Piper whispered as she reached up on her tiptoes to press her lips to my jaw before bailing on me to greet a customer.

Teddy approached, his expression unreadable. "Dane," he said, his voice gruff.

"Hey." I worked my jaw back and forth as I fought to keep my composure. "You came all the way from Colorado for a bakery opening?"

A hint of a smile tugged at the corner of his mouth. "Heard the cinnamon rolls were to die for," he said before playfully slugging me in the arm like he used to when we were kids. "Nah, little brother. I came for you."

My throat tightened as much at the familiar gesture as his presence. "How'd you find out about this?"

"Your Ol' Lady reached out to me about a week ago and invited me to the grand opening," he explained. "Said she wanted your kids to have a relationship with our side of the family. Figured the only way that'd happen is if you and I cleared the air."

I swallowed hard, unsure how to respond. Part of me wanted to pull him into a hug, while another wanted to deck him for showing up unannounced.

"Think we can step outside for a minute?" Teddy asked. "Might be good to talk somewhere a little more private."

Probably better that my wife didn't witness me getting taken down a peg by my fifty-three-year-old brother. I nodded, leading him out to one of the bistro tables set up on the sidewalk.

He settled onto one of the chairs, his joints creaking as he leaned back. "Sit," he commanded when I started pacing. "Ain't here for the reasons you think I am."

I dropped into the chair across from him, my leg bouncing with nervous energy. He studied me for a long moment, the weight of two years' worth of unspoken words hanging between us.

"'Bout time we sat down and hashed this shit out, don't you think?

Could have done it over the phone, but you won't take my calls... Not that I blame you with the way we left things."

I stared down at my hands, unable to meet his gaze. "You were right to react the way you did—"

"No, I fucking wasn't," he interjected, raking a hand over his weathered face with a heavy sigh. "You know why we chose Ghost for your road name?"

I shrugged, keeping my eyes fixed on the table. "Because I'm so quiet that people forget I'm in the room? I don't fucking know."

Teddy barked out a rough laugh. "If that were the case, we'd have called you Mouse." His expression grew serious. "It's 'cause you're just like our old man—haunted by every fucking mistake you've ever made."

He reached across the small table to grip my shoulder, his hand trembling as he squeezed. "I need you to know that what happened with Levi wasn't your fault."

A tear slipped down my cheek before I could stop it, and I hastily swiped it away, finally meeting his gaze. "If I'd just said something different or stayed on the phone longer..."

"It wouldn't have changed a damn thing," Teddy said firmly. "Listen to me. There was nothing you could have said or done differently that would have changed the outcome. Nothing."

I shook my head, the guilt that had been eating me alive for two years bubbling to the surface. "You don't know that—"

"Yes, I fucking do. You think that was the first time?" he asked, mashing his lips together to mask the quivering.

My head snapped back, shock reverberating through my entire body. "What?"

Teddy's jaw tightened, and he took a shaky breath. "About a year before... I found him out in our barn. We kept it quiet, thinking the less people knew, the better. By that point, we'd already been to a slew of child psychologists and psychiatrists who prescribed a fucking pharmacy's worth of meds."

He huffed out a bitter laugh, slowly shaking his head back and forth. "Kels and I went through every fucking fertility treatment just to have Levi, but it was like something in his brain was programmed to self-destruct, no matter what we tried to do."

All this time, I'd been carrying the burden of Levi's death, believing I was solely responsible. But there was so much I hadn't known, so much pain my brother had been silently shouldering.

"But at the funeral home, you said—"

"I know what I said," Teddy cut me off, his eyes shining with unshed tears. "I was hurting and looking for somewhere to place my anger. It was easier to blame you than to face the truth that sometimes, no matter how hard you try, you can't save the people you love."

He knelt in front of me, his rough hand moving to cup the back of my neck, bringing our heads together. "I'm sorry, Dane. For blaming you, for pushing you away," he said, his voice thick with emotion. "I know what it did to you, and it's why I've spent the last two years trying to reach out and make it right."

The weight I'd been carrying for so long began to lift, all the grief and blame I'd shouldered falling away as I let myself be held by my big brother for the first time in years.

When we finally pulled apart, both of us discreetly wiping our eyes, I cleared my throat and asked, "What about the stuff with Kelsey?"

Teddy dropped back into his chair, his hazel eyes flickering with pain at the mention of his ex-wife's name. "Everything revolved around trying to get Levi the help he needed, and shit with me and her kinda fell to the wayside. After he died…" He trailed off, shaking his head. "I think we finally saw how far apart we'd grown, and neither of us knew how to bridge the gap."

"So you threw in the towel and went Nomad," I said, recalling how he took off for Colorado shortly after the funeral.

He shook his head. "I didn't fucking throw in the towel. She did. I just didn't see the point of sticking around to fight her on it. Addie and Sky were already off at college, and we were sitting in that big ass house like a couple of strangers."

"Have you talked to her at all since then?" I asked, carefully studying his face and noting the deep lines etched around his eyes and mouth.

"We've exchanged a few texts about stuff with the girls when we have to," he replied with a shrug. "But that's ancient history now. We're both better off."

Something in his tone made me doubt the sincerity of his words. Teddy and Kelsey had been high school sweethearts, married for over thirty years before it all fell apart.

Not convinced he'd moved on so easily, I said, "Yeah, she seemed really happy when she and her fiancé stopped by earlier."

His face went red, the cords in his neck straining as he shoved his chair back and loomed over me. "Her what?" he said, his voice low.

"Her fiancé," I repeated, fighting a grin. "They were all loved up together on one of the couches. I can't remember if they ordered the Second Chance Scones or the Forbidden Romance Fruit Tarts, but they looked pretty damn cozy."

"Yeah? Hope he enjoyed it because he's a fucking dead man," Teddy growled, his hands clenching into fists at his sides. "Who the fuck is this guy? Did you get a name?"

"You know, for a guy who's moved on, you seem really...invested in your ex-wife's love life," I observed, crossing my arms over my chest as I leaned back in my chair.

He deflated before sinking back into his chair with a scowl. "You're fucking with me, aren't you, you little shit?"

I ran my tongue over my teeth with a grin. "Of course, I'm fucking with you. I haven't seen Kelsey in years." I studied him for a moment before adding, "But it's pretty obvious you're not over her. Have you thought about maybe talking to her? Seeing if there's anything left to salvage?"

Teddy shot me an irritated glare. "I'm the oldest. I'm supposed to be the one doling out advice, not you."

"Yeah, well, sometimes even the oldest needs a kick in the ass," I replied with a shrug.

"Enough of the emotional shit," he said gruffly before standing and clapping me on the shoulder. "Let's head back in so I can try one of those famous cinnamon rolls."

Nails was waiting by the door when we walked back in. "Holy shit, look what the cat dragged in. Thought that was you, Crow," he said with a grin, clasping my brother's hand. "Been a minute, brother."

"Too fucking long," Teddy agreed, pulling him into a quick hug.

I caught Piper's eye across the room, and she made her way over to us, a tentative smile on her face. In the midst of launching her business, my wife had taken the time to reach out to my estranged brother to mend the fences I'd been too damn stubborn to.

I pressed my lips to the top of her head, overwhelmed by the thought and care she'd put into orchestrating the reunion. "Have I told you lately how amazing you are?"

"Not in the last hour or so," she teased, tilting her face up for a proper kiss.

I wrapped my arm around her waist before turning to my brother. "This is my Ol' Lady, Piper. Piper, this is my brother, Teddy."

Teddy grinned at Piper's extended hand before pulling her into a bear hug instead. "Pleasure's all mine, doll. Thanks for reaching out and inviting me. Means more than you know."

Her eyes were glistening when she pulled back. "I'm so happy you're here."

"Speaking of family," I said, glancing around the bakery, "where's the little stink at? I want to introduce her to her Uncle Teddy."

Piper pointed under the table where Avery was happily munching on a cinnamon roll while watching her movie. Almost every square inch of both her and the tablet was streaked with frosting.

Teddy followed my gaze, his dark brows lifting when he spotted her. "And who's this little cutie?"

"This is our daughter, Avery," I said, crouching down. "Hey, darlin'. There's someone I want you to meet."

She looked up from her tablet, her green eyes wide and curious. "Sim-woll?" she asked, clenching the soggy remains of her cinnamon roll in her little fist.

I chuckled, gently wiping some of the frosting off her face with the wet wipe Nikki passed under the table. "Yeah, that's a cinnamon roll. But I want you to meet someone. This is your Uncle Teddy," I said as my brother squatted down to her level, his eyes crinkling at the corners.

Avery tilted her head, studying him intently before raising the soggy pasty with a shrug. "Uh, sim-woll?"

Teddy barked out a laugh, letting her guide it to his lips. "Super weird initiation, but okay," he said, leaning in to take a small bite.

"Mmm...yum!" she exclaimed, bobbing her head emphatically.

"You're right. That is yummy...and wet. Wasn't expecting that."

She grunted her approval before reaching up to smear frosting across his forehead. "Sim-woll," she repeated as if christening him into our family.

"Someone's been watching *The Lion King*," he said with a soft smile, the kind I hadn't seen on his face in years—not since his own kids were little.

She dropped the rest of the pastry onto the floor and curled her hands into claws before bellowing, "Yion...rawr!"

Teddy roared back at her, and Avery dissolved into a fit of giggles before crawling onto his lap, apparently deeming him worthy of her affection.

He wrapped his arms around her, his eyes clouding with emotion as he cradled her close. Seeing traces of the man my brother used to be before grief and loss hardened him left me with a lump in my throat.

Piper looped her arms around my neck and whispered, "I'm glad y'all worked things out."

"Thank you," I said, wrapping my arms around her waist and pulling her in as close as I could with our son in her belly. "For all of this, for reaching out to him, for giving our kids a chance to know my family."

She pulled back to rest her chin on my chest with a soft smile. "This biker I had a one-night stand with told me that family is everything, and I'm inclined to believe him."

"You keep bringing him up, darlin'. Sounds like he really rocked your world," I said with a chuckle.

"Eh..." She lifted her shoulder in a shrug. "He was okay—"

"Just okay?" I tickled her sides until she was squirming against me with giggles and pleas for me to stop before dropping my mouth to her ear. "I'll remember that when you're begging me to come later tonight."

"We'll see about that," she said with a confident smirk. "Oh, by the way, the rest of your family should be here soon."

My eyebrows shot up in surprise. "The rest?"

Piper nodded. "I may have invited your parents and brothers to the grand opening too."

A mix of emotions washed over me—anxiety, excitement, gratitude. It had been so long since I'd seen any of them. "You're something else, you know that?"

"Try to keep that in mind when you're edging me later," she quipped before heading back to the counter to greet a new customer.

Maybe it was the baker in her or some sixth sense unique to her, but she always seemed to know exactly what I needed, even when I didn't.

And I was the luckiest son of a bitch alive.

Piper had a knack for taking seemingly incompatible elements, like romance novels and pastries or two estranged brothers, and forging them into something amazing.

Two years ago, I never would have imagined sitting in the same room as my older brother, watching him play with my daughter. Yet here we were, reconnecting in the space my wife had dreamed up and brought to life.

I'd spent years trying to outrun the pain of my past, but there was a certain beauty to be found in the dualities of life. The worst night of my life—losing Levi—had also become the best because it was the night I met the love of my life. It was the night we made our little girl. Funny how grief and joy could exist in the same space, neither taking away from the other.

Teddy caught my eye and smiled as if he was thinking the same thing. There was a lightness to him I hadn't seen in years; the hard edges softened by Avery's infectious giggles and frosting-covered fingers.

The road hadn't been easy. We'd endured more loss and heartache than I cared to remember. But standing there, surrounded by family and love, I knew every struggle, every setback, and every moment of darkness had been worth it. It had led us all here.

We were all a little older, a little wiser, and with a hell of a lot more scars.

But that was the thing about scars.

They made for some pretty damn good stories.

The End

Thank you for reading THE KEEPER! I hope you loved Dane and Piper's story.

Want to get to know the club? The SPMC ride begins with Grey and Celia's story in THE DESERTER!

I grew up in the dark.

Right and wrong?

In my world, it was kill or be killed.

I spend my time in the shadows, doing what I want when I want. I refuse to follow anyone's rules—I own this town.

They might not see me, but my club controls everything... including her. I took Daddy's little princess and defiled her to send a message. Now, I want to keep her down here in the dirt forever.

She's crazy not to run.

Around here, there's no right or wrong. I'm the judge, jury, and executioner, and god help any fool who tries to lay a hand on what's mine.

If you're looking for a hero, you're in the wrong place.

One-click THE DESERTER now!

———

Keep reading for an excerpt from The Mercenary, Carnage and Harper's story, coming later this year.

And if you enjoyed Dane and Piper's story, please consider leaving a review on Amazon. I appreciate your help in spreading the word, even by telling a friend. Reviews help readers find new books to fall in love with.

Upcoming Side Character Stories:
Ivy, GQ, and Duke, Nikki and Nails, & Teddy and Kelsey

Want to be the first to know when these stories are coming out? Sign up for my newsletter, join my Facebook group, Shannon Myers's Fan Group, and/or Follow me on BookBub!

Turn the page for an excerpt from The Mercenary.

THE MERCENARY

CARNAGE: FEBRUARY 2020 (AGE: 36)

"Blood//Water" by grandson

We struck as Oklahoma was battening down the hatches for a blizzard. An arctic cold front had moved into the area four days prior, delivering subfreezing temperatures and making surveillance a bitch to pull off. The cold had settled into my muscles and joints, triggering old wounds that left me feeling much older than thirty-six. Every ounce of pain was worth it, though, because we finally had him.

Cobra.

Finding the biker had been easier than expected—almost too easy.

The possibility of a set-up weighed heavily on my mind. But one hundred sixty-eight hours of recon and another forty-eight spent running SDR—a surveillance detection route that would have smoked out even the most experienced units—turned up nothing.

Not once in the last nine days had Cobra given any indication he was aware we were on to him.

I'd accounted for everything.

Except her.

She lay sprawled across the king-sized bed, a sunny yellow sweatshirt bunched up over her hips, chest rising and falling with each deep breath. Pale pink sheets wound around her toned calves like snakes, as if she'd been thrashing in her sleep. One arm rested against her bare stomach. The other was twisted in the long silvery-blonde hair fanned across the pillow beneath her head.

I could easily make out her features, down to the sparkly purple nail polish on her fingers, thanks to the soft yellow glow cast by the nightlights scattered throughout the room. I'd counted at least seven of the damn things upon entering.

How the hell she managed to sleep with her room lit up like a goddamned runway was beyond me.

There was a dull thud downstairs, courtesy of Mike or Zane, but the woman didn't move a muscle. She slept on, oblivious to the monster beside her bed and those lying in wait one floor below.

For over a week, I'd watched Cobra coming and going as if he didn't have a care in the world. If she was being held against her will— I paused to check her wrists but found no abrasions or markings.

There was a crystal chandelier hanging over the bed and ornate throw pillows on a pink velvet loveseat in the corner of the room. If Cobra was holding this woman captive, it didn't show. No, I'd bet my ass she'd handpicked each item in here, along with the farmhouse crap I'd passed downstairs.

But who the fuck was she? And where the fuck had she been hiding for the past nine days?

I crept toward the nightstand, searching for clues among a picture frame, water glass, and prescription bottles for *Topamax* and *Metoclopramide*. They weren't medications I was familiar with, nor did I particularly care what they were prescribed for.

What I needed was an identity.

A lover?

If that was the case, then it seemed more likely she would have been in the main bedroom downstairs.

The toe of my boot connected with something solid, sending it into the nightstand with a sharp *clink*. Any illusions of her being a prisoner vanished as soon as I realized it was a weapon.

She mumbled something in her sleep, and I held my breath, waiting until she went still again before dropping into a crouch to retrieve it.

I turned the dainty revolver over in my hands, ignoring the protest in my stiff joints as I studied her face, trying to guess her age. Mid-twenties, maybe. Certainly much younger than Cobra, who had to be pushing sixty. Some type of sugar daddy arrangement, then. A place to live in exchange for fucking a man old enough to be her father. I let my gaze roam over her body again, deciding that even with the lavish house, Cobra had gotten the better end of the deal.

Unfortunately for her, she'd unknowingly signed her death warrant the day she moved in.

There was an alliance in place—one signed by every club in the nation. An attack on one was a declaration of war on all. If it got out that a Silent Phoenix officer had been on the Crows' turf without going through the proper channels, the peace treaty that had held for the past three years wouldn't be worth the paper it was printed on.

No witnesses.

The club had made that mistake once before, when our former Pres, Grey, stormed a strip joint in the Outlaws' territory, wiping out their partners, Los Dictadores. Decades of fighting followed, along with a war that had damn near decimated every club before the syndicate reformed.

Cobra had been all too willing to let us take him without a fight—had wanted us to believe he was alone in the house. Perhaps we could use her as collateral to obtain what we needed from him. The thought of a former Serpent down on his knees, begging a rival club member for his fuck buddy's life, brought a smile to my face.

I pocketed the bullets from her gun and was in the process of lowering it onto the nightstand when the picture inside the frame caught my attention.

In it, a much younger Cobra knelt beside a blonde-haired ballerina who couldn't have been older than five or six. My smirk faded as I compared her to the woman in the bed. While the roundness in her cheeks was gone, the bone structure was the same.

She wasn't some fuck buddy.

She was his daughter.

An uncontrollable shudder swept through my body as I worked to extinguish every source of light in the bedroom. As long as she didn't see my face, she couldn't identify me later.

What was I doing?

I couldn't leave her alive.

There was a reason Bear, the club's current Pres, had asked me to assist the two detectives. Mike and Zane were more than capable of retrieving Cobra and delivering him to Grey, but each had his own reason for coming. Reasons that would get them both killed if they let their emotions cloud their judgment. I was their handler—here to ensure everything went according to plan and nothing led back to the club.

Cobra had been a willing participant—a soldier—in the Sons' war. But this woman was a civilian, a pawn in a game she didn't even know she was playing. It went against what little humanness I still possessed to hold an innocent woman accountable for the sins of her father, but I was going to have a hell of a time convincing the two downstairs to see things my way.

After grumbling something unintelligible, she rolled over, putting her face inches from where I crouched, debating my next move.

Unfortunately, I didn't have long to decide.

The sound of glass shattering downstairs sent her bolting upright in bed with a startled gasp.

A section of the downstairs hardwood squeaked out a protest, like the rubber sole of a shoe on a basketball court. Cobra's subsequent groan of pain killed any chance of her chalking the whole thing up to a dream and going back to sleep.

She crouched at the foot of the bed, her breaths ragged. I expected a scream, or at the very least, a whimper once she realized I'd turned off all the lights. Instead, with a calmness that could only have come from extensive training, she slowly turned and drove her foot into the side of my head before scrambling toward the nightstand.

I launched myself at her with a low growl, my temple throbbing from the kick. The mattress dipped beneath my weight as I landed on her back and let the momentum carry us both over the edge to the carpet below.

The impact knocked the air from her lungs, and I didn't waste a single second. I looped one arm over her shoulder and the other under her left armpit, getting her into a rear mount. With my legs hooked around hers, she was completely powerless.

"Nice try, Twinkletoes," I murmured into her hair, fighting my body's automatic response to the feel of her curvy ass grinding against the front of my jeans—a painful reminder of how long it had been since I'd had a woman beneath me.

Sensing she wasn't going to escape, the woman went limp with defeat, and I relaxed my hold, planning to use the zip ties I'd packed for Cobra to bind her wrists. I was still working out the details of what to do from there, but I'd gotten out of worse jams with far less working in my favor.

She waited until I reached for the ties before pulling her lower leg back and rotating her hips until my knee was pinned beneath her tailbone. I moved to hook her again with my legs, but by then, she'd already planted the soles of her feet against the carpet and scraped her hips over, escaping the lower hold completely. The new position made it damn near impossible for me to put her in a chokehold. Seemed Twinkletoes had some martial arts experience.

We grappled for control until she managed to break the tension in my arms enough to roll toward me before wriggling out of my grasp completely.

Click.

Christ, she'd gotten the gun. She tried again, making a small noise of frustration upon realizing it wasn't a misfire.

Click. Click.

I snagged the zip ties with a low chuckle, unaware of the revolver coming at my head until it was too late. The tiny weapon cracked across my cheekbone, sending a jolt of red-hot pain down into the roots of my teeth. I worked my jaw from side to side as it began to swell. While nothing felt broken, I would be sporting one hell of a bruise in the coming days.

I'd add it to my collection.

After deflecting the next attempt, I knocked the gun from her hands with a snarl. If she was trying to take me down, she was failing miserably. So far, she'd only succeeded in pissing me off.

I popped up, straining to find the little nightmare in the dark. The last thing I needed was her snagging another gun, namely one I hadn't unloaded.

Instead, she'd decided to make a run for it, so focused on getting away from me that she missed the six-foot-seven obstacle looming in the open doorway. Her body collided with Zane's, and the force of the impact sent her hurtling back toward the carpet with an agonized groan.

"Thought you might need a hand," he drawled with a rare smile before jerking his chin to where the woman now lay writhing at our feet. "What do we have here?"

"A problem," I snapped, making quick work of getting the hellcat onto her stomach and securing her wrists before retrieving my knife. Zane's eyebrow ticked up, but he remained silent as I yanked the hem of the woman's sweatshirt away from her body.

"No," she panted, bucking her hips to try to throw me off-balance.

"Calm the fuck down, Rambo Barbie," I growled, slicing off a thick strip of the material to secure around her eyes. "I don't wanna hurt you—"

"Fuck. You."

I hauled her up by the collar of her sweatshirt and leaned down until my mouth was against the shell of her ear. "Sorry, Twinkletoes. You're not my type. Now, shut your pretty mouth unless you want to be gagged next."

Zane didn't question the blindfold or ask why she was still breathing. Instead, he let out a low whistle and dutifully followed me downstairs. Unlike another detective, who never seemed to know when to shut the fuck up.

Or apparently, what in and out with no trace meant.

It was precisely why I was here. Sullivan may have been Grey's son, but he lacked the man's patience and control. As an old friend and fellow biker had often said, he ran into things with his dick hanging out.

That man was gone now—another casualty of Cobra's war. Now it fell to Zane and me to keep the asshole in check.

"Somebody forgot to RSVP to our party," Mike tsked as we entered the kitchen, narrowing his eyes at me. "What did Daddy say about doing our fucking jobs?"

Somewhere between Lubbock and Edmond, he'd gotten it in his head that he was in charge. One of these days, someone was going to put a bullet in his head to shut him up. At the rate he was going, that someone would be me.

I cracked my neck and stared him down until he wisely chose to move on to someone else. His daddy wasn't the Pres anymore, and I had no problem giving him a hands-on reminder.

"Friend of yours, Cobra?"

A muscle twitched in the biker's corded neck, but otherwise, his expression remained neutral. Bored, even. Nothing like the man I'd pictured in my head for years—one who had supposedly favored diamond cufflinks and custom suits. With his charcoal cotton robe and slippers, he looked like any other middle-aged man. Minus the bloody nose and handcuffs.

"Hooker," he bit out, refusing to look at her. "Told the bitch she could leave once we were through. Thanks to you idiots interrupting, I'll be forced to pay extra."

Twinkletoes flinched at the term, confirming what we both recognized was a lie. Even if I hadn't seen the truth, I never would have believed her to be a whore. Sex workers had a hardness about them—a steel barrier they built around themselves to cushion against the people who used their bodies. This woman grasped how to fight, but she was soft.

"Now, hold on here," Mike said with a wide grin. "You're telling me she's a prostitute? *Her.* When did you pick her up?"

"A few hours ago. What do you want next—a location? Never pegged you for the desperate type," Cobra muttered dryly. "It's funny. Last I heard, you'd met the Reaper on a colleague's front lawn, leaving behind a widow."

"Yeah? Well, last I heard, you knew how to lie. We've had eyes on the place for days—seen no one but you."

"It's true," she said, her body tensing against mine. A tremor worked its way down her spine, but she kept her voice steady. "He hired me for the month."

I raised my eyebrows and shook my head. Someone had seen way too many movies.

"Right," Mike drawled, dragging Cobra to the kitchen island. When the old man saw the combat knife, he began struggling to break free.

With a sigh, I pulled my sidearm and held it to the woman's head. He settled instantly, and Mike undid the cuffs.

"Interesting ring," he noted, holding Cobra's hand up for inspection. The band winked under the pendant lights over the island —a diamond thirteen. "I feel like I've seen it before. Oh, that's right. You branded someone with it—a woman who's like a mother to me—"

Twinkletoes sagged against me but wisely remained silent.

"Just marking my property," Cobra interjected, forcing his lips into a cruel smirk.

Mike slapped Cobra's palm against the granite and instructed Zane to hold him down. While tracing the outline of his hand with the tip of the blade, the detective whistled a tune that sounded eerily similar to the opening music from Disney's *Robin Hood*.

I knew what was coming. Given the sweat beading on his brow, the biker did, too. Even the girl's breaths had become short pants as she struggled to determine what was happening.

"Marking your property," Mike mused to himself, still toying with the blade. "Is that what the kids are calling it nowadays?"

"You should leave the torture to your old man. It's clear you're out of your—" Cobra's words cut off in a sharp hiss of pain as Mike brought the knife down, piercing the skin directly above the ring.

"Now, let's try this again. Who's the girl? Tell me nicely, and I'll let you keep the finger."

"A whore!" the biker spat. "She's a fucking whore who has nothing to do with why you're here! Now, be a good little boy and take me back to your daddy!"

The blade made an unholy screech as it scraped against the granite, and Cobra roared through clenched teeth, straining to break Zane's hold before passing out from the pain.

Mike held the severed digit up like a trophy before dropping it and the ring onto the island. "And now, for my next trick—"

He retrieved a lighter from his pocket and began whistling the creepy tune again, tapping the heel of his boot to the beat as he held the flame to the open wound. The scent of burning flesh reached my nostrils as Cobra briefly came to with a howl of pain.

Twinkletoes shifted like she was going to make a run for it before turning her head to vomit onto the hardwood floor with a low moan. I lowered the gun to grip her shoulders, holding her hair back as she retched.

"Breathe through your mouth," I commanded in a low voice, trying to keep her together. She couldn't lose her shit. Not now. Not when there was a look in Mike's eyes I didn't entirely trust.

Not once during the five-and-a-half-hour drive up or in the week following had he mentioned torture. I had survived war zones by always planning fifty steps ahead. Last-minute deviations got people killed.

"He's out again," Zane said, looking to me to make the call. "Let's clean up and go. I'd like to be back before sunrise."

I agreed. Mike hadn't simply veered off-course with his little stunt, he'd created a fucking crime scene. He was too close—too fucking volatile to be trusted in this situation.

"Not yet," he argued, snapping his fingers in front of the unconscious man's face. "Cobra, pumpkin? You still with us?"

The old man blinked slowly before turning, not to look at the bloody stump where his middle finger had been, but to her.

"There you are, sunshine. Now, I hate to be a party pooper, but we're gonna have to skip the rest of the magic show and cut right to opening the presents."

I gave Mike a stiff smile, my jaw tightening in irritation as I reminded him, "We need to go. In and out, remember?"

"And we will, sweetie," he crooned, guaranteeing himself a split lip before the night was over. "As soon as Cobra here answers my question."

"I've told you already—"

"Yep. Hooker. Got that. Thing is, most men aren't willing to lose a finger for a whore. You know what? I've got an idea. Let's try your method. Bring her here."

"The hell?" Zane asked, his eyes bugging out of his head. "That's not part of the plan—"

"New plan," Mike interjected.

I didn't budge from my position, forcing him to come to me. She'd stopped vomiting but was now shaking violently in my arms. And she had every right to be. I knew what Cobra's method was—hell, anyone who'd ridden long enough had heard the rumors of what the biker and his buddies had done to Grey's Ol' Lady, Celia.

Sullivan was many things, but a rapist was not one of them, making his statement all the more confusing.

He ran a finger down her cheek, and she jerked her head to the side, trying to escape his touch.

"The fuck are you doing?" I growled, taking a step back. I didn't know this woman, but I wasn't about to hand her over to a man who had clearly lost sight of the mission the moment he stepped inside.

"Getting answers," Mike answered, his gaze suddenly cold. "The same way he did."

"Don't you fucking touch her!" Cobra snarled, his face turning red.

"You'll have to jog my memory, pumpkin. Is it beat, rape, brand— or brand, rape, and then beat? I just want to make sure I'm doing this right."

"Please," she whispered through chattering teeth, sounding as if she was on the verge of hyperventilating. "I'm nobody—"

"Shhh…" Mike smashed his index finger against her lips, silencing her. "The grown-ups are talking, sweetie—"

"You've got me, detective!" Cobra roared, bucking against Zane's hold. "Let her go."

I jerked my attention to the biker, wondering if he realized what he'd done. Blindfolded or not, Mike wouldn't let her leave the room now that she knew he was a badge.

A small wooden sign that read *thankful* leaned against the white tile backsplash near the stove. A sign I knew she had chosen, along with the mason jar of fresh tulips and light green slipcovers on the kitchen chairs. The little things always seemed to stand out most—a pair of children's shoes lying amidst rubble after a bombing or the half-full cup of black coffee still waiting on the table for a biker who had come home in a pine box.

I'd been fighting in wars since I was seventeen—both overseas and at home—and it never got easier seeing the stuff left behind. Something about the sign being in Cobra's house—knowing she was responsible for it—spurred me to regain control of the situation.

"Enough," I said, tucking her small frame to my side. "That's enough."

"But—" Mike protested.

I straightened to my full height and snarled, "I swear to god, if the next word out of your mouth is *sweetie* or *pumpkin*, I will put a bullet in your fucking head and tell your family you fled the country to start a new life! You listen to me, you little shit. You've had your fun, and now it's time to clean up the goddamn mess!"

Cobra stopped struggling against Zane and smirked. "Better listen to your boss—"

"As for you," I growled. "You're going to shut the fuck up. You keep running your mouth, and there's not a chance in hell she's making it out of this alive. You get me?"

Mike pulled his sidearm with a chuckle. "Oh, she's definitely not getting out of this alive."

"Yeah? You gonna be the one to pull the trigger?"

Twinkletoes shrank back with a choked whimper, treading over the toes of my boots with her bare feet as if she could escape the impact of my words.

"Why not? Not like I haven't done it before." He pressed the barrel to her forehead and stared up at me with a manic expression. "That's a nice shirt. Be a real shame to ruin it."

We were playing a game of roulette, and I was no longer sure Mike would wait until I was out of the line of fire before pulling the trigger.

I glanced down at her and then over to Cobra. "You gonna tell him, or am I?"

The biker shook his head, proving he was identical to the Sons and their ilk—men who considered family members fair game if it got them closer to their enemies. Despite what he believed, giving up her identity would be the only thing that saved her.

"She's his daughter," I announced to the men in the room.

Mike lowered the gun in an instant before turning to Cobra for confirmation.

He nodded slowly, eyes still fixed on me. "She is. But whether that will help or hurt her remains to be seen."

"I'll do it," she whispered to the room. "Whatever you want. Just let him go."

Jesus.

The silence was broken only by the continuous ticking of a large wooden wall clock hanging in the eating nook.

I cleared my throat, and Mike looked up, fight gone and face ashen. "Time to clean up your mess. Do not leave a single trace of evidence. Think you can manage that... *sweetie*?"

"Please," Twinkletoes begged, her chest heaving with each ragged breath.

Mike blinked rapidly and stumbled back a step, his gaze suddenly unfocused.

Family was everything to him.

His twin girls would be turning three soon. Maybe he was picturing them in a similar situation, offering up their bodies in an attempt to save his sorry ass. Or perhaps he was remembering the time his now wife, Lauren, had met the business end of my M17 when she barged into the bar *Leather & Lace*, demanding answers for her mother's death.

Even the notoriously stoic Zane had gone pale at the revelation, probably thinking about how close his wife and sister-in-law—Grey's daughters—had come to death at the hands of club enemies.

Bikers or not, they lived and died by code. Same as me. And it was now on my shoulders to determine this woman's fate.

Zane kept a firm grip on Cobra, even though we both knew he wasn't going anywhere. His secret was out; now, he'd do anything we asked if he thought it would keep her safe.

The biker watched me carefully, probably wondering if I was the type to brutalize his daughter to get to him. I may have looked every part the beast, but I wasn't taking an opportunity solely because it presented itself.

That was his game.

I nodded to Zane, still weighing the pros and cons of what I was about to do. "Once he's done, we'll go."

"She's—" Cobra pressed his lips together in a grimace as if whatever he was about to admit caused him pain. "She's already seen one parent die already. Please don't make her do it again."

Fuck.

There would be no mother she could run to once he was gone.

Eliminating the last remaining threat from the war meant leaving this woman an orphan.

"Daddy—no!" she cried, struggling to reach him. "I said I'd do it! Take me instead. Please!"

"Enough, Harper," he growled. "Remember your training—"

"Fuck the training—the protocols—all of it!" she roared before lowering her voice to a whisper, speaking only to me. "You have the wrong guy. My father, he's retired. He hasn't been in for almost three years. It's not him. He's not your guy. Whatever you think he did... it's not him. Just—please—take me instead."

Retired? What the hell was it she thought he did for a living? Bikers didn't retire. They might step down when age took its toll, but every single one knew once they patched in, they were in for life.

In by blood. Out by blood.

Twinkletoes ground her ass against me as if I hadn't recognized what she was offering when she begged me to take her. On any other man, the act may have worked. But I didn't miss the mechanical way she moved. Hell, I could practically smell the terror seeping from her pores at the thought of handing herself over to be beaten and abused.

Still, she would do it to save him—a man who didn't deserve an ounce of sympathy from anyone. Cobra had clearly let his daughter believe he was some secret agent or spy instead of a low-life who preyed on those who were weaker than him.

He'd been destined for a bullet since the day he came into this world.

I wasn't aware I was still clenching her hair in my fist until she began squirming to free herself. With a sharp tug, I yanked her head back. "Shhh... no one's going to hurt you. You have my word."

Harper shook her head in denial, still struggling to break my grip as she vowed, "I won't let you do this. I won't—"

"Take him," I ordered Zane, meeting the hate in Cobra's eyes with a cruel smirk. "If you so much as blink the wrong way, there's no deal. I'll tie a ribbon around her neck and deliver her to the Outlaws myself. After what your buddies did to their president, I imagine they'd love to get their hands on her."

His face paled. I had him over a barrel, and he knew it. Silent Phoenix may have abided by a specific code, but that didn't mean other clubs did. The Outlaws were one of many who had a bone to pick with Cobra. And if they couldn't have him, they'd happily settle for his daughter.

He nodded in understanding. "If you'll just give me a moment with her—"

"Not part of the deal," I coldly stated over the sounds of Harper's incoherent pleas.

Mike's head shot up from where he knelt, mopping up blood, face screwed up as if he'd bitten into something sour.

This was on him.

If he wanted to allow the man a moment alone with his daughter, then he should have kept his emotions out of it and stuck to the plan. As it was, we were already behind schedule, and I was completely and thoroughly pissed off.

"I am asking to hold my daughter one last time. Are you going to deny me this?" Cobra growled, making no attempt to hide the tears glimmering in his eyes.

Zane shook his head slowly as if he didn't see the harm in what the man was asking and couldn't fathom why I wasn't granting the man's last request.

Because I wasn't a goddamned genie in a bottle, doling out wishes. Letting him speak to her came with too many variables. Mike was unpredictable enough and the primary reason we were in this FUBAR situation in the first place.

I couldn't risk leaving one more thing to chance.

"What part of *no* did you not understand?" I asked, enunciating each word.

"No! Please," Harper begged, failing to mask the rising panic in her voice. "Let me say goodbye!"

"You just did. Take him."

"Harper!" Cobra jerked against the handcuffs as Zane snapped them back on, his muscles straining beneath his robe. "Wait—Harper! Please!"

With a tired sigh, I released her hair and looped my arm around her throat, resting the barrel of my gun against her skull where he could see. "Last chance, and then we do this my way."

His feverish gaze moved to Mike, who turned away with a

regretful shake of his head. Realizing no one was going to intervene on his behalf, Cobra released a long exhale, the fight draining from his body almost instantly.

"Harper," he said in a voice choked with emotion. Tears ran freely down both cheeks. "I love you, my girl."

It was almost enough to break even my resolve.

"Daddy?" she questioned, sensing the defeat in his tone. "Wait. No, not like this—I'm not ready!"

Mike ran a bleach-soaked towel over the counters and floors, removing the last traces of blood and vomit before chucking it into a full garbage bag. "Let's go," he muttered to Zane, refusing to look my way. They led Cobra out through the kitchen side door, all three of their faces etched in grief.

Good. At least the drive home would be peaceful. I'd finally have the quiet I'd craved since leaving Lubbock.

"Not like this!" Harper pleaded, straining against me. "Not like this—please! Daddy!"

"Shhh," I breathed into her hair. "I'm putting the gun away now, okay?"

She quieted, her heart pounding furiously beneath my arm as I returned my sidearm to its holster. The door closed with a definitive *click,* and she brought her heel down on the toe of my boot, fighting me with everything she had.

"Let me go," she rasped as I locked her head in the V of my arm, reaching my hand toward my opposite shoulder. "You didn't let me tell him I loved him—I didn't get to say goodbye!"

Nothing she said or did would change her father's fate. He'd chosen death the moment he laid hands on Celia. Whether she bid the fucker farewell or not, the end result would ultimately be the same.

Still, I wasn't willing to inflict more pain if I could help it. So, I let her claw my stomach with her bound hands and gritted my teeth when she drew back and kicked me in the shin.

"Believe me, it's better this way, sweetheart," I said, tucking my other arm behind her head. Knowing I was beyond redemption, I lowered my chin, breathing in the scent of her hair like a man starved of oxygen. She smelled like citrus and vanilla—a combination I found intoxicating.

By the time she realized I had her in a rear naked choke, I was already applying pressure, savoring the feel of her body going limp in my arms.

ACKNOWLEDGMENTS

A big thank you to *Swoonworthy Sourdough Artisan Bakery* for allowing me to use your fabulous name for my fictional patisserie.

If you're near Luling, Texas, check them out at:
627 E Davis St
Luling TX 78648

ALSO BY SHANNON MYERS

From This Day Forward Duet

(David & Elizabeth's Story)

From This Day Forward

Forsaking All Others

Operation Duet

(Dakota & Zane's Story)

Operation Fit-ish

(Kate and Nate's Story)

Operation Annulment

Silent Phoenix MC Series

(Main Storyline)

The Deserter (Book One)

The Protector (Book Two)

The Renegade (Book Three)

The Traitor (Book Four)

The Savior (Book Five)

Standalones within the SPMC universe

The Keeper

The Mercenary (coming soon)

Fairest Series (Can be read as standalones)

(Charm & Neve's Story)

Through The Woods

(Killian and Ari's Story)

Wait For It

<u>Fictioned Series</u>

(Hayden & Jake's Story)

Protagonized

ABOUT THE AUTHOR

Shannon is a born and raised Texan. She grew up inventing clever stories, usually to get herself out of trouble. Her mother was not amused. In junior high, she began writing fractured fairy tales from the villain's point of view and that was the moment she knew that she was going to use her powers for evil instead of good.

After an unplanned surgery in 2014 and a long pity party, she decided to pen a novel about the worst thing that could happen to a person to cheer herself up. She's twisted like that. Thus, From This Day Forward was born and the rest, as they say, is history.

She resides in the Texas desert with a posse of men (nothing like she'd imagined in her fantasies) and a plethora of fur babies.

Find her online at: http://shannonshaemyers.com
Or in her fan group: https://www.facebook.com/groups/630229377127363/

facebook.com/shannonmyersauthor
x.com/shannonsmyers
instagram.com/shannonsmyers

www.ingramcontent.com/pod-product-compliance
Lightning Source LLC
Chambersburg PA
CBHW030638020726
47493CB00006B/1776